About Darry Fraser

Darry Fraser's first novel, *Daughter of the Murray*, is set on her beloved River Murray where she spent part of her childhood. *Where The Murray River Runs*, her second novel, is set in Bendigo in the 1890s. Darry currently lives, works and writes on Kangaroo Island, an awe-inspiring place off the coast of South Australia.

Also by Darry Fraser

Daughter of the Murray
Where the Murray River Runs
The Good Woman of Renmark

THE
WIDOW
OF
Ballarat

DARRY FRASER

mira

First Published 2018
Second Australian Paperback Edition 2019
ISBN 9781489281036

Published by
Mira
An imprint of Harlequin Enterprises (Australia) Pty Ltd.
Level 19, 201 Elizabeth St
SYDNEY NSW 2000
AUSTRALIA

® and TM (apart from those relating to FSC®) are trademarks of Harlequin Enterprises Limited or its corporate affiliates. Trademarks indicated with ® are registered in Australia, New Zealand and in other countries.

A catalogue record for this book is available from the National Library of Australia
www.librariesaustralia.nla.gov.au

Printed and bound in Australia by McPherson's Printing Group

Susan Parslow, you are a champion of my stories.

One

Ballarat, Victoria, December 1854

The coach juddered and rocked as it thundered over the rough road. Nell Amberton's hands trembled in her lap, and not only from the dangerous ride away from the explosive violence at the Eureka stockade this morning. That she could still see her hands, or anything at all, out of one eye, was a blessing but little comfort.

Never had she trembled at anything—in fear or rage—as much until her husband Andrew had barged malevolently into her life. At her father, perhaps, but he was no match for Andrew. He was shouting now ever louder over the grinding whir of the coach wheels as it banged and bounced over the pockmarked road.

'… Until you are delivered of a male child, I will continue to administer punishment as befits the chit you are.' He glared and pointed at her eye. 'I see you didn't attempt to hide the results of your comeuppance this time.'

The ugly bruise was over her left eye. When she'd last checked early this morning, it had looked darker. Her eye still felt puffy. And, because she hadn't been able to hide it completely this

1

morning—there'd been no time as they'd fled the township—she'd fully expected a tirade. But expecting it never prepared her for it.

' ... proof to anyone that you are wilful and unruly, and that I am forced to take swift action.'

Her fingers touched the little sprig of yellow wattle she'd pinned on her hat earlier to remind her of courage. Its leaves had drooped, she was sure, as much from the heat already in the day as from her mood. *That would not do.* She needed all her strength of mind and body to protect herself from her husband. She straightened as she adjusted her bonnet.

'And so you *should* cover it up. It is not a badge of honour. I will not tolerate your insolence in my household ...'

Andrew Amberton was a cruel man who'd escaped transportation from England—his family had packed him off to the colony to be with his widowed sister, Enid Wilshire, and her son, before the law could do it for them. His crimes back there could only be imagined.

Last night, angry, bellowed words between Andrew and his nephew Lewis had echoed back and forth from the parlour to Nell's room as she'd lain in the marital bed. Wanting sleep desperately, she'd covered her ears with the pillow and finally dropped off. Then in the early hours of this morning, she'd been harshly roused and ordered to dress, to make haste, and then hurriedly propelled into the coach. There'd been no violence visited on her this morning; she'd only had to listen to Andrew rant and rave about having to pay for the coach ride in advance, and in gold. Two heavy bags had been shoved under the seat behind her skirt.

He was still blustering. 'But at last we finally have this conception ...'

Oh God, no.

Andrew's earlier attempts had all resulted in him spilling on her as he'd held her down, before he was able to complete his assault. She'd paid for his failings on those days. Then she'd paid again when, with the arrival of her monthly course, she'd been pressed to announce that she had not been with child—how could she possibly have been? He must have known that much. Or perhaps in his madness he didn't want to remember he had failed.

Nell shut down the memory of the only real coupling—rough, short and painful—weeks ago. It was his one successful attempt in a scant three months of marriage. But any possibility of conception had again been dashed when last week her course had come early. She'd hidden it from him, not wanting to endure—

'I should have left you to fend for yourself in the camps at Ballarat, but you submitted to your duty …'

Never willingly.

He'd assumed that she had conceived because he'd managed to penetrate. Believing he would cease the beatings, she hadn't corrected him. He'd blared to his sister that he would soon have an heir.

He was still shouting. '… otherwise cast you off as useless, sent you back to your lying cur of a father. A good thing my sister is now informed of the forthcoming issue. She will see to you in your confinement.'

Nell couldn't remember if she'd heard Enid's whining voice during the altercation last night, but if Enid was to see to her in her confinement, why were they bolting away from their home now?

'She agrees with me, however,' he continued, loudly, bouncing about the seat they shared, his hip squashing hers. 'You're just like your predecessor, a weak baggage.'

His first wife, Susan, poor girl, was blessedly free of him, and of this earth. She hadn't been able to endure his beatings, and both she and the babe had died in premature childbirth. Had Susan's father betrayed her too, like Nell's father had betrayed her? He'd taken her by the arm in a punishing grip to Susan's funeral. There, they'd witnessed the dead woman's only relative, a brother, just back from some war in Europe, shaking uncontrollably, distraught with grief. And afterwards, finally threatened with abandonment by her father, Nell's hand had been forced. She'd grudgingly consented, accepted her fate and mere weeks after the funeral, Nell was married to Amberton. Too late she'd learned from Andrew that he'd paid her father to entice him into handing her over like some prize sow. If there was any consolation in this humiliation, it was that Andrew would have despised paying.

Her lip curled now. All this because her father, Alfred Thomas, had a new wife to support. Dora had firmly urged him to move along his hard-to-handle spinster daughter. Never mind that Nell worked the family laundry business alone.

But perhaps her doing so reminded her father that he'd failed as a land owner, failed as a provider for his family, and the once-comfortable life that afforded his daughter her education was now gone, thanks to his drinking and gambling. That his daughter's own manual labour had to support him prior to her marriage.

The money Amberton paid for her must have given her father and his new wife reprieve from having to work the laundry themselves and they'd closed it down. Typical of her father. It would be a short-lived financial reprieve—the recently wed Dora was a spending force to be reckoned with, a rival to his own.

Andrew hadn't paid for Susan; he'd somehow, by thuggery or otherwise, acquired a loan from Susan's father instead. Nell had spied a paper to that effect, witnessed by Andrew's nephew, Lewis Wilshire.

The coach jolted, and a grunt escaped her, turning her thoughts. *I will not be beaten down. I will not have the same fate as Susan. I will do anything to survive.*

Nell's ire thrummed. Andrew Amberton's fists might well be intolerable, but she would not break under his aggression. She'd fought back at first, physically, but it wasn't worth the punishment, which was part of the game for him. There had to be another way—if she could just stay strong. He might kill her, but until that time, she'd be staunch and endure at all costs. If she stayed alive and bore him a son, she might have a life she could manage—if she could escape his killing her afterwards.

'It would have to be a boy, mind, and not a female child,' he said, and the smirk appeared. 'It's declared in my legal papers.' Would he ever stop repeating it? 'Even a stipend for you depends on your delivering a male child and only if I were to meet an early death. Which of course I have no intention of meeting. So much more fun to have.' His voice jumped and quaked again as the wheels cracked over the corrugations of the road. Then he grabbed her hand and thrust it over his groin. Her gut surged in revulsion. She snatched her hand away, trying to hold back the rising gorge.

At least if she vomited, he'd continue to believe that she was with child. Then he'd berate her for such a lack of control.

Too late she saw it coming. His fist cracked into her chin, but its power was lost in the shudders of the carriage. He cursed, and turned his attention to hanging on to his seat.

What ill spirit pervaded his soul? What kind of man …

And yet, if Andrew were to die today somehow—if it pleased the god she barely had faith in any longer—would she be safe from the destitution and life on the streets that her father had threatened? The law would protect her, a wife—a widow—wouldn't it? She didn't know. She didn't know!

Nell's thoughts were a tangle of trails and tracks and footsteps that took her nowhere but back over the same old ground.

Since her wedding, she'd feared for the health of her mind. Her rationality had struggled under his constant beating.

Think straight. Think straight ... but she couldn't think beyond surviving. *I must surely be mad, believing I should stay and not run fast and hard and take whatever fate befalls me. Perhaps my mind is already lost that I stay and stay and stay ... Would death be better than this?*

No. She *had to stay* to survive. Touching fingers to her forehead, as if that would stop the rattle of words in her head, she knew there was a chance—if she stayed alive. That's all she had to do. He'd beaten her when she'd admitted there was no pregnancy. More horror would later await if again there was bloodied proof that no child was quickening in her womb. There was still time to conceive if he could manage ... Oh, dear God, she couldn't bear to have him touch her again. Despite her roiling gut, a voice whispered, 'Survive. Survive.'

A gunshot boomed in her ears, so close she thought a bullet had roared through the window. Perhaps the murderous troopers had caught them.

Breath was flung out of her. The coach skewed to one side and for one terrifying moment, it swayed precariously on its axle. Fright clutched at her throat. Gripping the windowsill, she gaped as the baked earth seemed to rise. Andrew's bulk slammed against her, surely forcing the coach to crash onto its side. It swung back dangerously. Her head cracked on the timber doorframe and bounced off.

Sparks shot before her eyes.

Perhaps nothing mattered now. It would all be over.

Two

Finn Seymour knew it was close. A pale red dusty cloud rose in the air just beyond the jutting rocks of the wide curve in the road. It signalled the coach would round the bend towards him in less than a minute.

Why did the bastard choose this morning of all mornings to run? Amberton should have been with his miners, looking out for them after the deadly clash.

In the early hours of this morning at Eureka Lead, one of the digging sites where Amberton had claims, the government troops had attacked a small group of miners and their families—fired on them while they slept in tents behind the stockade they'd built. For fifteen deadly minutes, the shots exchanged between the troopers and the miners—those who'd roused quickly from their sleep—had boomed throughout the camp. Some of the miners who'd been wounded, unable to escape, had been bayoneted. Wives and families behind the barricade had been trampled, some butchered, when the troopers rushed them in their tents.

The rest of the Ballarat camp—some thirty thousand people—had been woken. By the light of dawn the horror had been plain to see.

And where had Amberton been? Running for his life like a scurrying rat. He was a coward. A wife beater, a wife murderer, and now he'd abandoned his men.

After what had happened to Finn's sister Susie, nothing about Andrew Amberton surprised him. The man was known to bribe the mounted troopers, and the traps—the foot police—to escape paying extra license fees for his three workers. He was known to pay his miners a percentage of the finds, but it was also known that he cheated them, and lied. Was known for his cruelty. The man was repugnant.

Today, that man would die.

Finn's roan gelding danced underfoot, shuddered and snorted. He pressed his knees against the horse's middle and the animal quietened. Alongside him, the saddled-up but riderless bay gelding shunted against the other horse.

He brushed aside a fleeting tremor in his arm, a warning. *No time for nerves now, Finneas, my man. This is your best chance at him.*

His gut clenched. Sweat popped on his forehead, dripped down over his brows and ran to soak into the kerchief over his nose. Another trickle slid down his back. His hot, gloved hands gripped the two sets of reins. He checked the three single-shot pistols tucked loosely into leather satchels on his saddle. They wouldn't let him down. He'd make damned sure Amberton was sent to hell. If the bastard somehow got off a lucky shot, so be it. As long as he killed him, Finn didn't care that he might die too.

The rumbling of the coach's wheels grew louder. The lone driver, Ben Steele—well known to Finn—could be heard shouting over the din for more speed. A short whip cracked and cracked again.

Saddle creaking, Finn adjusted his seat and planted his feet in the stirrups. He checked the plain kerchief over his nose and mouth. Firmly in place, it was a nondescript match for the pale shirt and cotton twill trousers he'd donned for today's work.

Ben would drive as normal, hard and confident, and Finn would bail him up. That was the plan. The coach, pulled by two blinkered, charging horses, careened into view.

Only thirty yards more, closing fast. December sun beat down on his head, his hat the only protection that kept his brains from cooking in the midday heat.

On the coach, Ben snapped the whip high over his horses' flanks.

Finn kicked the roan. They leapt onto the rough road and stopped right in the path of the oncoming coach.

Pulling a revolver from the satchel on his saddle, he yelled, 'Bail up,' and fired a round into the air. His horse wheeled, but Finn had no time to spare on nerves for horse nor man.

Ben pulled hard on the reins to haul in the coach horses. He looked to be struggling, fighting for control. Horses squealed in protest. The coach rocked dangerously from side to side.

'Go 'round, man. Go 'round,' a voice shouted from within the coach. 'Forge on!'

'We'll go off the edge of the track and roll the coach,' Ben called in return. 'I'm pulling up.'

The harnessed horses snorted at the rude tugging on the reins, and at the snarls and grunts of their driver. Within only feet of Finn, the coach came to a standstill. Ben's hands shot into the air.

'Brake, and get down,' Finn ordered. 'Stand where I can see you.'

Ben bent and wrenched on the brake. Then with his hands back in the air, he clambered from the driver's seat to the ground.

Finn squinted at him. Ben had a strange look on his face and was winking at him like a mad person.

Another roar from within the coach. 'What do you want, you scum?'

Ben stood stock still, glaring at Finn. 'Mr Amberton,' he shouted over his shoulder. 'Keep yourself calm and you *and the missus* won't get hurt. These bushrangers like good manners, sir.'

'Bollocks to that,' was the shouted answer from within.

Finn returned Ben's glare. Ben had said Amberton would be the *only* passenger. But now he was saying the man's wife was on board? Christ, the bastard didn't waste any damn time finding another victim.

'Shit,' he said under his breath. He beckoned Ben. 'Come at me, hard, then get the hell out.'

Ben hesitated, his hands still in the air. 'Jesus, Finn. He could kill ye,' he said, low and desperate. 'I know ye don't care but—'

'Then the bastard will die with me.' Finn gave him a short nod. 'I want no witnesses. Come on. Tussle.'

Ben let out an almighty roar and flew up at Finn atop the horse and pulled him to the ground. Finn's empty revolver skidded across the dirt.

From inside the coach, another shot rent the air. Ben swooped up his hat, leapt onto the bay and, shouting to the passengers that he'd get help, galloped off back the way he'd come.

Finn scrambled to safety behind the roan. He pulled a loaded revolver from the saddle, aiming it at the window of the coach. 'Amberton, step outside.' His pulse throbbed hard in his throat, his chest tight. His hand shook a moment … *Not now. Not now …*

No movement from the coach.

Finn grimaced. 'Step outside, you coward, or I'll shoot you where you sit.' He heard the growl in his threat.

'My wife's in here, you braggart.'

But still no appearance by the fine, upstanding, courageous husband. 'Don't hide behind her skirt. It's not the good lady I want.'

He heard the sputters from within the coach. 'There's gold in bags here under the seat.'

Finn fired at the coach, under where he presumed Amberton sat. His ears rang with it. A scream rent the air, and not a female one, it seemed. His shoulder jerked. His hand shook. *Not now* …

A guttural, urgent voice snarled from within the coach. 'Get up … Get up and stand in front of me.'

The door, a canvas drop curtain swinging against it, opened and Finn stood stock still. A young woman, gaunt, dressed in a white blouse and dark blue skirt, bent in the doorway of the coach. One of her arms was held in a grip by a large hand, no doubt her husband's, who couldn't be seen.

Finn lowered the empty revolver, slipped it into the saddle's bag. No time to reload that one, but the third one was still unfired. He settled a hand over the butt of it, ready. If he withdrew it all the way, the woman was in danger of being shot, either by him or by her husband. 'Step down, Mrs Amberton.'

Except now he could see she couldn't step down. Her husband had grabbed both her forearms from behind so that her body shielded him.

Finn's glance flicked to her face. It was partly in the shadow of her white bonnet, and sturdy sprigs of yellow wattle on it jiggled as she shook. A strong chin, a straight nose, and he imagined her a fair woman, not a beautiful one. What hair he could see was soft blonde. She might once have been slender, but was now thin, the blouse loose over her bosom. Young, but not a girl. Just Amberton's type. Her eyes, though downcast, were wary. The brief study showed him her mouth was grim, her jaw set.

'You know me, scum. How is that? And you call me coward yet hide behind that mask,' Amberton shouted, yet he still held his wife in front of him in the coach doorway.

'The mask is for your wife's sake. And I know you because of Susie.'

Amberton blurted a cough, a choking sound. Hesitated. 'Liar,' he grated.

'I said to step outside.' Finn's hand, still steady, tightened around the butt of the next gun.

'And I said the bags of gold are under the seat, in here,' Amberton yelled. 'I'll throw them out. Take 'em. Take them. It should be payment enough.'

Gold? A trick, no doubt. Finn's patience wore off. 'Step down now, Mrs Amberton.' He knew she would have to lower herself to the step, then slide to the ground. He would not be availing her of the foot step that jutted from the coach, nor would he assist by offering her his hand.

Awkwardly, with only one arm now in her husband's grasp, she gathered her skirt, struggling to stay upright. Lifting her booted foot over the step, her heel caught and she lunged forward, nearly wrenching out of her husband's grip.

Amberton shoved her the rest of the way over the edge of the step. She dropped to the ground with a cry. He was now a wide target in the open doorway of the coach, and his hand-gun came up to take aim.

Finn's hand began to shake violently. He tried to snatch the pistol from the saddlebag, but his fingers wouldn't close over the butt of the gun—

The rifleman, hidden from the coach behind an outcrop of low boulders, loosened his stance. Settling the butt of the long Enfield rifle-musket into his shoulder, he concentrated his sight only on Andrew. It wasn't a difficult shot now. The range wasn't so long; he had skilled precision. He'd been shooting at game since he was a young child, so he was used to succeeding with moving targets.

And Andrew was a large target, objectionable, and barely mobile. It would almost be too easy.

A deep, sharp sting in his side, courtesy of an earlier bayonet slash, brought a grunt to his throat. His guts squeezed, which made it worse, and the pain was a brutal reminder of events that had followed the fiery, doomed stockade battle.

Even so, intent on his mission, just moments before now, he'd found this bend in the road. His vantage point would be clear, the coach an easy target. It would be travelling at speed but would take the sweeping bend at a slower pace. His shot would be dangerous, perhaps even lunacy itself, but luck had been shining. No need to imagine the horror of mistakenly killing horses, or an innocent coach driver or—God forbid—Nell.

It was luck of the best type and a most convenient thing: the appearance of a bushranger who'd bailed up the coach. A stationary coach with an easier target than ever if Andrew stepped out. And he did. Just after Nell appeared then fell to the ground.

He fired. The butt hammered his shoulder, and the juddering shock burrowed deep, down into the cut in his side. He rocked, light-headed with the throbbing agony of it. Steadying, exhaling low and long, he checked the coach through the sights again. Blinking and swiping at his watering eyes, he waited.

Two shots rang out, one from Amberton. But the other?

Finn's horse danced and snorted beside him. Holding the reins fast, one-handed, his stare fixed on a spout of blood erupting from Amberton's chest.

Mrs Amberton screamed. She scrambled under the coach as her husband pitched face forward into the dirt. As the body landed, she scrabbled backwards. Wordless, she panted and desperately tugged at her skirt, the hem caught under the wheel. Finn stood, blank, wondering in a split second if Amberton's shot had hit him. He looked down over his front. No blood spurting. No pain. He hadn't been hit. And his horse still danced by his side.

He sprinted to Amberton and fell to his knees alongside him, checked for a pulse in the broad neck. Nothing. A sightless eye stared off into the distance, as if from where the shot had come, the other stared at the dusty road under it. Finn squinted at the terrain where Amberton's last glare was aimed. He scanned the landscape, saw nothing untoward in the scrubby bush and small rocky outcrops of the one hill that overlooked the road. No glint of light off a gun barrel, no movement in the scrub.

Finn glanced over at the coach. Mrs Amberton was under it, tearing at her skirt, frantic to free herself. He heard a great rent give way and then she scrambled out the other side.

The shudder rippled through him. He clutched his elbow, couldn't forestall it. He stayed on his knees, hunched over the arm wracked with tremors. 'Stay where you are,' he grated. As she scampered away, he raised his voice. 'I would not want to come find you.'

She stopped, just beyond the coach. The horses shied and stamped their feet, then settled, their eyes wide, ears pricked.

Rolling back on his feet, Finn lurched upright, arms held tight against his chest. His right shoulder jerked and a spasm splayed his fingers, and then it left, as quickly as it had arrived. He shook out the stiffness in his hand, and steadied himself. He looked over his shoulder, sure that if a gunman was on the hill somewhere and intent on more murder, he would have been shot at by now. And so would the woman.

Expecting she might yet have fled up the hill, he spun back. He didn't want to chase her, catch her up there, risk his identity, or worse—offer a target if she was the objective.

Instead, she had stood up, was dusting herself off, and seemed in no hurry whatsoever. Half her skirt was missing—there was a piece caught tight under the coach wheel. A simple white chemise showed, torn in part, falling short of her ankle boots. As she sucked in draughts of air, her chest rose and fell. The bonnet gone, her hair hung loose over one eye, and her forehead creased in a frown.

'How I hate gunshots,' she said through her teeth. Without looking at Finn, she asked, 'Is he dead?'

Finn stared at her, not sure he'd heard correctly.

'Is he dead?' she demanded, louder.

'Yes.'

Then she lifted her one blue-eyed gaze to his. 'Well?'

Still he stared.

The frown deepened. 'If you're going to kill me, it wouldn't be a very good idea, would it?' Her voice wavered only a little. 'To kill your only witness to self-defence.' Her chin lifted.

Is it fear? No, it's a calculation. She seemed to be weighing him up. 'I've no intention of killing you, Mrs Amberton. I had only intended to kill him.' He pointed to Amberton's body. 'But as you can attest, I was beaten to it.'

She gave a curt nod, then backed up against the coach. 'So, what now that someone else has made your mission redundant?' Her hands found the thorough-brace suspension and she sagged a little.

Guts. She had guts, this one.

He spread his hands as if to say he had no idea. Which was true. And then he saw it fully—a dark puffy bruise above and below her left eye that coloured her cheek with a deep sooty smudge. 'You're hurt.' He tapped his own eye.

'A blow landed. 'Twas nothing like the usual,' she dismissed. Her glance darted to the body and back to him again.

'He used his fists on you, too.' He eyed her face, searching for other bruises, other marks on her. None he could see, but he knew there would be more. He knew the Amberton of old. His sister had married him. Had died at his hands.

The woman pointed at his arm. 'You are injured.'

Surprised she even cared to mention, he said, 'A jarring, is all.' He rolled his shoulder as he came closer, flexing his arm. As he advanced towards her, she pressed back and watched him in taut silence. Her chin puckered as she held on to her distrust, her good eye growing wider as he approached.

He held up a hand. 'I would not harm you, Mrs Amberton.' Finn was only a few steps away. 'But what should I do with you? I'd only come to dispose of that pile of garbage.' He pointed again to the prone body of her husband. 'I'm not sorry for it, but it was not something a lady should've witnessed. Especially his wife. And for that, I am—'

'Do not be sorry on my account. He is not worth it. And I have not seen your face.' She indicated the kerchief. 'I can't identify you.' Attempting to stand upright, she wobbled and so remained where she was. 'You sound like a gentleman, as if you have had an education, are perhaps gentry.' The twitch at her chin appeared again, and she turned away from her husband's prone form. 'Yet, a gentleman would not have left me … in these dire circumstances.' Her eyes did not meet his as she waved towards Amberton's body.

Taken aback, Finn cocked his head. 'Oh, I'm sorry. I gave no thought to your dire—'

'I will be destitute,' she cut in sharply over his quip. Darting him a glance, her booted feet scuffed at the dirt, scraping, tapping.

Ah. It was money she was after. A pay-off, perhaps, for her silence. In that case, a greedy, grasping woman was by far more easily dealt with than a crying or beseeching one.

Finn pointed to the coach with one of his guns. 'He said there was gold in there.'

She flashed him a look. 'And for how long will I have that in my possession?' This time she stood up and braced against the coach.

'Theft was not, and is not, my intention,' he said.

A moment's confusion crossed her face. Then, 'It will not last me long when I have to—'

'He liked to boast he had a couple of large estates, and that he is a wealthy man.' Finn shrugged, not apologetic. 'Was.'

Mrs Amberton glanced at the body, and blood seeping out from under it, muddying the dirt. She began to cough, or sob, or gag—he couldn't decide. She settled, took a couple of breaths, smoothed her skirt. Her hands at first seemed agitated, then she firmly pushed at the heavy fabric against her legs. 'A wife does not inherit.'

Now Finn understood. Unless her husband had instructed that a stipend from his estate be awarded to his wife upon his death, she would have nothing on which to survive. He knew it from his own marriage. That was the ancient Dower law, and she would indeed be left for the poorhouse without it. Clearly, this woman believed it had not been put in place for her. He knew of old that in her husband's family there were no kindly relatives, only Amberton's sniping sister, and a nephew he knew little about. Finn rubbed his hand over the kerchief. Unfortunate circumstances indeed, even for this lovely, avaricious lady. But surely not his concern—

'I have to produce an heir for the family, a male child, to gain financial support.' Her voice wobbled, low and gravelly, but her stare was direct.

It challenged him. It wasn't greed but something else. Her eye, intense, darker blue now, never wavered from his. Instantly he knew what she wanted. Her jerky breathing, her chest rising and falling. He knew as a peculiar heat from his gut crept up his neck. As another simmered deep down inside, he knew.

'And do you carry a child?' He surprised himself; it was indiscreet, bold. He took a step closer, her stare firing his blood.

Her head shook just a little. Her gaze fell to his chest, then lower where it lingered before travelling back up again. 'Not yet.'

A primal surge bolted through his belly. But he recoiled in shock. At himself, at his sudden reaction. 'I have never committed rape, madam, ever, and I never would.' A burst of anger scorched through him, but as her face flushed a deep red, it dropped away.

One of her hands lifted and dropped, as if in apology for decrying his honour. 'It would not be rape.' Then she fingered the neckline of her blouse. 'There would be time before anyone comes.' She faltered but there was a resolve in her bleak stare.

Had she just spoken those words? He backed up a step and looked down the road where Ben had bolted. No one would come soon—the military had shut down the town and had it under martial law. The diggings were eerie, quiet as death.

Is this some trickery?

He looked back at her. Her eyes, searching, seemed not to have left his face. This time he saw another woman in the hollow of her gaze—a desperate woman. It wasn't greed he had seen before. It was strategy—the swiftly devised plan of a survivor.

She could not really want this...

When he found his voice, he said, 'It would not be his child, even if there was—' he hesitated, '—conception.' He stood there, agape at the nature of the conversation.

A quick frown. 'I'm perfectly aware of that.'

Testy? He could hardly believe his ears. 'Even if you were to become—'

'No one would know it wasn't his. No one would ever know any different.' The woman shook her head. 'It would be only another base act, in itself that means nothing to me. It could produce a male child for this God-bereft family and secure my future,' she said. 'And I know the time is right.' She held his stare, swiped the back of her shaky hand over her mouth. 'I know it.'

Another base act. Means nothing … His hands clenched as tightly as his gut. 'But you might not become … as you want, and you would have sullied your—'

'I will take a chance.' She licked her lips and a frown darkened her brow. 'If it happens, I gain everything. If it does not, I would have gained a little time to squirrel away some funds. But either way, no one will know except you, and me, and I don't even know who you are.' Her words came fast, urgent, desperate. 'But if not now, there will be no other chance. They will force me out onto the diggings, or the street.'

Too many words coming at him, he couldn't take it in. He forestalled again. 'But it might not be a boy.'

The woman dragged in a pained breath. 'I have prayed to every god I am aware of, if any are left above this world, that it would be a boy.'

He stood dumb. Why was he even discussing this? *Get your brain back in your head, man.*

'Is there something wrong with your grasp of my situation?' she snapped.

More than testy. Finn shook his head. 'No, there is not. But nor is there good sense here, either.' He pointed in the direction of Amberton's body.

She didn't glance at it. She stood taller, a little unsteady, and he saw a flicker of what he thought was hope in her good eye. She took in a long, deep breath. 'It's not sense I need. Just do not show me your face.'

What man would not oblige on such an invite? He hesitated. What would it matter? He would surely be hanged for the hold-up and what it appeared he had committed, not to mention taking a woman on the very same roadside and risking her blurting to the troopers.

Since returning from the war, he hadn't cared if he lived or died …

His thoughts turned over. The back of his hand went to the kerchief as he searched for any ploy, any coquettish flutter of eyelashes. He saw nothing in her one open eye. Her direct, proud stare was blue, intense, and clear. And suddenly it mattered a great deal to live. To be alive. To fight for life. A flash of clarity wedged in his head.

He didn't want to be a dead man anymore. He wanted to live.

Back-stepping, he drew a deep breath. 'But I need sense, madam. Regretfully, I must decline your request.' He damned the lust, damned his better sense. 'Very regretfully. I am not your solution.'

She stared. Bleak. Bemused. Then, exasperated. Finally, she shied away from his scrutiny, her head bent. 'You leave me in a situation, sir.'

Finn pointed towards the body again. 'He is dead. Whatever your situation now, it is a better one than before. Yours and mine, both.'

She didn't look in its direction. Instead, she looked at Finn, appeared to want to shout, or scream; her rage was palpable. Then her shoulders dropped. She sighed as if resigned and pushed herself upright. She seemed awkward a moment until she brushed down her skirt and slapped at the dirt at her knees and the hem.

'My hat,' she said without looking at him.

He glanced around for the white bonnet and found it, not far away. The little yellow flowers attached were bedraggled, and he brushed them gently. They seemed a small light in an otherwise dark day. He returned the hat to her and silently she placed it on her head.

Finn's own hat was by his horse's forelegs. He left the woman to snatch it up, took up the reins and turned back to her.

'Help will be along.' His voice was terse. 'You should sit back in the coach and wait, if you can bear to be near that,' he said, indicating the body with a tilt of his head. 'I'll put the driver's gun in there for you.' He took Ben's rifle from a sling strapped off the side of the coach and slid it inside. 'Don't attempt to drive away. The road might be crawling with unsavoury types. Bushrangers, for instance.'

Mrs Amberton's gaze flickered. 'You have been a gentleman to me today.'

Finn snorted. 'I have not provided you your solution, but I would be damned either way, madam.' He scuffed the dirt at his feet, aware of his profanity.

'Please, no apology. That would indeed be ungentlemanly.' Her smile was wan. 'And as for him—' She nodded towards the inert body on the far side of the coach. 'I only wish it had happened earlier.' She looked at Finn. 'I would gladly have done it, had I the capability.' She lifted her face towards him, her mouth set, her eyes darkened by the frown that twisted her brows. 'He was a monster. I should thank you.'

'But I did not do the deed. Both you and I should be thanking another.' He put a hand to his hat and tugged it more firmly on his head.

She started, worry creasing her features. 'Do you have to go?'

He barked a laugh. 'I am a bushranger, Mrs Amberton. You might not be safe from me. And I would hang for this if the troopers arrive and find me still here.'

A beat later she asked, 'Why did you want to kill him?'

Finn thought about his answer, thought about not answering her, aware that time was speeding along. This was not an afternoon tea party, even though his guest was becoming more intriguing with every minute. He said, 'He murdered someone close to me. If not by one blow after another, then it was by degrees. I was away.'

Mrs Amberton seemed to sag. 'He was a monster,' she repeated, her voice a hoarse cry. 'I hope you and yours are now safe.'

Her colour was fading, perhaps the shock of all this was taking over. Finn's gaze roved over her. 'And you? Will you be safe?'

A short breath, a quick shake of her head. 'I will survive whatever comes next. I have up till now. Everything will be easy after life with him.' She waved in the direction of the body then clasped her hands. 'It must be. No matter what my situation is now.'

Before he could stop himself, he said, 'I will see to it that you are safe when you are returned to your home. Sit in the coach and wait. The driver will be back soon.' He indicated he would help her inside and took her proffered hand. It fit snugly in his, her clasp confident, like it belonged. Confounded by that, and everything about this encounter, he stepped back.

Steadying, she climbed into the carriage and turned to sit. 'It is strange to thank a bushranger, but I do. For all.' As she withdrew into the shadows, he heard her goodbye, a breath over a resolute voice.

As he turned from the coach, horses' hooves beat in the distance, fading away. A rider, leaving from somewhere close.

Jesus Christ … had whoever killed Amberton remained, watching? The shock of it hit Finn in the guts. He backed up against his horse in a sudden confusion, a thick fog at the edge of his mind. His legs were unsteady. He reached around to grip the saddle, stepped a foot into the stirrup and swung up.

No tremors, no shakes. Not yet. Without a backwards glance, he urged the horse into a gallop, and tore north across the rough country into the harsh summer wind. The more distance he put between the coach, the woman, and possibly, the other rider, the better. His face burned behind the kerchief.

All he saw was her proud stare. Her alabaster skin, dotted with the smallest dusting of freckles, pale against dark blonde, furrowed eyebrows. Her wide generous mouth. She was beautiful to him, not just fair as he'd first thought.

Amberton's widow. Beaten, but not broken by him. A strong woman who would now find herself, indeed, in dire circumstances. A strong, beautiful woman. Someone ready to do whatever it took to ensure her survival. Perhaps he should have, after all—

Take your mind out of your trousers, Seymour. And what the hell just happened?

Not just that the woman had nearly seduced him—he snorted at himself—but because he hadn't murdered anyone. Someone else, with one crack shot, had killed Andrew Amberton stone dead.

Three

Finn woke slumped against a tree trunk. Horses' hooves had snapped him out of sleep, and he palmed his eyes against the glaring midafternoon sunshine. He blinked up at Ben, who cantered into the clearing, reining in his mount. Neither rider nor horse looked like they'd been riding too hard.

'I know from takin' Mrs Amberton into town that you didn't get yourself killed,' Ben said and slid to the ground. He threw the reins over the tangled shrub where Finn's horse was tied. He still wore his driver's shirt of heavy cotton, sweat-stained at the armpits, sleeves rolled revealing tanned and wiry forearms. His trousers fit snug on his youthful frame. 'And I can see the billy's on.'

Stabbing a thumb at the small campfire, Finn said, 'Help yourself.'

Large flies came from nowhere in the still air and buzzed a lazy hum. Ben squatted at the fire, and dipped a tin pannikin into the billy suspended over low flames and glowing coals.

He sat his backside in the dirt, landed the cup by his side and flicked off his hat. 'That was certainly some morning's work.' A quick scrub of his head relieved the itch of sweat in his coal black hair. He returned the hat to its place shading him from the searing sun. Blowing into the cup before slurping a mouthful, his eyes downcast, he said, 'I counted five shots before I took off proper for town.'

Finn, his back against the log he'd slept by, spread his hands over bent knees. 'I wasn't expecting the woman.'

Ben threw down another mouthful. 'But you didn't shoot her.'

Finn rubbed his nose. 'I took two shots. And warning shots at that. I didn't shoot anyone as it turned out.' He checked his memory again. 'And Amberton only took two.'

'Eh?'

'Did you see anyone else?' Finn asked.

Ben stared at him. 'Not a bloody soul.' He shook his head. 'Not till I got back closer to town and got to the troopers.' He cupped the hot pannikin and tapped his fingers against its heat.

'Amberton, dead, by the other shot. Not mine. I know not mine. I nearly got myself killed because of these damned shakes.' Finn held his hand up in front of his face. Steady. The surge of excitement, of danger, or whatever-the-hell else afflicted him, was gone.

Ben's eyes widened. 'Did his wife shoot him then? She told the troopers that some bushranger killed her husband. I reckoned that was you. Other than that, she hardly said a word.'

Finn shook his head. 'Someone behind me shot him.'

'Revolver?'

Getting to his haunches, Finn reached across to snatch his pannikin from the dirt. He dusted it off on his shirt and dipped it into the dark billy tea. 'I would've heard if someone was close behind me. And Amberton, or the woman, would have seen someone.' He shook his head. 'Rifle, I reckon. Crack shot to the heart. And over my bloody shoulder.' He checked his free hand for the shakes again. Nothing.

Ben whistled low, between his teeth. 'Shite, mate.' He scratched an ear, a frown creasing between his brows. 'Would have to be a good shot.'

Silent, Finn nodded. Thoughts stampeded through his head again, none of which slowed enough for him to catch them. *A shot over his shoulder …*

As Ben slurped his hot tea, his frown deepened. 'And no one else knew we'd be there?'

Corralling his thoughts, Finn tried to piece together the hours prior to their ambush of Andrew Amberton. He swiped at a low, insistent blowfly. 'Not from me.'

'Me neither.' Ben loaded up his pannikin again, his fingers tapping once more at the heat from the cup. 'Amberton must have told someone. He'd already booked me to drive the coach out and then, bugger me, the diggers decide to have a riot. Nearly bollocked up the whole thing.' He looked up. 'He had gold on board too, and he sure had a big mouth. Someone else must have known. Did you get any of it?'

Finn shook his head again. 'Not the purpose of the exercise. How much was there?'

'Don't know. Amberton stowed it in the coach before we started out. When I got back there with the troopers, his missus was shaking my gun at everybody, real nervous. Troopers got a bit twitchy then. The horses played up. There was a few mad yells, all that nonsense, and then we all calmed down when she recognised me and she let go of the gun. She had me move the bags when we loaded the body—might have been a fortune in there, the bags were heavy enough. And the troopers didn't have a clue. Too busy bein' scared of bein' shot by some bushranger.'

Finn rubbed his mouth, mulled it over. 'Where was Amberton going and what was he doing with all that gold? Did you hear anything about it—where it came from?'

'Out of his mines, maybe. All he said when he paid me was that he wanted to go to Bendigo.' Ben shrugged. 'Amberton was lucky getting the gold that far. The troopers are crawling all over the place, locking it down. Maybe whoever shot Amberton wanted the gold.'

Finn tasted the bile in his mouth. 'Then they'd have had to kill me to get it. And kill his wife.' Sweet Christ, had he left the woman there at the mercy of another? Surely not. No, no. He'd heard someone ride away. 'So, the troopers cooperated when you got back to town?'

Ben scoffed. 'Scared of their own shadows, but a bit of convincin' with a couple of small nuggets and two of 'em finally came back with me.'

Finn waited. 'And?'

'And the coach was right where we left it, with my gun in Mrs Amberton's hands, aimed out the window. She prob'ly wouldn'a hit anything two foot in front of her.'

'Wouldn't be so sure of that,' Finn said. 'She saw no one else?'

'I expect she would'a said so if she had.' Ben frowned, recalling. 'She was shaken up a bit, is all, she reckoned. She had to sit up in the driver's seat with me when we needed to put the body in the back. And then we came back to town. Took the body to the camp hospital, and after, troopers said I could go home.' Ben looked over and Finn met his gaze. 'Wouldn't worry. He's one of fifty or more, they reckon, dead or dying.' He kicked the dirt at his feet, his mouth a grim line. 'No official count yet, but they're sayin' about thirty diggers dead, five troopers, so far. And there's at least one woman dead, and other women and kids shot at and stabbed too. There's plenty of men been shot bad still in hiding. Some trampled. Dead bodies have been hacked by troopers, the bastards.' Scuffing a boot heel back and forth, he flicked a glance at Finn. 'Amberton will be forgotten soon enough, his killer not even looked for. They've more important people to look for. Lalor's still not found. Heard someone say the Catholic priest hid him till they whisked him away someplace.'

Finn grunted at that. He commiserated with the diggers, and their spokesman Peter Lalor, in their fight for better rights, for freedom from oppression and freedom from the crippling gold-mining fee. It was a poll tax, raising money only for the government coffers—if it got to the coffers. Corruption was rife, and the miners had had enough. But Finn's fight was elsewhere. 'You know what happened to Amberton's wife?'

'Troopers said I could take her to her house in Ballarat town. Off-loaded the bags, carried 'em inside for her.' Ben aimed the dregs of his tea into the dirt. 'Don't worry about his wife, mate,' he continued. 'If anything, she looked calmer than the rest of us. Didn't even want me to go get family. I thought she'd be scream-ing her head off. After all, some dashed bushranger chappie had just murdered her old man.' He laughed a little at his feigned accent, his grin wide. 'Just wasn't you or me.'

Finn's gut settled. He wiped a hand over his mouth again, thought of those calculating eyes. Those bleak eyes. Proud, blue eyes. *You have been a gentleman to me.*

'You're sounding different.' Ben saluted him with his cup. 'Somethin' else happen at the coach?'

'Aye. But don't know what.' Finn thought of that moment of clarity, that point at which he no longer wanted to be a dead man.

He exhaled. *Don't even think about her, Seymour.* But he did think about her. The town would be in lockdown, its occupants fearful of the troopers, or of more uprisings. It would be a danger-ous place for a woman on her own.

Forget about it. Forget about her.

But his mouth was away with him. 'So, Ben,' he said. 'Just for my information, for tying up loose ends …' A finger rubbed a sweaty brow. 'Which house in Ballarat did you take her to?'

Four

Nell sat rigid in the kitchen room of Amberton House. The late-afternoon sunshine poured in the open back door, casting a long illuminating glow over her hands as they rested on the small table. She flexed her fingers, testing them, noting they'd finally stopped shaking. Earlier, her heart had been racing, as if expecting an attack … someone jumping out at her, or Andrew waking from the dead. But the feeling of impending doom had receded, and her pulse had returned to normal.

She closed her eyes and thought back to being alongside Mr Steele on the coach-driver's hard bench. She'd gripped the rail alongside, holding on grimly as the vehicle pitched and swayed its way back into Ballarat at less frantic a pace than earlier in the day. It had meant she could hear her dead husband's bulk as it rolled on the floor inside the coach.

Was it only this morning she'd been on a wild ride out of this town with a madman for a husband? Her hands shook again. She clasped them, squeezed tight. Her neck hurt, her shoulders were tight, and pain tore up the back of her head. Breathing deeply, she tried dropping her shoulders, sitting straighter. Her heartbeat thudded in her ears.

You are safe. Order your thoughts. Calm yourself.

She couldn't. Looking for distraction, she gazed around the bleak interior of the room. She'd never thought of the house as hers, though now for all intents and purposes, it was. *Andrew was dead. Dead, dead, dead.* So, until a court took the house away from her, it was hers. For all its fine-sounding name—Amberton House—it was just a normal-sized cottage built of timber. And it held no happy memories.

Leaning forward, her elbows on the table, trembling fingers steepled and tapping on her mouth, she eyed her crumpled and torn clothes in a pile by the stove. On her return, the moment she'd found herself alone, she'd hurried to the bedroom, tossed the dusty bonnet to one side, peeled everything else off in a fumbling, tearing hurry—filthy dress, blood-stained at the hem, torn chemise, underwear. She'd stepped into clean underclothes, grabbed a faded housedress and had shrugged it over the top. She'd slipped her feet back into her laced boots, the only things kept of this morning's foray.

What would her hair look like? Fingers flew to her head and she twisted loose strands back from her face. Hard to manage with skill when her hands quivered so much.

And now—what was it, six o'clock perhaps? She was back here, a widow, and in another precarious position. Still, nobody but the coach driver and those two stupid drunks who passed as troopers knew she was back. She had time to think, to chart a way forward. Calmer now, her breathing was easier. Her head had stopped thumping once the tight band across her shoulders had loosened up.

No one would bother her today. The troopers were not interested in dealing with bereaved relatives, and the paperwork—if any—for another dead body. There'd been panic in their eyes at the camp hospital. The first stop had been to deliver the body, and, apprehensive of reprisals by surviving miners, the troopers had escorted the coach no further. They'd dragged her husband's body out of the coach and dropped it to the ground. Then they'd ridden off leaving Ben to do the rest.

Nell had clambered down from the driver's seat, unaided, forgotten, and climbed into the cabin of the coach. She'd torn off another part of her ragged chemise and dropped it over the dark pool of blood underfoot. Though much of it had seeped through the floor timbers, she was glad to cover it from sight. Then shaking incessantly, she'd kept herself well hidden from the pandemonium that was the hospital tent. The wounded had to be hauled from where they'd been found in the dirt to the relative safety under the medical canvas. There'd been pitiful calls for help on the bloodied stretchers of the injured, and the dying. There were many, many casualties.

Ben had come back, it seemed only moments later, with men to help him load Andrew's body onto a stretcher. They'd been directed to bypass the medical tent and go directly to the morgue tent. When he returned to his coach, Ben had driven her back to Amberton House, deposited her and her possessions—the bags— and left.

That had been hours and hours ago. No visits from anyone, no other disturbances. At least her incessant shaking, which had been powerful at first but was now only intermittent, would not be witnessed by anyone else.

Calm, and with a steady heart rate, she studied her emotions. Did she feel anything but revulsion for Andrew? *No.* Did she feel anything for his death? *Relief.* His demise was nothing but a blessing and that was all encompassing. Heady, even.

He had no power, now. He was gone forever. Someone had shot him, and it wasn't that bushranger. Someone else had hated him. And now she would waste no more time on Andrew. Not one moment more. Though she had been a wife for only three months, she'd administer her affairs until the law stopped her. And surely it would, because a married woman had no rights over her husband's financial estate.

Her thoughts turned to her immediate future. Who else knew of the gold bars and nuggets now in her possession? Her gaze darted to the bulky canvas bags alongside her discarded clothes and bonnet. Someone from the Amberton family would claim it, she was sure, even though that amount of gold certainly wasn't from Andrew's hard labour—because there hadn't been any. Andrew hadn't laboured—he made others slave for the wealth he had enjoyed.

Still tapping her lips, she knew the gold was tainted simply by way of it having been in Andrew's possession. She should hide it, use it to survive if she had to. She shifted uneasily. That wouldn't be right. Even if she did feel right about it, she couldn't spend it; trying to make any exchanges would arouse suspicion, especially from his family, and the law would soon find her. She would most likely go to jail for having it while not being able to prove it was hers, or even Andrew's for that matter. And there was so much of it. Best to leave it hidden for a while, especially from Enid and Lewis, until she planned a way forward.

She leaned back in the chair, touched her fingertips to the puffy flesh of her eye. Lord knows, she'd look a lot like many others would today, wounded by events out of their control. For some, the wounds would heal. She would be one of them. She would have no scars from the few months in Andrew's grip. It was a promise to herself.

Coals still glowed low in the oven. It would be sensible to light a candle or two, a lantern perhaps. Standing, steadying, she reached for a candle stub on the shelf, took it to the stove and pointed the wick to the flickering coals. Guarding the little flame, she set the candle in a holder on the table.

Enid. She'd have to get that battle over and done with, and she'd survive it better than any battle she'd had with Andrew; Enid wouldn't take a fist to her.

Then Nell would have to find her own way, or perish. The goldfields were full of enterprising women who worked as their own bosses. Enterprising, but still not thought of so highly. Even if widowed, women were suspect if they had no supporting family. And she would never return to her father's tents, even if the new stepmother would have her. Relieved of Andrew's yoke, she would never take a step backwards and swap it for her father's.

No matter. She was not so despairing. She'd fought despair before. Sometimes it had felt like her mind was going, and she'd fought with the last of her strength. When Andrew had treated her worse than garbage, she'd fought on. Fought to keep her mind on the straight and narrow and not to retreat into feebleness, or detour into wrong-minded thinking. She had done it, she had stayed strong. She would never go backwards. Never despair.

Her life wouldn't crumble now.

A little excitement grew. He was right, that bushranger. *Whatever your situation now, it is a better one.* She would remember it.

Her face flamed with the memory of her proposition to him, then flamed again at the light in his eyes. At the light in her heart when he'd looked at her, studied her, when he politely rejected her desperate advances. She laughed at herself. *Imagine that, a bushranger with manners.* But her laughter stopped. That's how low she'd become, reduced to begging a stranger to put a child in her womb so that she could survive—begging a man who'd been intent on murder. What had possessed her over these few weeks, the last days, to have given thought to such a thing? He would think her a terrible woman, that bushranger.

Oh, what did it matter? He was a man outside the law, and their paths would never cross again. That thought caused a mixed reaction. He had been kind. She'd seen it in the way he looked at her, those green eyes watching, studying. She'd had a little hope.

What rubbish, Nell. Your thoughts are skewed.

He would think her loose, and wanton, dismiss her as being the ranting, wretched woman she'd sounded like. Even the bush-ranger had higher morals than she had.

That was the state of her mind, skewed with a madness borne of Andrew's mistreatment. And all to survive. Taking in a deep, steadying breath, she looked around the kitchen again. It was just a kitchen. The parlour was just a parlour. The bedroom was just a bedroom. Would his menacing presence be forever here? Shuddering, she thought she'd burn the bed.

She eyed the bags of gold. What hope would a lone woman have, out on the street, trying to flee, and carrying a bag of gold tucked under each arm? As if she could carry it, besides. She could barely manage to drag one bag at a time.

Mr Steele had said that no one could get in or out of Ballarat, that the murderous troopers would still likely go on a frenzied rampage if they thought they could get away with it. He'd told her that the military had put the whole place under martial law, and that eight hundred more militia were arriving. Thirteen miners had been arrested for their part in the uprising, and the authorities were clamping down. There was a curfew already. If any one was seen out after eight o'clock in the evening, or with lights on in the tents at camp, it meant swift arrest. Did that mean no lights in the few houses as well? Nell didn't know and wouldn't go venturing to find out. If someone came for her because of her candles, she'd plead terrified ignorance. Though from what she'd heard, innocent women would not be spared, either.

She needed a better plan. She needed time. But how much time before she'd have to find Enid and Lewis and report Andrew's death?

She sat for a while longer, and her hand rested on her belly. She was so glad there was no child of Andrew's growing there. But would she want another man's? Her thoughts strayed once again to that bushranger, a man with kind green eyes, and a low, well-spoken voice. A man who'd told her he would see her safe. Was that a man with no scruples? When she'd offered herself so brazenly to him, wouldn't an unscrupulous man have taken her there and then?

The flame bloomed in her face again. The man at the hold-up had been a gentleman. She knew it, but how could she trust it in the light of what she knew of men?

Finn Seymour tapped a long sprig of yellow wattle against his leg. He turned for only a moment to watch the last of the setting sun drop over the horizon.

Fool.

Although the light would be reasonable for a little time yet, he risked being hauled off by the troopers if he was caught idling in the street. In any street. Ben had warned him of a curfew and Finn was in no mood to be swept up in the repercussions of the 'riots', as the government men were calling the Eureka debacle. Guessing he'd have about fifteen minutes before he needed to be under cover somewhere, he knew he'd have to make haste.

Staring at the unassuming timber house on the opposite side of the street, he watched a glow appear in a window as a candle was lit. She would be in the back of the house. It appeared there was no one else with her, and likely not going to be by now. Would she be sitting in the peaceful night trying to recuperate after her ordeal?

She might have been desperate and out of her mind on the roadside. But here, at her house, no doubt she would be resting, attempting to make sense of what had happened, like he was trying to do. It wouldn't be in his best interest—or hers—if he marched up the path and hammered on her door.

But the need to extend the tenuous connection with her gnawed at him. He had to do something. Anything. *Hurry.* He loped across the road and sidled around the back of her house. The door was open, and for a moment he froze, undecided.

He stared down at the wattle in his hand.

This was certainly not the act of the gentleman *she thought you to be, Seymour.*

Walk away.

The evening was slipping into night, and the silence outside was eerie. Nell had taken the candle to wander through the rest of the house, and, mindful that it was wearing down, she headed back towards the kitchen room outside.

She needed a purpose, needed to be busy. Didn't need to feel this awful terror, anticipating the troopers pounding on her door.

The first thing she'd do, now, tonight, was stuff those bloodied and torn clothes into the oven and hope the room didn't choke with the smoke. One piece at a time should be all right.

As she passed the doorway of the bedroom, she checked it, held the candle high. Perhaps later, if burning her clothes was success-ful, she'd burn the remaining bed linens, too.

Resting against the doorjamb, she inhaled deeply, relieved not to feel sick with tension, and not to have a thunderous headache. Expecting it still might come, she closed her eyes a moment and drew a long breath in and let it slowly out.

At the hold-up, Mr Steele—

Her eyes snapped open.

At the hold-up. The bushranger had two horses with him, one of which Mr Steele had jumped on before riding off. Her mind worked. Why would a lone bushranger have two saddled horses with him? He'd certainly given no indication of wanting to kidnap Andrew, or her for that matter, so why two horses? Very convenient for Mr Steele to ride off on one.

Mr Steele. Did he have something to do with the hold-up?

Reaching across, she pulled the door shut to the bedroom and stood for a moment in the hallway. She knew where Mr Steele's business was situated. Knew he owned the coach that Andrew had hired. She would pay him a visit. Had Mr Steele been in collaboration with the bushranger? If so, to what end? The gold? That couldn't be right. There were many opportunities for him to—

No, no, no—too many thoughts flinging about in her overwrought mind. Why should she venture to seek out Mr Steele? Did she really even want to? Vexed at herself, she headed for the kitchen room. The back door of the main house was open and in the lingering light she saw moths and mites attracted by the candle. She snuffed it out, and hurried, keen to close the house and sit in the kitchen room that was outside the main dwelling. She'd light another candle there as she used the oven.

Perhaps tomorrow or the next day she would venture a walk to Mr Steele's. Her heart sank. First, she would have to go to Wilshire House and inform Enid and Lewis of Andrew's death. Her mood dropped further. She'd have to wait until after that to see Mr Steele.

Taking a step or two more in the hallway, she stopped in her tracks. A shadow was thrown across the lingering light at the back door, and something fluttered to the ground.

She stiffened, heart thudding. She wanted to get to the kitchen room to light another candle, but if someone was out there waiting to pounce ... Nothing moved. Nothing shifted. She heard nothing. No footsteps.

The light was failing quickly. Panicked, she burst out of the house and dashed to the kitchen room, slammed the door, shoved home the bolt. Heading straight for the candles stored on the mantle, she found a taper and with shaking hands pushed it into the oven, hoping there was enough heat left in the coals to give a spark. She smelled a little smoke then saw a tiny flame. The wick caught, and light glowed around her. She tried to be calm, tried to breathe steadily. Tried. *Tried.* Safe. Barricaded behind a sturdy door. Hot, stuffy, no air. She reached out and grabbed the fire poker.

But—what if it was someone injured, someone looking for safety? Her heart thudded again. She put her ear to the door and heard nothing. Tried to peek through a gap in the timbers but the light outside was no good.

She retreated, sank to her knees and slumped on the floor, and the poker clattered by her side. The candle flickered. She couldn't spend the night in fear, not after everything else that had happened. This would not be her life from now on, full of fright and anxiety.

Breath hitched in her throat and, her mouth dry, she rested the poker by the door, got to her feet, and with the candle in the other hand, slid the bolt open. Bending to close her free hand around the poker, she nudged the door open with her foot. If there was someone out there meaning to hurt her, she'd give them a good run for their trouble.

Nothing. Nothing but warm air, a faint scent of burned timbers on it.

As she stepped onto the dirt outside her door, her foot fell across something. The candle glowed as she bent and picked up a sturdy twig of yellow wattle.

Five

Reaching for the cloudy, corked bottle on the small bedside table, Lewis Wilshire groaned aloud as his damned shoulder ached. The bruise of the rifle butt had surprised him. He'd practised shooting of late, so he should have been prepared for it.

Everything seemed to ache. His damned shoulder, his damned side. His damned head.

On the edge of his bed, facing away from the small window overlooking the street, he carefully unwrapped the rag from around his middle. It had been a shirt only yesterday.

He pulled the cork with his teeth and splashed a little of the bottle's contents onto his side. Crude alcohol was better than nothing. Stretching his mouth as the still raw spots of the wound stung and burned, he believed he was past the worst of it. The newly healed skin had only been a little chafed by the hard ride earlier today, and he assessed no permanent damage.

He'd have to sacrifice another shirt if he was to keep a firm bandage around his middle. After the miners' conflict, bandages were in short supply, so a shirt it would have to be.

Bloody bastard trooper. The bayonet had sliced him in the left side, just below his ribs.

And how to keep that from his ever-suffering mother? Not that losing a few shirts bothered him at all. However, he did not intend to explain to her that he'd sided with the rebels—in fact, been almost under the Australian flag, the Southern Cross, when the Canadian, Captain Henry Ross, had hoisted it weeks ago. Or that he was by the captain's side again in the early hours this morning when the government troops had struck. Poor bastard, Ross. He'd taken a musket ball, bad. Lewis knew he'd been mortally wounded.

How to keep all that from her, along with the fact that, at the first notion of trouble, her mad bloody brother Andrew had run like the stuck-pig coward he was.

After seeing Lalor shot and dragged to safety, Lewis had scarpered to escape the trampling hooves, the blazing tents, and the brutal bayonet stabbing of defenceless men and women. He'd been picked up by strangers in the melee and slung into the bottom of a cart. It had charged madly beyond the reach of the mounted troopers, who'd been crazed by bloodlust and had spied easy victims in the other direction. He'd been dumped for safety, with others, well away from Eureka Lead.

He'd lurched up a short rise and down into the sparse cover of some remaining scrub, only to come across the rape. Enraged, his frustration and horror had boiled over. He'd snatched up a short, thick rod of gum tree and had thrown himself bodily at the trooper. The screaming woman had been pinned underneath the bastard and Lewis's momentum had shoved the man off her.

The dirty grub might have had his pants open, but his gun, bayonet attached, had been within easy reach. He'd grabbed it and swung at Lewis, who'd felt the quick stinging slice in his side. Lewis swung back, his grip on the piece of wood.

Thwack! A sickening, deadly crunch.

Luckily there had been a natural hollow in the ground, and the shallow grave, with the body covered with leaf litter, would not be discovered for months, if at all. It had already been days past, and no one had sounded an alarm about it. Everyone was too busy looking after themselves to bother with a missing trooper—thugs and criminals the lot of them. Lewis wouldn't waste curses on another dead man who was on his way to hell. This one to the special hell for men who rape. *Bastard.*

If anyone talked, if anyone came forward to name him for being there, anyone who'd seen him, he'd be hanged. But there'd only been him, and the woman, and the dead trooper. He was sure neither of them would talk.

She had simply stopped screaming as soon as the trooper dropped lifeless at her feet. She'd stared hard at Lewis, scrambled upright, adjusted her skirt, and pressing a hand low between her legs, had bobbed awkwardly to him—a nod her only thanks before she'd gazed in horror at the blood colouring his shirt. Then, crying, she'd clambered into the bushes and out of his sight.

Now, at home, he winced as the cotton stuck in some scabby spots. He dabbed at it with a damp rag and eased it off the healing wound. He knew from a medic friend at the camp hospital that if wounds were not cleaned, he would get the sepsis. It was a new theory, still barely believed by the medical hierarchy, but Lewis had seen enough success after bad accidents at the diggings to trust it.

Only nicked him … The long gash, which hadn't needed stitching as he'd first thought, looked pink and was clean. No evidence of infection or the slime of pus oozing yet.

The rebels, so-called, were saying to wait while the law decided what action it would take against them. It was said they would not be prosecuted; no one would dare prosecute in the face of the witnessed atrocities. All the same, Lewis would lay low and the death of the trooper would pass by.

About the death of his uncle, he'd do what was necessary.

He laid back on his bed. Every so often the flat, low voices of his mother and of his uncle's widow reached him, drifting up the short hallway from the cheerless parlour room.

Nell's news two days ago had been met with a shrill cry, then his screaming mother had dropped to the floor. Nell had stood by as Lewis bent, carefully, to help Enid up and into a chair. He'd tried to soothe her. Nell had remained standing, coolly delivering the details of his uncle's fate as if she were relating a tale that belonged to someone else. Her features, dulled by the yellowing bruise covering half her face, hadn't showed emotion.

But his mother. Dear God, his mother. If she had any idea what he'd done … that he'd killed her brother. Well, that truth would never reach her ears from him, like all the other truths he'd hidden from her.

It had certainly been fearful for him as a young boy when his uncle had first arrived. If his mother had ever known of her brother's sudden temper and the thumping Lewis would get as a consequence, she'd never said.

This house, Wilshire House—it sounded so damned grand, but wasn't—was his uncle's, as was the one Andrew had occupied with Nell. Did both houses now belong to Nell as Andrew's widow? If it were so, there'd be nothing his mother could do about it, except for that medieval bollocks that was supposedly his uncle's will. In the name of all things holy, what could have possessed the lunatic bugger to write such a thing?

Nothing natural had appeared to help hasten Andrew's departure from this world, not even his madness, which, of late, had seemed to fester and sicken his spirit even more. He'd flung himself into another doomed marriage to try and avail himself of an heir. Had not even given his family the courtesy of forewarning, only the sudden announcement, and with his first wife's grave still fresh. The new bride Nell had looked dumbstruck at the nuptials, her father beaming like a cat with cream.

So far, no news that Andrew's loins, from which his uncle had hoped a son would spring, had planted anything. Or perhaps the springs were not as tightly coiled as Andrew would have his men believe. Lewis grunted his scorn.

Lewis had now seen the blackened eyes of both his uncle's wives. The first wife had died delivering a dead baby. The evidence of his fists on her poor ravaged body prior to the birth had been unmistakable to the midwives. How was it that the man continually proclaimed that he wanted a son and heir, yet made sure it was very nearly impossible as he badly beat his wife? The midwives had told Lewis that his uncle had exploded in an uncontrollable rage over something Susan had said. Nothing Susan could possibly have said would have caused uncontrollable rage, and certainly not in a true man, a *real* man. One of the midwives had demanded to be paid for her silence, the other had fled in terror for her own life. The troopers had not come to take his uncle away. Andrew should have stopped there before he risked being committed to stand trial for murder. He should've left it at that … He was in no state to beget a child. But no, he had to continue, didn't he?

Lewis was now Andrew Amberton's successor, was he not? The eldest surviving male in the family. Except if there was direct issue, of course … he could still be usurped by law, by pieces of paper, a marriage certificate, a birth registration—if there was to be one—and a will. It was a ridiculous thing. His uncle wasn't fit in the mind. If Lewis had taken it to a magistrate and ordered the will to be rescinded or revoked, or whatever in God's name the term was, he'd have had his uncle committed to an asylum.

The look on his mother's face when he'd suggested it had stopped him flat. So he took the only other solution he had and dispatched his uncle—without so much as a hitch in his breath.

He would revisit the situation with the will. His mother had informed him that the lawyer, Mr Campbell in Bendigo, would have it read. Lewis would ask Matthew Worrell, Andrew's ledgers man, who worked with his cousin the lawyer, to introduce him. Always best if one had an introduction.

There was, of course, the chance that Nell might well be with child. He hadn't heard—surely his mother would have said—but if Nell was with child, he would not direct any harm on her. She could be useful—in the face of Flora's rejection of his marriage proposal, offering marriage to Nell might be the best way forward. A comely wife, a fortune to administer and, perhaps, children of his own.

After he'd witnessed the damage his uncle had inflicted on Nell the last time, he'd decided he would not wait any longer. Would not stand by and let the possibility of another woman's death occur at the hands of his uncle. His own mother might turn her eye, but not he. As Lewis proclaimed to himself, the estate would not go to waste under his administration if Andrew were to 'pass away' suddenly. His uncle was repugnant, and Lewis would ensure he was assisted off this mortal coil. The injuries inflicted on Nell had simply brought his solution forward.

So after the massacre, as it was now called, and his little detour with the trooper in the faint early light of morning, he had limped home. It wasn't far. Then just after dawn, struggling with the nuisance cut in his side, he had checked that the Enfield rifle was secured to his saddle, that the cartridges were in the bags, and had clambered atop his horse. He'd ridden to his uncle's house, only to see him hastily alight a harnessed coach, after shoving his wife inside, and depart town. All the better.

Careful, Lewis kept a lookout for any troopers. He'd always known where his best vantage point on this road would be and he headed there as quickly as he could. He took the rough terrain cross country to position himself before the coach rounded the big bend.

That bushranger could have upset things. But the man hadn't spooked overly much, except for what appeared to be a short fit after the shots were fired. Only moments later, he'd regained his senses and stood there, talking with Nell, as calm as day, Andrew's body ignored. Lewis couldn't make out their words, but it seemed the man was *discussing* things with his surprisingly composed aunt. Then he'd approached Nell at the coach and Lewis again had steadied his eye at the rifle.

The bushranger had put the driver's rifle inside the coach for her, had helped her inside. A gentleman. Absurd, but there it was. No need for more killing, just yet. Lewis needed to leave before that *gentleman* bushranger decided to come looking for him.

Now home, again on his bed, he closed his eyes, the relenting need for sleep still catching him unawares. Before he gave in to it, his plans were foremost on his mind. Plans that might now have to include Nell Amberton.

Oh, dear God. Flora, what will become of us? Flora.

Six

Ballarat, Christmas Day 1854

Noise from the streets was restrained; life after the killing fields of Eureka Lead and the stockade remained quiet. A stillness had descended on the town, shrouding the misery. The camp itself hummed with a low energy, like a grumbling dog not yet ready to rise again.

At the diggings, the burned tents had been cleared. There was a dreadful discovery of bodies that had been caught and burned in the night's fires as the deadly soldiers and troopers stormed through Eureka Lead. It was a horror witnessed by the survivors and reported indignantly by the *Geelong Advertiser* (for Mr Seekamp, the editor of Ballarat's own newspaper, the *Ballarat Times*, had been imprisoned for sedition after the battle). What other dreadful atrocities had been inflicted that were now only coming to the light of day? The troopers, and those who condoned their cowardly acts, should be damned for eternity.

Nell watched as Enid dabbed at her reddened eyes once again. It had been weeks since Andrew was killed, and his sister was clearly still much overcome by it.

Now the woman glanced a watery eyeful at Nell. 'I am glad we did not prepare to have Christmas. Wouldn't be right,' Enid said, picking up her fan and flapping it a few times in front of her eyes. 'After the death of my dear brother. And your husband.'

It was hot, more than one hundred degrees. Nell lifted her own fan. It would have been far too stifling in this heat to have readied any sort of Christmas celebration. Not that it would have been a particularly festive one. 'I am certainly happy we did not prepare for Christmas. Very happy,' Nell answered, her glance veiled.

Enid's eyes leaked tears, it seemed all the time. There hadn't been any agonised weeping. After screaming the first time upon hearing of Andrew's death, she had been somewhat dignified and had held most of her woe inside. Her face would stretch in the distress of high emotion, distraught and pained, but in silence.

In that, the woman was certainly not like her brother, neither in stature nor in temperament. Yet her features were an eerie reminder of the monster that had been Andrew Amberton. Enid had her brother's low forehead and wide eyes, a nose, which, when her emotions were high, flared at the nostrils. Her hair, the same pale ginger as her brother's, and receding the same way, was thin and drawn back from her gaunt face in the fashion of a dec- ade past.

A sigh turned Nell's thoughts. One day, when she was free of all this, free of these people, she hoped she would have a child, a wanted child. Perhaps one with kind, searching green eyes, and chestnut-coloured hair, like that of the man she'd thought of for weeks. Perhaps her boy would have the same auburn-tinged brows, and long lashes the colour of the darkest night. Maybe when he got older, his razor-scraped cheeks would show a fine shadow, or a stubble glinting with grey and flecked with red after a day or two without a shave. Her heart gave a little leap and her cheeks heated up.

Nell closed her eyes and sat back in the chair, a cushion at her back and her feet on a little stool. The window was open and the wisp of a breeze, warm and dry from under the shade of a gum tree outside, teased at her neck. Wilshire House had a far more pleasant outlook than the home she and Andrew had occupied.

'You seem to get a cooler breeze here through the warmer months,' she murmured to Enid. 'I'm grateful you offered me a room here. I was uneasy after the first night alone and seeing that mysterious shadow. Perhaps it was not danger at all, only my excitable nerves.'

Enid sniffed. 'Lewis felt it was the right and proper thing to have you here for the interim. But you will return once our affairs have been settled.' The fan flapped again.

Nell nodded absently. 'As soon as I can.' She could feel Enid's sour glance.

In the weeks past, she'd accepted the room here at Wilshire House, knowing it certainly hadn't been offered out of the goodness of Enid's heart.

Enid had stared frostily at her when Nell had agreed to take it up. 'If you would return the gold that Andrew left, as well,' she'd said, politely, as if it were just another ordinary subject of conversation. 'It will be kept in trust, of course, and Lewis will administer it once the estate has cleared probate.'

Lewis, reading the Geelong newspaper at the time—the local *Ballarat Times* hadn't been printed since the Eureka debacle—had glanced up, startled. 'Gold, Mama?'

Nell had only shrugged. 'Andrew left me no gold.' Which, she reasoned, was true.

Enid had not been deterred. 'Lewis and I will check the house for ourselves when we come to collect you. Andrew might not have wished to bother his dear wife with such things.'

Nell had swallowed down a retort. Mildly, she'd said, 'Of course.'

When Lewis arrived with the hired cart to transfer Nell to Wilshire House, Enid herself had gone through Amberton House with a fine-toothed comb. She hadn't found any gold. Lewis had been satisfied with that.

For the few anxious days and nights that she'd remained at Amberton House before the move, Nell had secreted bars and nuggets throughout the house and the yard. She'd sewn the smaller nuggets into her skirt's hem. The day they'd had come for her, Nell had been relieved that the gold pieces hadn't clack-clacked softly as she'd made her way into Wilshire House.

The remaining gold at Amberton House would wait for Nell to retrieve it when she could. It was safe in its hiding places for the time being.

Now, Nell couldn't wait to go back to Amberton House. She was ready, her bruises healed, her appetite returned. The gloom of Amberton House would have to be endured, for it was the lesser evil at present.

Today, she wore a plain skirt of black linen, and a blouse of dark cotton over a chemise, all fresh from the clothesline. She refused to dress in anything more drably respectful for her mourning attire. If she'd ventured out, which she had rarely chosen to do, Enid had loaned her a black jacket to cover herself. It was too damned hot to wear that dreary dark fabric, so it was easier not to venture too far.

However, of late, she'd become restless. Trying to keep modest in this heat was an effort for every minute of the day and night.

'I will be glad of some new clothes, I have so little as it is,' she said, idly. 'These mourning weeds are too hot, by far.'

Enid made a noise. 'You should be thankful my brother insisted on good clothing for you. He might not have been the richest man on the fields, but his tastes stretched to the best he could afford,' she shrilled.

Or steal, Nell thought. 'I have hardly any clothes,' she corrected. 'A few undergarments. So a couple more pieces will do me.'

'You were to have a tea gown, he told me,' Enid went on, a huff in her voice. 'I, myself, have never had a tea gown.'

Nell didn't bother looking at her sister-in-law. 'A nice thought, Enid, but I can assure you, it had not been about to happen. He would never have bought me a tea gown.'

Andrew wouldn't have risked purchasing a tea gown for Nell; that would have been far too expensive and would have put her above her station, and questions would have been asked about Andrew's dealings. He wouldn't pay his workers fairly, and men were imprisoned for stealing from other men—he was very aware of that. It appeared he'd fled the fields rather than pay up. Fled while his miners, men he'd mistreated himself, bore the brunt of the troopers' savagery.

Enid sniffed, dabbing again at her nose. 'It was to be a Christmas gift, he said.'

Nell riled at the haughty statement. 'I wonder where he put it then, for clearly neither of us has found it,' she said lightly. 'It's better that such a gift was not made. Many families will have foregone Christmas this year because good people have gone unfairly to their graves.'

'Yes, he was a good man, but you sound ungrateful for all his generosity towards you.'

Nell shot her a look. 'Don't believe your own lies.'

Enid flushed. 'Well. You can be thankful you're back in rude health after the ordeal at the hands of that bushranger. My brother was not so lucky.'

Nell's ordeal with Andrew had been far worse than any bush-ranger could have imposed on her. 'I am glad to be in rude health, Enid, and all I yearn to do is to laugh again, to be free to choose my own way.' She would remain as civil as she could.

Dabbing her handkerchief some more, Enid said, 'We should not quibble. We should be more concerned with that terrible turn of events.'

'Which of the terrible events?'

'That we should have had to bury him with those rebel men,' Enid said.

I would sooner have left him for the crows. 'It was best,' Nell replied. 'Others have had to suffer it as well for there were too many deaths for one undertaker. And too hot this year. Most had to be quickly buried in the mass grave.'

'There's nowhere to mourn him. And who will bring his killer to justice?'

Nell decided to refrain, but if she'd been a blaspheming woman, she would've told Enid to go to hell.

Rather, she murmured assent to Enid's whining, which had become a habit. Nell almost didn't hear Enid's grief, and could barely spare her any commiseration. When Enid had visited Amberton House, she had not so much as offered a sympathetic hand clasp when Nell would appear, her face swollen, or her eye blackened at the hands of the woman's brother.

Her sister-in-law's only saving grace was her son, who had taken leave after his breakfast this morning. To rest, he'd said. Lewis had taken to 'resting' in his room through the day for some time now, Nell had noticed. She'd wondered if his slight stoop and a shortness of breath lately was an indication he was unwell. He had always been polite towards her, so if he was an ally, tentatively speaking, she hoped he was not becoming ill.

Lewis would be the sole trustee of the estate. Perhaps he would be kind to her.

Thoughts drifted as the breeze, only a slight respite from the heat of the day, tickled at her throat.

'I should have insisted,' Enid went on. 'I should have made them give him a separate place in the cemetery.'

Nell glanced over. Enid's face was splotchy and damp, probably not so much from weeping as from the hot sweats she endured from time to time. They were doubly terrible in this heat, Nell was sure. Enid's eyes were swollen, and her nose, chafed by hours of wiping, looked sore.

'It's too late to lament it,' said Nell. 'Perhaps you can purchase a plot in the cemetery. Erect a headstone over it once the will is read, and his estate belongs to Lewis.' She held her breath. So far, Enid didn't know there was no baby.

Enid shot her a quick glance. She frowned then the squint disappeared. Her mouth pulled a little as she spoke. 'At least his affairs ensure you won't have to go and find work in this town derelict of decent men and women.' She moved her shoulders, stiffened her spine.

There seemed to be no doubt in Enid's mind that she was the only law-abiding person left alive.

'I am sure there are plenty of decent men and women here,' Nell said mildly, without looking over. 'If I asked for it perhaps there are some who would take me on to work for them.'

She heard Enid's catch of breath. 'You will not go to work. We must press on for the sake of the future. For the child.'

In the moment's silence, Nell could almost feel Enid's thoughts. She waited.

'If there is indeed a child,' Enid finally muttered.

Inhaling deeply, Nell kept her tongue.

'You are not showing,' Enid said, another pointed remark.

'How would I? It is so early. But if it is so, and all goes well, he will be delivered early August.' Again, Nell kept her voice mild, a soft but firm confirmation.

Enid blinked. No doubt doing her count. More dabbing at eyes, more pulling of her mouth. 'We will have a doctor confirm—'

'That would be best.'

'And you don't know it will be a "he".' More of Enid's clever deductions.

'A manner of speech. And no matter if not. I will find my own way.'

Enid scowled, her mouth thinning. 'You wouldn't survive without us. Without the name.'

'Hence why I would have to find work. And I assure you, if I didn't have to carry this name, I would not.' Nell turned to look fully at her sister-in-law, who, after some seconds, turned away, her mouth pinched, her eyes narrowed.

Fully aware she had to take some steps to garner against poverty— for surely Enid would adhere to her dear brother's wishes—Nell closed her eyes and let out a deep, silent breath. There would be a way to keep safe and secure. It just hadn't shown itself yet.

She settled back, and at once saw the searching gaze of those kind, green eyes. She revisited the idea that Mr Steele held some clue to the identity of her bushranger. *Her* bushranger. Was her memory becoming crowded with silly thoughts because her belly tingled and her heartbeat sped up when she thought of him?

He was not a thug. She knew it as much as she knew herself. What had he said—that his mask was to protect *her*, that he knew Andrew because of … of who? Nell searched her crowded memory, but no name came forth. Why was it still so foggy?

But she remembered the awful tremors as he clutched his elbow, his arms crossed over his abdomen, as he bent double. Remembered the struggle he had trying to control them.

Awful tremors. Shaking uncontrollably.

With a little start, and a flush heating her cheeks, she inhaled a sharp breath as her memory tweaked again. Had she seen him somewhere before?

She needed to visit Mr Steele.

Seven

Nell held onto her hat and looked up at the bold sign above the wide doorway. *Steele and Sons Coach and Cart* stood out proudly in green outlined in red. Inside, a wide and long dray sat along the far wall. Leather and oil, dust, sweat, and manure reached her nostrils.

Four horses stood in a small corral, watching her, nodding their heads. Nell saw him, his back to her, a tin in one hand, a greasy rag in the other as he wiped oil along the foot board of his coach. 'Mr Steele?'

Startled, he turned sharply. 'Mrs Amberton,' he said. 'Good day to you.' He wiped excess oil from his hands onto the rag and stuffed it between the spokes of a wheel. Bewildered, he said, 'What can I do for you, missus? I hope you are well after—'

'I am well, thank you.' Nell had practised what she would say, something about perhaps helping him clean the inside of his coach, which would have been a sensible excuse. Instead she stood dumb in front of him, her little drawstring purse dangling from her hands.

'That's grand, Mrs Amberton. Grand.' He looked around. 'Would you have a seat? I think maybe this box here. I could—'

'No, I'll stand. I won't take up much of your time.' She looked beyond him into the interior of the coach.

'It's been cleaned,' he said, matter-of-fact. 'Strong lye will scour just about anything.'

'It will.' She nodded. 'Did I thank you for your help that day, Mr Steele?'

'You did. Terrible day, Mrs Amberton.'

'For many people.'

He nodded. He looked younger than she'd thought him to be. Black hair, oiled here and there with grease from the can no doubt, hung in strands that he tossed back from his face. He had a patchy day-old stubble on his cheeks and jaw. He also seemed nervous, but she supposed she was a new widow, and one who had aimed a rifle at him upon his return to the coach that day.

May as well come straight to the point. 'Mr Steele, the day of the hold-up, the bushranger had come with two horses. The spare horse also saddled.'

He blinked as if recalling. 'Yes, he did. You're right. And a good thing, too.' He shifted his weight and rolled his shoulders a little.

Nell glanced around the building and looked back over at the horses. How on earth would she tell if any of these horses was the one Mr Steele rode away on to get help that day? She'd taken no notice at the time.

'Why do you think that was?' She tilted her head. 'It has played on my mind.'

He shrugged. 'Strange thing.' He was not able to hold her gaze.

Nell clasped her purse in front of her to stop her hands shaking. 'I could barely speak afterwards, as you know,' she began. 'But now, after some time to recuperate, I felt I needed to come and see you today. I want you to know that the bushranger was ... did not seem a thug to me.'

Mr Steele looked confused. 'A good thing he was behaved, Mrs Amberton,' he said finally, and scratched his head.

'And that he was, in fact, kind to me.'

A nod in response, a kicking of dirt at his feet.

Nell's nerves settled somewhat. She knew she was right. Mr Steele did know the bushranger, it seemed to be written all over the poor man's face. 'I hope the police have not bothered you too much over it all,' she said.

He looked up, surprised. 'Not one bit. They don't care. Still chasing their tails, tryin' to be the big men but can't. Heard some have deserted already, knowin' they'll be in trouble for what they did at the stockade.'

Nell looked around again. 'You have a good business, it seems. A big dray for heavy work. The coach for hire, as well.'

He stared at her, waiting.

'My husband knew you ... how?'

He thumbed at the dray. 'He would purchase implements for his diggers from a merchant I cart for.' He lifted his chin towards the coach. 'He knew I had a coach as well. There's some talk a service might open from here to Bendigo if the road gets some work. I mentioned I'd like to drive it. And then, he—'

'Yes. Bendigo. I hope you are successful. It would indeed be a good service. I've heard it's quite the place to be. When I was younger, my family was supposed to move there, but it didn't happen.'

He only nodded, seemed to know he wasn't required to say anything.

Nell opened her purse. 'Mr Steele, can I leave something with you?'

Wide eyed, the young man waved a hand vigorously. 'Uh, no, Mrs Amberton. Your husband paid me before we left. It was part of our deal because I wouldn't take him anywhere unless he paid—'

'I know that.' She clearly remembered Andrew storming about it that morning before the coach arrived for them. She looked at her hands, now steady. 'I meant that I would very much appreciate leaving a message for your kind friend.' She withdrew an envelope from the little purse.

He made no attempt to take the envelope. 'I don't have no kind friend.'

Nell placed the envelope on the step into the coach, avoiding the oiled foot board. 'Of course. Even so.' She stepped back, fearful if she didn't she would snatch up the envelope and run away. 'Good day, Mr Steele.' Her voice sounded rough to her own ears, and when she left, he was gaping at the envelope.

'Good day,' she heard him say.

Nell's heart pounded. She hadn't seen signs of anyone else there, but the young man's response to her was telling. Even if her bushranger wasn't close by, he would certainly have her note very soon.

Eight

Rain pelted the parched earth and had dropped the temperature unseasonably. It would extinguish the burning tents from memory, the sooty scars from the land and from the hearts of men.

Nell scoffed. Nothing would remove the stain of Eureka. Nothing would change the fact that once again a government and its military had—with gross arrogance—used brutal force for unfair advantage on a much weaker adversary. She hoped the lives lost had not all been for nothing. The *Geelong Advertiser* was not giving the government favourable press, and it might have been making a difference—there was talk of a new Goldfields Commission of Enquiry. Perhaps Governor Hotham might now be listening to the pleas of ordinary people for a better life under his authority.

She stood at the front window, watching the heavy shower crash to the dust of the road. The only thing the rain did was stop her walking to the main store. She needed to step outside this oppressive house and take some air.

She rested her head against the sill and felt the cool air of outside chill her cheek. The time at Wilshire House had rallied her strength, rested her mind, and given her thoughts safe ground once again.

Even Enid had been tolerable. A twinge of guilt burrowed deep inside. Since she had her strength back, and her monthly had been, it was now time to make it known that she was not with child.

Folk scurried, some under sturdy brollies, some clutching the hands of their children, as if in desperate need to never let go. The memory of that night three weeks ago and the horror of the losses would never leave the living who remained. But here, as Nell watched, life went on.

'You look well, aunt,' came a voice from the doorway. 'Even in so few weeks, you have gained better health.'

Turning, she acknowledged Lewis. He was only a scant year older than she, but he had aged this last month. His strong frame still seemed stooped. Tiny creases had formed at the edges of his blue eyes, and his hair, a much darker shade of ginger, and much thicker than his mother's, looked unkempt, as if slept on and not brushed for some days. Nell had never met Lewis's father, Mr Michael Wilshire, who'd died and left a poor stipend for his wife and young son, but he must have been a handsome man. There was little of Enid's countenance in her son, and therefore little of Andrew, for which Nell was glad.

'Better than you are, I'll wager, by your look. Are you not well?' she asked.

He leaned on the doorjamb. 'I'm well enough to wager at the races today, though I believe this rain might hamper quite a few of us. However, I'm better these days than I was before.' He looked past her to the view from the window. 'Like most of us since that night.'

That was certainly true. And Lewis might have been talking of the murderous brawl of the stockade, or of his uncle's demise, or both. She didn't feel the need to make comment on either. 'Will you come in and sit? I have some tea.' Nell gestured to a small pot on a table next to where she had sat.

'Thank you, but no tea.' Lewis pushed off the doorway and, in measured steps, headed to a chair in the middle of the room. Its back was to the fireplace, which had the makings for the next fire. The weather had turned cool, strange in the middle of summer, but it wasn't cold enough yet to light.

Lewis sat and stretched out one leg, levering his body into the low chair. 'And how is your health, my dear aunt, after everything?' His eyes held candid concern.

Waiting a beat, Nell composed her features. 'I am well, so far.' His gaze didn't shift. 'It will be a joyous day to have a child in the house,' he said.

Enid must have told him what Andrew had wrongly assumed. Nell inclined her head. She folded her hands in her lap and met his steady gaze with her own.

His hands gripped the arms of the chair. 'I wonder what possessed my uncle to charter a coach to drive to Bendigo so early on that terrible morning.' Then he scratched his head. 'I would assume urgent business, but of all mornings ...'

Nell lifted a shoulder. 'He needed to see Mr Campbell, his lawyer. For what, I don't know.' She looked away, as if by turning her head the unsavoury events of that morning would not come forth.

'Sad business. I'm sorry, aunt, that I mentioned it.'

Deflecting, she said, 'Please don't call me aunt. It makes me feel as if I should be in my dotage.' The last thing she wanted was to comment on how she felt.

'Hardly dotage.'

'Nell will do,' she said, and turned back to him to offer a small smile.

'It must have been frightening for you, the appearance of a bushranger.'

Not nearly as frightening as it was relieving. Nell nodded. 'It was a dangerous drive, as well. Mr Steele was ordered to go ever faster. Up until that bushranger bailed us up, we'd been driving like the devil was behind us.' She took a breath. 'Perhaps he *was* behind us, in the wake of the madness of that night. And then when Andrew was shot—'

Lewis sat forward, eyes wide, listening attentively.

'Well, after the terrible attack at the diggings earlier that morning,' Nell went on, 'it was too much. The police have spoken to me again.'

He seemed to relax. 'It was too much, I agree, and I have asked the constable that his men should now leave you alone. After their visit here last week, they have their statement from you and have no need to return.'

'Yes, no need. My memory is quite clear. Nothing will change.'

'I believe it. My mother said you seemed remarkably calm giving your statement.' He shifted in his seat at her surprised glance. 'She said that you had very clear recall.'

Nell kept her voice calm. 'I knew well what to tell them, and how.' She clasped her hands. 'It was a strange experience, the hold-up, the shooting. It was as if it were not happening to me. As if I was watching it unfurl before me, and I was quite removed from it.' She remembered screaming, and that a sharp clarity had descended on her once the bushranger had threatened to chase her.

After a moment, seeming satisfied, Lewis said, 'I know my mother can, at times, be …' He searched for a word but failed to produce one. 'Anyway, I just wanted to ask after your health, myself.'

His eyes seemed full of concern. Nell felt her cheeks warming. Lewis's attention had never gone beyond what was proper before, and nor would she have expected it to, but there was a subtle difference in him now. Since that terrible day, something had changed in him. Perhaps he was preparing for his new responsibility as head of the household; stretching his wings, so to speak. Becoming a little bold? As he studied her, she became increasingly more uncomfortable.

But Lewis had a sweetheart, Flora Doyle, and the two women knew each other reasonably well. Surely then, Nell was wrong in her assumption about Lewis's attention and her blush was because of her own embarrassment, nothing else.

He slapped his knees. 'Now I need to go to Bendigo to make an appointment to see Mr Campbell. A formality, of course, to have the will read. I'll also meet with his cousin, Mr Worrell, who looked after my uncle's ledgers.' He let out a laugh. 'I confess, I know only what little Uncle chose to impart. I will need to acquaint myself of the books fairly quickly.'

It was true. Andrew had kept Lewis working in a junior capacity in Ballarat, until he felt the miners in his employ were 'getting too big for their boots'. He'd then sent Lewis to note their grievances, to cajole and plead, to placate, to pay a few pennies more, but Lewis would come back more on the side of the miners than of their employer.

Nell spoke up before he could rattle on. 'And when will Miss Doyle visit again, Lewis? I presume we will be seeing more of her.'

Lewis ducked his head. 'Flora has decided that perhaps I am now too high and mighty for her.' He examined his fingers. 'Though it seems a laundrywoman with her own customers can earn more money than I, so I wonder who is the more high and mighty?' He gave Nell a rueful smile.

He seemed genuinely saddened by Flora's apparent rejection. It likely had something to do with Enid. Lewis's mother had probably made a no-nonsense visit to young Flora, unbeknownst to Lewis.

'I'm sorry to hear that,' Nell said.

'She deemed herself unsuitable as my wife, though it seemed to me to come out of thin air.' He shook his head as if he were baffled.

It seemed unlikely, though, that Flora had made a hasty decision. What Nell knew of her—a young, dark-haired Irish woman whose mother also worked as a laundress—was that she was a forthright person with her own strong opinions. Nell liked her. They had struck up a friendship on the fields long ago, when in passing they discovered they were both laundresses. When life at her father's laundry became too oppressive, Nell would seek Flora. There was warmth and companionship in her darkly witty conversation.

Lewis had met Flora while using the services of her laundry. By chance, Andrew had accompanied him and enquired about Nell, Flora's visitor. The next day, Andrew had shown up at Nell's own laundry. Weeks later, Susan had passed away.

If Flora had any reason to reject Lewis, it would be because she'd clearly appreciated that, once married to him, she would have to work just as hard, and for little in return, *and* with Enid as a mother-in-law.

There was an understanding on the goldfields that women had as much right to paying jobs as the men. How Nell suddenly envied Flora her freedom. Was that a way forward for her— working for herself? Sometimes the women did better financially than the men, and set up shop charging for work that a man would not do, or had no time to do.

Perhaps Enid and her ilk clung too tightly to the preference of *being* a possession rather than *having* possessions. Enid would not approve of Flora earning her own living, yet many women on the diggings did just that.

Nell's life would take another turn very soon. A visit to Flora might be the thing to do; there would be much to talk about.

Lewis gave a short laugh, as if exasperated, which brought Nell back to attention. 'I will have to find myself a wife, a suitable wife, soon, if I'm to look after this family.' And then his gaze became a study of her again, polite but steady.

Nell allowed a breath to fill her lungs deep into her belly. When her eyes met his, she wondered if he'd intimated marriage. Surely it was only her nerves conjuring innuendo. The next days would be fraught, so no use reading any nonsense into what might just be simple concern. But as she and Lewis were not related by blood, was it such a ridiculous thing for him to consider a marriage to her? It would certainly fix many things all at once.

People didn't marry for love, she knew. Oft times it was for convenience only. *Hah!* As it could be said of her own marriage to Andrew—*his* convenience. How could she even think to enter into marriage with Lewis? Clearly, she wasn't as far removed from addled thinking as she'd hoped. She wanted to leave this whole family behind her.

Realising he expected her to comment, she said, 'Well, if it's not to be Miss Flora, I'm sure you will find a deserving wife, Lewis. A gentleman such as yourself would have no trouble securing a good match.'

'My choices on these fields are quite limited to few and far between,' he said, a little wryly.

Nell deftly skirted what he might have meant. 'I agree, there are not so many single women of marrying age,' she said. 'As for Flora, however, I should like to maintain my acquaintance with her.'

'By all means, if you wish it.' He gave her a small smile, and a slight raising of his brows. 'And on that note,' he said as he carefully stood up, 'I will take my leave and find a friend who might partake of a drink with me.' He dipped his head. 'Good day, Nell.'

'Good day, Lewis.'

The door clicked shut. In her mind's eye, she saw the look on his face again, and the small smile. But could she be sure he'd understood her? She would not be his 'deserving wife'.

Nell closed her eyes, wondered if the bushranger had received her note. Wondered if she had a right to expect to hear from him. After all, a bushranger … She laughed at herself. She shouldn't be thinking of that man at all. Or any man. She would be free of all of them.

Her own mother had told her a long time ago, 'Make sure you have running-away money, if you can get it.' There was still a little time to earn some, if she was clever.

Nine

Ballarat goldfields, January 1855

Nell ventured onto the digging fields. Bad enough she had to walk around this hellish campsite as a lone woman, but at least she wasn't enfeebled with child. There had been horrible stories coming out since the skirmish, or the *massacre*, as the papers were now calling it. She shuddered. People were saying that even women—some of whom were carrying their unborn—and little children had been murdered, that innocents were sacrificed.

There were thirteen men languishing in a Melbourne jail, awaiting trial for sedition over the event at the Eureka Stockade, as the *Geelong Advertiser* had called it. This was no simple 'miner's skirmish'. Mrs Seekamp's editorial in the local *Ballarat Times* was scathing in her attack on the government—she was fighting for her husband's release from jail, and had taken up editorship of the paper in his absence.

At least Nell could take a walk, and she was grateful. Many others from that terrible night could not. Her usual good health had fully returned, her battered body recovering better than she had expected. And as for her mind, well, each time she caught a thought about Andrew and how worthless she'd felt while in the awful marriage, she pushed it aside. She couldn't feel, couldn't *be* worthless if she was to survive. No one on the fields would be safe, including her, if things turned bad again. She had to be strong in mind and body.

Now, here, the very air at the camp was charged with an atmosphere she hadn't known before. Prior to her marriage, at her father's tents, life and business had been conducted as it always had. She'd worked as a cook and a laundrywoman for her father's team. She'd sewn, baked, and toted her wares along the avenue for a mile each way, bringing home nuggets, or minted coin, or promissory notes in exchange. Things had dramatically changed when, soon after the death of her mother, her father had married again. It changed to far worse when he'd married her off to Andrew. Yet, as Nell looked around, many things had stayed the same.

Rows of tents, people shouting, men bent silently over their sieves at the creek, or shovelling clods of earth out of deepening holes in the ground. Women rocking puddling cradles for gold, or cradles for babes—sometimes at the same time—or trudging from site to site with baskets and sacks laden with goods, chattering endlessly. Children scampering about, and generally into mischief—they ought to be in some sort of school, not just the Sunday School. Other men scarpered to certain tents here and there, with a gold nugget in their hand and hope in their trousers.

Nell knew where she was going and kept her head down to watch for potholes and broken bottles. People knew her in her father's area of the camp, but here on the other side and closer to the burgeoning township, she was almost anonymous. Here, she hoped her father might never discover her. She would be just another face in the crowded, rowdy, ramshackle tent town. And her father would have no reason to look for her; she was useless to him now and would have been discarded from his thoughts and manipulations on the day of her wedding.

As she picked her way deeper into the camp, the rowdy din grew. Gathering her skirt, she stepped over a child's mullock heap and steeled herself against the cacophony of noise she'd almost forgotten. Tied-up dogs barked at her. Some lunged, some crawled forward pleading for a kind hand. Always, the competition among dogs alerting their masters to trespassers was deafening along the meandering waterway where the diggers panned and sluiced their sieves. The cries of female voices reached her, the screech of a child just born, the yells of children playing. The shouts of men, some angry, some elated, some frustrated.

Was he one of them, her bushranger? She glanced about, not sure she really wanted to see him, or even imagine she would recognise him, but sure she could feel his presence.

How stupid. Why would he be here? Why would he risk it?

She stopped. An uncanny quiet had descended as two pairs of police on horseback trotted by, two abreast, forcing men, women and children to leap out of their way. Fists waved behind their backs, but neither trooper nor digger risked a confrontation. Not now.

It was said that Peter Lalor had lost an arm to the surgeons and was somewhere still in hiding in Ballarat. Another whisper was that he had been spirited away to Geelong, or beyond, to garner more support. In truth, no one knew where he was, and tensions still ran to fever pitch. Would he marshal another uprising, or had he died and his death been kept secret? No death certificates had been issued for the miners who'd lost their lives, or the women who'd died; no pardons nor amnesty had been given for the so-called insurgents. There were no answers yet for what had happened, and the mood in Ballarat was edgy.

Now that the troopers had passed by, there was noise again, blustery and tense. People spilled from the raucous so-called lemonade tent, and staggered off to their patch of dirt, the day's gold dust or nuggets gone to buy a few pannikins of illicit grog.

Nell moved quickly. In the near distance, she could see Flora's laundry fires and the washing tubs. It hadn't been easy escaping the ever-watchful eye of her sister-in-law, but without Lewis by her side, Enid had no leverage to keep her indoors. It was a mystery to Nell. Surely Enid wanted her gone as soon as possible. Perhaps she was worried Nell might steal something. Ah. That was most likely it. A laugh escaped her. The last thing she wanted was to touch anything that belonged to that family.

She stepped her way along the edges of sandy holes and heaps, careful to avoid turning an ankle on the debris of the camp, the discarded bully beef tins, the pans, rusty cups and pots. Scorched canvas still lay on the dirt in some areas or hooked on lone shrubs. Others had been raked and haphazardly piled in a heap, making way for new tents. Compensation had been denied to many of the diggers, and yet more than one man sat by his new tent gazing into its empty space, a new pan and sieve and pick by his side.

The hoots and whistles of men, some squatting over their pans, or their mines, became loud in her ears. Startled out of her thoughts, she looked up and was greeted with a leery grin, a mouth devoid of teeth.

'Young miss, a man could use those pretty hands.'

About to assail him with the only useful thing she'd learned from her father—a mouthful of his irreverent vocabulary—she was stopped in her tracks. Something swished by her and cracked the man on the head. A small rock.

He dropped, disappearing down his shallow hole with a yowl. Yelps of laughter and hoots and whistles followed, and two of the man's nearest neighbours trotted over to peer down at him.

Nell spun around, unsteady on her feet, the ground uneven.

Flora Doyle stood with one hand on a hip, and a crude sling-shot wrapped around the other. Her hair, a usually wild black mass with chestnut streaks weaving through, was held back in a laundress's cap. A long apron covered wide, man-like trousers tied at the ankle. 'Good day, Miss Nell. It pays to watch where you're goin', and not to daydream over these diggin's.'

Laughter at the man down the hole drifted away. He yelled obscenities at his detractors.

'Good day, Flora.' Nell dusted down her skirts, and tapped one booted foot on the other to remove excess dirt. 'You're so right. I was distracted by such noble sights.' She lifted her chin at the miners still tossing gibes at their colleague. Chuckling, they left him to his own devices.

The young woman cast a look about her. 'Fools.'

Nell was staring at Flora's trousers. 'Are they what the newspapers have called "bloomers"?'

'They are at that, though I've fashioned them a little more to suit myself. I've sewn them so they're not quite so wide.' Flora smacked a hand against her leg, and a small cloud of dust arose. 'Means I can bend over those damnable tubs and not be at the mercy of useless fashion, or gibes from those *eejits.*' She lifted her head towards the still chortling miners. When she looked back, she stood up straight. 'You're a long way from home.'

'Not so far,' Nell said with a wry smile. 'I'm more at home here than in the town. My own father is still in this mess of a place, though I'm not in any hurry to find him.'

'In that case, why are you here, Miss Nell?'

'I heard you might not be visiting us again, so I thought I'd visit you.' She dropped the smile. 'And stop calling me Miss.'

Flora wiped her forehead with an arm dusted white. Washing soda or some such thing, Nell thought. How she remembered those days. But, unlike Flora, she had not earned a living from it. Didn't even earn her keep, according to her father.

'You're a lady, now and all.' Flora's soft Irish lilt was tinged with a smile. She turned and headed for the washing tubs.

Nell fell into step with her. 'Hardly. I'm just a plain widow, like a lot of others.'

'I heard that about you. I should be sorry.'

'Don't be,' Nell said. 'You of all people know how I came to be his wife. And what being his wife was like.'

'I couldn'a stood it.' Her stare was fierce before she dropped her gaze. 'I'd'a killed a man like that,' she said, low and hoarse.

Nell dropped her voice to match. 'I wonder why I did not. He is not missed. No dying under the flag for him, Flora.'

A voice called from within the tent behind. 'Ah, that flag, daughter. 'Twas beautifully stitched afore God, it were, and now torn down and gone only He knows where.'

Flora raised her brows in Nell's direction. Moving past the tubs containing dark water and grey foam at the edges, she flipped back the canvas door of her main tent. 'Ma, we have a visitor.'

A plump woman seated on a timber stump, sewing on her lap, looked up. 'That's better, Flo. More light and a breeze. Whoo, it's so hot, I must have been off with the faeries for a bit.' She squinted at the needle in her veiny hand, then at Nell. 'A visitor, is it? Oh, 'sake's, I think I've lost me thread, Flo.'

Her hair, the same wave as Flora's, had faded in colour to a soft brown, streaked with grey. Clearly brushed, it had been pulled neatly into a ribbon at the back of her neck. She looked serene and happy.

'Hello, Mrs Doyle.' Nell looked into a blank upturned face.

Flora took the needle from her mother's hand and checked the thread. 'It's Nellie Thomas. You remember Mr Alfred Thomas? His daughter.'

'I remember a young girl by the name of Nellie, but not you. But that's what's wrong with me, isn't it?' she asked her daughter. 'I don't remember yest'dy. I do remember a bastard by the name of Alfred Thomas, though.' She took back the needle Flora held out for her. 'Bastard, he were.'

Nell didn't hide her smile. 'He still is that, Mrs Doyle.' Her father had thrown punches at his wife and daughter. Had drunk most of his earnings and had threatened time and again to abandon them to the streets. Nell's mother, Cecilia, had died of consumption before she could be turned out.

Flora raised her brows at Nell's words. 'That's the Nell I remember.'

Mrs Doyle nodded. 'Seen him t'other day. Right gormless, he are.'

Nell glanced at Flora, who shrugged. Mrs Doyle took to her sewing again, still nodding. Startled, Nell stepped forward to help the older woman. Flora touched her on her arm, spoke softly. 'Leave it be. Ma's doing a wonderful job.'

Nell was shaken. Flora well knew that her mother held only a rag in her hands. Mrs Doyle was sewing the same thing over and over, the stitches neat and even but doing nothing. 'Flora. I didn't know,' she whispered.

Flora patted her mother's arm. 'Ma, I got the billy boiling for tea. All right?'

Mrs Doyle held up the rag, turned it, settled it back on her knee and continued. 'I'll be out as soon as I've finished the lad's shirt here.'

Flora beckoned Nell to follow her out. She secured the canvas flap open, dropping a stick into its grommet and shoving it into the ground.

'Flora,' Nell said, concern creasing her brow.

Lifting her shoulders, Flora looked to the sky. 'I'm all she's got. Apart from the "lad's shirt". I'll be looking out for her till the day she dies. No mistake.'

'Of course you will, no mistake,' Nell agreed softly. 'At least you still have her to look out for.' Her throat tightened.

Nell thought of her own mother. Not a frail-minded woman, but a woman lost in this man's world, all the same. Now long departed, and gone too early, Nell keenly missed her. Right now, it came with an overwhelming thud. The sun beat down on her, the noise of the neighbouring miners and their tin pots, pans, sieves and shouts, crowded her ears, and she groped for a place to sit. Another sawn-off tree stump suited perfectly. Once her bottom hit the seat, she calmed herself.

'You've gone a pale shade of white,' Flora remarked.

'I miss my own mam.' Nell patted her face clean of tears, wiped her hands on her dress. 'Or maybe it's the heat.'

Flora eyed her. 'Have yer gone soft, after all?'

'I worry about that sometimes, these days, after … whether my brains were mashed by the punches.' Nell looked around. 'How do you manage with all this and your ma, too?'

Bending over the fire pit, Flora dipped a tin cup into the billy and handed Nell some tea. 'I just do. Before dawn, past dusk. Even Sundays when all these *slabs* are on a day's rest.' Her Gaelic scorn and her language were still strong, it seemed. The word sounded like 'slobs'.

'But your mother?'

'Oh, she seems happy enough. I need to take her to the latrine, but apart from that, she sleeps all night, wakes and works on her shirt all day. I give her other small sewing jobs. She would've helped sew the flag if they'd let her, she bein' Catholic and all. She loves her seams, her stitches.' Flora lifted a shoulder. 'She drinks tea, eats, talks to me. It's all right. She's company, and she's not always off with the faeries. Sometimes she's as sharp as a tack.' She blinked back bright tears in her dark eyes.

Distracted by a sturdy man dragging a small cart, Nell held her tongue. The man pulled up in front of the washing tubs. 'A job fer yer, Flo.'

'Just land it on the mat there, Tillo.' Flora pointed to an empty mat next to her tent. 'Come back tomorrow before evening.'

The man was stout and puffy cheeked. His dirty, grease-stained hat was missing bits, his shirt nearly clean and badly crinkled. He upended the cart's contents onto the mat. 'I got a bit of gold dust this morning. Can't get the assayer till day after.'

Flora looked at the pile of rough shirts, trousers and under-wear. 'Your boys woulda paid you up front for me to do that.' She pointed. 'It'll be a pound.'

He grunted. 'Big heart, Flo.'

'But not big pockets. One pound before you go for the grog.'

'Tomorrow.' Tillo turned the cart and trudged off.

'Not taking payment in gold, Flora?' Nell asked.

'Sometimes, when I know they're honest.' She turned her head at the retreating Tillo. 'He's only honest when it suits him. So, I trust a pound coin in my hand, mint issue.'

'Wouldn't he go to some other laundry, one of the teams that Mrs Pardeker runs, perhaps?'

'There's lots she won't have, and lots who can't afford her. This here is a good business, and while it lasts I'm going to work hard on it, and be hard in it.' Flora sat across from the fire pit. 'Feeling better now?'

'I am, and I'll be better still, as soon as Andrew's blasted will is read.'

'Surely it should have been on the day of the funeral?'

Nell shook her head. 'Had to be put off after the stockade. But soon, and then I will be free of this family.'

Flora's gaze darted to Nell's waistline. 'So, you're not—?'

'I'm not.' She took a sip of tea and lifted the cup in salute. 'Oh, how I've missed tea like this. The insipid stuff I get in the house makes me think Enid has used the tea leaves more than once by the time it gets to my cup.'

Flora snorted. 'That's how they have a lot of money.' She swiped a hand over her eyes, as if she had dust in them. 'Will they do the right thing by you, then? That family can't be as bad as—'

'I don't want anything to do with them if I can help it. And that brings me to my visit.' She looked up as Flora frowned. 'No, no. I'm not asking for money. I need money, yes, but I'm looking for work.' Nell toed the dirt at her feet. The hidden gold was not hers to use, and no one else knew of it. It would stay hidden until she decided how to deal with it. 'When I tell them there's no child coming and they put me past, for surely they will, I will have to work to keep myself. I might leave the fields, perhaps even leave the area, if I earn enough.' She smiled uneasily. 'Out loud, that sounds like a sweet story.'

Flora's frown deepened. 'That family won't support you even now? Even as you've—thankfully—been made a widow?'

Nell swallowed down a rise in her throat. 'No child,' she said and patted her belly. 'No support.'

Flora stared. 'How can that be right?'

'It's in Andrew's will. His wishes.'

'That can't be a legal thing. You're his widow.'

Nell shrugged. 'What do I know of the law? A father can sell his daughter, a man can put his wife by.'

Flora scowled. 'No. They can't. It's against the law.'

'The law,' Nell scorned. 'It might well be true but it's not my experience. My husband and my father must have come to some sort of arrangement because if I hadn't agreed to marry Andrew, it was the streets for me. That much my father did tell me.' Nell shifted on the stump. 'And fighting Andrew's will. How? By complaining to a magistrate? Ha! I've heard of women who stood before a magistrate to get an order to stop the beatings, but it only made it worse. A letter to the governor instead, perhaps,' she said, a twist on her mouth. Looking off to the distance, she said, 'So I must work. You do, and I used to. It's not that bad. Better than being with Enid.'

Flora shook dust from her bloomers. 'Nellie, it's hard work, laundry work. Have you forgotten? Scrubbing all day, lifting heavy tubs, lugging water. Over fires in this accursed heat.'

'I can't forget that. That's how Andrew found me, remember?'

'That's another me mam would call a bastard.'

'I could help you with your mother, too. And laundry's not dangerous work.'

'It can kill yer all the same.' Flora met her gaze. 'You could help with Ma, that's true.' She leaned forward to pour herself some more tea. She tugged on her bottom lip and sat back. 'An extra hand … We'd have need then of another washing tub, maybe another boiler.' She stared off down the way, at Tillo's back, and her eyes narrowed.

Nell slumped. 'I can't buy one, yet, but I will be able to, soon.' It wasn't enough of a reason to use any gold, but if needs be she could borrow a little of it …

Flora held up a finger. 'Wait here.'

She marched away from the fire pit and Nell watched her follow Tillo. She called out, and the man stopped and turned. Flora stood, first with her hands on her hips, then a thumb pointing back to her tent site. The other hand was palm up.

Tillo shook his head. Flora clamped hands on her hips again as she spoke. Tillo threw his in the air. Flora stood taller and waited. Then he said something in reply and she threw her head back and laughed, turned smartly and made her way back to Nell.

'A new half barrel will be here tomorrow. Might stink of rum … I mean *lemonade*,' Flora said, and laughed again. Few folk legally distilled rum and sold it on the fields. It was always disguised as lemonade of some sort. 'For a pound's worth of laundry, we will have an extra tub. I'll build a second stand tonight for one more boiler. I reckon Tillo will find us another for later.'

Nell's chest expanded. 'A pound, that's it? Nothing more? Just what would you owe him?'

Flora gave a short laugh. 'Nothing more than his washing, Nellie. I've never done business on me back. Doing the laundry is hard enough on me back as it is.' She sat again, looked around and pointed at a pile of rocks. 'I'd gathered those a while back. Now they'll come in useful. They'll make a bigger stand than this one.'

'I appreciate it. I'll help you build it.'

'It's hard work, Nell.'

'I know.'

'I mean all of it. Hard because we're doing it on our own, for ourselves. There's them that don't like it.'

Nell nodded. 'But times are changing.'

'And your sister-in-law? How're you going to get around her?'

Nell's mouth pursed. 'As far as she's concerned now, there's nothing to worry about. The will says it all.'

Flora kept her eyes down. 'And Lewis?'

'Lewis's only worry was that I might have given birth to a boy. Now he can have the will read and not feel as if his life has been stripped from him.'

Flora looked up then. 'So, he inherits straightaway?'

'It all goes to the surviving male member of the family. I believe Lewis will hear the will, then he'll begin to grow his assets. I'm not secure in either house.'

Flora kicked at the dirt, bent to toss a few twigs onto the fire. 'So. You'll leave there. You're a widow. You'll take a job here on the diggin's.' She looked at Nell. 'That's brave.'

'It's necessary, not brave.'

'And speaking of brave,' Flora said, waving away Nell's scorn. 'You haven't told me of your adventure. How brave were ye when you got bailed up?'

Nell rolled her eyes. 'Not brave at all. I tripped and fell out of the coach, and when the gun went off again, I scampered like a baby underneath it, screaming my head off. Got my dress stuck under a wheel and couldn't move until I tore bits off it. Might've got myself trampled by the horses or driven over by the cart. Not brave. Stupid as a rock.'

Fascinated, Flora chewed her lip. 'Why did he not shoot you?'

Nell stilled, remembering the low voice, the tentative, *'You're hurt.'* And then the other thing he said came back to her. *'He used his fists on you, too.'* As if he might have known how Andrew treated his first wife. Why did that suddenly come to her, now?

She looked at Flora. 'I don't know. After the shot killed Andrew, lots of things fled through my mind. I was scared for my life, but not once did I think that I would be killed by the bushranger.' Nell tried to recollect more. 'I said a very ridiculous thing to him, and as silly as it sounds, he seemed a gentleman.'

'A gentleman? He murders your husband—wait, I see it now. It would seem a gentlemanly thing to do, murdering Andrew for ye. Ha!' Then Flora winked at Nell and crossed herself.

Nell inclined her head. 'I should cross myself, too, but the bushranger didn't shoot Andrew. That shot came from behind him.' She shuddered. 'Either a lucky shot, or a very good marksman. It could easily have been me killed by that shot.'

Flora's eyes flickered in thought, then her gaze fell to the fire and she was silent awhile. 'A marksman, you say?' she said when she looked up. She took a deep breath. 'You were lucky the bushranger didn't have his way with you then, over his shoulder and off to his lair.' She waggled her finger in the air.

Nell said, 'By the time I'd found my tongue, I didn't believe I was in any danger. Not from the bushranger, anyway.' She burned, remembering her proposition, and cursed Andrew again for her feeble state of mind at the time.

'What is it? You've gone red in the face, Nellie Thomas.'

'He *was* a gentleman.' Nell thought of the kind eyes, of the polite rejection. Of honour. Her embarrassment flamed once more, and she wondered if she would ever see him again. She was hopeful that perhaps she would, if her note had been delivered, yet she had no clue how she would ever manage to hold up her head in front of him.

'Hmm. By the look of those bright spots on your cheeks, is it a pity you couldn't have made his acquaintance?' Flora laughed.

Nell glanced up. 'A fine thought.' She tapped her fingertips on the pannikin, and changed the subject, tossing her tea into the fire. 'But it won't help find a place to live, especially if Enid and Lewis decide against letting me take up the other house.'

Flora slapped her knees. 'It just might help if we knew where he was, this gentleman bushranger of yours. Perhaps he could swoop you up and take you off with him.' Then she shrugged. 'Failing that, your new lodgings will have to be a tent here in camp.'

Nell looked about her, at the rough and tumble of the camp, at the dust and the dirt, the hard, worn-down faces of men and women alike. The white people, the black people, the yellow people, myriad languages, the bellowing, the brawling, the children of all races on the diggings, scampering about, their dirty faces and patched clothes evidence of the fickle luck on the fields. Her heart banged. 'Yes, I know. A tent here in the camp.'

Ten

Nell decided it was time to inform Enid that she was not with child. She'd had a few weeks of calming herself in the relative safety of Wilshire House, but now she should move elsewhere, away from Enid's constant disdain, and begin to make a new life.

On the verandah—a narrow strip of boards only a few feet from the street front—she found her sister-in-law fanning herself, silent and frowning. Composing her features, Nell began. 'Enid, it appears I am not with child.'

Enid's tenuous civility evaporated like fog on a summer's morning. A glint of light showed in her eyes. She sat forward in her seat, the fan forgotten. 'I had the sense that you were not.'

Enid's vehemence and acid glance gave Nell a prick of fear and reminded her of her husband's violence. But Enid was not Andrew, and Nell was not in danger of being punched and beaten. She debated whether to sit or to turn away and run down the hallway, throwing something at the wall as she went. Drawing in a shaky breath instead, she decided to be more determined—for her future, for her old self, the confident and no-nonsense Nell. Wrangling with Enid would set things straight and would out the undeniable truth. She breathed more deeply as she drew out a chair to sit alongside her sister-in-law.

'You will also note that I am not unhappy about it.'

Enid glared. 'You should be on your way, then, not getting comfortable.'

Nell settled in the seat, her hands still in her lap. 'One of your midwife friends had said that she'd seen many beatings, and that mine were not the only ones Andrew doled out. That he could have actually murdered Susan.'

The snort from Enid could have been derision, but it sounded more like she was choking on the accusation.

'She said that trauma such as I had suffered,' Nell continued, and watched Enid's gaze dart away. 'You know, the beatings, the black eyes and jaw, the cracked ribs and bruised stomach,' she went on as Enid now seemed to squirm. 'All by Andrew—although the midwife didn't have to actually say that—'

'So, only *you* say,' Enid hissed, quick to clarify. She chewed her lips, her face screwing up and twitching as she held on to her outrage.

'All that, and his murder before my very eyes,' Nell resumed, swallowing down the nerves, 'would be enough to send the womb hysterical. The woman was sure of it. Do you remember she said as much to you, too?'

Enid put her nose in the air. 'Of course I remember what she said. The most terrible event of a husband's murder would have been a great shock for any woman,' she conceded, obviously not caring to address Andrew's violence.

Trying not to bare her teeth, Nell said, 'His brutality was something no woman should have had to endure.'

When she looked at Nell, Enid's eyes were wide and glassy. 'I don't believe one word you say, Nell Thomas, about what you were supposed to have endured. My brother was a—'

Nell's wrath boiled over. 'Your brother was a loathsome man,' she rasped. 'And you turned your eye from all his barbarisms to ensure that you and your son survived. You let nothing get in the way of that, not even common decency.'

Enid rounded on her. 'What did you expect?' she spat. 'You, only a laundress, forced upon him by your father—a failed squatter because of his gambling, his drinking. A man who set up a laundry and had his daughter work it.' She leaned over. 'I told him often that you and your father were only after his money.' She fanned furiously.

Nell returned her glare, frowned darkly as her voice thrummed. 'And you were not? If it meant that your son was once again his sole heir, and that you were not turned out, you'd turn an eye to anything, even my murder.'

Enid's mouth thinned. A shrewd calculation showed in the squint of her eye. 'Lewis is now the heir, plain as day, anyway, as you have so kindly advised. Your accusation is baseless. Moot, in fact. You are a disgrace.'

Was Enid about to smirk? Nell scorned. 'I hope the madness of your brother stopped with him and that his insanity, and your malicious traits, have not been inherited by your son.'

Enid's small eyes popped, and a deep red flush spread over her features. She slapped the fan against her chest. Breathing in angry snatches, she muttered, 'You ungrateful hussy.'

Nell's rage erupted, and she shot out of her chair. Alarmed, eyes fearful, Enid thrust back into her seat. Nell bent to her. 'It was only sheer chance he managed to rape. His apparatus almost always failed. Then he would attack me for it.' Shaking with fury, she watched Enid scoot her chair back.

Enid's mouth worked before her voice sounded, sneering. 'You lie. Susan carried almost to full term. She was weak, they said, the baby coming too early, dead in the womb, is all—'

'An innocent,' Nell exploded. 'She and her baby did not deserve their most horrible fate.'

Enid faltered, her mouth working at the harsh reality of Nell's words. She took a moment, then rallied. 'You … make all this up, this … these stories.'

Nell throat squeezed. 'Why do you hide from it? He was *insane*.' Her hands balled into fists again. And as suddenly as it boiled up, her rage cleared, its flare dropping away. Letting go of the breath she was holding, she rocked and rocked in the warm air. She had to calm herself. There was no point to this. *No point.*

Enid only shook her head, denying. Afraid.

Releasing her hands from their clench, Nell flexed her fingers. 'It was a cruelty on Susan that caused her death, I'm sure of it. And I am glad his madness does not grow on a child within me.' She beat down the last of her fury, but raw emotion shuddered in her voice. 'Your brother can no longer harm anyone. The bullet was too quick a death and hell is too good for him.'

Enid blanched, and for a moment her mouth dropped open in shock. Then the squint twitched. 'Well, then,' she said, breathing raggedly, clearly feeling no longer in physical danger. 'You know what that means.' Her lips flattened before she enunciated each word between her teeth. 'You can pack your bags.'

Nell knew that had been coming. She'd already made plans to move back into Amberton House and take her meagre possessions with her. 'I will certainly do that. But I will stay here just a few more days before I make my final departure.'

'You will leave today,' Enid snapped.

'I think not,' Nell said firmly, evenly. 'While I don't want to stay in this hostile place a moment more than necessary, I need more time to secure myself properly. Lewis is now the head of the house. I will negotiate with him.'

Enid propelled out of her chair, drew to full height and pushed past. Nell's thudding heart made her giddy, but she'd done what she'd set out to do.

Carrying her sewing kit in a basket, Nell got to Amberton House later that afternoon. She'd needed somewhere out of Enid's way. By the time she arrived, she'd built up a thirst. The water carter had delivered a barrel some time ago, long before they'd left that fateful morning in the coach. She headed out the back for it. A pitcher still sat next to it on the short dry-rock wall that held it off the ground.

Odd. Here was another lone sprig of yellow wattle, its flowers faded a little, lying beside the pitcher. She looked around. No flowering shrub in sight. Perhaps a bird … She sat stock still when she spotted another sprig of wattle atop the wall further around, and yet another older sprig, withered, at the foot of the wall. Ahead of her thoughts, her heart raced. This was no bird dropping twigs. The sprig was in the exact same place as before.

Who's been here? Children? Why wattle? Her own shrub had lost all its blooms. She'd hastily grabbed the last of it on the morning she and Andrew fled. She remembered she'd needed to be reminded of her courage. The bright yellow balls of colour had resembled the sun shining. She'd tucked the sprig into her bonnet, a quick flick of a pin to hold it in place …

The bushranger had handed her bonnet back to her. He'd stared at the wattle, brushed his fingers over it. Had he been here? Her heart pumped harder.

She bent and picked up a sprig. Little yellow dots, like dust puffs, flew off. It had dried, had been here a while. Had the bushranger left sprigs, and perhaps at least twice more since? He'd said he'd see she was safe when returned to her home.

So, had he come? It could have been him who came the first night after the hold-up. But how would he have known where she lived? *Ah, of course.* Mr Steele.

She'd been frightened that first night, believing it to be a thief, an opportunist after the massacre. Not for one minute had she thought it would be the bushranger. She had scurried to stay at Wilshire House, too fraught to stay on her own. And now she was scurrying again, away from there.

Alarmed, she shook herself at the direction her thoughts were turning. She'd wanted him to find her, that's why she'd sent the note. But what sort of dangers would that attract? Her mind must still be addled. Dear Lord, what was she doing? *Stop. Think.*

The weight of the gold dragged on her. Foremost was her safety, but afterwards the gold had to be her priority, and only then could the distraction of her clandestine visitor be addressed.

She perched carefully on the edge of the wall. Lifting the lid of the barrel, she leaned over, cupped her hand and dipped it in the bucket. As she trickled cool water into her mouth, the words that had shouted inside her head when she was speaking to Flora returned.

A tent in the camp. She sighed. There were thousands camped there already, and she well knew the life. As long as she avoided her father, it wouldn't be so bad. He still lived somewhere in that maze of humanity, eking out an existence on God only knew what. Not that she'd be interested in ever seeing him again, nor listening to his chortling over his own daughter's downfall. He hadn't cared a damn for her anyway, as long as he'd gotten his money. Nell shuddered. She owed him nothing.

But gold was at her fingertips. Almost literally. Bending to pick out a loose rock in the wall, she felt behind it for one of the bars she'd slid into the hollow. Still there. Replacing the rock, she tapped it into position with her foot. She knew where each one was secreted. She would have to begin her sewing and work quickly. A new garment each day would have to be loaded with as many of the nuggets as it would take without pulling it out of shape. Then she would go to the laundry and work with Flora.

She headed to the back of the house and threw open the doors to air the place out. Today it seemed different to her. She might prevail upon Lewis to gift it to her after all, or rent it to her cheaply. At least that way she would have respectability, and she did have to live somewhere. If Enid had a say in it, the chances of Lewis doing anything of the sort were slim. She wouldn't want to share her brother's estate, especially with Nell, if she didn't have to.

Then again, Lewis seemed a sensible person. Showed nothing of the debauchery that afflicted his uncle. Or she hoped not. *Horror.* She'd never succumb to that again. So, was working on the fields as good as she could come up with? But what else to do? What *else* to do? Flora had told her to return tomorrow. Nell needed to put a plan together.

The light was fading now, so she had to work fast. She hurried to the bedroom. On the bare but foot-worn floorboards, she knelt and dug under the mattress, a wool affair—an expensive one, so Andrew had said. It had been his pride and joy. He'd pinched her and punched her and pushed her off it when he took a fancy to. She hadn't had the strength to drag it out of the house and burn it. Enid had insisted it came with her to their shared house and Nell had insisted it stayed where it was.

It wouldn't bother her to sleep on the thing now. The bed linens had been washed, and washed again at the other house, much to Enid's consternation. Nell hadn't been able to burn them before she left the first time and Enid had taken them to be laundered. At least Nell would be able to nod off without fear of being abused in the middle of the night. She'd gone well beyond hating Andrew—she had a much more satisfying emotion than that. She despised him.

There were times lately she'd wake suddenly in the dead of night, her heart racing, her skin clammy, and imagined she could hear him snoring beside her.

Pushing that ugliness away, the foreboding aside, she continued to grapple her way under the mattress for the promissory notes stashed in an envelope there. Andrew had thought he'd hidden them from her. Not this time. They'd help her start a new life and be easier to pass off than the bars and nuggets, which would have to wait until she could get them weighed and exchanged without causing a fuss. Other nuggets were hidden in the mantel above the cooker.

Oh, too much worry and bother. She huffed as she withdrew her arm, tiring in the heat and the stuffiness in the room. Resting on her knees a moment, she wondered what on earth she was doing. Going back to the diggings would be the best idea. Many women worked for themselves there. She would be all right.

Then again, maybe not. The promissory notes—she should gather everything possible to ease the way. More groping under the mattress. Where was the blasted thing? Again, she withdrew her empty hand, sure that the envelope had been within easy reach. Slumped on the floor, frowning, she suddenly recalled. Good lord, her mind was as woolly as the mattress. Enid had sent a woman in to clean the house after Nell had moved out. She'd been instructed to 'turn the house upside down' and so Nell had shifted her cache before the woman had a chance to flip the mattress.

Pushing to her feet, her head swimming just a little, she steadied and turned for the small dresser. Pulling out the drawer that had been packed with her smalls—all cottons and plain apparel—she felt at the back on the frame itself for the envelope wedged in a corner.

Sighing with relief, she cursed her dull mind. Tugging the envelope out, she fell beside the dresser and with determined fingers, found the notes and a tiny button of gold within. At least it was something she could redeem without attracting any notoriety. Mrs Willey's store, the one Andrew had frequented, would honour the notes. She would secure the envelope to her person along with a few other nuggets sewn into her hem.

She set to work in the parlour room, close to the window to catch as much light as possible, and unpicked the tight neat stitches of her skirt. Her sewing needle flew over hems already freed and she tucked lumpy nuggets inside. There'd been just enough daylight, and no need to light a candle.

She wouldn't be able to do all of it at once, there were too many nuggets. And what amount of money would there be? Thousands of pounds worth, she thought.

She stood up and checked the weight of her garment. Satisfied she could carry herself without attracting undue attention, Nell gathered herself for the walk back to Wilshire House. She wasn't looking forward to it, but it was part of the plan. Twilight was nearly gone now, and soon the streets would be dark and deserted, and dangerous for a lone woman.

As she turned for the back door of the house, her breath stopped in her throat. Her pulse banged at her temples.

A figure blocked the doorway.

Eleven

Handing over the note the moment Finn arrived at his stables, Ben had been hopping foot to foot. 'I get twitchy all over thinkin' about it. Thinkin' that Mrs Amberton worked out I was part of the hold-up.'

Finn had read the note, his chest expanding. *Sir, I am soon to reside at the house to which Mr Steele delivered me that terrible night. I should like to thank you properly for your unintended kindness to me and would be grateful to have you visit me at your convenience. NA*

Inordinately elated, he'd held back his surprise, and looked at Ben. 'She hasn't mentioned any such thing in here at all.' He waved the letter, a smile on his face.

Ben paced. 'She didn't say it to me in so many words, but she'd figured it out, all right. She picked it that you brought two horses.'

'Ah. Clever woman.' Finn hadn't bothered concealing the getaway horse meant for Ben. Amberton was the only one he'd expected to see at the coach, so it hadn't mattered. He'd scanned the letter again. 'For what it's worth, mate, it seems she doesn't give two damns about that. Just keep denying it anyway, and no one will be able to prove otherwise.'

'Yeah, well, I dunno.'

'I don't reckon there's any chance you're in danger.'

So here he was. At her house, as bidden. Since Finn had received the note, time and again he'd tried to reason with himself, to resist. Her note was bold, yet innocent. Tantalising, but naïve. Her invitation fraught with danger. And how he wanted to see her. He wanted to touch that proud face, stroke her hair and feel her in his arms, this strong, intelligent woman. He hadn't felt like that in all the years since his wife Louisa had passed. Never looked at a woman again for anything other than physical release.

He didn't want to frighten her, didn't want to sneak up on her. He'd watched her enter her house, alone, and knew it was not a trap. Then he saw nothing. She had no candle, no flame or tinder to light one, so he couldn't track her movements. It was clear she hadn't been expecting anyone, and just as he was about to call out, she appeared in the hallway near the back door.

She stopped, her breath hitched. Her eyes were wide in shock. Fear.

'Nell.' His voice was sharp, but he stopped dead in the doorway. He had frightened her, dammit, taken her by surprise, and the kerchief hadn't helped. If she wanted to run past him screaming now, he'd not stop her.

A moment passed. 'And what do I call you?' Breathless and imperious.

He ignored that. 'I came to see that you are safe. I said I would.'

Another moment passed as she battled her breathing. 'The wattle. You have been here before.' Shaky.

'I have.'

'Then you would know that, at present, I don't live in this house.' Clipped, still short of breath.

Yet she made no move to pass him. Did she feel trapped, perhaps? He stood aside and said, 'If you would rather not remain here now, I will walk you to wherever you are lodging.'

A short sob escaped her. 'I have no wish to go there, either. But it is a roof over my head for a short while.'

'So, you are not as safe as I'd hoped.'

'It's not ideal, but I have other plans.' Another shaky breath expelled. Not so imperious now.

A light fragrance of lavender reached him. In the deepening night, her hair looked darker than the pale blonde it was. Her face seemed to have lost its gaunt hollows but that might only be a trick of the fading light.

'I'm pleased to hear that,' he said. 'And I'm sorry I frightened you just now.'

'A man appearing at the door wearing a kerchief is frightening.'

'I am still a bushranger.' He leaned on the doorjamb.

She gave a short laugh. 'I—Now I don't know what to say.'

'In your note, you invited me.' Or did she regret sending it? He drew in a deep breath and turned to look out into the night. The stars were beginning to emerge in the darkness. He looked back, testing the moment. 'So I wondered what you might want, and here I am.'

'I only wanted to thank you,' she said quickly. 'In person. I said so.'

'You'd already done that.'

She stared a moment longer and seemed at a loss for words. Then, 'You saved me.'

Finn shook his head. 'Ah. You forget that someone else saved you.'

'It's true. The shot that killed Andrew was not yours, but you saved my … you saved me from myself, from being further undignified in such a …' Inhaling deeply, she went on, firmly. 'I'm not the sort of woman that I seemed to be then. I was in a desperate situation.'

'You were, indeed.'

Her eyes were intent on his. 'I am normally a virtuous person.'

It seemed she was determined to advise him of that. He let out a breath, hoping she didn't notice that it shook. 'I have no doubt of that.' He wanted her, virtuous, without virtue … Christ, he wanted her now, but not here. Not a furtive fumbling. Not just to release an urgent need. Not just *another base act*.

She took a step. 'I didn't want my letter to have been a mistake, but perhaps I was too bold, too full of my own—'

He straightened, wouldn't trust himself with her. 'Don't come closer, Nell.'

She stopped. 'I want to explain my actions that day. I was desperate … You deserve an explanation from me, some honesty from me.' Her hands clasped.

Finn's heart pounded, his fingers flexed. He wanted to take her where she stood. 'I don't deserve a thing. You confuse a lowly bushranger, madam.'

'You're not that. I know it.' She settled herself and took a deep breath. 'There were many things that drove me to—' Shaking her head, she lowered it. It seemed she wouldn't go on. Her hand came up again as if she would touch him, but she didn't. 'I just want you to know I'm not such a desperate woman. That here, now, my situation is my own.'

Disappointment hollowed in him. But he should have guessed. Her letter had been naïve after all, and she was just a flighty woman. He'd been a fool coming here. He pushed off the wall, preparing to get the hell out of there. 'Well then, I'm very happy for you.'

'Wait—I'm not finished.' Her eyes were still on his and she caught her bottom lip as if deciding something before she continued. 'And, at this moment, now you're here,' she said, 'I want you to know that my feelings are not at all virtuous.'

It was that forthright stare that caught him, the unblinking blue gaze. He seized her outstretched hand, pressed her other behind her back, locked her to him. He swung her round so in the doorway the glow of a rising moon illuminated on her face. Clear eyes stared back at him, no fear in them. Her breath came in quick gentle sighs. He felt his legs tense, his belly grip. His penis hardened and would be evident against her.

'Neither are mine, but this is another madness,' he whispered, and dropped his chin to the nape of her neck. He pushed down the kerchief and his lips found her warm skin.

Twelve

The scratch of his whiskers on her shoulder sent feather-like thrills tingling over her breasts. Irresistible, and a torment. She couldn't move, was held fast against him from hip to breast. One more tingling scrape against her neck and his head came up, the kerchief now back in place.

No, no. Her fingers took the edge of it. 'Oh, but I want to see who you are.'

His hand took hers, smooth and swift. 'For the while, it has to remain in place.' He rested his forehead against hers, chest rising and falling, solid, warm. 'Are you not afraid?'

'Of what?' she breathed, searching his green eyes under a puckered brow.

His arms were either side of her, his hands sliding down her hips. Glancing at her face, a short breath escaped him. Hands bunched her skirt, and hard knuckles brushed against her thighs. She gripped his shoulders, her fingers digging into him, drawing him closer. Quick to grasp her wrists, he stopped her, and she frowned at the loss of him under her hands.

He hesitated. 'He hurt you.'

Her heart swelled, and emotion choked out her cry, 'But you will not.'

He blinked, frowning, and after a sharp breath, he dropped his face to her neck again. 'You're right.' He wrapped her in his arms and stood holding her tight, hugging her. 'You're right, I will not hurt you.'

As they stood, her heart entangled, her mind blank, long moments passed. All that she knew, felt, wanted, was that his arms were around her.

When he lifted his head, his voice was muffled, a thrum against her ear. 'And now, if you are ready to leave for your residence, I will see you safely home.'

Thirteen

Later that evening at Wilshire House, with Lewis still not home and Enid her only company, Nell prepared a light meal of potted meat and potatoes. The sisters-in-law shared it in strained silence for the most part. Enid had told her, a little snip in her tone, that she'd informed Lewis there would be no baby.

Nell's thoughts were barely on Lewis as she reserved a plate, piled high, for him. She'd gathered her wits enough since arriving back at the house to wonder what plan he might have devised, now he knew Andrew's estate belonged to him. Her nerves were tightly strung after her encounter with the bushranger. Her stomach was fluttery, making it hard for her to concentrate, but the boiled potatoes had tickled her taste buds. Her heart had still been racing but food was sustenance and thankfully, had settled her.

Enid watched her, eyes narrowed. 'Are you not well?'

Nell stood to remove the scraped plates into the tub under the kitchen window. 'I am well, Enid. Thank you for asking after me,' she said amiably, not turning to look at her. Nell could feel the packet of her cache scratch against her ribs, and though it was a moment's discomfort each time she moved, it was worth keeping it there.

Enid made a noise, a grunt either of assent or indignation.

Nell hoped to change some smaller pieces of the gold tomorrow, and perhaps would find a better place to hide the rest. The promissory notes would have to be carefully, quietly exchanged. She wouldn't alert anyone to her sudden good fortune.

Her thoughts returned to the bushranger and her heart skipped a beat again. He was indeed a gentleman, and for the second time had not let her send herself down a road to ruin. She felt a sudden rush of discomfort as she remembered what she'd offered again, but at least she knew he was as willing as she. Was that a bad thing? Surely not. Her circumstances put her well beyond worrying about what it might have looked like to him.

She'd walked swiftly back to Wilshire House, part embarrassed, part filled with joy, part bewildered. He'd stepped behind her, promising to keep her in his sights. At the Wilshire's, she'd turned to lift her hand in thanks, but he'd already gone. And although she had no way of knowing if she would see him again, her spirits were high.

The night passed uneventfully. Restless and wide awake, Nell heard Lewis come home. He'd stomped about the place, and the subsequent scrape of furniture and occasional slurred expletive indicated how he'd spent his evening.

She hadn't been disturbed by it. In this house, before they'd moved to the other, Andrew had hammered a bolt across their bedroom door on the outside to prevent her leaving the room, although he'd only used it one time, thankfully. Lewis had reworked it to the inside for her. To assure her of her security, he'd said, now that Andrew was, ahem, gone. Things like that made her wonder if her suspicions about Lewis were wrong. That sliding bolt had given Nell the peace of mind to easily drop off to sleep most nights. It did nothing to prevent her waking later in a sweat, only to remember, when her racing heartbeat settled, that Andrew was gone.

She chided herself. A bolt on her bedroom door was one thing, but hardly a deterrent if anyone really wanted to attack her. *Damn Andrew.* She still had to be vigilant. Until her head was clear, it could well be that everyone was suspicious now.

Morning burst through her window as it was wont to do, its brilliant light refusing to be ignored. It seemed a much different day today. How could that be? Just because a man had given her a little delight, mystery, and some manners, didn't mean the world had changed for the better overnight. But this morning it felt a bit like that. The wariness of the night before was a little distant after her first unbroken sleep in months.

Nell felt a moment's unease that while the bushranger knew where she lived, she had no more information about him. Perhaps with a calm day ahead, her memory might return the teasing bits and pieces of that day of the hold-up, and more of their conversation would come back to her.

Needing to visit the privy, she tucked her feet into her slippers, and quickly donned her dressing gown over her night dress to venture outside. As she opened the door, Lewis was exiting his room. His face looked sallow, his hair tousled, and before he saw her, he rolled his tongue around in his mouth and smacked his lips together. He was shirtless, but at least his pants were buttoned up. His feet were bare.

Nell stood in the doorway. 'Good morning.'

'Good morning, aunt. Nell,' he corrected, and looked uncomfortable in the small hallway. He ducked his head. 'I came in late last night. I hope I didn't wake you.'

'You didn't.' She saw that he had a bandage around his middle and stared.

He held up his hands. 'A slight problem falling off my horse. Damn thing was drunk,' he said. 'Pardon my language.'

She indicated she needed to pass. 'If I may?'

'Of course.' He retreated inside his room and shut the door.

She wondered what he'd fallen on … after his drunken horse had tossed him. Still, since the fracas last month, many men had appeared to be injured. Perhaps something nasty had happened to Lewis and he hadn't said. Had he involved himself with the diggers' unrest? Was he still involved, even now?

Perhaps he had simply fallen off his horse and hit a rock or a stout stick. Either way, if he was healthy enough to spend his evenings getting drunk somewhere, the accident had not seemed to inconvenience him.

She'd heard here and there that there were some men, injured in the blockade, who'd been taken into hiding before the troopers had been able to find and butcher them, or had been able to haul them off to the authorities. It was all over town that casualties—deaths and injuries—were many and varied in number. At least one woman dead, and God forbid, more women and children had been shot at, too. Nell had been told that a Mrs Smith, shot on the night, might not survive her wounds. Some women, and pregnant women as well, had been injured by the troopers, some immorally, it was whispered, long after the skirmish itself.

Governor Hotham was still turning a blind eye to almost every plea for compassion and mercy.

If sick and injured men could be hidden on the fields, in tents, under beds, in cupboards and behind bushes, then surely a woman tending laundry could well hide in plain sight. It was said there were nearly thirty thousand souls or more on the fields. Nell could very well hide among them.

As she returned from the outhouse, soft snores were coming from within Lewis's room. Perhaps he would not be making another appearance for some time, after all.

Enid was in the kitchen, her night cap still in situ, wisps of hair showing from underneath. The kettle stood on the stove top, a light steam coming from it.

'Oh good,' Nell said. 'Tea. I'll make it.' She might be able to get a decent cup if she got to the tea leaves first.

Enid sat heavily at the table, her chair groaning as if she were too heavy for it. It might need repairing, for her sister-in-law was not a stout woman. Nell glanced about at the other chairs. None looked to be in decent repair. She hadn't noticed before, and wondered why disrepair had been tolerated. Well, no matter to her. Now they could afford new chairs using Andrew's money.

'I have need of tea,' Enid said. 'I am to go to the town this morning to help start to fit out the entertainment tent for the ball, Saturday week. A number of subscriptions have come in late, believe it or not.'

Of those on the fields who could write, answering the subscription invite might not have been high on their must-do list. There had been a big nugget unearthed recently, and the frenzy for more had taken over. The fields were a hive once again; panning had been less successful, digging deeper more so. Nell's morning with Flora the day before had been a mine of information.

Enid's musing brought her back to the conversation. 'They are expanding the tent, adding another for seating so there will be more seats to dress, and more tables for food. You must attend with me, Nell,' she said, and held out a cup to receive tea from the pot. 'We have need of more helpers, even if you are in mourning. There will be many widows among us today.'

Nell held the pleasant smile on her face as she poured. 'Not for me, thank you.'

'We will go after we do the chores here.'

Enid seemed not to have heard her. Nell's smile was still in place as she dropped the kettle back to the cook top, and turned to her sister-in-law. 'I have no interest in assisting the fit out for the ball. I am sure there are many ladies far more qualified than I who could help.'

Enid blinked at her. 'Nevertheless.'

Nevertheless. Whenever Andrew uttered that word, it augured his next episode.

A shiver sped up Nell's back. The involuntary shudder was obvious. Enid was startled. 'Damn your *nevertheless*, Enid.'

Indignant, Enid's face pinched. 'I—'

Nell leaned over the table. 'I will not be assisting at the entertainment tent.'

Lewis appeared in the doorway. 'Nor should you, aunt. I'm sure the good ladies of the Ballarat diggings can arrange the tent without your help. Isn't that right, Mama?'

Enid turned, her face still reflecting Nell's effrontery, and gaped at her son. 'You are not correctly dressed for breakfast.'

'We are not at the governor's table, dear Mother, nor likely to be. I am dressed for breakfast in my own home, with my relatives around me. I am wearing a shirt, trousers and my socks.' He rubbed a hand through his sleep-tousled hair then pushed off the doorjamb. 'Some tea, if you will.'

Enid was for a moment frozen and pink at the rebuke, then stood and stared at the kettle before reaching out for it.

Nell took a seat at the table. It was one thing to argue with Enid to her face, but quite another to see her embarrassed by her adult son, the man who stood to inherit everything.

Lewis took a chair across from Nell, accepted the cup of tea from Enid, and nodded to her. 'Thank you.'

Was he flexing his muscles now that his uncle had gone? Or perhaps Nell hadn't noticed before how poised and mature he was. It appeared that he was very much at home as head of the family.

He sat comfortably in the silence and gazed candidly at Nell before setting down his tea. 'I will be going to Bendigo, probably tomorrow. It seems the time is right to have the will read and check my uncle's estate.'

Without looking at Enid, Nell heard a short, sharp intake of breath from her sister-in-law.

'I should accompany you, son,' Enid said from behind Nell.

'It's an arduous day's journey, Mama. No need to take an uncomfortable coach ride. I'm better alone, on horseback. I can fully report to you on my return.'

Enid came back to the table, the blackened kettle in hand. She landed it with a thump on the table. 'I should be there.'

'I believe I am named as Uncle Andrew's successor, so it would stand to reason that I undertake the business at hand. Knowing Uncle's intentions, the meeting with Mr Campbell should be very straightforward.' Lewis scratched his nose with a forefinger. 'Besides, I should think the journey would tire you too much. And, as Nell is my uncle's wife, uh, widow,' he corrected and ducked his head in apology to Nell, 'I am saving her the unpleasant ordeal of having to be present.' He looked up at her from under his brows. 'I should say how sorry I am to hear of your other recent sad news, aunt.'

Nell nodded, embarrassed, partly because Lewis at least had the good grace to appear sympathetic where Enid had not, and because Lewis had even alluded to such a thing. A gentleman usually did not, it being women's business that she might have miscarried. He didn't seem to appear gleeful about the inheritance all being his, either. And she couldn't care less about being saved the 'unpleasant ordeal' of the will being read. As soon as she was gone from this awful house and away from its occupants, the better.

Had she for one moment entertained ideas of marrying Lewis? To become Enid's daughter-in-law by it? God forbid she should have any more of these ridiculous ideas. Certainly now she couldn't blame any silly thoughts on being worried about being pregnant. Clearly desperate circumstances had forced her brain to conjure desperate solutions.

'Besides, Mama, you've just said you'll be helping at the entertainment tent. Much better for you there than struggling in a cart all the way to Bendigo.'

Smoke rose in a thin curl from under the kettle. Enid snatched it off and stared in dismay at the scorch mark left on the table.

'Look at this,' she hissed before turning smartly and dumping it back onto the iron cook top. 'Go then. I would not stand in your way as you undertake your responsibilities.' She turned back with a squinted glance at Nell before she addressed her son again. 'In the light of Andrew's passing, we will decline to attend the ball itself. I will assist with the fitting out of the tent, but it would not be—'

'Mama, we will be attending,' Lewis interrupted. 'Even if I, too, have to wear black to satisfy some matrons. We are not in the Old Country, nor do we bow overly much here to the old ways.' He set his cup aside and laced his hands on the tabletop. 'Please don't look so shocked. The races went ahead despite many men losing their lives mere weeks earlier. I saw a number of women there and even some in apparel that was indeed black.' He looked at his mother, glanced at Nell. 'And I say that you both shall attend.'

Enid's voice had stopped in her throat, her mouth open. Nell brushed her skirt down, concentrating on the task.

He took the last of his tea. 'I will partake of that bread, Mama, and some cheese if you have it, then I must go to the diggings.'

Enid moved herself smartly and gathered thick slices of damper, and a chunk of cheese from a muslin bag. 'I don't believe Nell should attend the ball,' she insisted, stiffly.

'Even so, Mama.' Lewis turned his gaze to Nell. 'Your subscription invitation will stand as before,' he said. As Enid thumped a plate in front of him, he took to his breakfast. 'It's to be support for a miner's hospital. Good cause, wouldn't you think? Don't look so stricken, Mama. We can afford to flout the rules, here and there, eh?' He didn't wait for an answer. 'I will be back by Friday. I look forward to next week's social engagement. It will be just the thing for all of us.'

Andrew had bought tickets on subscription for them. Nell hadn't considered attending a social gathering since his death, but it seemed Lewis was intent on having the family present at this next one. For what purpose, she couldn't surmise. Perhaps it was a last kindness to her, even though it seemed to have upset his mother no end.

Nell remained silent as Lewis ate, her thoughts spinning. If he was to be away for some days after tomorrow, she would have to find a quiet moment today, without Enid in earshot, to broach the subject of the other house with him.

If an invitation to attend a ball was still open for her, perhaps he would be conducive to the idea of her occupying the other house, after all.

Fourteen

Bendigo, January 1855

'Mr Seymour, good afternoon. Please. Have a seat.'

Finn Seymour reached over and shook Mr Worrell's hand. He took the proffered chair, a polished leather affair with dark timbers, smooth under his hand, and heavy. So like Joseph Campbell to have good, solid furniture.

He sank into it. 'Thank you. I know your cousin well, the venerable Mr Campbell, and consider him a good friend. I'm happy to finally make your acquaintance, Mr Worrell.'

'And you, too.' Young Worrell waved a hand towards the door. 'Mr Campbell—'

A voice spoke from behind. '—Will catch up with you in due course, Finneas.'

Finn turned to look at the man in the doorway. His face split into a wide grin as he got back to his feet. 'Joseph.' He gripped the other man's hand. 'Good to see you.'

'And you. I see you've met the younger, good-looking one of the family.' Joseph nodded towards Matthew. 'He's also got brains, thank the Lord.'

Mr Worrell laughed. 'You're not so much older, cousin.'

'That is correct. I just feel it.'

Finn could tell there were some years between them, maybe ten, if that. His friend Joseph did indeed look much older than Matthew, but then, he'd always looked older than his peers. A tall man, the good life appearing around his middle as if he was carrying something spare, he would barely be in his late thirties. His light brown hair seemed always receding but had never receded too much. A big nose, the kind that made you think of a bare-knuckle rules man, and kind eyes. Intelligent eyes. Eyes that when their gaze pinned you down, you blustered out all the truths of whatever matter had brought you before him.

'Mr Worrell here is taking me over my ledgers.' Finn nodded back towards the younger man.

Worrell did not have the look of his cousin; he was of sturdier stock, though he appeared to be as tall. His nose was not that of a boxer's; it was more patrician. His intense blue eyes were light and clear. His dark hair and pale skin attested to his roots—Welsh, perhaps. It was the added presence of a dark mole on his left cheek that made him look as if he might have carried Romany blood. He had the look of a man who knew his business.

'You are in very good hands, my friend. When you are finished, we'll attend to your legal matters in my office.' Joseph nodded at both, and walked off down the short hallway.

Finn returned to his chair and eyed the documents in front of him on the desk. 'So, Mr Worrell, what do you say? How are things looking?'

Matthew Worrell flattened his palms over the papers a moment, then reached across to open a ledger. 'There's no doubt about it, you are in a very good position. Your implements and tools merchandising business is doing well. That is, until the stockade affair interrupted it somewhat.'

Finn leaned forward. 'It didn't last for long. Only a few implements, considering, were confiscated from the miners as weapons.' He peered at the numbers.

Mr Worrell nodded. 'That's true. I have entered purchases up to last week, and the subsequent sales.' He ran a finger down a line of neat figures. 'In fact, it looks as if your business even outperforms that of a digger's finds in some cases.' He smiled then, a bright wide-mouthed grin that returned youth to the face that had been serious so far.

'I've heard the same from other merchants. A man can't give away a dairy cow but can sell a pan and a shovel for the price of someone's soul.'

'A sign of our times, I fear. It is said that the man who supplies the diggers easily wins the gold. Do you hold any mining licenses yourself?'

Dropping his chin, Finn studied his boots. 'The law states that "all persons connected with the search for gold" must have a license.' He looked up. 'That includes me and my business, so I do have one, but don't use it to dig. It's almost criminal to have to pay it. I'd rather supply diggers the tools than be the one constantly looking over my shoulder from a hole in the ground.'

'The troopers?' The younger man's eyes lit up. 'Are they as bad as—?'

'And the rest.' Finn shifted the conversation. 'You haven't decided to try your own hand at the diggings, Mr Worrell?'

Matthew tipped his head towards the door, his eyes wide. 'I have heeded the advice of my wiser cousin. He is far more sensible than me, though I am still interested in new opportunities. He says men have a need for good ledgers and solid legal advice, and that this is where we will sustain our future. So, for the time being, here I sit.'

Finn detected a regretful tone. 'And that also makes you a wise man.'

'Besides,' Matthew leaned back in his chair, and smiled with a broad grin, 'Bendigo has much civilisation, such as timber and brick dwellings. Far superior to the canvas tents of Ballarat.'

'Ah yes. I admit to happily foregoing life in a tent.' Finn settled back, his hands across a flat belly. 'And Bendigo is eminently more comfortable because it's not in a state of morbid fear.'

'Hopefully, that business in Ballarat has settled. Now, let's get down to it.' Matthew Worrell checked his line of figures again. 'I'd say your business has sustained its level of stability. If anything, it's clear that demand for your supplies is growing.'

Finn nodded. 'And certainly so if we can successfully negotiate the road from Melbourne before winter comes. Some leave it too late, and bullock wagons get bogged. Horses pulling carts get bogged. It can be terrible. Most often death for the animals if they can't be pulled out.' He briefly looked to the ceiling while he thought of his next words. 'Would the business attract a purchaser, were it to go up for sale?'

Mr Worrell's eyes widened. 'For sale?'

'I am increasingly weary of the rush for gold.'

Matthew Worrell stared at him. 'Weary of the greatest economic surge in the history of mankind?' He blinked at his own audacity. 'I mean—'

'Precisely that, Mr Worrell. I look around on the fields and see greed, envy, death, scourge, and a lot of poor people.' He frowned. 'Oh, some of them might have held a good few nuggets, but they're not the majority. They are mostly fools with nothing more than hope. The rest are drunks, men who abandon their families, and women who ply a trade because of those men. Yet I see there are a great many women who do better than the menfolk with their enterprises. But we know that won't last.' He inhaled, a long intake. 'No. My time there has a limit. And I have my eye on another venture.'

Mr Worrell was taking in Finn's speech, his mouth open and finally closing. He dropped his gaze to the figures before him. 'There seems to be much more money to be made.'

Finn sat forward. 'True. But the life there sickens me. The only family I had left was lost to the greed of the fields.' He laced his hands. 'My father started the business just as the fields opened up, but the boisterous noise of the diggings grates on me. The lack of privacy, the barracks life of the tents, the constant gunshots for no good reason…' He thought he felt a tremor begin and clenched a fist. 'I have no need to remain there.'

The young ledger keeper lowered his voice. 'And my condolences. I heard that you'd had a bereavement while you were away—'

'There were two family members who passed away during that time.' Three, if one counted Susie's unborn child, Finn thought, though the law did not.

As he hoped, his reply stopped Mr Worrell taking the conversation any further in that direction. To his credit, the man only tapped his fingers on the papers under his hands. 'To answer your question, you are in a good position to sell.'

'I thought the skirmish might have panicked business people. It appears not so.'

'You're right. Should you realise a sale, your cash assets will be very healthy. But consider this, Mr Seymour. The moment word is out that you wish to sell, there might be opportunists who would simply start up a run of supply from Melbourne in competition.'

'You are good at your job, Mr Worrell. That could happen any time. I wonder if the diggers would be too busy to think of it,' Finn countered. 'But you're right. I should consider it a possibility. Perhaps we need to make a more discreet approach to businessmen who might well be prospective buyers.'

'In that case, could I help in any way to prepare a proposal, or a sale document for you?'

'Certainly. And when the time comes, I will take the documents you prepare to the banks, if necessary, to secure a loan for my next venture.'

'And, if I may ask, what is the next venture that so interests you?' Mr Worrell had the light of adventure in his eye.

Finn warmed to his subject. 'You might have heard that a Mr Cadell and a Mr Randell, river captains and competitors, successfully navigated the River Murray upstream to Swan Hill.'

'An exciting race last year, it was. I'm very interested in news of it.'

'It's the beginning of a new trade route between three colonies,' Finn stated. 'And I believe a very lucrative one at that. I'll look at building paddle-steamers to carry freight and produce up and down river.'

The ledgers man nodded at Finn. 'That would require considerable starting capital,' he cautioned.

'I have my late father's affairs to administer. There is an inheritance awaiting probate.'

Mr Worrell dropped his gaze to the figures on his ledger. 'Ah. Yes. I believe you are seeing my cousin to discuss your—options.'

Finn continued, ignoring the small warning signalled by Mr Worrell's comment. 'A very exciting project. The port at Goolwa is in its infancy. Many opportunities there, I believe.'

Matthew Worrell looked up. 'Sounds promising,' he said. 'I might look at the place myself.'

'I have only a halfway decent rum here, Finneas. I still can't get a hold of any good whisky, either by illicit stills or otherwise. Seems there must be a gap in supply at present.' The solicitor held out two cloudy, stout glasses, halfway filled with dark golden liquid.

Finn laughed aloud as he took a glass. 'As if you'd acquire anything from contraband, Joseph Campbell.'

'It would be a gift from the gods if the stuff was worthy, contraband or not. It's good to see you. How long have you been back?'

'I landed mid October. Was just in time for Susie's funeral. Too late for my father's.'

'My heartfelt condolences. You have come back to sorrowful times.'

Finn inclined his head. His father's death was not unexpected, but had come sooner than he thought it might. Susie's death weighed heavily on him. He took a breath and eased himself into one of Joseph Campbell's large and exquisitely crafted chairs. 'Christ, Joseph. These chairs are going to last you into the next life.'

'That is my intention. There is a fine timber craftsman and a fine upholsterer here. I have a new desk and a new chaise on order.'

'A little luxurious? They're enormous.'

'One has to be comfortable.' Joseph Campbell pulled out a heavy chair, spreading his hands over each of the arms as he took his seat. 'For a man of my size, building a custom-fit is the only answer. And the leather is the finest I've seen.' He slapped his hands on the arms. 'But you haven't come here to discuss the finer points of tanned cow hide and well-constructed bits of timber.'

'Passes the time of day, especially with this fine rum in hand.'

Mr Campbell mused over his glass. 'Fine rum. Is that a contradiction somehow?'

'Better than some I've tasted lately,' Finn allowed. He felt a quick shudder in his arm again and glanced at his hand. He had written Joseph a letter, about—among other things— the tremors, and now the lawyer would perhaps see them for himself. He put his glass on the desk.

'So, the affliction has not subsided?' Joseph asked.

Finn still stared at his hand, now steady. 'Sometimes, I feel it has, a little, but the shakes still manage to surprise me. I have nightmares, but not often.' He frowned and took up his drink again, frowning some more. 'Thankfully not the sweats so much, either.'

'Unfortunate thing.' Joseph Campbell tapped his desk lightly while he seemed to gather his thoughts. 'The mail is so slow now from England, from Europe, thanks to the war, that there's been no real news for months. Everything we get is three months old.'

Finn tested a fist, clenching and unclenching. It was steady. 'There was an ill-fated charge by the Light Brigade in October just gone. The news of that event is not fully reported, even though my correspondent had heard directly.'

'Think yourself lucky you got a discharge and found your way home. I don't pertain to a man dying for a reason not of his own.'

Finn let out a long breath. 'War does no man any good. And you're right. I'm for Queen and country, there's no mistaking it, but that is one skirmish I was glad to be out of.'

'Yet you took armed service, voluntarily.'

Finn scoffed. 'Barely a boy's own adventure, at the time. In hindsight, visiting my cousins in England turned out to be a badly timed mistake. But after the death of my wife, it seemed a good idea. I would certainly not have gone had Louisa been alive.' He rested the rum on the arm of the chair. 'They were all primed up to fight for some cause, any cause, and they found one. I was stupid enough to think I could join up to look after them.' Flicking a fingernail against the rum, he ducked his head. 'Then it turned real. Too real. Russians, Turks, British, French. I saw enough death and maiming to last me a lifetime, and the real fighting hadn't even begun.' He held up his right hand. He flexed his fingers, moved his steady hand into the line of sight. 'But I don't understand the shakes. They got me posted home because

I couldn't hold a damn gun straight. It doesn't just come upon me when I'm vexed, it's any time. Could be anything—'

'A fearful memory, or perceived danger, perhaps?'

'But not necessarily one thing or another. Nor each time I come up against a challenge.' Finn thought then of the bail-up on the morning after the stockade attack, and of the woman. He shrugged it aside. 'To the army, I was a risk.'

'They lose a lot of good men to that sort of risk, I would suspect.'

Joseph was nothing if not dry in his humour. Finn let that comment be. It was more accurate than his friend would know. He checked that thought and looked again at the lawyer, his battered face and thickened knuckles. *Or perhaps Joseph knows more of that than anyone.*

Finn said, 'Those fools should never have been in charge of troops. They send more good men to their unnecessary deaths every engagement.'

'And the fighting is for …?'

'Started over religion. Moved into politics. Some say it'll end on the Crimean Peninsula. Probably right. The Turks are mad for it, as are the Russians.'

Campbell took a swallow of rum. 'And your English cousins?'

Finn lifted his shoulders. 'When I was discharged, they were still fighting, and then were being deployed to a place called Gallipoli, a staging point between destinations. They could still be there, for all I know. No one here knows what's happened at this point. Information is slow getting here because they deployed our mail steamships to carry troops back and forth to the Mediterranean for this war.'

Joseph looked at his friend over thin spectacles. 'By now, your cousins are probably sitting at home with their cigars and their port wine. It was a good thing you made it home when you did.'

'All left to chance and to coincidence. These blasted tremors, the ship's sailing schedule, the kindly weather … But still I was too late for my father, but more so for Susan.'

Joseph Campbell let out a breath, his lips vibrating as it expelled. 'Yes. Poor Susan. I fear she could not wait any longer.'

Finn studied both hands now. The shakes were absent. His broad hands were lightly tanned, fingernails chipped here and there, but overall, the clean and calloused fingers were steady. 'I should never have left her with only our father here. He must have been already poorly.'

'My good friend, you were not to know. No one knew.' Joseph leaned back in his chair. 'He didn't seem unwell when you left. And Susan was already being courted by the devil himself, and nothing was going to stop him. And your father agreed to the match.'

'I should never have left,' Finn repeated. 'Amberton was brutal.'

'I know.'

Finn heaved in a breath. 'I imagine she thought it would be different for her.' He looked up at his friend. 'But that's never so, is it? Does no one think to forewarn these women about men like him?'

'People tell me that they mind their own business.'

'I should have known better than to leave.'

'And you would have done what? Forbade her to marry? As it turned out, your father made a—' He stopped.

'Yes, we should get to my father's affairs. I admit, I have struggled to meet this moment, but after the events of the past six months, I need to move forward with some clarity. Put some of the past to rest.'

Joseph nodded. 'You will.' He tilted his big head. 'But before we go back to your father, did you know that someone has put a stop to Amberton? You'll be pleased of it, if you do know. Some-one has made a widow of his second wife.'

Finn turned to stare out the window. Clouds moved across the sky, a scant breeze nudging them along. There was no threat of more rain, not that it would have been a threat. It would be welcome ... He stopped procrastinating. 'I do know that he's dead.'

'Wouldn't ease the pain, or the anger for you, I imagine. Susan had no one here to protect her from him. I know that weighs heavily on you.' Joseph leaned across his desk and laced his ungainly hands. 'The new widow at least has Amberton's sister, Enid Wilshire. No doubt a help for her.'

Finn did his best to appear disinterested. 'No doubt. And the widow's own family—where are they?'

'Her family are not clients directly of mine, so I can tell you. Her father is an old tyrant, well known on the fields for being a conniving old sod. Sold her off, I've heard.'

'Like a dowry thing? Obsolete, now, isn't it?'

'Still prevalent, when needs arrive. Not illegal,' Joseph said, a glance at Finn before he leaned forward to refill his glass with a tot. He lifted the decanter in Finn's direction. 'I believe he was heard to say, "daughters need to be auctioned off". Seems she had previously refused all his efforts at matchmaking.' He replaced the decanter when Finn declined with a shake of his head.

'And where is he?'

Joseph caught Finn's enquiring glance. 'The widow's father? Still on the fields, I hear. Last reported to me, he was bragging new-found wealth. He should beware bragging about money. It's a common precedent to an early death.'

Finn wondered why the man's whereabouts were reported to Joseph. He wouldn't ask; wasn't his business however curious he was. Besides, it might pique the lawyer's curiosity and he didn't need that. He'd make his own way learning some more about the new widow, Mrs Amberton.

That might be a stupid thing to pursue in the light of the other night. It would have to be carefully thought out. He had made a mistake by answering Nell's invitation. How had the bushranger got himself this enmeshed?

'You must hear a great many things,' Finn deflected. 'I'm sure that's only one of the sorry stories of the Ballarat fields. For myself, I'm looking beyond.' Then a tremor started. His left hand clamped the right. He glanced an apology at his friend. 'A moment until it subsides, Joseph.' He felt sweat trickle under his shirt. 'I'm no good while it ails me.'

Campbell stared a moment then said, 'Let's concentrate on the matter you need to attend, Finneas.'

Finn held his elbow and hugged it to his body. Breath puffed out of him as he felt a band constrict over his chest.

Joseph started to rise to his feet. 'What can I do?'

Finn lifted a hand to wave him away. 'Nothing.' His gaze travelled over the small bookshelf behind his friend, on which the sturdy tomes looked regal and scholarly. He checked the carpet under his feet, clean and, no doubt, of good quality. He looked at his boots, a little dusty. He rubbed one against the other leg to clean it off. Breath still puffed out, but the constriction was easing. 'They say a legacy of war, not a physical one. A survivor's sickness, perhaps.'

The lawyer raised his brows.

Finn grunted a laugh. 'I see you thinking. If the wound is not physical, it must be that I'm weak in the mind. I can assure you, it's not so.' He inhaled deeply as the constriction finally receded. 'I am determined to move forward from it.'

Joseph took up his own rum again. 'I cannot imagine it would stop you, nor what would cure you.'

'They say nothing but time.' Finn shrugged. 'This bad business of the Eureka Lead. It decided me. Too much aggression and greed.' He looked up, reached across for his rum. 'If this ailment is to be with me for some time, I cannot abide unexplained noise. Gunshots, for instance, it seems now.' Finn gazed into the deep swirl of molasses-coloured rum. 'I had occasion to shoot a firearm recently, which hadn't brought this on before—when I am doing the firing, that is. This time, however, tremors resulted.' He flexed his right hand's fingers. 'Well, nearly got me killed. I couldn't control it.'

'I don't understand. Were you at the stockade?'

Shaking his head, Finn said, 'Afterwards. My grip was so fumbling, I was nearly not able to defend myself.'

'If you require legal—'

Dismissing him with a shake of his head, Finn said, 'Just something got out of control. Done with, now.'

Joseph spread his hands. 'Things have been out of control—if there ever was control.' His mouth downturned. 'You reported it?' he asked, then scoffed. 'Stupid question. I fear there's few to report to. Thank God, you came out alive.'

Indeed. Finn threw back a long swallow of rum, felt his eyes water. It was reasonable rum, but his tolerance was low. He set his glass down again. 'My head was clear, but my hand … I need to find a gentler climate, so I'm looking much further afield. New frontiers, so to speak.'

'Our colonies are certainly not short of new frontiers, but whether they are gentler is open for discussion.'

'I have heard—and your cousin, Mr Worrell, was able to enlighten me—that new company laws are to be enacted soon.'

Joseph nodded, and did a quick search amid the ledgers on his desk. 'The emerging company law is quite interesting. I won't have up-to-date information for some time—the slow ships.' He uncovered a thick file, opened it and squinted at a sheet of paper on which he could see flowing handwriting with a crest above it. 'Law Society edict of last year, warning us of changes. Why would it be of interest?'

'I told Mr Worrell that I wanted to sell up and build paddle-steamers for the Murray. Take freight from Goolwa in South Australia to Swan Hill and back again. The country in both colonies looks set to open up so I want to be ready.' He leaned forward. 'There have been tentative interests already in Goolwa, where there's a new port built, and I don't want to miss out.'

Joseph Campbell steepled his fingers, the oversized knuckles like knots in a tree trunk. He nodded slowly and pursed his lips before he said, 'In the first instance, your present company structure would adequately suffice. We will eventually receive mail from England—if this war is ever to cease. For now, I'd say continue as you are.'

Finn felt the tickle of a warning again at the words but ignored it, shaking his head. 'I told Mr Worrell I need to realise some capital.'

Joseph rested his hands on his desk. 'You have adequate funds to continue your merchandise business, and no need of the bank's backing. Stay a while. There is still much money to be made. You'll have need of the sort of business you own.'

Joseph's lack of enthusiasm for the new venture struck Finn as odd. A tremor warned again, and he gripped his elbow. 'I need to move quickly, to capitalise on opportunity. My father's estate would assist the building of a couple of steamers, small ones to begin with.'

Peering over his spectacles, Joseph said, 'Which brings us, good friend, to our real business. Your father's affairs.' The gnarly fingers locked and unlocked. 'It seems there was money exchanged for Susan's hand in marriage.'

'Christ. A *dowry?*' Finn sat forward. 'Worse than I knew—'

'It wasn't a dowry, not as we know it. It was a loan. But the recipient is dead, his estate all a fraud. If there were any funds to recoup, they have evaporated.'

Fifteen

Lewis Wilshire stepped into the foyer of the suite of offices. Inside, as the heavy door clicked shut behind him, the noise of the street was silenced.

Bendigo was robust, its population enjoying civilisation brimming with commerce, merchants trading and building, and hardworking families. The goldfields were rich and rivalled the Ballarat fields.

Carriages rolled up and down the streets, pedestrians rushed to their stores and shops. Talk was that Cobb and Co would soon be coming there from Melbourne. Churches and schools and entertainment halls were plentiful. The town was even changing its name, and 'Sandhurst' seemed to be favoured.

Lewis, like others, preferred the original name 'Bendigo', but popular vote was not considered. It was a sturdy town. He wondered if Ballarat would ever become as strong as Bendigo, teetering as it did now on the brink of further unrest, and government-sanctioned murder. Until now, Ballarat had been quiet and orderly, and Bendigo the rowdy town.

He gazed around. The short hallway, with its high ceiling, polished floors and architraves, had an almost reverent hush about it. In the eerie quiet, he turned to listen for Justice herself.

Not here, he decided. Advice was dispensed here, not justice. *He* dispensed justice. He smiled to himself. What would Flora make of that sentiment? He could hear her derision. She would throw her black wavy hair—tied into an unruly plait—over her shoulder, and she'd stand, hands on hips, laughing at him.

He loved her pluck. Could she still be the wife he needed? Was it even sensible to think like that? He shrugged inwardly. It would all be moot as soon as the will was read. He could do as he liked, and with whomever he chose.

Pushing aside the memory of her, he looked about for a place to hang his hat. After shucking his coat, he hung both on the hook and rail along the wall alongside another coat and hat. Dusting himself down after the short walk from his hotel, he was ready for his meeting.

A sign above a door on the left read 'Appointments'. Lewis knocked, opened it and entered. He faced a stout man seated at the desk. His neatly clipped beard and droopy moustache were the same salt-and-pepper grey as his wavy head of hair.

The man came to his feet. 'Good afternoon. Mr Wilshire, is it?' He extended a hand.

Lewis took the proffered hand, the grip firm and short. 'I am, sir.'

'Pleased to meet you. I'm Mr Bagley. Give me a moment to check I have all your details.' He sat again. 'Mr Campbell still has someone with him, and when he becomes free, I'll inform him that you've arrived.'

Lewis supplied his full name and particulars, though he was sure he had put the same in his letter requesting an appointment. He sat in one of two high-backed, leather-seated chairs, side by side, and settled. He didn't have to wait long. In an office off to his right and behind Mr Bagley, voices rose, chairs scraped, and the vocal tones of business being finalised reached him. A door opened.

A tall man, slightly stooped as if to disguise his height, he knew as Mr Campbell, but of his client, who walked grimly ahead, he knew nothing; he did not recognise him. These days between the two towns and the burgeoning population of both goldfields and surrounds, it was impossible to know who was who any longer—newcomers or original settler people.

He nodded in acknowledgement of the man, who murmured a 'Good day' to him with a perfunctory nod, a deep frown on his face.

'Allow Mr Bagley to get your hat and help you into your coat.' Mr Campbell nodded in the direction of the door.

The man flexed the fingers on his hand, stretching out his arm. 'No need. You see it is back in good working order,' he said. 'Thank you, Mr Campbell,' he said and shook his hand. 'And you, Mr Bagley.'

'Pleasure, sir. I will see you out.' Mr Bagley left his seat to escort the man to the front door.

Keeping the confidentiality of their client, as befitted those working in a solicitor's office, neither Mr Campbell nor Mr Bagley provided any clue as to who the man was. In any case, his identity was neither here nor there.

Turning his attention, Lewis shifted in the chair, preparing to be invited into the inner sanctum of Mr Campbell's office. In the moments before Mr Bagley returned, another office door opened, and a younger man stood in the doorway. Lewis got to his feet.

Matthew Worrell tucked a paper into his waistcoat pocket, then offered a handshake. 'Morning, Lewis. I know you're here on business, so I won't dither with the usual pleasantries. Mr Campbell will see you first, then if necessary, Baggles will come get me to join you.' He nodded towards Mr Bagley, who was returning. 'I'm just finishing up some work here.'

Lewis dropped his hand. 'Of course, Matthew. Then I thought we could perhaps reacquaint with a drink—'

Matthew waved him off. 'Have to run now, but maybe see you later.' He returned to his office, shutting the door.

Resuming his seat, Lewis waited for Mr Bagley. It was a good thing Matthew would attend the appointment at some time. He had taken care of Andrew's ledgers, and would bring the most recent figures pertaining to the business's holdings. Pity he seemed to be a little dismissive just now. Perhaps just busy. A good sign.

He was a few minutes early for his appointment, so he settled back as Mr Bagley took his seat and recommenced his work. Lewis shifted as the wound in his side gave him a twinge, compliments of the long hard ride from Ballarat. Other than that, he was comfortable enough.

He'd arrived late in the afternoon yesterday, as the setting sun was still glowing long into twilight. He'd found a hotel, and paid for a good bed in a private room, a hot bath to be drawn, and his horse to be stabled. Damper and mutton stew at the bar downstairs in the hotel had satisfied his appetite. He felt he'd deserved some comforts on this occasion. He was preparing to take over his birthright.

Refreshed this morning, and barely sore in his side, he'd shaved, donned his clean shirt and trousers and prepared for the meeting. As he sat waiting, he gave thought to his uncle. He easily dismissed the death at his own hands of a man known for his brutality to women, and clearly to women with child; a man whose madness could only be stopped one way. The fact that Lewis would directly benefit from killing him did not prick his conscience. The man had been an atrocity in nature. Lewis's vigilante action had saved Nell, he was sure. Perhaps even his mother—who'd have known if Andrew's raging temper would finally spill over onto her?

He had not devised a plan in time to save poor Aunt Susan, Andrew's first wife, before she'd met her death, but it certainly accelerated a strategy. Why his mother had tolerated the madness in her brother he had no hope of understanding. He knew that she had arrived in the colony long before Andrew, had married, had a child and been widowed, so perhaps she just had no way of dealing with it. Andrew had arrived a little after Lewis's father had died of apoplexy.

But Lewis recalled a long-ago memory. His uncle had raised a fist at him, and had been seen just this once by Enid. A bitter exchange followed behind closed doors between his mother and his uncle, and after that Andrew always hid Lewis's subsequent thrashings.

As physically volatile as Andrew was, his mother had a waspish tongue, sharp and as nasty as they came. Now that he was head of the family, Lewis would ensure that her vitriol towards Nell, and others, was reined in.

That would suit him well where Flora was concerned. Flora had been aghast that Nell, whom she'd come to know as a friend, would be so treated by Enid. And then to learn of black eyes, and bruises to Nell's arms, and likely elsewhere, perpetrated by the woman's brother! Flora had taken Lewis to task over his mother's apathy.

He had tried to spread his hands as if helpless, but when Nell had appeared after a bashing, Flora exploded. She had broken off their relationship in the street immediately outside Enid's house and then confronted his mother with her anger.

Lewis scratched the back of his head as he recalled the altercation. Flora had aimed some colourful language at him, but she left the greatest derision for his mother. 'Your sort of woman is the worst,' she snapped at Enid. 'If we women don't put a stop to this, how will it ever be fixed? Your brother needs committing to an asylum for his actions, and yet you do nothing but blame his wives. You turn your eye, and that's evil too.' She'd aimed a deadly look at Lewis. 'Your mother and your uncle both disgust me. If I so much as glimpse your uncle near my laundry again, I will yell blue bloody murder.' And she'd stormed off.

With neighbours gawking, and Enid's mouth opening and closing, her hand at her throat, Lewis had directed her quickly back inside. He'd torn outside to follow Flora but hadn't been able to find her.

The decision had been made. He'd fixed the issue of his uncle, and once all this had been settled, once he'd obtained his inheritance, he would follow Flora. He would put things right between them—

'Mr Wilshire.' The lawyer himself stood at Mr Bagley's desk, offered his handshake and beckoned Lewis to follow into his office. 'Please sit.'

'Thank you, sir.' Lewis's heart thudded in anticipation as he sank into the chair Mr Campbell indicated. On the wide desk, he could see the lawyer had his letter of request open atop a clean blotter for a dip pen and ink pot, which stood nearby. A small stack of papers was alongside.

As Mr Campbell looked at him, Lewis was taken aback by the youth of the man. He could be no more than a dozen years older than he, yet he had the demeanour of a much older person.

He pulled his spectacles low over his nose to peer above the rim at Lewis. 'Your letter states that you believe you have your uncle's business to attend.'

Lewis wondered if he'd misheard the tone of voice. He frowned. 'Well, yes, Mr Campbell. My uncle, Andrew Amberton, had a considerable estate and now he has passed away, I believe I am to administer his assets.'

Mr Campbell laced his big knuckled fingers. 'Since receiving your letter, we have investigated as is usual, and have no reason to believe that your uncle left a will. We have not found anything lodged with the Office of Births, Deaths and Marriages.'

Lewis stared. 'No will?'

'In fact, unless you can recover such a will—from your residence perhaps—it would appear that your uncle died intestate.'

Lewis sat forward, felt his guts chill. 'He always spoke of a will, and of his wishes and stipulations that were in it.'

Mr Campbell raised his brows. 'Indeed. However, I have knowledge that there are considerable debts held against him. Any asset that he alleged he owned might have to be sold to cover these claims on his estate or passed on to his successor to pay.' He tapped the papers.

'Debts?' Lewis scowled despite a gnawing doubt. 'He has a strong business. Mines on the fields at Ballarat. Income in gold. Two homes in the Ballarat township.' He leaned forward. 'He spoke of his own farming land in the Western Districts, and he'd bought land north-east, newly surveyed, on the Murray.'

Mr Campbell rested his hands on the desk. 'He may very well have spoken of such things, but in truth, it appears not to be so. None of it, except the mining business. You might check that the licenses are all as they should be, especially in light of the riots.' He tilted his head towards the small stack of papers by his arm. 'Your mother instigated a public notice as she registered his death, citing this office as contact for any outstanding debts. She might not ever have imagined this, but these are the many claims on his estate that have come into my office since.'

Eyeing the papers, Lewis cleared his throat. 'And they are for what?'

Mr Campbell took the papers and set them in front of him, one by one 'As you can see, the debts are considerable.'

Lewis picked up the closest paper. 'This is for the house he and Aunt Nell occupied.'

Mr Campbell leaned forward, reading upside down. 'Yes, a rental amount due.' He tapped the page.

'Rental?' Lewis squinted at the figure. 'And for the house my mother and I occupy?'

Mr Campbell lifted a page. 'Same. Rent owed.' The finger tapped again.

Lewis looked up. 'I believed that he had purchased those houses.' His stomach rolling, he asked, 'Did he actually own land in the Western Districts?'

The lawyer tapped another page. 'He put a down payment here, took out a loan, settled, and has since neglected to repay anything, defaulting on the loan. The bank is about to foreclose. Mr Amberton cited security with a counterfeit title to this property—' he said as he shuffled the papers and withdrew one, '—here.'

Lewis squinted. 'Counterfeit. How?'

Mr Campbell lifted his loose shoulders a little. 'A clever copy. And a lazy clerk who didn't follow procedure. It was not discovered until the default.'

Lewis sat back. 'Did he own anything?'

'It appears not.' Shuffling again, Mr Campbell came up with another paper, handwritten. 'It seems he also took out, shall we say, a loan from his previous father-in-law.'

Rigid, Lewis stared. 'What do you mean?'

'This is a loan receipt for five thousand pounds made out to Mr John Seymour.'

Lewis closed his mouth but couldn't mask his shock. What in God's name would his uncle want with a loan for that huge amount? Where were the ill-gotten gains? It certainly wasn't in property, according to Mr Campbell. Perhaps it was to pay for all the other debts … No wonder he'd been bolting out of town as quick as he could, the mad, lying, cheating bastard.

'I am at a loss,' Lewis said, shaking his head, staring at his hands, listening as his birthright, his inheritance whooshed away on thin air.

'Understandable,' Mr Campbell replied. 'Now, tell me, is the mine still operating, Mr Wilshire?'

Lewis rolled his hands together. 'I've simply conducted business as usual. It is well known I am the manager …' He looked up sharply. 'Am I personally liable for these debts?'

'No. But I suggest you continue to operate the mine as usual, until this mess is sorted out. As there is no will, therefore no administrator, the proceeds from the mining, a license being still in his name—'

Lewis snapped to attention. 'He's dead.'

'—might well have to pay off these creditors.'

Nodding, Lewis dropped his head to his hand. He would have to let Andrew's licenses lapse, stake the claims as his own. But how would he keep control of the mines without the other men to work them? He'd have to get things in his name, in place, quickly. But would he still be liable somehow?

'You could apply to administer, as you are one of Mr Amberton's relatives. That way you can manage matters.'

Lewis's head snapped up. 'And what ramification does that have for me?'

'I suggest you agree to release the land in the Western Districts and forfeit Mr Amberton's initial outlay. I would also suggest that the rent on the houses needs to be paid in full if you are to continue to occupy them.'

'If I apply to administer—'

'Do you want to administer his affairs?' Mr Campbell tapped the papers in front of him, drawing attention to the amount owing on rent.

Lewis blanched.

'I didn't think so.' Then Mr Campbell gave him another shock. 'But this loan of five thousand pounds will have to be repaid. It has your name and signature on it as guarantor, and the family wants it back.'

Sixteen

Ballarat

Nell dug her knuckles into her back and stretched. She'd forgotten what working over a washing tub felt like, or how the skin of her hands would begin to crack as they dried out. How the biting odour of lye would linger in her nostrils.

The morning was already hot, and the sun beat down mercilessly on a cloudless day. Heat from the fire underneath the boiler throbbed up, and her perspiration evaporated before it could drip anywhere.

Noise, even this early at the diggings, was incessant. Men shouted at each other, some in derision, some in jocularity. Dogs barked at any moving thing. Children ran, unchecked, playing chasing games, squealing with delight or bellowing with rage. Women emerged from tents to work, fossicking, child-minding, cooking, mending, doing laundry. Their day was only done at the moment they fell asleep.

Nell stared at the scene laid out before her. The children scampering about, free as birds when they weren't ordered into their families' mining activities. Why weren't they at school? Her mother had taught her to read and write; perhaps she'd begin her mother's work again, and take some of these children in to teach. But it didn't appeal overly much, it was just something she could do. She looked at the mountains of dirty clothes. First things first, then she might think more about it.

Nell took the long, sturdy rod again and plunged it back into the frothing water, pulled the clothes this way and that, dirt and fat and oils streaming in their wake. Not only was the pile of clothes and bed linens beside the boiler half as tall as she was, but the supply of soap needed to wash it had to be replenished. It was her turn to make it, and this would be her next job.

Soap making was a necessary skill, and an art, Flora had said, and Nell knew it well. Saving most of the ashes from the fires, Flora used it in barrels with a layer of hay over a drain hole in the bottom. After she poured hot water slowly over it, leaching it, a tub underneath caught the run-off solution, the lye. Then pounds of lard were required to boil with the lye over a slow fire. It was a skill she needed to brush up on, much to Flora's gleeful delight.

Hot work, dawn 'til dusk, on a day with the sun shining. At least she was alive.

She pulled and pushed once more on the rod and determined that this tub of clothes was about as clean as it was going to get. Heaving in a deep breath, she tested the heat of the water with a hand, then plunged it in to pull out sodden clothes. Squeezing out excess water from each article, she dropped them into a tub of cold water and pulled and pushed the rod once more.

Oh, to have one of those new machines where you wound a handle round and round and pushed clothes through two tight rollers. Water would squeeze out effortlessly and the garments or linens would be ready to hang out to dry. Flora had shown her newspaper advertisements. They pondered together whether it would be prudent to save for one. No one here had yet seen one of these magical washing machines, but they couldn't come too soon, if Nell had her way.

After dumping more filthy clothes into the hot water to stew for a bit, she wrung out the rinsed trousers and shirts and flung them over the drying ropes. Flora had strung a series of lines between six-foot posts sunk for her by eager miners. Nuggets had been found in the holes dug, so the posts were haphazard. Sturdily sunk, but not exactly in straight lines.

Flora poked her head out of her tent. 'I'm just getting Ma organised—'

'Me name's Josie,' Nell heard a voice call loudly from inside the tent.

Flora rolled her eyes. 'I'm just getting *Josie* organised with her sewing, Nell. I won't be long. Put the billy on, will you?' She ducked back inside.

Nell, glad of the break, filled the billy from their water barrel and set it over the kitchen fire pit. She sat on a rough-hewn bench and threw in a handful of tea leaves grabbed from the plain packet Flora kept in a tin nearby.

Murmurs of encouragement, gentle complaints and rippling laughter reached her from Flora's tent. The lilting Irish notes of mother and daughter was a sharp reminder of the loss of Nell's own mother.

Her heart gave a lurch. *Ma, my beloved ma. I miss you every day.* A breath caught in her throat as she thought of her mother's last few gasps. They'd laboured harder only for a minute or so, signalling her passing from the consumption. Then, with Nell's hand holding hers, and hearing Nell's whispered words of support for her to go, Cecilia had left her daughter for the next world. Nell's father, Alfred, had been at the pub.

Flora emerged from the tent, smiling, tilting her head at the vagaries of her mother's affliction. 'Not so long ago, there'd be folk who'd say she was touched by *fae*.'

'Don't they still?' Nell asked, poking a thin stick into the brew and giving it a stir. Aromatic steam hid her eyes from Flora, but not well enough.

'What is it, Nell? You're sad.' Flora sat beside her on the bench, took the stick and stirred the brew some more.

'*Fae* or not, you're lucky you still have your Josie. My ma's been gone two years now.'

Flora wiped the back of her hand over her forehead. 'I'm sorry for it, Nell. I remember Mrs Thomas fondly.' She reached over and squeezed Nell's arm.

'Much has happened since.'

Flora sighed. 'And much has stayed the same.'

They both looked across at the laundry tubs.

'That's true enough,' Nell said, and gave a short laugh. 'And it won't do itself.'

Flora flicked a hand at the tubs. 'Sit awhile. Your boss says it's all right.' She dunked a pannikin into the billy and set it down for Nell and did the same for herself. 'I heard you're going to the Subscription Ball.'

'Though not for want of trying to get out of it. Lewis is insisting for some strange reason. I can think of nothing worse than going to a ball. Widow weeds, and all that, and then there's Enid.' Nell looked at Flora. 'And how did you hear I was going?'

Flora dusted off her apron over the soft folds of the wide bloomers. 'Lewis found me at the butcher's tent before he went to Bendigo.'

'Did he now?' Nell took up her cup and gave it a gentle swirl before sipping.

'Aye, he did. Said he couldn't find me here, so he came lookin'. Says he wants to walk out with me again.' Flora studied her hands, palm up, palm down. 'Says you asked him to be occupyin' Amberton House.'

Nell was surprised Lewis had said anything to Flora. 'I did. But if I tried walking from there to here before dawn,' she waved a hand at the tubs, 'and walking back after dark, I would have rocks in my head. If the laundry doesn't kill me, the walk to and fro Amberton House would.' Not to mention the dangers of walking alone, in fields pock-ridden with holes, mullock heaps, tents, and drunken men. 'When I asked about Amberton House, he said to wait until after his visit to the lawyer.' It was a fair answer in the scope of things.

'You can still put a tent here.'

'I might have to.' Nell frowned. If Flora had agreed to see Lewis once more, Nell wouldn't be confiding in her, especially about Andrew's gold. 'And so, you agreed to see Lewis again?'

'No, and not sure I will. He returns today from Bendigo, no doubt the big man of an estate.' Flora blew in her tea to cool it. 'He would be coming back far too well-to-do for the likes of me, and I think that's where I'll be leavin' it.'

Nell smiled a little at that, remembering Lewis's comments about Flora. 'He will certainly have a job to manage the businesses, if the way Andrew always went on and on about it was any indication.'

Flora took a swallow of tea. 'Does it not bother you now, not having the life Andrew married you into?'

Nell stared at the low flames and the embers glowing under the billy. She lifted the pot away from the fire and dunked her cup again to top up. 'What life was it? If I even cared, there's naught to do about it. Enid has made herself clear. And to answer you directly, no. I have no wish for it. But Lewis hasn't said what he'll do.'

'I think he would be kind, Nell.'

'Do you?'

Flora made a face. 'He'd look after his own first, o'course. Like I would.'

Nell looked at her. 'Then in that case, it might be best for me to put a tent here.' She drew in a breath. 'And will you be going to the ball?'

Flora looked skywards a moment. 'To be sure,' she said, wryly. 'Me and me mam here will bring out our finest flounces and ribbons and pop along.'

'Anyone can go if they pay their three pounds, you know,' Nell said, chiding.

Flora snorted. 'I'll not be wastin' my hard-earned cash on the frivolous goings-on of a ball. But I am happy to donate to the cause. I'll give you a sixpence to take for the pot.' She stood up, dashed the dregs of her tea into the embers. 'We best get along. As you said, that lot,' she pointed at the tubs, 'won't do itself.'

Seventeen

Crushed under the weight of Mr Campbell's news, Lewis had found a pub in Bendigo. He had sat and brooded for hours before he'd decided to ride into the night for home. At first, he'd chugged down the rum, but then he considered the ride home and the ugly hangover he'd have if he didn't stop the drinking. He'd also save his coin, which would be more prudent than ever.

Now he sat opposite his mother in the kitchen of their house. He was dog-tired, dirty, and he could smell himself, but that was the least of his worries.

In the early evening light, Enid's face was ashen, the colour his own must have been when Mr Campbell had uttered the words that shocked him.

'Nothing?' she asked, short of breath, her small eyes as wide as possible.

'Only debt,' he answered, flatly. 'For the most part, I can operate the mine and pay off the rent on the houses. Hand one of them back to its owner after that.'

'And good riddance to Nell Thomas,' Enid hissed.

'Nell Amberton, Mama,' he corrected. 'She legally has Andrew's name and will remain here in this house with a roof over her head.

The problem lies squarely with Andrew. None of this is Nell's fault.'

'It's her fault, all right—'

Lewis fist hammered on the table. 'He was the worst type of scoundrel to her, and to poor Susan if you would care to remember.'

Enid ignored him. 'It was in his will that she is not to be supported—'

'What have I just finished telling you?' Exasperation caused his voice to rise and he went on. 'There is no will. There is no fortune. No grand houses. No estates. No land anywhere. Only large debt.' His side pained with a quick, deep sting, and he calmed himself. The ride home had been bad enough without stirring up more aches to bother him. 'And Nell is rightfully his widow.'

His mother's colour returned in a rush. She picked up her fan and flapped it in front of her face.

'This debt,' he went on in her haughty silence, 'is a debt I have somehow guaranteed. And how is that possible, eh? The man must have forged my signature.' He drummed his fingers on the table. 'The mine will have to deliver, we will have to explore more ways to extract the gold.' His thoughts jumped from possible solution, to improbable outcome, and back to blame. 'He was a liar, damn him,' he snarled.

Enid flinched, swallowed down her emotion.

'He was a thief,' Lewis stormed on, his brows taut. 'He was cruel, and controlling, and it was good—' He stopped. He was too close to announcing the murder he'd committed.

His mother hiccupped, and wiped her nose with a handkerchief.

He burst out instead, 'But what possessed him to forge my signature on a document like this?' He flattened a palm on the agreement to repay the loan, which was spread out on the table.

'Five thousand pounds, Mama. It's a monstrous amount of money. Did he say a word to you, about any of this sort of thing?'

Enid pressed the handkerchief to her eyes. 'No.'

Sitting forward, his head in his hands, he let out a breath. 'What possible reason would he have?' He looked up, bleak. 'Unless he intended to betray us as well. Unless he intended to keep this money to himself all along and ride off.' He stopped, stared at his mother's crumpled face, but hardly noticed it.

He'd shot and killed his uncle—a mercy to all those who suffered, certainly. And yes, yes, there was a small matter of Lewis being bypassed for succession, of inheritance, but now there was nothing to inherit. Had never been. Had he been outwitted by Andrew all along?

Enid sobbed soundlessly into her handkerchief, her shoulders hunched.

Lewis knew his signature on the loan document was fraudulent, illegal. He had no funds to take it before a magistrate and declare the guarantee invalid—even if there were a magistrate to be found who could give a damn. In the present climate over the goldfields it would be nigh on impossible. But he'd put it to Mr Campbell to challenge it as soon as he could think straight.

The lawyer had simply said, 'Let's see your signatures,' and asked him to sign his name on a loose sheet of paper for comparison. Sliding the papers side by side, they both stared at the signatures, Lewis's fresh one against the one on the loan document. Lewis knew he was in trouble. The forgery was very good. He looked at Mr Campbell, who just shook his head. Even the signature and name of the witness—which neither of them recognised—looked to be as fraudulent as it was illegible.

He was now in debt to the tune of five thousand pounds and he was thinking fast.

'It was a special kind of madness,' Lewis mused aloud, staring past his mother and into the cast iron gloom of the old stove.

'I presume you are speaking of Andrew,' Nell said as she stood at the door, just in from working at Flora's laundry. She held her boots in her hand and had slipped her feet into house slippers before entering the kitchen.

'I am.' Lewis nodded, and stood, facing her. 'There is some terrible news, Nell.'

Nell looked at Enid. Her sister-in-law rocked a little back and forth, her face covered by hands bunched around her handkerchief. The silence of it sent a hollow feeling to her stomach and she glanced back to Lewis.

'What is it?' she demanded.

Enid's nose blared into her handkerchief. She reached for another in her lap and wiped her eyes with it.

Preparing herself, Nell set her boots outside the door and asked again, 'What is it, Lewis?'

'Before I explain,' Lewis said, and indicated she should sit at the table, 'I would ask if you ever saw my uncle's will?'

Nell sat in a chair at the table and took another glance at Enid. Her sister-in-law stared at the broad, black cooker squatting in the bricked alcove. Its heat, necessary but overwhelming in the small room during summer, made Nell's armpits trickle and her scalp crawl. She felt the dirt of the day gritty on her skin.

'I did not. I never saw any papers to that effect,' she answered. 'He said he sent it to be registered just after we were married.'

Lewis sat again. 'It was never registered, if indeed there ever was a will.'

His words took a moment for her to comprehend. Nell rested the palms of her hands on the hard timber table, its smooth well-worn surface cool to her touch. She leaned in a little. 'It was all he talked about near the end,' she said.

Enid sniffled.

'About that, and his land, and these two houses,' Nell continued. 'Of the mining. Of how great a man he was.' She heard the bitterness of her words and stopped, sinking back in her chair. 'I don't know what it means if he has no will.'

Lewis thrust a hand through his hair. When he looked at Nell, she saw his usually calm, clear eyes were shot with red, the rims bright against the white. 'No will, no inheritance, and no money. No holdings, no houses. Nothing except a huge debt of five thousand pounds owed to his previous father-in-law, John Seymour, and the family want it back.'

'Five—? John Seymour, Susan's father?' Could that be where the gold had come from—Susan's family? Breath hitched in her throat. There could easily be that amount in gold in those bags. That she still had hold of it sent waves of shame through her. Fear came fast on its heels. Her thoughts rushed over the bags of gold, what she'd hidden, how much there might have been. The certainty of its true ownership struck her dumb.

'Yes. Susan's father. There's nothing else, not a farthing, only what comes in from the diggings, is all. I must take up the licenses to ensure we have that income, at least.'

Enid straightened, shot a look at Nell and bristled. 'We?' she asked.

Nell ignored Enid. 'No houses? Not this one or the other?'

Lewis shook his head. 'Not owned. Rented only, and with much rent outstanding.' He looked at her. 'It means I will have to surrender one of them to the owner. I will try to find the back rent for it, but Nell, it will have to be the one you had hoped to occupy.'

'Of course.' She clasped her hands over the table. 'Of course,' she repeated, thinking quickly. 'I have some possessions there.'

She looked at Lewis. 'Nothing I can't carry in a basket, some clothing only. A few papers, old letters.'

'There was nothing there when I checked that day,' Enid snapped, her handkerchief coming away revealing angry, thinned lips.

'But there is now. As you know I had intended to leave this house and live there again. I had taken a few things back. I will need to retrieve them, and soon, that's clear,' Nell replied as evenly as she could. Good God, she would have to go back to the house and retrieve the bars and nuggets, hide them somewhere else, somehow. That gold was not Andrew's to have, nor Lewis's to keep. Nor hers, for that matter. She was certain it belonged to her predecessor's father and should rightfully go back to his family.

Some of John Seymour's money must have been exchanged for Nell and paid to her father by Andrew Amberton. She was now sure that's what had happened. Stunned, Nell stared across the room.

Enid pushed away from the table, took a nub of candle and poked it into the stove to light its wick. She lit others from it, and their low glow softened the night's arrival as the sun began to set. Insects flew to the candles; some perished, some escaped only to return. Mosquitoes buzzed lazily overhead.

'What do we tell people?' Enid said to her son, turning back, a candle in her hand. She set it on the table and took her seat again.

'Nothing,' Lewis said. He tapped his fingers on his knees. 'Say nothing. The miners will still dig for our gold. We will pay out the rent, first on the other house. We will have to be frugal from now on, and for the foreseeable future.'

'I will not be able to face the ladies—'

'Mama, no one need know any different.'

'But we will not be able to go to the ball, and people will ask why not, especially as we have accepted to go,' she reasoned weakly, her eyes on her son.

Lewis stood up. He reached over to the mantel and took another stub of candle, lighting it from the ones on the table. His lip curled. 'If I so chose to use an excuse, we would have poor dear Andrew's demise to hide behind. But I do not choose. We will all still go to the ball. The tickets are paid for, and we have them as proof of payment. We will not allow any of this to escape this house and will carry on. As normal.' He walked past Nell to the doorway. 'I am going to wash and then I will go to the pub. Pity the Bentley's hotel was burnt down before the riots. It would have suited me well to be seen tonight in Ballarat's finest establishment.'

Ballarat's finest? Nell wondered at his patronage of the Eureka Hotel, now gone, and its owner James Bentley, who'd at first been exonerated for the murder of a drunken Scotsman, then incarcerated for manslaughter. Talk was it had justified the diggers' actions. It had fuelled the disastrous events of the stockade battle, unified the miners against the corrupt government and police. Had Lewis more to do with the darker side of life on the diggings than she had imagined? She would need to be more vigilant. An eerie flutter spread through her chest, as if a cool breeze had entered her body.

Lewis headed out but turned back and looked at them. 'Best foot forward, ladies. We will sleep on plans to secure the future.'

Enid stared after him. 'He goes to the pub,' she said, ruefully. 'He acts as if this is not the worst thing to happen for us.'

Nell didn't answer. If this was the worst to happen, Enid was a fortunate woman.

Eighteen

Five thousand pounds. A fortune. Since departing Joseph Campbell's office with the news—the crippling news of his father's loan to Amberton—it had bedevilled Finn. He'd thought of nothing else.

Shaken, and numb with the futility of rage, he'd left Bendigo immediately instead of enjoying the town on Saturday and Sunday as he'd planned. He'd ridden for Ballarat and, long hours after dark, dismounted at a stand of gums that reached high to the moonlit sky. Small scrubby bushes dotted around what looked like a natural clearing, and he'd found a hollow that would suffice as a place to sleep. Leading his gelding off the road, he checked the night sky, and, not fearing any thunder and lightning tonight to bring limbs crashing down, tethered him nearby. He rubbed the horse down, gave him water poured into his hat from a travelling flask. He bunkered down in the hollow, his saddle a pillow.

The night was warm. A breeze would drop over him and move on, so he hadn't needed to pull the horse blanket over him. Before sleep came, an intense tremor shook his arm. It pulled his chin to his shoulder and curled his fingers into a painful fist. As it passed, and muscles relaxed, his fingers released, the echoes of bullets whining by his head and canon shot booming in his ears receded. He thanked God he was by himself. Bad enough it had to take him over in Joseph Campbell's office, but he knew he couldn't hide it from everyone. It set upon him with no warning, and it wasn't mindful of the company he kept.

He'd take his chances if the tremors erupted in public, unannounced. There were folk who knew he'd returned from armed combat near the Crimea, but none other than very few knew why he had been discharged. Some folk were known to say of these afflictions, that if there was no physical wound, the afflicted man must be soft in the head. These men must have been, they said, so greatly disturbed by *fear* that its manifestation was made apparent for all the world to see. *They were not war cripples*, they'd said. *These men were cowards*. To be wrongly accused of cowardice simply because his body shook inexplicably enraged him. Yet he could do nothing except bear it. The tremors would lessen over time, he was sure of it, hopeful of it. He'd try to find someone who could advise medically and confirm that hope.

Finn took deep breaths. His mind was whirling away his reason and he had to stop it. He was no cripple, no coward, and would press on through these tremors, make light of them where he could. He hoped that a catatonic state did not descend on him as he knew had happened to others.

He had to focus on getting his father's loan repaid. And he knew without a doubt that the gold in Amberton's coach was his by rights. Over the years, his careful father, John, had secreted much away, he knew that. But the loan papers Joseph had shown him horrified him. Amberton had somehow wheedled the loan, had stolen his sister, killed her and then had died at the hands of another. Had Finn only known of the loan at the time of the holdup, he would have taken the gold there and then. Justice done.

He checked his thinking. Mrs Amberton knew where that gold was now. And she had guarded it carefully, according to Ben, when they'd come for her.

His arm shook a little again. He lay on his back and he braced his elbow, but nothing more came of it. Waiting a few moments more, he relaxed and flexed his limbs.

The woman's intense blue eyes, wide, imploring, and proud, came to his mind as he readied to sleep under the night sky. The way she'd pressed against him, the way he'd reacted to her. They were the last things he remembered for the night.

He rose just before dawn. Breakfasting on bread he'd bought before departing Bendigo, and downing water from his flask, he rode on to his home on the edge of the digging fields.

Late in the afternoon, bleary-eyed and weary, weighed down by Joseph's news, Finn walked his tired mount into the two-stalled stable at Steele and Sons. Ben was already there, rubbing down another of Finn's horses.

The work cart, empty now and ready for a journey to Melbourne to pick up more supplies, stood outside, timber gleaming, wheels oiled, and clean. A huge canvas tarpaulin lay folded neatly in the back, coils of thick rope on top of it. Ben's coach nearby rested on its draught poles and chocks of rough-hewn tree trunk were jammed against the wheels.

'You made it back in one piece,' Ben said in greeting, and kept rubbing as he grinned up at Finn. His shirt sleeves were rolled up to the elbows, his baggy trousers stained with oil and axle grease.

'You could say,' Finn replied and led his horse to the other stall. He loosened the girth strap and lifted the saddle off, slinging it over the rail with a grunt.

'Didn't expect you this side of next week. How'd it go, the lawyer's visit?'

'Looks like I'll be hauling picks and shovels and pans from Melbourne for a while yet.'

'You could haul what's left in that musty old store of your pa's and sell it off if you ever cleaned it out.'

Finn gave Ben the eye. The old man's store had stood filled to the brim with saleable items. Finn kept putting off throwing the doors wide and trading from it. Instead, he'd shoved the excess merchandise from his trips inside, closed the door and walked away. Now, he might have to face it sooner rather than later.

Finn snorted. 'Either way, no building riverboats for me in the foreseeable future.' He loosened the horse's halter, removed it and tossed it to the back of the stall. Grim, he snatched a rag, and started the rub down.

'That so? Well, there you are. Good reason to stay and sell off that stuff before you can't sell it.' Ben leaned his arms on the withers of a healthy roan, its flank broad and well-muscled. 'Still, would be a shame—no riverboats.' He ducked under the horse's neck to peer over the rail into the next stall. 'Would be a rollickin' new adventure.'

Finn grunted as he rubbed, and his horse shied in protest. 'My father had a small fortune set to come to me after he died. Seems while I was away, when Susan married, it went in a loan to her husband, Amberton.'

Ben's eyes popped, the irony not lost on him. 'Jesus. You mean your gold paid for his ride with me that morning?' He thumbed over his shoulder at his coach.

Finn's jaw set. 'I hope to get most of it back.'

'I've still got the nugget he paid with. Don't worry, it's yours. But if Amberton took a loan from your father—'

'Amberton's got no assets, apparently.'

Ben sputtered. 'The wife had gold in those bags.'

'Aye. She did.' Finn did a quick calculation. 'Gold is three pounds an ounce, so if Nell Amberton does have my father's gold, it would weigh nearly as much as she does. She'd never lift it. It would be hidden elsewhere, or perhaps already exchanged. But if the family did know of it, chances are it's not with her now, anyway.'

Ben gave him a look. 'I can tell yer plannin' something.'

Finn knew where she lived. Perhaps, after a night's sleep in a proper bed, he would venture out. 'The bags might be hidden in plain sight, at her house.'

'Daft thinkin',' Ben growled.

Finn agreed. 'True. Ridiculous.' *For now, be calm, man, be calm.* He should heed Joseph Campbell's last few words to him before he'd left his office. *'Let me deal with the family, Finneas. A letter might be all it takes if the funds are indeed still real.'*

'Ben, it was gold my father found as a squatter.' He rested his arm on the horse's flank. 'He'd hidden find after find on his property near here in the late forties. Others would have known there was gold too and hidden their finds.'

'It's a wonder word never got out then,' Ben said. 'Gold brings all them blasted loudmouths.'

Finn shook his head. 'Might have been rumoured here or there but the New South Wales colony had jurisdiction and it suppressed any real news. My father was lucky, and shrewd. He kept it quiet. But afterwards, it was too big, it wouldn't stay quiet. The Ballarat diggings became a frenzy. And here we are.'

'Good thing Victoria got up as a colony,' Ben said. 'All that gold goin' off to New South Wales woulda been criminal.'

Finn nodded. Victoria had become a separate colony in 1851 and that's when his father had set up the merchandise store in Ballarat. Two years later John applied for a digger's license, enabling him to own the gold he'd found before and, cautiously, go public. His funds grew substantially. He bought and sold well.

'At some point,' Finn said, brushing down the horse once again, 'my pa's mind must have started to go, probably after ma died.' Finn hadn't noticed the decline in his father; he'd had his own grief to deal with after Louise had died from an aggressive cancer. He'd gone to England in a blur of heartache and numbness by turn. 'I didn't see it. I left. But Andrew Amberton must have seen it and pounced.' That he'd missed the old man's crumbling state of mind sat sorely on Finn.

Of everything his father had worked for, the merchandise store was all that was left, it seemed. A store of jumbled tools, and hard memories. He'd have to face it.

After a last rub on the horse's rump, Finn said, 'I will think more on what to do. If there's anything, any gold to fight for, I won't let it go without a fight. Mr Campbell wants to try something first, but he better be quick.'

He blew out a long breath. Had Nell given him a performance the other night? Had she been ahead of him, played him for a fool? Any strategy he would plan around her was a matter for another day. Joseph Campbell's strategy would have to suffice for the moment. It gnawed at him, having to wait, having to follow the law, but his mind needed to be clear. Today, he had a business to run, had money to earn, and so far, had good health returning.

He flung the rag into a corner and turned back to Ben. 'So, for the time being, Seymour's Implement and Merchandise needs to hire Steele and Son's Coach and Cart for a buying trip to Melbourne.'

Ben threw his hands in the air. 'All right. You know I'm yer driver. And then after that, we fix that store of yours.'

Finn grunted. He wasn't sure if he agreed or not.

Nell had pleaded for the afternoon off. Flora waved her away grumbling, extracting a promise from Nell that she would return before lunch on Sunday, the next day. Most of the single men who could not afford laundry services did their own on that day before church. Those who would go to church, that is. On Sundays, Flora and her mother would convert her fires to cooking fires, and roast many potatoes and a joint of meat for grateful diggers who were happy to pay. Nell would be a welcome extra hand.

Hurrying from Wilshire House, Nell slung a tote-bag over her head and shoulder. It swung ungainly, empty except for a sewing kit neatly tucked inside, until she held it close. Walking smartly over the dusty road, she headed towards Amberton House. Hot and breathless as she pushed open the front door, she headed straight for the pitcher of water she'd left in the kitchen the last time she was here. Pouring barely a cupful, she gulped some down. Tepid, but it would have to do.

Working quickly, she plucked at the plug of timber in the hollowed mantel. Teasing out the closest nuggets, she sank to the hearth. Unpicking the hem of her day dress, she tucked a nugget into it, deftly sewed it closed, tucked another nugget alongside and sewed it in. She tried for another five or six nuggets around the width of the skirt, then stood to gauge the weight of her dress.

Moving back and forth, Nell paced until satisfied that the nuggets were not too cumbersome and didn't noticeably drag on the dress or bang against each other as she walked. She could comfortably go back to the other house without staggering under the weight of them. Now for the other nuggets left in the mantelpiece …

She reached in and coaxed out the others; the last one she needed to guide out with a long twig from the kindling basket. She tucked what remained into her tote-bag and slung it again over her head and shoulder, a little more clumsily than when she had set out from the other house. It was weighty, no question, but it disguised its contents well enough not to alert a passer-by to her mission. The bars that were tucked into the wall under the water barrel would have to wait for another day.

Steady on her feet, she went into the bedroom and emptied the tall-boy drawers of her few underthings, stuffing them into the tote. At least if Enid hovered when she got back there, she had the cottons to prove she'd done what she said she would. There were no letters to retrieve, no papers as she had said, so if asked about them she would say she'd burned them as unnecessary rubbish. She still had the old envelope tucked close to her person, the dot of gold and promissory notes safe for now.

Back in the kitchen, she stilled, willing herself to concentrate on whatever else might be here for her to take. Only bad memories, she decided, and they could well remain. Gulping the last of the water, she left, pulled the door shut on her life with Andrew Amberton, brief as it was, and walked away, her steps measured, her breathing calm.

Her mind blanked then filled with a spark of hope. Finding a hidey-hole in her current abode at Wilshire House would be nigh on impossible, but hiding gold in her new tent on the goldfields might just be a stroke of genius.

And now she desperately needed to write to Mr Campbell.

Each night since the riots, life had steadily got back to normal, everyone had got back to being liquored up again, and this Saturday night was no different. Drunks and their carts, carriages and horses straggled back and forth between establishments. The curfew having been lifted, or barely enforced, meant Finn was free to roam where he wished. On foot, he had no trouble easing his way unnoticed through town to the small timber cottage where he knew Mrs Amberton had lived.

Cautioning himself about the wisdom of these stealthy visits, he told himself he would stop after this one. Someone might eventually note his loitering and besides, he wouldn't jeopardise whatever Joseph might have put in place.

He'd have to be careful this last time, more than usual. He steered clear of any sightings of troopers. They and the traps, the foot police, were still a dangerous bunch of thugs and some, guilty of the massacre and having deserted, had not so far been found. Finn knew most folk didn't expect that they'd be brought to justice. He'd be on the lookout.

The setting sun took its time. He walked past Mrs Amberton's house, well after twilight had lost itself to a dark but starlit night.

He didn't see any sign of life in the house. No glow of candle from room to room showed through the uncovered windows. No movement detected. She had not returned.

Either side of her house was cleared space, the dirt tumbled in places, rocks and stones jutting out of the dry earth. On one side, it was clear that there was to be another abode built. Sawn timber, pots of nails, and roofing iron were stacked on a horseless cart a short distance away.

Finn wondered where she was, the woman with the bright eyes and hair the colour of pale corn-silk. It seemed she wasn't here now, but until he got a closer look, he wouldn't know if she still lived in the house.

Crossing the road at a normal pace, he headed for the back of the small house. He wondered if Amberton bought it from the proceeds of his father's loan. He stuffed that thought down as the ire beat at the back of his throat. He doubted Amberton owned it, for Joseph had said the man had only creditors, and no viable assets other than his mining licenses. For Finn, that was next to useless. If you paid your thirty shillings for the license each month, you owned the right to mine. If Amberton's nephew continued to pay, the licenses would be in his name, not his dead uncle's.

No dogs barked close by, no humans shouted at him, he heard no noise except the carousing of some pub revellers in the distance. Flattened against the wall of the house by the back stoop, he listened for signs of life inside. Nothing. The kitchen room was in darkness.

The good Mrs Amberton was not here. She must still be at the other house, the one he'd escorted her to. He tested the door, turned the handle and opened it. No low glow from the cook stove. It was clear, now that he was inside, that no one lived here any longer. Finn relaxed, and a long breath escaped. Adjusting to the dark, he headed straight for the stove. Cold to touch. No fire had been kept alight here for days.

In the shadowy dark, his hand swept over the table. He reached out for a shelf of the hutch beyond. Nothing on it. Nothing to sweep aside. He pulled open two drawers under the shelf, felt all the way up to the back of them. Nothing.

Back outside, he tested the door to the main house and once again, it opened freely. Without the stars to give him even some dim light, he waited until his sight adjusted.

He stood in a hallway. This was the same as other houses of its type—four rooms, two to the left and two to the right. Inside the front rooms, the windows allowed him to peer out into the night. He turned back and as he stood, his back to the street, he didn't believe there was anything of value left in the house.

He turned for the hallway, listened for sounds other than his heartbeat, or his breath, or the soft footfalls of his boots.

Floorboards barely creaked, iron on the roof had finished con-
tracting after the day's sunlight and heat. It was silent.

But he couldn't help imagining the sounds of Amberton's
punches. Landing first on his sister, Susan, whose light frame and
lithe form had not withstood such beatings.

His mind reeled. *Susan. No one deserved to get what you did.*
They'd let him see her before her burial, and his guts had churned
at the pathetic, battered sight he faced. There wasn't much a goldfields mortuary could do to cover it up, and when they placed the
lid over her, Finn turned away and threw up his horror. He'd seen
a dead body before, plenty recently, but none had been a family
member in such a state.

Amberton said Susan had fallen at the house, and bedridden
with premature labour delivering a dead female child, had passed
away. Then at her funeral, there was the bloody smirk on the bastard's face. He'd stood over her grave, flicked his wrist and tossed
the clod of earth on her coffin without a backwards glance. Finn's
tremors had seized him, but he didn't miss the jeer Amberton flung
at him, nor the blank stare of the vacant eyes as he stalked past.

Finn squeezed his eyes shut at the memory, fell against the
wall, hands clenched as frustration and futility tore through him.
Then rage screamed up from his innards. He opened his mouth
to howl his anguish silently into the night and a tight band constricted his chest. He slumped, had to breathe, had to keep his
temper capped and his mind safe from the poison that had been
Andrew Amberton. Susan was gone. There was nothing he could
do now, nothing to avenge for her.

But Finn couldn't leave those thoughts behind. The new Mrs
Amberton, though a little taller than his sister, would not have
fared any better. When he'd first seen her at the coach, she seemed
slight, but not weakened. Her eye had recently been blackened,
but her pluck was evident. What horror had she endured after

Susan? How much longer would she have survived …? What had she said at the hold-up? *I would gladly have done it, had I the capability.*

Suddenly he couldn't go where his mind would take him. *Amberton, the monster.* Now beyond Finn's revenge. He thudded through the house, out through the back door, which he slammed shut. He held his elbow, just in case, but as he hurried off the property and back onto the dusty road for home, he knew his body would not vex him tonight.

He should have strangled Amberton with his own hands and stared him in the eye until he was dead.

Nineteen

Outside Melbourne

Finn squinted skywards into the wide expanse of blue and the unrelenting glare of a bright, late summer sun. He whipped off his hat, wiped his forehead, and jammed the hat on again. 'Maybe one more trip before the rain comes,' he remarked to Ben alongside him on the cart. He flicked the reins and the horses trudged forward, only a little faster.

'Perhaps two more trips if it stays dry. Depends on how quickly you move this lot off.' Ben thumbed over his shoulder to the stacked implements piled high in the back of the cart. 'Then I say we get into that store of yours and clean it out, once and for all.'

'In time.'

'Finn. There's a lot of stock in there your pa bought years ago. You have to get it sold,' Ben said. 'It'd mean you wouldn't have to make so many bloody rushed trips. It would tide you over for winter and beyond. Keep you in front.'

'And how is it you have a head for my business all of a sudden?'

'Hardly "all of a sudden". You moped around it before you left, and you're still mopin' around it. Time to get on with it.' Ben flicked his hand in the air.

Finn had heard Ben's case before. Facing what was in his father's shop was proving difficult. It felt like he'd lose what was left of his father, of his legacy. Selling off the stock would somehow set the past free and he wasn't sure he could let it go. And yet, he heard his father's voice, loud and clear. *It's stock, Finneas. And stock is money.* How many times had he heard that?

Finn looked over his shoulder at the cart, top heavy with new tools ready to go straight to the fields on their return. Pans, shovels, sieves, picks, axes, buckets, and a couple of large soil-washing 'puddling' cradles on order for two of his more affluent customers. There were windlasses and winches for those men now digging shafts. After finishing with alluvial gold, which was becoming harder to find, miners needed heavier tools to continue striking it rich, or hoping to.

Laden to the hilt and beyond, the cart journey back to Ballarat had been a slow one, as usual. Finn's mind was on the off-loading. He wondered how quickly could they make another trip before the road to Melbourne became a winter wreck with horses and bullocks bogged all along the track, perishing if they couldn't be dug out. Finn had only seen it once, and never wanted the experience to be his again.

'You might be right,' he said. Thoughts of how to go about cleaning out the store floated, and he had to give grudging credence to Ben. It was time to—

His arm gave a sudden jerk and it snapped to his side. He grunted, waited for the inevitable, but like the last few times, nothing eventuated.

Ben glanced across. 'Another one?'

'A half start,' Finn replied, stretching out his arm and flexing his fingers. 'The damnedest thing.'

Levelling a rifle over his knees, Ben sniffed and spat. 'Whatever it is must be on its way out. You haven't had a full-blown attack for a while.'

'Who would know? I don't want to put a wager on it.'

Silent for a while longer, they listened to the clop of horses' hooves over the track. They passed men travelling on foot with swag and spare boots over one shoulder, tools or a gun strapped to their chest, each hopeful of a find on the fields.

Here and there, men shouted for a lift. Good-naturedly, Ben fobbed them off. He turned to Finn. 'Last camp tonight before Ballarat tomorrow. You'd miss this if you went off boating up and down the Murray.'

'Sure enough, I'd certainly miss this,' Finn gibed. He gee-upped the horses and used the slack reins to flick the flies away. He watched men walking on either side of the cart as they headed north. Hope and dreams were in each one—young and older, excited and jaded, well clad and not-so-well clad. All manner of nations walked this road, and today, at least, it was a quiet affair.

Finn's arm stiffened a moment, muscles twitched and bunched, and just as quickly relaxed. Another half start. He spoke to Ben but looked straight ahead at the road. 'It came to me as we were going south that I wouldn't be able to be around the building of a steamer. Too much sudden noise, too much steel and banging of hammers on anvils.'

'Seems to be the sorts of things that set you off.'

'That was one part. If I got past the building of the damn thing and took to the wheel of a steamer, could my body keep a crew safe? I don't know.' He glanced across. 'You've already grabbed me twice to stop me going off the cart.'

Ben lifted his shoulder, shifted the rifle. 'Like you said, we could buy passage on a steamer at Goolwa, take a week or two to see if you could abide it.'

The plan was that Finn would hire Ben to accompany him for a reconnoitre as much as for a safeguard for himself. He didn't know if the engines would set off the tremors, and there was only one way to find out if the shrill, ear-splitting blast of the steam whistle would do it. Would he risk it?

'Don't want to topple off deck and have you follow me in,' Finn said. 'I've heard the river's a treacherous waterway.'

Ben grunted. 'I've heard it, too. Never stopped an adventure before.'

'Never did.' But Finn's heart was heavy. He wouldn't risk it. Not yet. Certainly wouldn't risk the life of another.

Under the boiling sun's rays, Finn concentrated on the road ahead. Tomorrow he'd be home. Offload this lot, sell, and begin it all over again. Maybe clear out the store. Maybe not.

Not even the memory of the intense blue of the woman's eyes, nor the soft blonde tendrils at the nape of her neck lightened the load he carried today.

Twenty

Ballarat

Amid the steam of the laundry tubs, and between the wringing of rinsed, sodden clothes ready for hanging on the line, Nell's tent took shape.

Flora hammered a peg into the ground. 'Please God that I strike a nugget as big as my fist,' she muttered.

Nell stood over her. 'Have you paid a license fee just in case you do, Flora?' she asked, a tease in her voice. She held on to a sturdy rod once meant as a stirring dolly for the tubs; it would now act as the spine onto which her canvas would be hung and secured.

Flora stood up, swiping the perspiration from her forehead. 'Ha. I certainly have, and I have to anyways, gold or no. But if I found a nugget I'd hold off yellin' about it until things changed around here. There's talk of a new franchise from the government, a new fee, but it might take another uprising before that happens.'

Nell lowered her voice. 'Is that sedition I hear?'

'Sedition, perhaps. Hand me that other peg, would you? Hotham hasn't come down out of his castle yet, and no one is being compensated for all the murder and ruin, so now we're waiting to see if our boys will be hanged for their trouble.'

Nell knelt beside her, holding the guy rope taut while Flora hammered the peg home. 'There's lots of talk, Flora, but I hope nothing bad will happen again.'

'Aye. No action while we all keep our heads down, and our loved ones safe.' The soft Irish lilt was whispered.

'I'm hearing that no jury will convict even one of the men they have in prison.'

'As you say, lots of talk. Gossip only, too early by far for anyone to know that. I'm hearing that Lalor is alive and keeping *his* head down until there's amnesty, but who knows what the government has in store for us.' One last hammer blow and Flora fell onto her backside. 'Uh. Hard work in this heat. Wouldn'a do diggin', myself, for anything. I druther my laundry. Come on, one last thing to do.' She clambered to her feet, grasping Nell's outstretched helping hand.

Together they fitted the rod between two poles set six feet apart, fashioned to hold it high overhead, and grappled and hauled the canvas over it. With a few last shoves, and cheers from the men around them, a great swathe of patched and dirty canvas fell over the rod and draped to the ground.

'Your new home, madam,' Flora said, out of breath, and gave a mock curtsy.

They carried a cot newly purchased from Tillo into the tent, then stood back, dusting off and admiring their handiwork.

'It's a beautiful thing. And that will have to do for now,' Nell said and turned back to the tubs. 'I'm back to my work.'

She would go back to the house after sunset and inform Enid and Lewis of her decision to move out from under their roof. She'd take her possessions from there to the diggings, use part of her wages from Flora to buy bed linen, a chamber pot, cooking utensils, some bloomers—though Flora said she'd have to order them in—and a sturdy, small tin box to bury somewhere safe.

It was time to make a life not beholden to any man.

Lewis had his bread in one hand and a fork in the other as he stared at her. 'And just when is it you think you will be leaving here, Nell?'

Candlelight flickered from a stub on the table, from the cooking mantel, and the hutch that housed Enid's crockery.

'I will move my possessions this next few days, if that is suitable, so I must ask for grace until then.' Nell wondered if Lewis was about to try and stop her leaving, but what reason would he have to do so?

'Is it completely necessary?' he asked.

Enid cleared her throat and moved her plate and cutlery.

Nell held his gaze. 'I would not want to be a burden to you, especially now, Lewis.'

He dropped his bread on the plate and pushed his chair back from the table. 'Especially now,' he repeated and glanced darkly at his mother, who turned away, before continuing. 'Surely life in a tent on the fields is not what befits you as Andrew's wife.'

Enid sat up, her back ramrod straight.

Nell took in a deep breath. 'Andrew made his feelings perfectly well known to you, and to your mother, about my being his wife.'

Lewis frowned. 'And you are well aware that he was not a man in control of his own mind.' He ignored his mother's quick glare. 'You are his widow. You were his rightful wife.'

Nell twisted her hands together. 'Lewis, with respect, has it not occurred to you that I wish to be as far from Andrew and his … estate as possible?'

Enid shot to her feet, her eyes ablaze. 'The effrontery,' she aimed at Nell.

Lewis reached over and laid his hand on her arm. 'Mama, you cannot deny—'

Enid's venom spat out of her. 'Married or not, he thought you nothing more than a doxy, after his money, after his gold, after his position in society and what it could do for you.'

Nell stood, her chair scraping as it was thrust back. 'I cannot believe even you think that—after what he did, and how often he did it. And it's more than clear now that he had no money for me to go after.' She faced Lewis. 'I am not asking your permission, I am telling you I am leaving this house, and that I will be gone as soon as I can. I will make no claim on you.' Resisting a glance at Enid, who was undoubtedly bristling behind her, she waited for his response.

He sighed heavily. 'I will assist you with the cart, so that you can make the transfer of your belongings without effort.'

'Thank you.' Nell gathered her plate and cutlery, picked up Enid's and took them to the wash bowl on the bench. 'I do not have to attend the ball, either,' she said, and brushed herself down as if she'd spilled crumbs.

'On that, dear Nell, I must insist you do, if just for my sake. I would like to show you that the Wilshires have some heart.'

Nell blinked at Lewis. He kept a straight face as Enid har-rumphed and marched out of the kitchen.

He pinched his lip, pensive. 'Oh dear, it seems I've upset my mother again.' He looked at Nell. 'Apparently I do it on a regular basis. Courting a lowly laundress, having a lowly laundress put me by, and now wishing to continue the courtship with the same lowly laundress, who still won't agree, I might add. Not to mention, defending my mad uncle's widow, and wishing only her comfort and safety, but also finding myself the head of a penniless family with debt up to my hairline.'

A small frown crossed Nell's brow. 'I'm sorry about all that for you, and that you're so out of sorts with Enid.'

Lewis held up his hands. 'There's no love lost between you, I can see it. No need for apologies.'

'It's not as if she invites even a friendship, Lewis. She never has.'

He dropped his gaze. 'I know she stood by and said nothing, did nothing when you were ...'

She let him stand in a moment's discomfort before saying, 'I heard you arguing with Andrew the night before we left.'

Lewis licked his lips. 'Yes.' He brushed crumbs off the table. 'I had seen the evidence on your face of his latest effort with his fists. I felt it my duty to intervene.'

Light-headed, Nell leaned back on the bench. 'Was it his fists that had you falling off your drunken horse?' Dear God. Had her husband seriously injured his own nephew?

Perplexed a moment, he tilted his head then snorted a laugh. 'Not Andrew. He wouldn't lift a finger against me, even in a rage. It wasn't the first time I had warned him.'

Nell nodded. 'Susan?'

'Aye, his first wife. Dear Susie.' He exhaled, shook his head.

Something triggered a memory, another voice, but before Nell could grasp it, Lewis continued. 'Unfortunately, when I stepped in there, he retaliated on her. I have never forgiven myself for that. Or him. Eventually she lost her life.' He glanced up, and a light in his eyes glinted. 'I was not going to allow it to happen to you too.'

The room closed in, the warm air a creeping weight on her skin. She was remembering Andrew's retaliation on her after her trip to the magistrate when she'd tried to intervene on her own behalf: her cracked ribs, a blackened eye, the bruises on her wrists. Yet the way Lewis spoke now, something ... A skitter of knowledge vibrated deep within then fled up her spine. She still couldn't grasp it.

The candlelight barely flickered.

He went on. 'Except that, on that night, if he hadn't promised to rein himself in, I would have done more than just argue with him. He needed to be put away, for good.' He shook his head again. 'But there were other more pressing matters than needing to remove him right at that point.'

Nell held her breath. What was he saying? What was she remembering? A patter of heartbeats clouded her thoughts.

He pulled the candle closer, poured melted wax away from the wick. The drops pooled in the dish underneath and the wick burned brighter. 'He was supposed to come to the Eureka Lead with me, to stand with us, the few men who remained under the flag. We were standing up for our rights, not arming ourselves in rebellion. We hadn't expected a massacre—God knows the so-called stockade was barely three-foot high in places. Half the men still behind it were sleeping off the rum. Instead, I found Andrew after the skirmish, hiding at the house, bundling you ungraciously into the coach he'd hired, and trying to go God only knows where.' He pursed his lips. 'I couldn't stop him. Not then.'

Nell eased herself into her seat again. 'He would have planned it.'

Lewis scratched his forehead, took up the chunk of bread and dragged it around the gravy on his plate. 'Do you know where he was taking you?'

'No.' Nell was still, her thoughts on the driver of the coach, Mr Steele. 'If Andrew told me, which I doubt, I have forgotten. I was not at my best at the time.'

'Of course not. I'm sorry. It's just that once again, I find myself perplexed at his behaviour. In some ways, even in his madness, he seemed organised, and calculating.' He took a bite of the bread and gravy, chewed and swallowed. 'I have another subject I'd like to discuss with you.'

Startled, Nell shot him a glance.

He seemed to be considering his next words. 'Though you do full well know our situation now, with only the mining bringing in some funds, I feel it my duty to offer marriage, Nell. Not just my duty, mind you.' He hesitated. 'I should say, I am delighted to offer marriage.'

Surprised, her breath short, she measured her words carefully. 'Thank you, Lewis,' she said. 'I must decline. You know it.' Her eyes met his. 'It's not necessary. There is no obligation to me, and no expectation from me. You don't need an added burden at this time.' She gave a faint smile. 'Besides, ours would not be a good match.'

'But perhaps it would,' he disagreed. Then, after catching her frown, he said, 'Perhaps it would not.' He pushed back in his seat. 'I don't mean to make you uncomfortable. But to go into the fields and work for yourself … It cannot last, this independence of women. Once the final glitter of gold has been dug up from Ballarat and everywhere else, things will return to normal and women will take their rightful place in the home.'

She waited a beat before her answer seethed out of her. 'If my rightful place was what I encountered in my father's home and then in my husband's home, I am not in a hurry to ever go there again.'

Lewis held her stare. 'Yes, but surely under a better man's protection—'

'I will take my chances alone. I will work while I can still earn my own living.'

'You might change your tune if you meet a decent man,' Lewis said. 'One who is not your nephew, I hasten to add.' He gave her a wry smile. 'When you marry, you will have to forfeit all that hard-earned income.'

'Unless he gives me leave to keep it, I will not be marrying him.'

Lewis nodded. 'Then I'll raise my glass to him when we meet. And on that note, I must insist you accompany us to the ball, Nell.' When she lifted her shoulders, unsure, he said, 'Because if you come, I think I can convince Flora to come.' He held out a ticket addressed to "A Lady".

She took it and blurted a relieved laugh. 'To think your marriage proposal might have come from the heart.'

'It did, Nell. It's just that my heart is equally delighted you declined.'

Twenty-One

Bendigo

Mr Bagley handed loose documents to Mr Campbell. 'I've just opened the mail, Mr Campbell. There are a couple of client promissory notes, and there's also something from a Mrs Andrew Amberton.'

Joseph Campbell looked at the paperwork in his hand. He tucked the notes one behind the other until he came upon the letter to which his clerk referred. 'Thank you, Mr Bagley.' He turned, took his cup of tea, and retreated to his office.

The notes could wait. The letter from this Mrs Amberton might be interesting.

Dropping all the documents to his desk, he sorted the promissory notes to one side to give to Matthew later and turned his attention to the neatly written, one-page letter.

Dear Mr Campbell, I beg leave to address you on a legal matter. I am the widow of Mr Andrew Amberton. He passed away suddenly after being gunshot when on a coach ride out of Ballarat. It was

early on the same morning as the Eureka massacre and I was of the
unfortunate circumstance to be with him at the time.

Joseph noted little sorrow in the few words so far.

On this ride in the coach, my husband was carrying two bags of gold
containing many nuggets and rough cast bars and weighing such that
I would not have been able to carry them myself.

Mr Campbell's brows rose. He shifted his spectacles further up
the bridge of his nose and read on.

As you might be aware, I am the second Mrs Amberton. My pre-
decessor, Mrs Susan Amberton, passed away mid spring of 1854.
It has come to my attention that the bags of gold were a loan to her
husband at the time, Mr Andrew Amberton, from her father and
was to be repaid to her father.

As you know, Mr Amberton died without a will and has many
creditors. I cannot in all conscience, knowing of its provenance, claim
this gold for his estate, nor surrender it to my husband's many credi-
tors when I am aware to whom the gold should rightfully be restored.
Currently, the bags and contents are concealed, and safe.

I also beg your leave again to ask that this remain private between
the writer and yourself as it is of a vexing and harrowing nature. I
am not without opportunity to be gainfully employed, and therefore
not unduly impoverished. Even if that were not so, I would gladly
return this gold to its rightful owner, repaying the loan to that fam-
ily, that being the family of Mrs Susan Amberton, neé Seymour.

Joseph dropped the letter in his lap and rubbed a hand over his
mouth. Good Lord. Wonders would never cease. He continued reading.

My new place of residence is at Miss Flora Doyle's Laundry on the
digging fields at Ballarat. A letter will find me there, but I beg you
maintain confidentiality and not trust this issue to the mail.

Yours faithfully, Nell Amberton (Mrs).

Joseph reread the letter. Could barely take in what he was reading. If it were true, and the woman's sentiments genuine, he had
scarce met someone of her ethics. He would be very interested in
meeting this woman himself, to lay eyes on a truly honourable
person.

How this would work according to the letter of the law, he
had yet to learn. It might put him in a dubious situation. Perhaps
he would need to consult a colleague for advice. Either way, if
the woman was to be trusted, he believed Finn would recoup his
father's funds—or most of it.

He leaned back in his chair, stretched his legs under the table.
Thought for some moments on the ramifications of the woman's
letter.

'Joe, you're deep in thought. Is it the Cooper problem?' Matthew stood in the doorway, a pencil tucked behind his ear, his
waistcoat open and his sleeves rolled up.

Joseph gave a short laugh. 'No. I wish it were that problem.
Here, read this. Tell me what you make of it.' He pushed Mrs
Amberton's letter towards his cousin.

Matthew frowned as he sat opposite, reading. He whistled
softly and kept reading. Glanced at Joseph and lifted his brows,
only to return and read the letter again. 'If I was a betting man,'
he said, eyes still on the single page, 'I'd say Mr Seymour might
see some of his inheritance, yet.'

'My thoughts exactly. However, I now have a problem.'

'Yes, I see that.' Matthew took the pencil from behind his ear
and tapped the letter with it. 'Mr Seymour is your friend, and you

are his solicitor. You are also the managing agent of the Amberton estate, such as it is.'

'And now, thanks to Mrs Amberton's letter, I am privy to a gold cache, the amount of which would surely come close to the loan amount owed by Amberton to the only survivor of the Seymour family, Finneas Seymour.' Joseph pushed his chair away and stood. 'I can't un-see her letter.' He faced the window, watched the carts and carriages on the street trail up and down the road.

'But surely if Amberton made a forgery of the loan document, and it could be proven, the gold has effectively been stolen.'

Joseph turned around. The pencil was tucked back behind his cousin's ear, and the dark brows rippled in a frown. 'His is a very clever forgery, and hard to prove different now. His nephew's real signature is as close to identical as you can get. Finn's father's dead, his sister is dead. And we know Amberton was handed the funds. Unless we find there's a witness to coercion …'

'An interesting situation,' Matthew commented.

'One we will think on,' Joseph said.

'You're the legal mind, Joe, but it appears to me that Mrs Amberton would not be at odds with the law.'

'We have to determine the rightful owner of that gold.' Joseph mused for long moments while Matthew reread the letter. 'Widow Amberton might well be left all the debts if it becomes known she is in possession of it. Her husband died intestate, so there are no papers of administration, or any papers at all that I've found. If anyone would have known about a will, aside from the widow, it would be the nephew, that what's-his-name who came in last week.'

'Lewis Wilshire,' Matthew provided. 'He's an interesting character. He was odd as a younger person, but a reasonable man by all accounts these days.'

Joseph turned back to the window again. 'Is he, now? He might not be if a bag of gold was found to be in his aunt's possession, especially if it could ease his situation.' He walked back to his desk and took a seat.

Matthew linked his hands behind his head. 'I would say that if Mrs Amberton surrendered the gold to you here, then much of the problem would disappear. Not a learned deduction, mind you.'

Joseph nodded. 'But I think you might be right. If I reason that the loan represents the greatest of the creditors, and Mr Wilshire is the suffering guarantor of that loan, I might be able to make a legal argument for returning it to the Seymour estate without it becoming part of the Amberton estate.' He put a loose fist to his mouth. 'But I am not a magistrate to make such a ruling.'

'Would it need to go before a magistrate? Is it not a separate issue?' Matthew held his right hand palm up. 'On this hand, the loan to Amberton to be repaid to Seymour because the funds are in the widow's hands and she has expressed a wish to return them.' He opened his left hand palm up. 'On this hand, Lewis repays the debts to the creditors of the estate by way of his mining license.'

Joseph tapped his mouth. 'Perhaps. Justice might be at odds here.'

'What is a logical solution?' Matthew asked.

'What is the legal solution?' Joseph countered. 'That is rhetorical for you, Matthew. I have to answer that one.'

Matthew sat up, his arms folded. 'Lewis would not be in a position to repay the loan without the gold. His other creditors can all be paid off, most probably in the course of a few months to a year. At worst, two years after good finds on the fields. But not a five-thousand-pound loan. It's a fortune. So I would say he'd be very happy to have that loan off his shoulders right now.'

'We would have to have the gold assayed.'

'We would. And by someone reputable. But how would we get it?'

Joseph pinched his nose, adjusted his spectacles over his ears. 'There might be a way around this. After all, Mrs Amberton is the widow, and in possession of the gold. Nothing willed to her, or decreed in a dower situation, because there's no real property—'

'Dower? Do you mean *dowry?*'

'Dower. An ancient law amended over centuries. After 1836, if my memory serves me correctly, a wife of a man who has property must have one third of real property awarded to her on his death, so she can continue to live in some small comfort. Often, it's not enough. Anyway, it's not the case here because we know there is no property,' he mused. Joseph tapped the desk top, searching his memory. 'I have a feeling Mrs Amberton should dispose of the gold as she wishes. Keep things separate, as you suggest.' He stopped a moment and glanced at Matthew over his spectacles. 'There might be a way around all of this, without need of the law, despite my seeing that letter. Are you willing to be a part of it?'

'Of course. What is it? I'm up for adventure, danger.' He rubbed his hands together.

'Adventure, perhaps. And I've already inadvertently danced into danger, not noticing both Finn's appointment and Lewis Wilshire's appointment were back to back last week. I'm thankful neither one knew the other.' Joseph Campbell looked at his cousin. 'Just a little bending of the rules around the posts, so to speak. My plan is, that in the first instance, someone will have to go to see Mrs Amberton, care of ...' He looked at the letter under his hand on the desk. 'Miss Flora Doyle's Laundry, Ballarat.'

Twenty-Two

Ballarat

Nell had the distinct feeling she was being watched. A glance behind her as she hurried from Wilshire House to the diggings had caught a figure slipping back into the shadows. It was behind the last timber house on the dusty track that led into the fields. The sun had only just begun to light the day, so it was hard to check for certain that someone was following her.

Picking up a little speed, feeling the sudden trickle of perspiration slide between her breasts, she prayed that the nuggets sewn into her skirt would not click-clack about, drawing attention. Thank heavens this was nearly the last delivery of the cache returning to the goldfields. The irony of it was not lost on her. Every day she'd brought back a few nuggets to the diggings camp to deposit into a tin in a hollow under her chamber pot. Exactly what she'd do with them from there was anyone's guess. No word yet from Mr Campbell's office. She could only hope that he hadn't thought to put the troopers onto her and demand the gold for Andrew's creditors. Surely he would see she was trying to do the right thing?

A shiver dashed through her, and the perspiration cooled. Despite all rationale, she knew she wasn't safe from any quarter. To be caught with that amount of gold, and no way of proving it belonged to her, would be a hanging offense. At least she had been able to pay for a current license by using the button of gold. Only after a short argument with the merchant did she feel she got the correct exchange for it. But if anyone found that tin box …

One last glance over her shoulder. Nothing. In the fiery light of morning, she could see the last house now in the distance, and no man hovered nearby, nor hurried along behind her.

A swift walk took her past a row of tents from where men emerged, adjusting trousers, doffing caps and cuffing the ears of dogs and children, but she kept her eyes on Flora's laundry ahead. Despite chafed hands, torn and ragged cuticles, reddened forearms and aching back, her heart lifted in relief when she saw Flora emerge with her mother, and head towards the latrine.

How strange to suddenly feel safe in the throng of so many men, most of them gold diggers, and snarly dogs and screaming, bratty children, sons and daughters of the last of the convicts transported. Some were children of free settlers, or of Aboriginal traders, or of the many Chinamen that came from afar, or of people belonging to that faith other than Christianity, who prayed towards the east. But not often did she ever feel so unsettled as she had just those few minutes prior. Not even when she knew Andrew was going to—

Stop those thoughts.

The moment she arrived at the laundry fire pits, she opened her tent and quickly divested her hem of the dull nuggets. She held them only for a moment, warm in her hand, close to her heart. Then she dug out the soft sand under her pot, pried open the lid of the tin, and placed them carefully inside.

Replacing the lid, she wondered how heavy the tin would have become. Not stopping to check it, she scooped sand into place, sat the chamber pot back in position, and dragged her chair over it. It looked as every other tent looked. Habitable for sleeping, waking and working.

Outside, she brushed the clinging dust from her hands and went straight to stoke the embers Flora had let smoulder overnight. She dragged dense logs over and tossed the ones she could lift into the pits. Flora would help her roll in the heavier ones.

She turned to eye the mountain of washing. As she threw off the old sailcloth tarp covering it, stale sweat, tobacco, wood smoke and grease rose around her. She set to, sorting through it, and by the time Flora had returned with Josie, there were three massive piles ready for the tubs.

'Good morning, Mrs Doyle. Morning, Flora.'

'Morning, dearie. Who is that again, Flo?'

'Nell Thomas. Come along, Ma, you've got the lad's shirt to do and I'm about to get you some tea.' Flora tried herding her mother into the larger tent alongside Nell's.

'I've a mind to sit outside today, Flora. I can do the lad's shirt out here. I'm watching out fer yer, there's been some skulking around here of late.'

Nell's blood cooled.

Flora didn't seem worried. 'You will need your bonnet.'

The older woman took up a seat on a log a little way from the fire. She sat patiently as Flora retrieved her hat, fitted it on her head and tied the string under her chin. The lad's shirt, a new colourful rag, was draped over her lap.

'I'll bring you the sewing kit directly, Ma.'

'And some extra pins,' her mother said, squinting in Nell's direction. 'That girl's bloomers have dropped the hem.'

Flora looked across at Nell, who looked down.

'And sure enough, they have, Ma. You'll need to fix that.' Flora shrugged as Nell protested. 'She won't give up until it's done. Best change out of them and into my other pair.' Flora ducked into her tent ahead of Nell and grabbed her mother's sewing box.

Shrugging out of her own bloomers and into an identical but older pair of Flora's, Nell thought hard about how she'd transport the last of the nuggets. She wouldn't be able to unpick Josie's handiwork on her bloomers without being found out, and certainly wouldn't be able to hide a fallen hem on Flora's.

Quickly back outside, she handed her bloomers to Josie and began the laundry work, stuffing the lightly soiled garments into the tubs first, thinking hard. Mrs Doyle sat humming as she began on Nell's hem. Flora tugged and kicked at the second pile of clothes and linens.

'Saturday next is the ball, Nell,' Flora called over the crackle and spit of the fire taking hold.

'What? Oh yes, it is,' Nell said, snapping out of her what-ifs. 'And then the day after, I'm here to stay. I'll bring the last of my belongings, such as they are. Lewis said he'd drive the cart, but I've no need of it.' Or would she? There were still many bars to retrieve from Amberton House. She dunked the dolly rod, frowning, and stirred the clothes, the fetid steam wafting up and over her.

At the mention of Lewis's name, Flora stopped her attack on the pile of dirty laundry. 'He still wants me to go with him to the ball.'

'Do you want to go, Flora?'

'She doesn't,' said Mrs Doyle, her eyes on her flashing needle. 'But I do. So the good boy is taking me instead.'

Flora flicked a glance at Nell, a short laugh escaping. 'He's not taking either of us, I told him. But I said that I'd be there, after all, taking Ma. She really wants to go. We can walk there.'

Josie nodded sagely, her needle and thread working fast over Nell's hem. 'That we can.'

Flora stood still, her hands on her hips. 'I'd be very pleased of your company there, Nell. I don't want it said that he and I are steppin' out again together.'

'I'll be there. He's told me I'm expected. And I don't mind so much, as long as I'm not falling over my feet, or his mother. They've another tent set up for child-minding and I've a mind to hide in there. Me being in my black weeds, it will suit. I've no interest in drawing any more attention to myself by dancing and laughing and having fun at a ball. I might be useless to you.'

'God forbid you have fun,' Flora said. 'You're not letting Mrs Enid and the gossiping old biddies get to you now, are you?'

'I don't want them fawning all over me as a grieving widow, either.' Nell cast a glance about their camp and across to others close by and lowered her voice. 'I don't regret Andrew's passing. But I do miss smiling again and laughing and dancing.'

Flora got back to work, casting her rod into the tubs, dragging the clothes back and forth. 'And what better place than a Subscription Ball to find some nice company to put that smile on your face?'

Nell gave a wistful smile, her thoughts on a pair of green eyes, and rusty coloured eyebrows. 'Nice? On these fields? I don't know.'

'You'll know,' Flora said. 'I might not have my sights set on anyone now, but I know they're not all like Andrew Amberton.'

Josie cut in. 'I'd have took that sort of company down the crick and drowned it afore it grew up.'

Flora barked a laugh. 'Ma,' she scolded. 'Nell, there's twenty thousand men here, they say. Bound to be someone.'

'Truth be known,' Josie commented again, eyes still on her needle. 'In twenty thousand, nary a one, I'll wager.'

Nell laughed at that. 'I've got this job, now. I've got my own wage, Flora. Why would I give that up?'

Flora straightened, frowned and pointed a finger. 'No one said you'd give anything up. But company might be nice.' Then her face creased again in a broad smile and she continued with the washing.

Indeed, company would be nice, but it would always come at a price. Since the coach ride, Nell knew the hold-up had gone by and had been barely noticed as a crime. The fact that a bushranger had supposedly shot and killed her husband and was probably long gone, meant that the authorities could put it to one side. No matter that Nell had told the police that the bushranger hadn't shot Andrew. Rather than investigate, it was too convenient to lay the murder at the feet of some mysterious ruffian who would never be found.

Lewis hadn't made too much of it, either. Putting it down to his aversion for his uncle, she believed he was relieved to see him gone. The only one not happy about Andrew's demise was Enid, and the authorities were not taking any notice of her.

Nell shook her thoughts away from the family. After this ball and moving the last of her meagre possessions from the Wilshire's house to her tent, she would not have need to go near them again. She would work on how to retrieve the bars from under the well.

Her head over the tubs, the rod pulling slowly through the water, the sharp lye in her nostrils, she missed seeing a figure approach.

'Help ye?' Nell heard Flora say.

Looking up, she saw a dark-haired man, perhaps her age but hard to tell, staring at Flora. He had his hat in his hands, wore a fine shirt in pale blue, waistcoat open, his brown trousers falling over good boots, dusty but well cared for. A coat hung loosely over one arm. His blue eyes were intense, and the frown as he stared deepened. A mole sat above a dimple in his left cheek.

Flora huffed a tendril of hair off her face, then tucked it back under her cap. 'If you have laundry for us, it's one pound a tub. Pick up, neatly folded, day after tomorrow.'

He still stared. 'I wish, most fervently, that I had laundry to leave every day if it meant I would need to visit here.'

Nell hid a smile. He hadn't so much as looked in her direction, his attention on Flora. A good-looking man, this one, and clearly not a digger. She shot a glance at Flora, who didn't seem to know what to do.

'We do laundry here,' Flora insisted, slowly. 'So, if it's not laundry you want doin', I don't know how to help ye.' She looked from the man to Nell and back to her tubs.

'I'll find some laundry if you give me a minute,' he said, with a smile and a candid stare. He took off his waistcoat.

Josie gave a shout of laughter. 'He's a lad, that one. I'll have a new shirt for him, soon enough.'

'Ma, shush.' Flustered, Flora dunked the dolly rod again and pounded the wash. Water plopped onto the ground underneath. She didn't look up again, just snuck a glance at Nell, pleading help.

The man moved closer to Flora's tub. 'I'm looking for Mrs Amberton,' he said, his waistcoat over his arm. 'I presume one of you ladies is Miss Flora Doyle and the other is Mrs Amberton.' He nodded towards Josie. 'And you must be Mrs Doyle. A delight to meet you, madam.' He bowed slightly in her direction.

Josie beamed at him. 'A lad with manners an' all, Flora.'

He stopped opposite Flora. Through the steam, dodging the sloshing water and the accompanying splashes, he said, 'I do hope you are Miss Flora Doyle.'

Nell, herself a little bemused, couldn't hide another smile. 'She is, and I am Mrs Amberton. Who might you be, sir?'

Stepping back from the tubs and a rosy-cheeked Flora, the man turned his attention to Nell and gave another slight bow. 'I am Matthew Worrell, Mrs Amberton, from Mr Campbell's office in Bendigo.' At her immediate hesitation, he lifted an envelope from his waistcoat pocket and handed it to her. 'I'm sorry I'm so very unexpected, but this will introduce me, my credentials, and my instructions. Could this be a convenient time considering the work to be done?' He shrugged back into his vest.

Now as flustered as Flora had been, Nell tucked the dolly rod under her arm, took the letter, opened it and read it. It was indeed from Mr Campbell. A few words he had quoted from her letter, and his offer of assistance, assured her that Matthew Worrell and his mission were genuine.

Flora stared at her. Nell stared back. Then, 'Flora, could I take a moment with Mr Worrell? We will walk, away from the noise.'

Josie piped up, holding up her sewing 'Take all the time ye want, young missy. These bloomers are done. They'll be in the parlour here, ready for ye,' she said and popped into the tent. 'I'm back to me lad's shirt, Flora,' she called.

'Right, Ma.' Flora lifted her chin at Nell. ''Course. Take all the time you need.'

Nell rested her dolly rod, wiped her hands on her apron and stepped down from the wash stand. 'Mr Worrell, shall we walk?'

He dragged his gaze away from Flora and took up alongside Nell. 'Thank you for seeing me straight away, Mrs Amberton. Mr Campbell thought the immediacy of the matter required some urgent action.'

They walked directly across from the laundry fires. Careful to note they were far enough away from big ears and bigger mouths, Nell dropped her voice.

'A shock, nonetheless, Mr Worrell. What is Mr Campbell advising me to do?'

'First, he has asked me to convey his thanks to you for being so honest about this matter.' Mr Worrell looked around and kept his voice low. 'He believes you are right in wishing it returned to its original owner. Can you be sure of its origins?'

They got to a space where no one could approach without being seen. The sun beat down on their heads and the flies were at their faces, but some of the clamour and shouting had faded with the distance.

Nell clasped her hands together then unclasped them when she realised her nerves would get the better of her. 'Very early in my marriage, I saw a note about the loan, and have not seen it since. It had my husband's signature on it, and my nephew's signature on it as guarantor. It was for a large sum. But I did not see if the currency stated was for nuggets or promissory notes, or pounds. However, I feel that the gold I have in my possession is rightfully the Seymour family's, on loan to my late husband.' She took a deep breath and straightened her shoulders, hands now by her side. 'I don't even know how much is there, or whether any of it has been spent.'

'I see.' Matthew glanced back at Flora, who resolutely dragged the dolly rod through the laundry. 'Mrs Amberton, if it is readily to hand, it could be easy, with appropriate receipting and signatures, to transfer it to its rightful owners.'

'Oh dear.' Nell thought of where it was in her tent.

Frowning, Mr Worrell continued. 'I know that this is unusual, but we have no other way of conducting business unless you agree to come to Bendigo.'

'I don't have the means to make such a trip.'

'Forgive us for presuming the same, hence why I am here. Mr Campbell is quite a trustworthy person, and his office carries a great respect in the colony, as he is well known in this area. You can be assured that the dealings will be scrupulous.'

Nell surveyed right and left again. A mere thirty yards away, men bent double over the shallow flow of the waterway, their pans slipping in and out of the water, swishing off the lighter pebbles and sand. Once or twice an excited yell erupted. 'It's not that so much, Mr Worrell, although you are right, I am reluctant to simply hand over the bag. It's more that it might be difficult to retrieve unnoticed, from where I have most of it, now.'

'I see.'

'It's a good deal of weight.' Nell swished away flies as she glanced around.

'I could assist if necessary.'

'You are not known, here, Mr Worrell and it might be suspicious if you were to suddenly begin to assist me.'

Mr Worrell nodded. 'Mr Campbell thought it prudent to ask if you have suggestions as to how we proceed.'

Nell lifted her shoulders a little. 'I have given it no thought.' All she could think of was the soft, sandy and deep indent under her chamber pot in the tent. She could not invite a young man into her tent and have it go unnoticed. She certainly could not lift the gold herself and bring it to him, nor would she do so piece-meal. That would attract as much attention.

He lifted his hat, wiped his forehead on his forearm and settled the hat back on his head. 'If there were a man hereabouts, who wouldn't be suspicious on these fields, could he then be of assistance in the retrieval of the bag?'

Nell thought hard. The problem was that the contents of the bags were mostly now in a tin in her tent. No man other than her husband would have any right going into her tent. Unless it could be by cover of darkness.

'I beg your pardon?' Mr Worrell leaned closer. 'Darkness, you said?'

She must have murmured aloud. She said, 'I don't know of such a man, personally. I will need some time to think on a suitable solution. Do you stay in Ballarat while you are here, Mr Worrell?'

'I will find lodgings and stay until Sunday, unless you and I need more time to conduct our business.' He smiled. 'I believe there is a ball being held on Saturday night. I should like to stay and attend if I can secure a ticket.'

Nell's mind twisted and turned. 'How will I get my answer to you?'

'I can be along here by early Sunday morning before I depart, if necessary.'

'Perhaps that is best.'

'Shall we?' he asked and indicated returning to the laundry. 'I should like to say goodbye to Miss Doyle.'

Flora was ready to drag the clothes from the wash tub to the rinse tub. She straightened up as Nell and Mr Worrell returned.

'Miss Doyle, I have to go now, but I will come back here for another appointment with Mrs Amberton before I leave for Bendigo on Sunday morning. Will you be in?'

Flora, already flushed with exertion over the tubs, blinked, and a frown appeared.

''Course she'll be in,' a voice drifted from the tent. 'She puts on a good roast lunch, too. See that you come by after your church, lad.'

Mr Worrell smiled broadly. 'Ah, thank you, Mrs Doyle. I'll be sure to do that,' he called in reply.

'There's many others eat here on a Sunday,' Flora said, ruffled, agitated.

'So I will be on my best behaviour. Until then, Miss Doyle.' He nodded towards her and turned to Nell. 'Thank you, Mrs Amberton. I hope you have found a solution come Sunday. Good day.'

'Good day.' Nell watched as he took one last glance at Flora. Then he turned and walked along the creek, dodging children, dogs, and miners at their work, until he was out of sight.

Nell's hands shook a little. She wondered about the solution she might or might not find. 'Well,' was all she could manage, and she looked at Flora.

'Well is right,' Flora grumbled, slapping her apron, and flicking escaped hair back from her face. 'Another mouth to feed on Sunday.'

'Somethin' lovely to look forward to, Flora, me daughter.'

Despite her sudden nerves, Nell smiled at the voice drifting out of the tent, while Flora frowned darkly.

Straightening up in the late afternoon sun, Nell bunched her hands on the small of her back and stretched. The last of her personal washing was done and hung out. There was enough heat left in the day to get it dry before dark, and it might only take an hour or so. She'd bring it inside her tent to fold and stack in the small crates she used for storage.

The hum of the day throbbed to a lull. Women left the digs to tend the cooking fires. Working children found their way home to dinner. Men began to amble back to their tents from the creek to sup and rest up. It wouldn't be long before those who took to drink would fire up the night, and gunshots and the bellows of the drunks would take over.

'Nice-lookin' smalls,' Flora called over from her tent, her own washing and her mother's flapping on the line behind.

'The only good thing I got from my marriage. Good cotton drawers and chemises.'

'Nice dresses, too.' Flora nodded at a pile waiting to be washed the next day.

'Only three I wanted to keep. Plenty for me now, especially if I give away wearing the black thing after the ball.'

'Good for you. Too dreary by far. And no one cares about who's wearing widow weeds, no one on the fields, anyhow.' Flora ducked back into her tent, the flap left open to let air through.

Nell wasn't so sure about that, but it didn't matter to her. Widow weeds were for mourning, and she wasn't mourning anyone, no matter that custom decreed she did.

As she bent to pick up the small tub she'd used to cart the wash from the fires to the line, she saw a horse and rider approach. A slow walk, unhurried, as if the rider knew exactly where he intended to stop. *Oh no.* He had a grin on his craggy face and a cabbage-tree hat on his head. His loose thin shirt opened at the neck, and patchy grey tufts of hair poked through. Her heart lurched.

'There you are, daughter o' mine. I heard you were on the fields again, an' then I saw ye, from afar, not long back. I can tell me own anywhere, I can.'

Nell stared. He would've been the one to follow her. A hundred retorts came to mind, but her voice stuck in her throat. From the corner of her eye, she saw Flora bob out of her tent.

Alfred Thomas reined in, leaned over the horse's mane a little. Settling in for a talk, it seemed. 'We feel a bit put aside that you, yerself, never told us your sad news.'

Still silent and staring, Nell tried to form words that just would not come.

'Now, I know that look. Means yer not so pleased to see me.' The grin barely moved, but he ducked his head a moment, before his eyes met hers again.

Nell felt the menace of him moving in waves across the short distance, flaring in her chest each time her heart thudded.

'I came to say that Dora and me are sorry to hear that yer now a widder.' The grin changed to an appropriate moue for her loss.

'Bit late, besides,' Flora muttered as she came to stand alongside. 'He's months dead.'

Alfred Thomas flicked a glance in Flora's direction and otherwise ignored her. 'And to see that you have what you need, Nellie. You always had what you needed under my roof, food an' sensible clothes. Got your letters from yer ma, got yer good spoken word. She loved her teachin', her music and dancin', God rest her soul. Well looked after, ye were.'

Nell gave a curt nod and resisted gripping her pinafore and bunching the fabric in her fists.

'And you'd be feelin' generous for it, I'm sure.' He looked around. 'But this—' he waved his hands, '—is not what I was expectin' for ye, as Amberton's widder.' At her silence, he said, 'I'da thought not to see you back on the diggin's. Yer had a nice house, good clothes.' He waved a hand at her bloomers. 'That's hardly best bib and tuckers.'

At her stubborn silence, Flora nudged her and whispered, 'Nell.'

Thomas's eyes flicked again to Flora, and back to Nell. 'Amberton not leave ye comfortable, daughter? Or did ye sell off all those trappings for yerself?' He leaned forward and the saddled creaked as he adjusted his seat. 'Yer dear old pa thought ye'd be grateful for marryin' up and—'

'Get away from here.' Nell's teeth had jammed together, and her voice shook.

Flora slipped her hand around Nell's.

Her father frowned, looked as if he was pained. 'Thing is, me and Dora need a few things. And Andrew, my dear departed son-in-law, promised to pay a little bit more. So I've come to see where it is, this payment owed to me.'

'Owed to you?' Nell's body shook. The rage built, squeezed her insides. 'You sold me to a monster.'

He let a laugh blurt between his lips. 'Sold?' he mocked. 'Was an agreement for me silence, is all. He got a good deal.' Shaking his head, he said, 'A monster. Yer make it sound—'

'A *monster* even worse than you,' she hissed. Flora's hand on hers squeezed tight.

Alfred Thomas sprang off his horse and flicked away his reins, a nimble action that took both women unawares. They leapt back together.

Flora bent and snatched up her dolly rod, her other hand still firmly holding Nell's. 'Don't come any closer.'

Suddenly Nell's father staggered backwards. He stumbled, and his hat flew off. A breath shot out of him and he clutched his chest, reeling. A bare moment later, his horse gave an indignant squeal as a large pebble lobbed off its rump. He jumped, stomped and trotted off ahead to safety, reins trailing on the ground.

Nell spun around to see Josie Doyle loading Flora's slingshot, drawing back another stone, her eyes fierce. 'I've a mind to slap the third one right between yer eyes, Alfred Thomas,' Josie called. 'Get yer filthy rotten carcass away from me girls.'

Flora gripped the dolly rod with two hands. Nell rushed to Josie and grabbed the slingshot, hugging the older woman, holding her still.

Nell's father rubbed a hand back and forth over his chest. He thrust a finger in Nell's direction. 'Yer still me daughter and I'm still owed what he promised me. And I know ye've got the rest of it hid somewhere. I know you, Nell Thomas.'

'Get,' Flora said, her teeth bared, and the dolly rod swung once or twice.

Alfred bent to snatch his hat from the ground, staring off a moment to check the direction his horse had taken. Then he jammed the hat on his head 'I'm owed, or it's the troopers next.' He waved his finger at the women then stalked away, one last glare at Nell.

Aware of the quiet about them, she glanced at the closest camp-site. A man had stood and was watching, pans in hand. A woman wrung her pinafore, and ducked into a tent out of sight, a child at her side. Down at the creek, a couple of diggers had stopped pan-ning and looked back at them.

All she heard was a dog barking, and nothing else. It seemed time had stalled. Then like a rushing wind, all noise came back. The folk at their campsites resumed their day, the men at the creek took to the water again, and Nell let out the breath she'd been holding.

She shot a glance at Flora as Josie shrugged out of her grip. ''Tis all right, lass. He's gone off, hopefully to the devil, though not by me. Weren't aiming to kill him or I would'a done.' Josie plucked the slingshot from Nell, tucked it back into her pinafore pocket and wandered back into her tent.

Nell stared after her, then checked her father marching away, the horse still further ahead. She stared back at Flora, her hands spread.

Flora tossed the dolly rod away. 'Ye've had, by far and away, one too many visitors today, Nell.' She shook dust from her bloomers.

Nell pointed at Flora's tent. 'Your mother …?'

Flora shrugged. 'Who do you think taught me to use the slingshot?'

Josie's soft snores in the next tent rhythmically marked the minutes of the night. Inside her own tent, well after supper, Nell stared blankly into the darkness. Lying on her pallet, dressed only in her cotton chemise, its length rucked up to expose her legs to cooler air, she thought of her father's threat. About bringing the troopers in if she didn't pay him whatever he believed he was owed.

Flora hadn't questioned her, but the dark frown and the thinned lips showed it played on her mind too. Alfred Thomas had put Nell, and Flora and her mother, at risk, and they were now in harm's way. He could very easily have brought the troopers back to take Josie away for assaulting him with a weapon.

Though, Nell supposed, even he might have been too embarrassed to do that. Dangerous as it was, a slingshot was thought of as a child's toy.

She rolled onto her side. How in God's name could she move the nuggets, and remove herself from the diggings to safeguard Flora and her mother?

She had no solution, and so, as she tossed on the narrow bed, the problem kept her from her sleep.

Twenty-Three

Finn answered the door to Matthew Worrell, who apologised for the unannounced visit. 'Not at all, Mr Worrell. Come in, come in. Partake of a rum with me. It's that time of day.' He had loosened his collar and removed his waistcoat when he'd come in from Ben's stables an hour ago.

'Thank you. And if you please, call me Matthew.' He dropped his bag at the door and brushed off his boots on the step. He entered the short hallway behind Finn.

'And call me Finn. Now, this way.' Finn indicated a room off to the right. 'Hat and coat here, if you will,' he said and waved at two vacant pegs on the hallway wall.

Finn led Matthew into the parlour room set with two chairs, a small table holding a decanter and two sturdy glasses. The window, open, with simple lace curtains on either side, allowed in a warm breeze. At least it moved the air. A chair in one corner, much like a dining-room chair, held a stack of newspapers. The fireplace, now empty, was clean but the faint acrid smell of wood smoke still permeated the room. On the mantle was a sketch of his parents, John and Celeste, and only one framed daguerreotype of Finn and his wife Louisa, on their wedding day five years past. There were no feminine trappings in the room.

Finn indicated Matthew take a chair by the window. Pulling the stopper from the decanter, he poured two generous shots. 'I take it your visit is for business.'

Matthew nodded and took up a seat. 'It is. I have here a letter from Joseph regarding the subject you and he last spoke of. For your information, I am also privy to its contents.'

Finn took the letter from Matthew's outstretched hand, opened and read it. His eyes widened, frowned and widened again. When he finished, he looked across at Matthew, the letter fallen to his lap. 'Mrs Amberton believes that certain gold she has in her possession is rightfully my family's.'

'That is correct.'

'And,' Finn said, struggling to grasp the situation, 'Mrs Amberton has only just become aware that the gold is not her husband's?'

'It seems so.'

'Astounding.' Finn looked down at the paper, wondering again if Nell had known at the hold-up. 'And Joseph is also concerned that I might take matters into my own hands.'

Matthew smiled. 'It would be a reasonable assumption.'

Finn snorted a laugh. 'It would. He also warns me against it. However, I am in no hurry to be dangling from a noose for my trouble.' He reminded himself that he'd very nearly taken matters into his own hands. 'I presume, therefore, that you are here to help me refrain from such folly. He says that you have discussed a possible solution.'

Matthew took a swallow of rum. 'We have. And today I had the pleasure of meeting Mrs Amberton in order to facilitate a handover, if you will, of the gold.'

Finn's mind ticked. 'You work quickly.'

'You'll agree, the matter would be best dealt with sooner than later.'

Finn remembered Mrs Amberton on that day, in her torn skirt, the ragged chemise underneath. Her startling blue eyes set in a gaunt face, one under a deep bruise. The memory of her desperation, and her desperate plea. Her unusual composure in the face of a dire threat. Her disdain for her husband and the lack of grief for his demise.

The gunshot from over his shoulder. Then he remembered the warmth of Nell against him at her house, sure of herself, offering …

He let go a swift breath between his teeth. 'She is well after her ordeal?' Finn's glass swayed in his hand. He had no desire to take a drink.

'Would seem so.'

Careful to maintain a neutral tone, Finn asked, 'And where is she now?'

'Ah. Client confidentiality, I'm afraid. But apparently retrieving the gold from where it is kept—and I hasten to add I'm not privy to that information—might prove problematic.'

'Hard to know how to handle the situation if two of the most necessary pieces of information are withheld.'

'Understand fully. But my cousin advises us to be prudent, and he is the lawyer in the family, not me. He believes we might only just be within the letter of the law and must proceed with the utmost caution. Delicate, for him.'

'Of course.' Finn's thoughts weren't on Joseph's delicate position, but on bright, intelligent blue eyes, a strong temperament and a curve to her hip he remembered under his hands.

Matthew continued, 'I'm his minion in this matter, so I am following orders. But he has given me some discretion, and should we decide upon a suitable course of action, and, all being lawful, perhaps we can proceed.'

Finn looked up. 'So you are here for some time?'

'I hadn't planned to be. Perhaps only into early next week, all being well.'

'That would seem optimistic.'

'I have no way of knowing how long it might take. Or even if we'll be successful this trip. All I can say is that Mrs Amberton is keen to finalise the matter.'

Finn shook his head. What a turn of events. The bushranger had made his bold feelings known to the woman from the coach. The gold in her possession he learned later was rightfully his. And she wanted to return it to a man she didn't know was the bushranger. 'Extraordinary.'

'Our thoughts exactly. It would be in our best interests to do the same and finalise quickly if possible.'

'And she wants no part of the gold for herself?' Finn remembered how desperate she was to survive, and what her desperation had driven her to ask of him. How brave and lovely she'd seemed in the empty house. How he wondered afterwards if she'd been scheming.

'She says that whatever she has in her possession is to be returned and, further, that she has no way of knowing if it's in its entirety.'

Finn spread his hands. 'I'm amazed.'

'The interesting thing for me,' Matthew said, and sat back in his seat, one booted foot crossing the other as he stretched his legs. 'Is that as difficult as she believes the gold is to retrieve, she won't have a man assist her. I think she murmured something about needing to be under cover of darkness, but she wouldn't elaborate.'

Finn sat up, wrapped his glass in both hands, but still didn't take a drink. The gold was hidden, that was obvious; it wasn't at the house that she'd occupied. He'd searched it as best he could. 'She must have it close by, somewhere,' he said, more to himself than to Matthew. How had she done it? How had she moved that much in gold without being seen?

'How so?'

Finn held up a hand. 'No reason to say. It just came into my head. But if she didn't want a man to help her, it was perhaps in a very private area, perhaps her bed chamber.' He frowned. Could it still possibly be at the Wilshires' house?

'Then that would now be her tent. I can't imagine it's there. Have you met Mrs Amberton?' Matthew asked.

Finn took a moment. 'Not formally, no.' He thought again of the woman who'd scampered under the coach, who'd so brazenly offered herself to him in exchange for … something she wanted, who'd asked to be handed back into the coach. Who later, at night, alone, at her house, had returned his embrace, leaving him in no doubt that she had wanted the same thing he had.

Strictly speaking, he had not met her. He had found her. It might be time for a woman in his life again. He dismissed the thought. What woman would want a man broken by something he couldn't name or understand? Then he derided himself. His self-pity was embarrassing to him.

He glanced at his wedding picture on the mantel. Louisa gazed out serenely, even though posing for the photographer at the time had taken a gruelling hour of restricted movement, aching muscles and ignoring a particularly insistent blowfly. It wasn't long after that day she'd noticed a lump in her breast. *Nothing we can do,* she was told. *It's too far gone.* Now, her soft laugh sounded around him, and her voice told him that he was wasting time, that life was for living and not for holding on to the dead. And she would've said it just like that. She hadn't needed to waste words, either.

He looked at the sketch of his parents. Kind people. Wise. He felt the acute need of them now. Both gone—his mother Celeste of pneumonia, long before his father. He could do with their stoicism, their wisdom.

Matthew's voice brought him out of his thoughts.

'Pity. She seems very fine. Perhaps one day you might meet.' Matthew downed his rum and stood. 'I should be off to the town, Finn. I must find lodgings, and some dinner. I hope to stay for the Subscription Ball tomorrow night. After that, we should put our heads together for a strategy.'

Finn waved him back to his seat. 'No need to find lodgings elsewhere. Stay here. There's plenty of room. And it's a short stroll to the tent where the ball is to be held. I have a ticket, and can assure you, for the right price, you could purchase a ticket at the door.'

'Very kind. If I'm not imposing.'

'Not at all. We can work on our plan for retrieval. Especially over a meal at the pub. We lost the Eureka Hotel late last year but there are numerous others. Last I heard the Duchess of Kent pub has a fine dinner on offer. It's not far from here.' Finn swallowed a mouthful of rum, waited as it hit his stomach. It settled warmly, so he took another swallow. A visit to the pub would test his nerves, but the time seemed right. If a tremor took him there, he would know he needed more time, and that his plans would indeed take longer to realise than he hoped.

'Thank you. I'd be delighted.' Matthew's eyes lit up. 'Lead me to a good ale and a hot meal.'

The hotel already had a crowd of patrons, rowdy, hungry and thirsty. Finn directed Matthew to a table just vacated and thrust aside the used dinner plates and empty ale mugs. He beckoned a serving woman and ordered. She removed the last patron's remnants as she left.

Tobacco smoke wafted thick and aromatic around them, and the hops of ale, the sweet spice of rum, and the mouth-watering scents of meat gravy hung in the air.

There were raucous tones of happy miners, groups of table-thumping Germans, singing Italians, huddled Englishmen, loud Americans, and colonial miners breasting the bar, awaiting plates of thickly sliced rich meat with gravy, oozing flavour and sustenance, and ladles of potatoes.

'Loud,' Finn commented as two pots of ale were delivered. He felt his arm shake, but nothing came of it.

'Might calm down once they all get a meal into them. Seems there's every country in the world eating and drinking here.'

Finn leaned across to be heard. 'Goldfields. They've come from everywhere. No different to Bendigo, except for the stockade fight, and that hasn't stopped anybody arriving. Though there's some still paying for the privilege of speaking up.' He nodded and pointed at a lone diner, a man whose slight body was jostled by those behind him as he sat staring into his dinner plate. 'Carboni. Tried for treason.' The man was restless, his red hair and close-cropped red beard giving him the look of a zealot.

Matthew looked across. 'He looks ill.'

'Released from prison recently. Dysentery. Maybe his meal is not sitting so well on him.'

'Any word on Peter Lalor?'

Finn shook his head. 'He's reported as being in Melbourne, perhaps Geelong. It's well known now he lost his arm. I've got the *Ballarat Times* back at the house if you're interested.'

Matthew raised his eyebrows. 'The *Ballarat Times*. It's all around Bendigo that Mrs Seekamp prints it now that her husband's in jail for his reporting the stockade incident. Poor fellow was a good voice for the people. Scandalous that a woman is at the helm,' he said in a mock furtive whisper, and laughed.

'She is much maligned for it, but she's a fierce advocate for the miners. And she's petitioning for her husband to be released after charges of sedition.' Finn thanked the woman who landed two steaming plates of meat, gravy, potatoes and cobs of hot bread in front of them. He reefed into his pocket for his coin purse and handed over a pound, waited for change plucked out of her pinafore pocket. 'Admirable, but for how long they'll let her stay at the helm, I don't know. You should read her editorials, they're feisty.'

'With great interest. One very surprising thing I noticed on the goldfields was the number of women working a trade, for their own benefit. And quite respectable women at that.'

Finn pushed meat and gravy onto a fork with a chunk of bread torn from a cob. 'And a number are publicans. The publican in this establishment is a woman, a Mrs Spanhake.' Finn pointed to a young woman surveying her patrons, hands on hips. 'They're merchants and traders, and quite capable entrepreneurs too. Interesting times.'

'Next they'll want the vote.' Matthew loaded meat and potatoes onto a piece of bread and took a bite.

'The working man has to get his vote first. That might be the only good thing to come out of this whole sorry mess. There's talk the mining licensing will change. Would also be a good thing if only the powers that be could properly govern their own troops.' Finn chewed, savouring his meal. 'They need to clear the charges laid on men who were unlawfully attacked.' He took a long draught of ale. 'My opinion only. Tempers are still raw here.'

Matthew looked around. 'Seem a happy lot, despite,' he observed. He took another mouthful, and nodded appreciatively.

'On the surface, yes. After a few grogs, not so happy. Any more than a few and the rot starts. In my business I hear it all. The good luck, the bad, the rotten troopers, the corruption, the lack of genuine concern from the governor's office. Unstable as it is, while the gold's coming out of the ground, and while this—' he said, holding up his right arm, '—still plagues me, I can still turn a profit here. But if there's another riot, more bloodshed … I have to plan ahead.'

Finn waited for a tremor, as if by mentioning it, one might occur.

Matthew piled another chunk of bread with meat and gravy. 'If we retrieve the gold, what would you do?'

'I would sell, as you are aware. I've had to revisit my thoughts on the paddle-steamer idea. I'm not sure my health would allow me to—'

'But if you had an agent, a manager?' Matthew straightened.

'To do what?'

'To oversee. To carry out your plans, to grow your Murray company.'

Finn considered what the ledger man was talking about. 'You liked the idea of building boats for the Murray?'

Matthew's handful of bread hovered over his meal. 'I did. I've thought of nothing but that since your visit to our office. However, I've no funds. The thought just came to me that I could be of assistance if someone were to finance the project.'

Finn dropped his fork onto his plate and pushed it away. 'I wouldn't be so financial to do that and keep myself as well. But I thank you for the offer. I'll look at that idea more carefully once the loan is repaid by the lady. Besides, Joseph would miss you at the office.'

Shrugging, Matthew picked up his pot of ale and downed the contents. 'Times are changing, as you said. In my work, I am fully aware of what might occur once the gold runs out, or the world economy is no longer hungry for it. I have to plan ahead, too.'

Finn laughed. 'You'll find something. I'm sure your quest for adventure will be tempered by a shrewd mind.'

Matthew grinned in return. 'One would hope.'

A large figure stopped by Finn's shoulder. 'Mr Seymour, I'm sorry for interruptin' yer dinner but I'm needin' some picks and some pans. Will ye be comin' to the diggin's tomorrow by any chance?'

Finn turned in his chair. A miner, Ned Francis, a customer of Finn's, stood, hat held in thick-fingered hands, his wiry black beard carrying crumbs from his own dinner. His digger clothes, the calico shirt, the rough patched pants and waistcoat, stretched over a stocky frame and the heat of the day came off him in sweat and dust.

'Mr Francis. I'll be at my store at six in the morning, loading my cart. Can you not send someone in?'

'Would, if my two lads weren't still laid up from the attack. Can't trust no one to manage if I'm gone.'

After the buying trips to Melbourne, Finn and Ben would often drive a cart to the edge of the fields, load a couple of barrows full of tools from the cart and push them into the rows of campsites, selling wares on the spot. 'Picks and pans it is, then. I'll find you soon as I can, after dawn.'

Francis blew out a breath. 'I'm grateful. Might be worth your while to load another cart, there's others in need of tools. Seein' as there's been more good finds lately, deeper than before, we're all runnin' out of things.'

Finn nodded. 'Good news.'

Ned Francis nodded at Matthew, then at Finn, and pushed his way back through the throng.

'And that request,' Finn began, 'has finished off my night here in the pub. I must load up a cart tonight. Try to find my driver. He'd be somewhere in one of the hotels, but I hope I don't spend half the night trying to find him.'

'I'd gladly give a hand if it saves you some trouble,' Matthew said, wiping his plate clean with the last of his bread. 'I was going to revisit the goldfields on Sunday, but an extra visit tomorrow would make me a happy man.'

'Some added attraction?' Finn asked. He stood, ready to leave.

Matthew stood with him. 'A very interesting entrepreneur has taken my eye.'

Twenty-Four

Ballarat, Subscription Ball for the Miner's Hospital

'That'll do us for today, Nell. You'd best get on back to Mrs Enid's house to dress.' Flora pulled the last of the pegs from the line and tossed them into a bucket at her feet. She rolled a pair of men's trousers, stiff after drying in the heat of the day, and tucked them under her arm.

Nell was clearing the line opposite. 'I'll fold this lot and be on my way.'

'Don't sound so happy about it,' Flora said, and laughed a little. 'You might want to cheer yourself up before tonight. Don't take no mind about your father's threats.' She lowered her voice. 'Wish he hadn't come here, though.'

'So do I and I can't help but mind.' Scooping up a pile of dried clothes at her feet, Nell looked over at Flora. 'If you weren't going to the ball, I wouldn't be going either.' She walked towards Flora's tent and the upended crates they used for folding the laundry. 'Don't forget, I'm the one being taken to the ball by Lewis and his mother, not you. Cheerful will be hard to do.'

'And after tonight, no more pretending for you. You'll be free of the Wilshires, and the Amberton estate, such as it is.' Flora walked to the crates as well. 'You could have knocked me over with a feather when you told me the news, that there's nothing of it, that it was all lies.'

Nell dropped her pile onto the first crate and pulled a shirt free, shaking it hard. 'Not free of his name, though. I wonder if I can call myself Nell Thomas again.'

'Don't see why not.'

'Not sure I want the Thomas name either, but it is my name.' She folded the shirt and picked up another. 'And what will I wear to this wonderful ball? I know,' she said holding out a huge men's shirt. 'I will wear my nice black blouse and my nice black skirt to keep Enid from grumbling.'

'Why should you care that she grumbles?'

Nell wiggled her eyebrows. 'I don't so much, but if she's grumbling at me, she's paying attention to me and I'd rather do without that. What will you wear?'

'I have an old dress of Ma's. It's a bit faded, more a pale green now than a dark green, but we worked it to fit, so it will do. Ma just wants her clean skirt, her blouse and a shawl. She can do my hair.'

Nell touched her laundry cap. 'I'll have to do my own. I won't be fussing.'

'I'm not fussing,' Flora said, quickly.

Laughing, Nell wagged a finger. 'Are you not? After that nice Mr Worrell came by again today, I'd have thought you'd take extra mind of your hair.'

Flora blushed to her roots. 'Bosh, Nell Thomas.'

Mr Worrell had indeed come by just after sunrise. From a distance, Nell had seen him alight a cart driven by another man.

They'd proceeded to fill a barrow with all manner of implements pulled from the cart. Then after a long look up the hill, the other man pushed it off in the opposite direction.

Matthew had come towards the laundry and once again, poor Flora had been somewhat dumbstruck. He informed them, and Josie, that he would be attending the ball this evening. He asked if they would also be attending and Nell had answered for them, that yes, they would. To which he replied, 'Then I await this evening with the greatest anticipation.' And he'd smiled warmly at Flora, the dimple in his left cheek rakish under the dark shadow on his jaw.

Josie had chortled from within the tent and promised him a jig, which he had accepted, delightedly. Flora had scolded her mother half-heartedly, and her burning blush at the time had taken some time to subside.

Mr Worrell lingered only a short while, made light conversation with Nell—who was the only one answering him—and when the other man with the barrow far down the hill whistled and waved a hand, he bowed slightly to both and made his departure.

'Not a word about it,' Flora had warned Nell, who hid a smile.

In the low light of early evening, Finn stood at his dresser, his hand gripping the elbow of his right arm. *Damn the thing.* He shuddered as the tremor took him. He backed up and sat heavily on his bed, doubling over to squeeze the blasted thing still. His insides clenched and the pain of it bit deep into his gut, breath knocked out of him. And now his right leg shook, shuddered uncontrollably, his foot banging on the floorboards.

It will pass, it will pass.

He fixed his gaze on the wall opposite. On his coat as it hung on the back of the door. On the chair by his reading light. He breathed in deeply and held on. It seemed to work, this concentrating on something other than himself, but he wondered about his strength of will, and how much longer he could defend himself when these attacks occurred.

Then his chest relaxed, the pain in his gut diminished and with each deep throb of his pulse it leached out of him. Releasing his elbow, his right hand fell into his lap. He waited a beat, waited to see if a second grip would attack, and let go of the breath he'd sucked in.

Flexing his right hand, making a fist and releasing it, shaking it out, he stood up and faced the mirror again, his heart thumping, his blood racing.

What had been in his head just now when it attacked? Nothing. He'd had his eye on his collar as he began to wind his necktie. So there were no thoughts of war, or skirmishes on foreign soil, of bloodied rivulets pouring into the hollow in the ground he'd occupied. No guttural Russian voices yelling as shots went off over his head …

And deliberately bringing these memories to mind now didn't affect him either. What *was* it?

Frowning at his reflection, he shook his head. What set it off? What kept it ambushing him night and day for no reason? He checked his hands once again. Turned them over, watched how steady they were. Not a beat, not a shake or tremor. Nothing. Perhaps it wasn't from the fighting at all. Perhaps he did have some malaise in his brain.

He rubbed his face in both hands, wiped the sheen of sweat on his trousers. A man would be mad to go into company tonight. He stared at his face in the mirror then squeezed his eyes shut, opened them, loosened his jaw. He wouldn't give in to this affliction he knew he'd contracted in the Ottoman city of Köstence—for he'd had no such affliction before the skirmishes there—and would now just have to bear the tremors, wherever he was. If some folk found themselves unable to be near him, so be it. He'd always tried to hide the severity of the attacks, as much for himself as for others.

It was the sudden onset that confounded him. No warning most times. And sometimes, like the time on the road with Ben, a false alarm.

He shook off the frustration and straightened up to his full height. Checking his collar and necktie once more, he glared at his reflection. Moody eyes returned the glare. He was not feeble-minded. He would have been carted away as an imbecile if so, but this thing vexed him sorely.

Bear the tremors he would, and he would do what he could to lessen the impact they had on his companions for this evening, if they were to occur. He reached into the top drawer of his dresser and brought out a large square of dark broadcloth. He deftly folded and knotted it, then fit the thing over his shoulder, sliding his right arm into a firm sling over his shirt and waistcoat. He slipped his left arm into his tailcoat and shrugged it on over the sling. If he buttoned it across his middle, the sling would keep his errant arm snug against him.

Ready to leave, he pulled open his door and saw that Matthew waited for him in the hallway. Faint strains of instruments preparing an assault reached his ears. 'I think I can hear the orchestra warming up. A short walk, no more, Matthew.'

If Matthew thought anything of his attire, he kept it to himself. He winced. 'Orchestra, did you say?'

They stepped outside, and the night sky was lit with a cloudless Milky Way.

The good folk of Ballarat had come out in their finest for *The Subscription Ball To Aid The Unfortunates Who Have Suffered.*

Nell stood at the entrance to the main tent. The gentleman who studied her ticket waved her inside with a cheery, 'Enjoy the evening, Mrs Amberton.'

Lewis stepped in alongside her, his mother on his arm. 'I see we are just in time. There are still places to sit if needs.' He glanced at Enid. 'Come along, Mama. Stop dragging your heels. If any old biddies say a word to you about being here, you just let me know who they are.'

Enid, keeping her head low, glanced here and there, checking the responses to their arrival. No one had as much as raised an eyebrow that Nell could see.

'I know perfectly well you'd have broken your neck to be here,' Lewis said. 'And here we are, so stop fretting. After all, dear Uncle Andrew did supply us with tickets.'

Enid pinched his arm. 'And remember that, my boy.'

'Oh, I do,' Lewis said and dropped his head to speak to her. 'So chin up. You and Nell are not the only ones that I can see in a little mourning dress.'

It was true. Dotted here and there were ladies who had chosen to attend, and they'd worn black, either in full or in part. There was some tut-tutting, or open whispers of shock, but that soon gave way. Gentlemen were not required to change their attire at all, but in deference, some had black gloves tucked, or shoved, into top pockets.

Enid straightened her shoulders. 'All right. Just for this one ball,' she said and craned her neck. 'Fanny Jones and Elsie Cartwright said they'd be in the refreshment tent. I can't see them here, so I'll look there before I come back to join you.'

'Of course, Mama.'

Enid flicked a glance at Nell. 'The child-minding tent is out that way.' She pointed outside and to the right. 'They are expecting you.' She walked off before Nell could answer.

'My mother is still in her happy mood. It seems this is as good as it gets these days.'

Nell watched as a black-clad Enid moved around clusters of women in their fancy clothes. Their fashionable off-the-shoulder dresses were in all manner of colours in bright contrast. Even Enid's severe hairstyle set her apart from the other women, but nary a glance was given in her direction as she left the tent. She hadn't been noticed.

'Take my arm, Nell. Don't go to the children just yet.' Lewis led her further into the tent. Already crowded, the huge tent's canvas sides billowed gently in the light breeze from outside and all the more, no doubt, from the hot air inside. Rows of benches suitable as seats had been set up around what would be the dance floor, and the outer walls of the room were kept free of encumbrances.

Nell gazed openly at the fashions of the day. Hairstyles with artful ringlets dropped over ears. Slim intricate little plaits looped up into hair parted from the centre and pulled to the back of the head, wound and secured with pins. Older ladies still wore the chignon, and some ladies of varying ages just kept a strongly pinned bun at the back of their head. Nell had tried to copy the more modern style, sweeping the hair low over her ears and taking it up in an elaborate winding of tresses pinned and secured with narrow combs at the back. Hopeless! She wasn't able to coax her hair into anything complicated and succeeded only in pinning thick plaits in a roll over her ears. Always a bane, her unruly hair was no better behaved because she was attending a ball, but she was past caring too much. The plaits proved too heavy for the fine pins she had, and her hair combs were nowhere to be seen at Enid's house. She wondered if all her remaining possessions there had been tossed into the streets. She had pulled it out of the plaits, drawn it as neatly as she could over her ears and wound it at the back of her head. The fine pins were all employed in keeping the bun secure.

And the gentlemen. Lewis certainly looked very fine in his high collar and necktie; it befitted a man of means. His tailcoat was darkest grey, his dress shirt white, matching his tie, and his trousers were black. His shoes, the dancing pumps that were favoured over boots for formal wear, were spotlessly polished. He looked a country gentleman. He guided her over to where other equally well-dressed groups of men and women had congregated. Nell felt an unease; these were not people of her station. Clearly, they were well-to-do traders and their wives, or some were perhaps high officials of some government department.

Lewis must have sensed her discomfort. 'Hold your head high, Nell. Should you not have been in your widow's outfit, your gown for this evening would have rivalled some of these ladies' gowns here tonight. For the sake of appearances, I would have made sure of it.'

She doubted it, but kept her countenance. She smiled back at women who smiled at her and dipped her head in polite greeting. At times a gentle, brief squeeze of a hand on hers would commiserate with her widowhood. Other times a brief flicker of acknowledgement before a back was turned. Some folk kept to the ritual of a mourning period and disapproved of her half-hearted apparel. Or perhaps Nell was just not of their ilk. Or worse, they thought her husband had been less than befitting their ranks.

Oh, to be free of this rubbish.

She could see Mr Worrell talking to a man who had his back to her. The right sleeve of the man's tailcoat was empty, as if perhaps he had lost an arm. She thought briefly of the news of Peter Lalor losing an arm but dismissed it. He would not be well enough to be back on his feet, and besides, he was still a hunted man, so it was unlikely he'd be here tonight. When Mr Worrell's friend turned sideways, she could see that his arm was in a broad sling under his coat.

Not Lalor at all. Of course not. Back before the riot, he was known to have a beard, and he had a full, roundish face. This gentleman was clean shaven except for long sideburns, and he certainly did not have a round face.

Her memory sharpened. Something about him …

Mr Worrell's head bobbed into her line of sight, but he wasn't looking at her. He was busy answering his friend, a little distractedly, in conversation, every so often checking the door. Perhaps he was looking for Flora.

'Our orchestra,' Lewis commented drily and nodded towards a motley group wielding violins and trumpets. A gentleman, already unsteady on his feet, tried to concentrate on a drum and his sticks.

'Surely not,' she said, and hoped that a proper orchestra of strings and woodwind would eventuate. Music and dancing had been part of her earlier life and the sophisticated strains of an orchestra brought her great delight. Nell and her mother had once sat on a hill and listened from afar to a visiting quartet performing in the town.

She released Lewis's arm, and as the growing crowd pushed inward, the air closed in around her. Voices rose to be heard above the chatter. Cries of welcome erupted every couple of seconds. Overly exuberant laughter of men and women seemed to be forced, as if it could disguise the unease on the fields. If they laughed long and hard, relief would follow. It swirled about her, and with each turn of her head, her nerves grated and her ears rang.

'I will visit the children's tent now, Lewis,' she said over the rising din.

Lewis was almost upon the group of people he had been moving towards. 'Very well, and if you see Miss Flora before I do, please come and get me so I might talk with her.'

Nell nodded, moved past him, heading for the doorway. It hadn't seemed such a great distance getting to the middle of the tent-room as it seemed getting back outside again, and with people stopping her to offer their condolences, or to pass the time of day, it took ages to escape the escalating din of the big tent.

Thankfully she had remained polite to all. She congratulated herself.

Outside, as the sun lowered for the evening, the air had cooled a little. At least in the open there was plenty of it to breathe, she thought, as she moved smartly between the two tents, arriving at the door to the child-minding tent.

Giggling and squalling met her ears at the same time. As she looked inside, young children in their best dress pantaloons and dresses played around cots and cradles that held swaddled babes. The din of a different pitch was just as loud in here as the other tent and Nell wondered how she was going to escape all of it.

If only Flora would arrive soon, then at least she'd have a companion to chat with. Before she was snapped up to mind this child or that, she retreated quickly and headed back to watch at the entrance of the main tent. There she was sure to see Flora and her mother as they approached.

Lewis availed himself of a rum and stood with men he knew from the fields. One—Robert Gregg, a robust man of middle age—offered his condolences over Andrew's death.

'Late in the show, Lewis, however, I should offer my commiserations on the death of your uncle.'

Lewis, his features now melancholy, turned to Gregg. 'Thank you, Mr Gregg. It was a sudden turn of events.'

'Yes, I understand. One wouldn't think that bushrangers still operated hereabouts.'

Lewis lifted a shoulder. 'Who's to say? With the massacre at the stockade, my uncle's death could have been perpetrated by any number of ruffians. No one has been brought to account for it.'

Gregg twisted the end of his dark beard, rubbing the spindly tufts of hair into a knot. 'Terrible thing. And bags of his gold gone, too, I suppose. Makes it difficult to settle the estate. And I beg your pardon for saying it, but I'm heartily glad I'm not one of his creditors. How goes it for you, Lewis, with all that on your head?'

Lewis's rum slopped in his hand. Bags of gold? 'Difficult,' he croaked. 'To say the least. Where did you hear of the bags of gold?'

What did my mother ask of Nell ages ago?

Shrugging, Gregg thought a moment. 'Not long after his marriage to the Seymour girl. He came out for a card game, just me and m' son, and a little rum loosened him up. Said he'd taken it off her old man by way of a loan.' Mr Gregg peered at Lewis. 'Shouldn't I have mentioned it? Still a secret, is it? I suppose so. You don't want that sort of information out, but if bushrangers stole it ...'

Lewis nodded absently. The man blathered on and Lewis nodded again, hoping he appeared to be paying attention. What had Nell said about it that day? She had, in fact, denied there was gold. He tried to remember his mother's query of Nell.

His mother. Had she known there was gold—is that why she'd asked Nell to return any? Couldn't be so. She'd have said. She'd have moved heaven and earth to find it and relieve their financial burdens.

What had Nell answered when his mother had questioned her? Ah, yes.

Andrew left me no gold.

So, what bags of gold was Gregg spruiking about? Lewis scoffed. Perhaps it was part of the same pack of lies Andrew had told over the years, part of the scurrilous legend he'd created for himself. His madness had known no bounds. Bags of gold, indeed. He'd have spent it, not kept it hidden. But it didn't sit well.

Lewis laughed to himself. He was right to have pulled the trigger, but even dead, Andrew was still playing with his mind. Lewis had waited a while hidden in the scrub after he'd shot Andrew. He didn't recall any bags at the scene, but they could very well have been inside the coach.

Nell certainly had not said any such bags had been stolen. Therefore, if there really was gold, Nell could very well still have it.

As Robert Gregg continued his monologue, Lewis scanned the tent for his uncle's widow.

Nell saw Lewis heading outside and she ducked behind a throng of people waiting patiently in line to enter the tent. She watched as he searched over her head, presumably checking for Flora's appearance. Then he made his exit and headed for the supper tent. He looked unhappy, but that was none of her concern. Flora could look after herself in that department if he caught up with her.

And in the queue, Nell spied her friend, arm in arm with Mrs Doyle. As the line moved forward, Nell fidgeted from foot to foot until Flora and Josie were inside the tent. She followed them inside and pressed her hands to theirs in greeting.

'You look very fine, Flora.'

Flora let go of her mother's arm and brushed down her dress. 'I think it'll hold up for tonight. But it's patched here and there, so I hope no one can see.'

'No one can see my stitches, Flora.' Josie moved in close to make comment.

'Of course they can't, Ma.'

Nell smelled the fresh-air scent of clean, line-dried clothes. Josie looked smart and matronly in her soft white blouse, a light cloth shawl and her full skirt of mid brown. 'And you do look regal, Mrs Doyle,' Nell remarked. 'Your skirt is very handsome.'

''Tis a good tweed this one, saved from me own ma's house. She had a bolt come down from Sydney just afore she passed on, God bless her.' Josie crossed herself. 'And now I'm looking for a drink of that punch,' Josie said and pointed at a lady holding a delicate glass in her hands.

Flora looked about a moment. Nell smiled. 'I'll get her a drink. Can I get you something, too, Flora?'

'No, I'll wait—'

'And here's that fine young fella from yest'dy, Flora. What's his name again?'

Matthew Worrell was by their side before Flora could answer. 'There you all are. I just said to my companion that I was waiting for at least two lovely ladies to arrive, and there are three of you. Just my good luck.'

'Ye'll go far, lad.'

He laughed at Josie, gave a little bow towards her, and to Flora and Nell. 'Allow me to accompany you to the refreshment tent.' He offered Josie his arm, and with a delighted chuckle she took it. Flora trailed behind with Nell.

'What on earth do I do with him?' Flora asked, close to Nell's ear.

'Why does he bother you so? He's seems nice. Of good intent, as far as I can tell. We need more of that around here, I think.'

'That's just it,' Flora said. 'He's being nice to me.'

Nell pulled a face. 'Oh, and that's terrible.' But she understood. After the type of treatment Andrew had dished out, anything kind was a wonder to her, and perhaps something to be suspicious of. Yet with the bushranger, no such thought had crossed her mind.

'Lewis always wanted something.' At Nell's askance look, Flora said, 'To improve me, to dress me up. God knows why he chose me in the first place if I needed improvin' all over the place, but I always knew where I stood with Lewis. I could always speak my mind without a care. I was never serious about him.'

The refreshment tent had filled as well, the men around the rum keg and the ladies hovering by the lemon cordial and the tea.

Josie had guided Matthew to the table where rows of four-sided brown gin bottles stood, some uncorked. Matthew paid a penny and Josie came away with a tot splashed into a pannikin.

'Dear Lord. Ma remembers she surely loves her tot of gin.' Flora thrust into a hidden pocket in her dress and produced a folded handkerchief. She unwrapped it, revealing numerous pennies, and headed for the lemonade. She came back with her own pannikin and poured the contents into Josie's. 'No more, now, Ma.'

Josie winked up at Matthew, who winked back. Her arm was still linked in his.

Nell leaned in to Flora. 'But you could be serious about this one,' she stated.

Flora blushed. 'He is too fancy for me,' she whispered dismissively as Matthew and her mother turned for the exit.

'No fancier than Lewis.'

'Mr Worrell is much more fancy,' Flora replied. 'I am much more suspicious.'

Nell laughed. 'Well, that's a good thing to be. Come on,' she said. 'We'd better follow and chaperone the two of them.'

Flora gave a harrumph. 'I'll get us some lemonade. Should you not be in the children's tent, by now?'

'The noise is as bad in there,' Nell replied and tilted her head towards the tent. 'I won't be staying long. Although now you have two suitors vying for your attention, perhaps I'd better.'

When Flora returned with two small cups of lemonade, they made their way back to the bigger tent. Matthew could be seen over the heads of the crowd and as he kept dipping below the level, Nell imagined he still had Mrs Doyle at his side and had bent down to hear what she might have been saying.

He caught her eye and beckoned them over with a lift of his chin.

'There you are,' he said as they approached.

His dark hair, the deepening dimple and the twinkle in his blue eyes had Nell glancing at Flora. There was that blush again, but this time Flora offered a small smile.

'I can look after Ma now,' she managed.

'Not at all. I've lost my friend somewhere, so I'd be all on my own if it wasn't for Miss Josie here.'

Clearly, Matthew thought that if he had hold of Mrs Doyle—Miss Josie, if you please—Flora would be hovering. Clever man.

'And who is your friend, Mr Worrell?' Nell enquired, looking about at the groups of men and women around them.

'Ah.' Matthew looked a little uncomfortable at that moment. He stared at Nell, then glanced away. 'Well, he's—'

Finn couldn't believe what he was looking at. There was Matthew Worrell with an old woman on his arm and two younger women close by. One of whom without a doubt was Mrs Amberton.

Amid the jostling of other ball-goers, Finn studied her, his heart rate speeding up as he tried to get a clear line of sight. As he well knew, the figure that had appeared gaunt and tired at the hold-up had indeed filled out. Her face was a handsome one—he could see it clearly now in the better light of the tent. His chest expanded as he stood there, as the bodies in the crowd bumped around him and helped hide him. Her wide clear eyes he remembered so well were unmarked by the result of a fist on them. She looked confident, and serene. She'd asked something of Matthew and he seemed at a loss to answer her.

His heart thumped. This was *Mrs Amberton*, merely steps from him. Casually chatting to Matthew. He should approach. He should—

Don't be stupid, man.

Did he think he could hide his identity after what had happened between them at the hold-up, and then at her house? Nell would know him immediately. Certainly, the kerchief he'd used would save him from a cursory glance, but not a meeting, not an introduction. And surely he couldn't meet her, not with both of them knowing now that certain bags of gold were at the centre of a legal matter. He would breach his obligations if he compromised what Joseph Campbell was trying to do. Had Matthew not thought of this? Or was she the 'entrepreneur' he spoke of the other night and Matthew's thoughts were on nothing but her?

Please not.

He glanced at the other woman, the dark-haired slim beauty by Nell's side. No, no—*this* was the woman Matthew had his eye on. Even in the man's momentary hesitation, he looked at this woman differently; his expression had altered, softened.

Nell kept her attention on Matthew's face, a smile in place until she was crowded a little by another couple, a man and a woman, the woman none too happy to see her.

Dora Thomas frowned menacingly at her stepdaughter. 'I see you are well-heeled enough to have afforded a ticket to the ball, even though you are in mourning.'

Alfred Thomas smirked. 'She is at that, Mrs Thomas.'

Nell braced, her glance on one then the other. She looked back at Matthew. 'Would you be so kind as to take these two ladies for some more refreshment?'

'Gladly,' Matthew replied, and he looked gladly ignorant.

Josie, still in his grip, cried, 'Goodo,' as Flora reluctantly accepted his other arm.

'Will you be all right, Nell?' Flora asked, dragging her heels a little.

'She is in her family's company, young woman. Of course she'll be all right,' Dora snapped, her ample bosom and cleavage covered by out-of-fashion lace ruffles.

Alfred Thomas leaned over towards Josie. 'You won't be aimin' yer shot at me in here, old woman.'

'Nay, yer too close, so a swift kick to yer nethers will do me just as good.'

Alfred stepped back swiftly, Matthew blurted a laugh and Flora groaned. 'Ma,' she chided hoarsely and urged Matthew out of the tent.

'That old hag needs to be taken off the streets,' Dora sneered. 'You would do well to seek better company,' she said to Nell.

Nell started to move past them. 'Indeed, and so I shall.'

'Just a minute, just a minute, Nell Thomas,' her father cautioned. He brought a finger up in front of her nose as she tried to step around him. 'Yer not so high and mighty, yet. I know that youngster Lewis Wilshire is in a bad place after his uncle died, leaving him nothin', it appears, except debt. He might be very interested to know that a certain great deal of gold is still about the place.'

Nell remained stonily silent, but her heart boomed, and her pulse raced.

'So, give it up to me, now, lass, and we'll say no more of it. Otherwise, me an' the traps will be watchin' yer every step.'

'So you said before. But say what you like, and to whom,' Nell muttered and pushed past them both. 'There's no gold for Mr Wilshire, nor for the likes of you.'

'Watch yourself, Miss High-and-Mighty,' Dora cried as she stumbled aside.

The brief spat had drawn the attention of a few, but not for long. The violins and the trumpets were warming up, and excited chatter drowned out anything else her father or Dora might have uttered at her.

Nell wrangled her way through the crowd, against the surge of folk coming into the tent to catch a glimpse of the band. Breathless, she stepped aside, allowed the press of bodies to rush past her and then, when the horde petered out, she slipped outside.

Everyone was pouring into the main tent. Perhaps her best hiding place was back in with the children, though all she wanted to do was to get away and back to some quiet place of her own. She hurried around the side of the child-minding tent, tried to block out the wailing cries of some, and the happy gurgles and giggles of others. Away from the lanterns that that now flickered dim light around the tents, she headed for a line of shrubs and a scattered group of chairs recently abandoned. The band had struck up a tune, stopped and started again. Laughter erupted, and she could hear a few jeers. Perhaps the music would not be the best tonight.

On the edge of the darkness, pacing, she wrung her hands. Too agitated by far, she stopped and found a chair, gripping the back of the seat.

Her father was an evil man intent on doing her more harm. He would hound her until she gave him what he wanted. In his desperate way he would stick with it.

He was right, she did have the gold, but how was he so sure of it? She had to think carefully. The gold was as safe as she could make it, yet for Flora and her mother it was in the most dangerous place of all. What had she done? How would Mr Worrell help her get rid of it and return it to its rightful owners?

Suddenly, hairs stood up on the back of her neck. She felt heat behind her and a low muffled voice.

'Don't turn around, Nell.'

Her stomach hollowed, and her pulse pounded ever louder in her ears. She didn't want to turn around. She desperately wanted to run.

Twenty-Five

Lewis bent to his mother's ear. 'Mama, have you seen Nell?'

Enid sat with her two friends, Mrs Jones and Mrs Cartwright, both fine upstanding ladies of the Ballarat fields who loved nothing more than a good gossip about the wrongdoings of everything and everybody. Nothing wrong with that, unless it was tonight when Lewis needed to speak to his mother.

The rapid chatter at this end of the refreshment tent made his eardrums rattle. He was the only male there. The ladies were in charge of dispensing cake and canapés, such as they were, and the lemonade and the tea. Gentlemen, at the other end of the tent, took care of the licensed hard liquor. There, voices boomed.

Enid answered her son. 'I saw her a while ago. No doubt having a fine time without minding her mourning period. She was with that Flora Doyle, and they were buying lemonade.' She glanced over at her friends. 'I honestly don't know what's happening with people these days. She might well be my sister-in-law, and young though she is, both she and that other girl need—'

'If you could spare a moment, Mama?' Lewis raised his voice, enough to catch his mother's attention. 'Begging your pardon, ladies.'

221

Enid excused herself, held her hand out for Lewis. He took her to a quiet corner by the table of small pies, breads and jams, and little cakes. It was nearly denuded and looked as if it had been rushed by a stampeding crowd. 'Mama, I've just heard it said to me that Andrew had bags of gold and that it was perhaps stolen from him when the coach was bailed up.'

Enid stared at him. 'Who would say that—someone who'd know?'

'Clearly.' Lewis related his conversation with Robert Gregg.

'Then Nell must have been aware of it, after all. I asked her at the time and she denied having any gold. She must have it somewhere. I swear to you it was not in that house she vacated.'

'It was indicated to me that it was a considerable amount. If Nell has it, where is it now, and how has she managed to move it?'

Enid's eyes narrowed. 'Perhaps with the help of your paramour. They are certainly very close these days.'

Lewis shook his head. 'I doubt that. But tell me, did Andrew ever indicate to you he had gold in a cache somewhere?'

His mother laced her hands, then smoothed the tablecloth, brushed crumbs from it. 'I felt he had something. Perhaps I heard him speak of gold. But I assumed it came from his miners, and that he was … careful with his funds.'

'Mama, we both know that to be untrue.'

'Well.' Enid, nonplussed, straightened the tablecloth again.

'I will find Nell and ask once more,' Lewis said, and rubbed his forehead. If Nell had the gold, he would be out of debt in no time. She might have come to the end of her usefulness.

His mother glared. 'It's not as if such a thing would have slipped her mind, Lewis.'

'Of course not. But neither is she living the high life and spending it,' he grated. 'If she has it, she has a reason to hide it. But I need it. We need it. After all,' Lewis continued, 'we are her family.'

He guided his irate mother back outside and was about to enter the entertainment tent when he saw Flora and her mother standing with a dark-haired man. He blinked hard as he recognised Matthew Worrell, the ledger man from Mr Campbell's office.

Under the starlit sky, and with a dozen lanterns throwing light in all directions, the scene looked eerie. And Flora was laughing at something Matthew was saying. Everybody seemed to be having a fine old time.

Enid stiffened at his side. 'And just who is that man she's with, now that she's given you over?'

As if Flora had heard, she looked across, her gaze locking with Lewis's before it flickered to his mother. Her smile fell away. She nodded, acknowledging both. At her distraction, Matthew looked across, as did Josie. Mrs Doyle's smile remained broad and aimed at Enid.

Matthew waved a hand. 'Lewis—Mr Wilshire. Delighted to see you,' he called over the few yards between them. 'I'll have a drink with you sometime tonight.'

Lewis nodded. 'Of course,' he called back. What was Matthew Worrell doing here? And how the hell did he know Flora? His skin prickled. Something was going on around him. Something was going over his head. Something was happening with people he knew, and with events that hadn't been run past him. He was missing *something*. A crack was appearing, a chasm widening; he felt the bottom of it dip and fall away under him. His gut trembled a moment.

Then it was gone. He freed his mother. Wiped a hand over his mouth.

Flora had gone back to her conversation with Mr Worrell, and her loudmouthed mother was part of the fun. Flora had met someone else—that was why she no longer wanted to be with him.

Flora.

'Papa! There he is.'

An excited female voice reached his ears, and he focused to see a finger pointing at him, then smartly drop, the owner knowing it to be rude.

Enid plucked his sleeve. 'Lewis, who is that young woman?' she enquired, her eyes widening. She gave him a quizzical look.

The young, dark-haired woman, a happy light in her eyes and a smile on her face, stood directly in front of Lewis, held her hand out by way of introduction as she spoke to the older man at her side. 'This is the man, Papa, who saved me from that horrible trooper and a terrible fate after the stockade.'

Twenty-Six

Nell held her breath. That voice. She recognised it instantly. Immediately, those green eyes above the kerchief came to mind. She couldn't see him, but his presence behind her hummed in the air between their bodies.

'You look very well.' Each word was a feather-like touch along her neck. 'You look extraordinary, in fact.'

Was he so close? Her hands shook, and she started—

'Please. Don't turn,' he said.

Fighting to keep still, she fixed her gaze on the tents in the distance, and the folk darting in and out, the laughter erupting around the pained strains of the orchestra warming up. Her chest rose and fell rapidly despite her struggle to control her breathing.

'Your situation seems much improved since our last meeting.' Each word murmured against her skin and glided along her shoulders.

The hum pulsed between them, more urgent as he'd stepped closer. She stood, not moving, wanting to turn, wanting to look at him.

225

He said, 'I'm sorry. I've frightened you once again. I'll not harm you, you know that, but you understand, I cannot allow you to see my face.'

That quiet, melodious voice. That accent. Was it part old country, part new?

'Who are you?' she asked, her words whispered on breath that beat out of her. 'Not your name, if you choose, but who are you that you seek me out? And why?'

Silence for some moments confused her. She started to turn, but his reply stopped her.

''Tis a strange thing.' His breath was warm on her nape, his mouth would be close. 'Though I hardly know you, I seem to have a care for you. But there are secrets between us already, and I cannot put you in any more danger until those things are set to rights.'

Nell blinked at that. 'Secrets? What sorts of secrets could I possibly have from you, a bush—'

'Ah, yes, a bushranger. It gives me heart that you have not given me up to the troopers.'

The heat of his chest was on her back, and perhaps, a bold brush of his fingertips trailed down the backs of her arms. Her hands clasped, and she squeezed them to stop the shakes. 'I don't know who to give up, if I would ever.'

'But my little kerchief would not hide much from an intelligent woman such as yourself.'

She shook her head in denial. 'After the night at the empty house, I gave no thought then to talk to the troopers. Besides, they'd seemed less than interested the first time.' That was the truth. Now she felt as if she was … identifying with him, allying herself with him—

'It's true,' he commented. 'They'd had a lot more to worry about then.'

Nell felt her nerve returning. 'Are we to continue to meet this way, where you surprise me and I am left to defend myself?'

He laughed. 'I wonder who needs defending.'

The flush of heat burned her cheeks and a quick retort escaped. 'I seem driven to do things I have not been driven to do before,' she said. 'And it makes me uncomfortable.'

'It makes me delighted. But I would hate to be the cause of discomfort for you.' And from under the kerchief his lips crept softly on the curve of her neck.

'You're laughing at me,' she cried faintly, every part of her attuned to his mouth, every nerve singing, waiting.

'No, Nell.' She felt the press of his mouth. 'I'm not laughing.'

She saw her father dart out of the tent, straining to see over the top of the crowds of people around him. Inadvertently, she shrank, stopped herself, heard the man behind her move. Alfred remained where he was, glaring into the night, shading his eyes with his hand against the light of the lanterns. Nell was sure he was glaring right at her.

'Just take one step back, and no one will be able to see you from over there. Are you being missed by a man curious as to your whereabouts?'

That unhurried drawl. That confidence … That part of her that couldn't resist the temptation of him. She started to turn, couldn't stop the girlish nonsense—

'Don't turn around,' he ordered.

That stopped her. 'I am long past doing what is bid of me.'

'Is that so? Just don't turn, Mrs Amberton.'

He wasn't going to harm her, she knew, she felt it, as clear as if she was facing him. 'How I hate that name.'

'Be still and you won't be seen.' His voice was in her hair, his mouth close to her ear and the twirl of that girlish nonsense was back, strong and propelling.

Fighting down the thudding beat of her heart, she stood stock still, watched her father. Alfred moved further from the tent, and as he did his light would have dwindled. He stepped back towards the doorway and disappeared inside.

She let out a sigh of relief. 'Don't call me by that name. Ever. It's Nell, and you know it.' The shrubs rustled. The warm breeze danced along her cheeks, tendrils from her thick hair whisked over her face. She felt him slip what seemed like a few dry twigs into her hand, and then he withdrew. Suddenly she had the feeling he'd gone. 'Are you still here?'

His voice floated back. 'I'll see you again.'

'Nell!' Flora was headed down to the shrubs. 'I can just see you. What are you doing out here?' She stalked the last few yards. 'I've left Ma with Mr Worrell to come look for you.' She stared hard at Nell. 'Are you all right?'

Nell was sure the man was gone, and she wet her lips, waved away Flora's concern. 'Just needed some air,' she said, puffing out her breath. 'Not only is Enid in there, but my father as well as my stepmother. It suddenly became far too crowded.' She slipped her arm through Flora's. 'Is Mr Worrell entertaining your mother?'

'Pfft. I don't know who's entertaining who. I don't know what he wants. Good God, you're shaking.'

Nell squeezed her arm. 'I'm getting soft like you said.' She would not tell anyone about the bushranger's appearance. 'And— it's your company Mr Worrell wants, Flora.'

They wandered closer to the main tent. 'No, it's not,' Flora stated. 'It's your company he wants. He asked where you were, said he needed another few words with you. When I couldn't find you in there I came looking. I got worried when I saw your father checking outside as well.' She stopped and peered at Nell. 'I look after me own, Nell, and your pa's dangerous for all of us.

You're still shakin'. Did your pa find you? Did something happen out here?'

Nell looked back towards the shrubbery only once, certain that her bushranger remained, hidden, guarding. 'I am a bit shaky, it's true. It's not only my father, it's all those people.' She didn't let her backwards glance linger. In the light approaching the tent, she opened her hand and saw the little twigs he had given her.

It was the same wattle she'd found at Amberton House, on the water barrel wall, and on the back step. Little puff balls of yellow, not brittle in her hands, but firm and fresh. It was his sign that he was looking out for her, silent, unseen and protective. He must live here in Ballarat. That was why he needed to ensure she never saw his face. Should that frighten her? It didn't. She slipped the sprigs into her pocket. It was her sign for courage.

Inside the tent, the din hadn't lessened. A voice boomed over the crowd and announced the band would begin. Nell's feet sank in the loose dirt underfoot. How anyone could dance in this she didn't know. Still, it wouldn't be stately waltzes, she was sure, so it didn't matter.

How much longer did she need to be here? How much longer did she need to be seen before she could slip away? Just knowing the bushranger had been here set her on edge. Why would he torment her with his presence? That thought made her shiver, but not with unease. It made her heart beat harder. It made her wish she could slip outside again and run back down to the shrubs.

Mr Worrell and Mrs Doyle stood in close conversation over by the far wall, on the opposite side to the band. Threatening whines from the violins became louder and then a hush descended, as the first tentative notes of 'God Save The Queen' sounded.

A few voices joined boisterously but dwindled away when the majority only half-heartedly began. People glanced at one another. Things were too raw, even today. *Would we sing for Queen and country when so many of the Queen's men had committed murder?*

The band played on until it, too, ran out of notes to play. A murmur in the crowd grew until someone shouted, 'Play something else, you dolts,' and a lively jig was struck. A roar of approval went up and couples surged forward.

Bumped away from the dancers, Nell made her way to Mr Worrell, and Flora took her mother's arm to go and watch the dancing. Josie's happy beam and the jig of her hips brought a smile to Nell.

'I think I will be away to my home, soon, Mr Worrell,' she said, raising her voice. 'Flora said you wished to speak to me?'

He bent to her ear. 'Our subject,' he began, and she nodded. 'We must devise a strategy.'

'I have not given it extra thought, just yet.' Nell felt the frown form, and her heart sank. The task would be nigh on impossible. 'I hoped there might be a little more time—'

'I'm sorry to say, not. We may have to resort to drastic measures to realise the preferred outcome.'

The jig was deafening but she didn't want to shout. She looked up into his blue eyes. 'I don't know how to—to deliver it,' she said as close to his ear as manners allowed.

'Can you at least tell me in which vicinity it is?'

Nell's heart was still beating a thud through her, now because of a different excitement. She looked away, looked across the bobbing bodies and the gleeful laughter, over at the overly enthusiastic and the subdued. Across the floor, she saw the man with his arm in a sling, talking to other men and laughing. His profile was a handsome one, his face etched, and the smile lines made grooves from cheek to chin.

He was a long way off, and on the edge of the dancing mob. Something about the way—

'Mrs Amberton, can you tell me what it's close to, at least? I could help, or I could find help if necessary.'

'This seems a strange place to be talking of this.' She wrung her hands, glancing back to find the man whose arm was in the sling, but he was hidden by the crowd. She stared back at Mr Worrell.

'Time is of the essence, Mrs Amberton.' He glanced about then his gaze came back to her.

No one had heard, she was sure. 'It's impossible to get it back from where it is,' she said, a little cry in her voice. 'It's too dangerous for others.'

'I've been thinking on that. Tell me, was it you who moved it to where it is?'

She nodded, spied her father coming towards them.

'Then,' Mr Worrell said and bent close again, 'could we not retrieve it the same way you delivered it?'

Yes. Yes—that was it. But now, Nell wanted to run. Her father, intent and angry, would cause a scene, and Dora was pushing and shoving in his footsteps. But Mr Worrell was right. She could extract it by delivering it in the same way she had brought it in, just not using her own clothes. It would mean enlisting Flora's help, and most likely Josie's too. 'Yes,' she said quickly. 'Yes, we could. My father's coming, so please just agree with me when I—'

He was upon them. 'Daughter,' he bellowed. 'I will not have ye ignorin' me and your stepmother.'

Nell narrowed a glance at him. 'I was enjoying myself. I can do both.' She saw Mr Worrell bite his lip.

'And you, sir,' Alfred belligerently addressed Mr Worrell, 'have no business with my daughter.'

'Matthew Worrell, sir. But I do have business with Mrs Amberton. And you are?'

'Alfred Thomas.'

Mr Worrell gave a slight bow. 'Sir. And a pleasure, Mrs Thomas, I presume,' he said and directed another slight bow to Dora, who puffed up like a pigeon.

'He does have business with me, Pa, and with Miss Doyle. He is a customer of our laundry.'

'*Our* laundry now, is it?' Alfred boomed. 'What a come down. Settin' up in someone else's shop, taking payment like a slattern workin' the fields. No longer pretending to be the lady he made ye.'

'You mock me, but I served your purpose,' Nell hissed. 'You and your wife didn't mind spending what I made for your laundry shop. The pay I earn now is mine.'

Dora glared open mouthed at Nell as Alfred said, 'My good wife does laundry fer us because her husband kindly provides for her.'

Nell seethed at her father. 'Provides for her on the money Andrew paid you for me.'

His good wife shut her mouth and turned to stare at him. Alfred blundered on. 'Yer might be right, Nellie-girl, but dinna Andrew have the means, so you wouldn'a have to work? I think he did,' he added slyly. He lowered his voice. 'I know ye got his gold, daughter, and I'm owed, so no lyin' to yer ol' da.'

Dora's affronted stare faltered.

Nell bristled. She turned her full attention to Mr Worrell. 'As you have told me, Mr Worrell, you have many, many shirts and trousers in need of laundering. You must bring everything to me—to our laundry at your earliest convenience. We will see to it all.'

A little bewildered, Mr Worrell said, 'I don't have so many—'

'And of course, you said you had your friend's laundry as well. Shirts and trousers, and bed linens.'

Dora leaned in, an unusual, sweet look on her face. 'Nell, it is not seemly to be doing business at a ball,' she chided, then smiled at Mr Worrell. 'Our daughter must be excused. She's bereaved just recently, and very taken with her new-found proprietorship.'

Alfred scowled at his wife. 'Her what?'

Nell caught Mr Worrell's eye. 'We are able to do this for you, but it will have to be delivered after lunch tomorrow.' She nodded, encouraging him to nod with her.

'Oh, but that's on the Lord's Day,' Dora said, clearly put out but smiling again at Mr Worrell.

'It's only a delivery, Mama Dora,' Nell said, grating against her own conciliatory tone.

Dora was stunned into silence at that. 'Well,' she finally said, but it was barely heard over the raucous din of the dance.

'Of course, Mrs Amberton,' Mr Worrell said. 'Of course, I will bring my laundry. All of it. And all my friends' laundry.'

'Very good. Now, will you accompany me to find Mrs Doyle?' Nell asked, and when Mr Worrell offered his arm, she took it, excusing herself from her father and her stepmother.

Finn was in the drinks tent talking to two men who puffed on fine-smelling cigars when Matthew found him and bent to his ear, beckoning him outside. After a nod and a shrug to his acquaintances, they waved him off good-naturedly and he stepped outside with Matthew.

'Did you say "laundry"?' Finn said, adjusting the wide swathe of cloth serving as a sling for his errant arm. They walked away from others talking in groups here and there outside.

'Yes, and lots of it.'

'I don't know that I have lots of it. Nevertheless, laundry it is, which you will deliver, I take it.' He remembered how, when he had delivered tools to Mr Francis, Matthew had gone in the opposite direction towards a laundry site. 'I noted your path on the fields earlier today.'

'I'm afraid my lawyer cousin would be disappointed in me, compromising the situation as I have. I am no detective police-man, nor trained in the fine art of subtlety and discretion. It wouldn't be difficult to deduce Mrs Amberton's new residence now.' Matthew did indeed look unhappy with himself.

'I can assure you,' Finn said, clapping Matthew on the shoulder, 'that I will be on my best behaviour and promise not to jeop-ardise the plan. I have noticed her here at the ball and have dili-gently restrained myself from going to her.' Finneas Seymour had restrained himself. The bushranger had not.

Matthew snorted and nodded. 'My thanks.' Then with a grave look on his face, he said, 'And let us hope that whatever plan is afoot, the cost of clean shirts and trousers does not take up most of your inheritance.'

Finn laughed. 'Let us hope.'

Twenty-Seven

The band's lively jig seemed to go on forever, certainly in Lewis's head. Finally, it came to a halt, and sweaty folk forged off the dancing area.

'... Papa, who saved me from that horrible trooper, and a terrible fate after the stockade.' The young woman was still beaming at him.

Her father seemed inordinately happy to have laid his eyes on him. 'Sir, I am indebted to you.' The older man gave a slight formal bow. 'May I introduce myself? Rufus McNaught.' The man's accent sounded American.

Lewis nodded, blank for a moment.

Enid shook his arm. 'Son,' she said into his ear, prompting a response, and nodding at him encouragingly.

'I am Lewis Wilshire. May I present my mother, Mrs Wilshire.' More slight bows.

'Mrs Wilshire,' McNaught said. He bowed a little lower towards Enid, and smiled.

Lewis watched the flush bloom across his mother's face and a smile begin. Her eyes never left McNaught. *Good lord. Astounding.*

McNaught turned to the young woman who was still smiling widely. 'And my daughter, Miss Annabel McNaught.'

Lewis took her proffered gloved hand and let it drop. 'Miss McNaught, delighted.'

She curtsied. 'Mr Wilshire.' She did the same to Enid. 'Mrs Wilshire,' she said, but she barely took her eyes off Lewis. Hers was a softer accent, but it brought no less ringing to his ears than her father's twang.

Rufus McNaught stood as tall as Lewis. His sandy greying hair was slicked down on his head, and the darker beard was bushy on his jaw. When he smiled, the gap-toothed grin didn't quite reach his eyes.

McNaught said, 'Begging the ladies' pardon, but there is something private I need to speak of, Mr Wilshire.'

Dear God, first Flora with Matthew Worrell. What is coming at me now?

Enid beamed at him and fanned herself. Then she smiled at Annabel. 'We should get some air, Miss McNaught,' his mother said. 'Perhaps some lemonade.'

Lewis stared at her. His usually staid mother seemed to be all of a gush. He watched as they stepped around other revellers and headed outside. Annabel took one last look over her shoulder at him.

His gut shrank. His senses were on high alert, but flight was impossible.

Mr McNaught waved Lewis ahead of him. Outside the tent, watching as the women entered the refreshment tent, the older man drew Lewis to one side.

'My daughter has spoken of little else since that terrible night.' He chafed his hands in front of him. 'I have often wondered who her rescuer might have been, and here you are. Right here, at the ball.'

Lewis's face burned. 'It was indeed a terrible night at the stockade, and after. What I stumbled upon, well, no decent man should have to witness, no woman to endure.' He looked at his feet in the dim light, ignored the jostling of others as they charged for the drinks tent.

McNaught was bumped and bumped again. 'There have been many such acts of that particular vileness towards womenfolk, that night, before, and after.'

Lewis nodded, his features grim. 'Indeed, I have heard those whispers. Abominable.'

'My thanks to you, sir, no enduring harm to her.'

'I'm glad to have been of service.' The band struck up again and for once, Lewis was desperate to be back there and dancing, even with his mother.

'Even so, for you, a terrible thing, to have to take a life.'

For a single split second, life halted for Lewis. Then rowdy laughter and foot stomping to the music thundered a pulse in his head. His temples ached. *Surely this buffoon is not going to give me up to the traps … No, no—I saved his daughter. He wouldn't. Would he?*

McNaught stopped the chafing and wiped his hands on his trousers. 'Fact is, it broke her courtship. Says her courting lad has scorned her because of it.'

Lewis blew out a long breath. 'I'm sorry to hear that. She looks a good young woman, she deserves to … put that day behind her and seek happiness.'

'That's true enough. It's all she talks about. The thing is, you see, she was to be marrying up. Her life would've been changing.' He tugged on his waistcoat, as if it had become a little tight. 'When the troopers rode up to our tents that night, they charged in on horseback, trampling my wife dead, shot my son and he's still badly injured. My daughter, well, she ran and ran, she says. And then that trooper found her.'

Lewis hung his head. His shoulders sagged a little as he listened.

'And now, well, until now, I saw no hope of her being in her right mind again.'

Lewis glanced at the older man. 'I am truly sorry that you are all so burdened. It was indeed a terrible night. Especially so for your daughter, of course.'

Mr McNaught straightened up. 'I should keep her with me now my wife's gone, and my son's sick. She's a good cook. A good housekeeper. She has her letters. But she'd fare better with a husband. Needs a husband to look after her, needs some children. She needs that more than I need to keep her. And she says there's no other man now but the man who rescued her.'

Icy prickles stung the backs of Lewis's hands. Something akin to an unravelling began in his gut.

McNaught went on, leaning in, his face earnest. 'This gold rush has made times mad, it's made men mad. I saw it at home, in California. I came here to—never mind. Lives are changed. Families abandoned. She needs a husband,' he repeated. 'Someone to have children with, to live a life with.'

Lewis set his teeth. 'Perhaps it would seem a better idea to go home to America, where much would be familiar.'

'I can't do that. Gold has not exactly leapt into my hands here.'

So that was it. He couldn't afford to feed and clothe her. Lewis stood straight. 'Sir, I do not know your daughter.' He thought of Flora, thought of a lie. 'And I might already be engaged to another.'

McNaught nodded, as if he couldn't stop. Then his voice dropped. 'I have been to where Annabel told me it happened.' He eyed Lewis. 'I've seen the body rotting there, almost unnoticeable, covered only by leaves that lift and settle in the wind.' He smacked his lips together. 'I want you to court my daughter with a view to marryin' her.'

Lewis felt wedged in some standstill moment of time, and the crushing pressure of it throbbed in his temples. He held up his hands. 'I'm not sure that is the best—'

'You have a bayonet wound in your left side, Mr Wilshire. You survived the unfortunate … incident, where another, one of the Queen's men, no less, did not.' The gap-toothed grin reappeared. Once again, the smile did not reach McNaught's eyes.

Shooting a look towards the entertainment tent, Lewis stepped closer. 'Will she speak of it?'

McNaught shook his head. 'She is aware of the need for silence in this matter. She knows her good name would be tarnished if she was to speak of it to anyone but me. She'd be blamed—they'd say she lured him there in some way.' The American dropped all pretence of good-natured negotiations. 'You well know, sir, how the law works for women in these matters.'

Lewis stared at McNaught, his mind working.

The older man narrowed his eyes and continued. 'I am sure you would be a gentleman, Mr Wilshire, for though she might be implicated if it came out, it would be you who'd hang for murder.'

The gentleman in Lewis could barely reply. Instead, he said, 'Self-defence would stand. There is talk the government will not prosecute miners.'

'But yours was not a rebel act. It was a long way from the stockade.' McNaught's squint deepened. 'My way is the better way.'

Lewis closed his hands into fists. He heard the painful strains of the fiddles tuning, and raucous laughter—now seemingly aimed at him—belted his ears. Perfume of lavender and of roses assailed him as chattering ladies moved past. Tobacco plumes and the sweet beckoning whiff of rum tempted his senses. And the menace of McNaught, and the havoc he could wreak, devoured him.

He stood, head bowed, breathing hard, thinking harder for some moments. He would not kill again. He *would not* kill McNaught over his threat. No need. Ludicrous—the man just wanted his daughter married. *Be sensible, Lewis …*

While men jostled around him, back-slapping their mates, chortling at jokes, his mind cleared. He looked about for Annabel again. It might not be so bad. A pleasant-looking girl. She seemed to like him, was grateful to him. How bad could it be?

He heard his mother's voice. 'We hope your discussion is finished,' she said, standing alongside him. 'The dance is to begin again.' Her usually pinched face had a small smile, and expectation lit her eyes. She was looking at McNaught.

The girl, Annabel, trailed along behind, delight on her features.

Lewis took one long look at McNaught. Then he nodded to his mother, and gave a bow, merely a movement of his head towards Annabel, a small smile only at his mouth. 'Your father has so kindly allowed me to court you, Miss McNaught, if it so pleases you.'

He missed seeing the thrill in her eyes, the indulgent smile of his mother, and the relief on McNaught's face. The only person he wanted to see now, tonight, was Nell Amberton, and he would find the gold she had hidden.

Twenty-Eight

Nell raised her voice. 'It's too crowded in here, Flora. I'm going outside. I might even return to the camp.'

'Where's our Mr Worrell?' Josie asked, and bobbed her empty pannikin up and down over the jostling revellers heading for the dancing floor. 'He put us here two dances ago.'

'Don't worry yourself, Ma,' Flora answered. She turned to Nell and took her arm. 'You can't go home alone.'

'It's not that far and the moon's out. Besides, there'd be others leaving. I'll be safe enough.'

'The fun's just started,' Josie said, nodding happily at everyone passing her by.

'Nell, wait a while. We'll come too, but I want me mam to have just a bit more time enjoying herself. Don't go on your own.'

Nell squeezed Flora's hand. 'I'll wait,' she said. 'I'll just be by the children's tent, then, getting some air.' A shiver rolled through her. She knew it wasn't fear but anticipation. Still, she reasoned, the bushranger wouldn't seek her out by the children's tent and besides, he was probably gone.

Well-dressed ladies passed her by and ducked into the tent, no doubt checking on infants and toddlers in the care of others. Talk was that the pay for the minders was good, and that those women fortunate enough to attend the ball were happy to pay to have an evening out, their children in safety close by, but not underfoot. It seemed a wonderful idea. As Nell sat outside the tent, around the side away from the main entrance, the squeals and giggles and chatter of little children had died down. The night had worn on, and the children would now be tucked up in their bedding baskets or boxes, sleeping until their parents retrieved them for home.

She closed her eyes, her thoughts rushing at her. For one thing, her father was looking for Andrew's gold. What had he said? Something about his 'silence'. Whatever that might have meant. Andrew had certainly not confided in her about anything owing to her father but why would he?

For another, Lewis and his mother believed Andrew had gold that was rightfully theirs, but she knew it wasn't so. The gold belonged to Andrew's first wife's family, the Seymours. Nell's mind wandered back to Susan's funeral. As far as she was aware, there was only one Seymour family member left. Susan's brother—

'You've got that look on your face, again, Nell. You've gone off in your head somewhere.' Flora pushed a cup of something into her hand. 'Here, I found a pot of Mrs Lark's fruit gin. It's not bad considering what other stuff is hidden in pots around here. Ma says it's real good.' Josie nodded her head but didn't have a cup in her hand.

'You didn't stay in there long. You don't have to keep coming to look after me.'

'It was Ma. Said you needed company in the fresh air.' Flora had hold of Josie who nodded at Nell, at Flora, and with a big smile to anyone who passed by.

'I see. Your ma said?'

Flora surveyed the comings and goings of the folk wandering from tent to tent. 'All right. So it was me. I'm worried, and there's more and more a feeling in there I'm not happy with. But what ails ye?'

'Too crowded by far, like I said. But I was thinking of the Seymours. I was wondering why my father forced me to Susan's funeral. We'd barely known her, or the family. She would bring the family laundry to our tubs, is all. I did know her mother, Mrs Celeste. She was a kind woman. Never met the father, or the brother.'

'True enough about Mrs Celeste. She wrote to that Caroline Chisholm about us emigrant women and children here on the goldfields, wanted to set up a school for us. Never came to anything. No subscribers for it, they said. At least we got the church schools now.' Flora looked at Nell, a frown creasing her brow. 'Why you wondering about the funeral? It's long past.'

Nell sighed and looked at her chafed hands, the skin dry and chapped from the laundry. 'Andrew had known me at our tubs, visiting my father, so he said. They must have made some sort of deal and it came into effect when poor Susan was barely cold in her grave.' She shuddered, wondered if her dead husband's dreadful claws would always remain in her.

'Wouldn'a put it past either of them,' Flora muttered. 'But why do you think that?'

'Andrew made for Pa as the first sod was shovelled back over Susan's coffin.'

Flora snorted. 'I should cross me heart against that sort of evil. But why think of it now? You're supposed be to be having some fun.'

'Aye, lass, fun.' Josie jigged alongside as the band struck another tune.

Nell crinkled her nose, shook her head. 'Something about that day. I watched from a distance, felt I was intruding. There was only one Seymour, the brother back from a war somewhere.

Their father had died while he was absent, and the son's grief was terrible. His whole body shuddered as if in some sort of fit, the poor man, and—' She stopped herself.

Wait. He was here! He was at the dance. It was he who Mr Worrell had been talking to, the man who she'd first thought might have been Peter Lalor until she saw his profile. She thought she'd recognised him—she *had* seen him before. So, perhaps not just his grief had created the terrible shakes, but a war wound, which meant his injured arm had to be encased in the large sling he wore tonight.

Flora, alarmed, glanced left and right around them. 'What is it?'

Nell straightened. 'I have to find Mr Worrell, to have him introduce me to Mr Seymour. He's here. I've seen him.' That way she could assure Susan's brother herself that she would deliver what was rightfully his as soon as she could. Best to put all that bad Andrew business out of her life as quickly as possible. Best to keep the gold as far from her father as possible.

'Why do that? It won't be a good—'

Josie nudged in between them. 'Well, sure. The lad will be happy to see us back in there,' she said, heading for the dance tent and pulling Flora along with her. 'I'll be glad of another jig with all them folk.'

Flora put out her hand as Josie tugged her by. 'Nell?'

'I'm coming.'

Nell strained on her tiptoes to see if Mr Seymour was still inside the tent. Jostled and bumped by the crowds, staggered into by two drunks, frowned at by the ladies into whom she was pushed, she made her way to where she could see Mr Worrell.

Tobacco smoke, spilled ale and rum wafted around her in a stench and she longed for the outdoors again. Josie was dragging

Flora through the throng ahead of her then struck out to the left, pulling her daughter alongside and disappearing behind bobbing heads and jigging bodies.

Nell lost sight of them and tried to follow. And then she came upon Lewis, who was staring down her father. She tried to backtrack, but was bumped hard by someone barrelling through behind her, and she got shoved into Lewis's back. He spun around, eyes watering as he rubbed his side. He stared at her, his breathing laboured.

'Nell,' he said, loud enough for her to hear. 'Your father believes you have something of mine.' Colour flooded his face and his brows furrowed low. 'And I want it.'

Alfred Thomas was equally enraged. He poked a finger at Nell. 'This needs to be dealt with away from all this bloody din,' he grated, the rum on his breath a sickly blast onto her face.

Nell stepped back, pressing hard against the bodies behind her. She thrust her way through the crowd.

'Not so fast, daughter.'

Wrenching out of the grip and at the merest glimpse of Mr Worrell over by the far side of the tent, she shot towards him. He was with Mr Seymour, thank goodness, and she doggedly forced her way forward.

Over the hum and zither of the fiddles, she heard the roared command of her father.

'Nellie Thomas, stop!'

She ducked her head, buried herself in the throng, pushing and shoving. Hoping not only to reach Mr Worrell, but to get out of here, to disappear and leave this place. To get rid of that gold, by any means, and into the hands of any man who would help her remove it from her tent, regardless of her reputation.

Mr Worrell caught her eye as she burst onto the periphery of the dancers. Mr Seymour, his back to her and gripping his own arm, slipped past them, and through the main door.

Flora and Josie were in view as Nell desperately struggled to break free of the crowd and reach them. Josie charged out of Flora's grip, flung herself past Nell and into the dancing, jigging mass. Flora yelled at her mother but held outstretched arms for Nell who pitched forward into them. Mr Worrell charged past, following Josie, elbowing his way behind her.

Flora propelled Nell behind her. 'Run, Nell. Hide somewhere. Come to the camp tomorrow, not tonight.' She thrust away into the crowd.

Hide? Where?

Staring for a moment, Nell saw her father burst out of the horde and stagger to the floor, clutching his groin, gasping for breath.

'Nell, wait!' Lewis roared over the crowd, bursting through before tripping over the prone Alfred Thomas. He landed heavily in a cloud of dust among the stamping, dancing feet. He let out a yell, gripped his side and rolled on the dirt floor.

Guffaws and whistles met her ears as dancers and onlookers pointed and laughed.

Dora came from nowhere to pull at Alfred, trying to get him to his feet.

Enid thrust herself through the crowd and dropped by Lewis's side.

Josie emerged, huffing and puffing, arms akimbo as she fended off the crowding mob. Flora followed behind and grabbed one of her mother's out-flung hands. She tugged her away from the swearing men on the ground and disappeared, Mr Worrell on their heels.

Nell took one look at Lewis struggling to stand with Enid's help, and her father still clutching himself, shaking Dora off. Then she propelled out the main door as fast as her feet could take her.

Twenty-Nine

Nell dashed past the children's tent. *Can't hide in there.* She kept going, down to the shrubs where she'd wandered earlier in the night, giving no thought to the bushranger. All she thought of was escaping her father, and by the looks of things, Lewis as well. After what he'd said to her, clearly her father had already had words with Lewis about the gold.

What to do now? Where to go? She'd fled but had no plan as to where to house herself tonight. Flora had said not to go to the tents, but wouldn't that be safest, where she would be with others if needs arose? Then again, she needed somewhere her father wouldn't find her.

Running into the darkened night, away from the many lamps surrounding the tents, she headed for the township. She wouldn't be far now from Amberton House, but a stitch in her side was beginning to pinch. She didn't want to slow down but had to. She had to.

Making out a hitching rail outside a lone timber dwelling, she slowed down and leaned against it to catch her breath. She looked around. Ducked away from the rail to lean against the house.

Where am I? Where am I?

Amberton House. She should go there. Lewis wouldn't think
to go there, would he? He'd never think of checking there, surely.
There was no longer any furniture, nor any of her possessions still
there.

There were the few rough cast gold bars still in the barrel
wall ... She could fashion a sack out of something, find anything
to carry four or five bars ... How heavy would that be? Too heavy.

Deep breaths. Steady yourself.

She'd have to sleep without bed linens if she stayed at that
house. So? She'd done that before when the house was full of furniture, thanks to her husband. She could do it again. Then, creep
back to the tents tomorrow and face ... what? And how to get the
gold out for Mr Worrell and Mr Seymour?

Yes, yes, sewn into their clothes, but how much time would
she have before either her father or Lewis Wilshire caught up with
her? Not to mention the danger in which she'd put Flora and Mrs
Doyle.

Think on that later. Later. She drew in deep breaths and let them
out. Slid to the ground and sat awhile, taking the time until her
heart rate slowed. She looked about again, couldn't see any life in
the street, couldn't hear anything except the faint strains of the
music from the ball.

Can't sit here all night. On her feet again, she dusted herself off
and peered into the deserted road. Now. Where was she? Oh yes.
She'd gone the long way without realising; she recognised a few
houses, ones she'd passed on errands before her marriage. Flickering candlelight in a couple of homes glowed softly and seemed to
shed a little light on her path as she picked up her direction. After
this corner, Amberton House was only a couple of blocks away.
She knew she had to make a left turn here at the cross road.

Gulping down air, she steadied then maintained a resolute
walk, head down, as she tried to pick out the road under the pale

light of the moon. Thank God it wasn't raining, or cold. Nights in Ballarat in summer might sometimes be relieved by a cool change, but not tonight. All the same, the shivers ran through her as she heard noises of the night all around.

A dog barked then bayed and a chain rattled as it must have lunged against its restraints. Breathless, she rounded the corner. Moving smartly, her steps confident, she was sure the house wasn't too far along now. Had Lewis paid the rent, or any part of it? Would a landlord have boarded up the doors? God almighty, where would she go if she couldn't get in?

Nell slowed. Her steps faltered, and she tried to focus on where she was. She could see a cart and building materials, timber stacked in a neat pile. Thank heavens. The empty site. Amberton House was only a short dash across the paddock now. She almost laughed and put a hand to her chest in relief.

No matter if it was locked up, she would find a way—

A shadow, darker than the night. A figure creeping around the side of the house.

She shrank back but under even the low moonlight she would be seen. She froze, waited until the shadow moved behind the house. Dropping to the ground, she crawled to the cart, for once thankful that she was wearing the black of widow weeds.

Dirt scraped her knees through her skirt as she scrambled on her hands and knees over tufts of prickly grass, sharp twigs, and hard pebbles.

Window shutters rattled in the dead of night. A moment later, a door rattled, then another. Whoever this man was, he was checking the house and finding it well locked.

Crab-like, she crept under the cart's draught poles and inched her way behind the wheel on the far side. Gathering her skirt close, she flattened herself on the ground, peeping between the sturdy spokes of the wheel to see the side of the house.

There it was again, the shadow. Furtive. Stalking from the back of the house to the front, bent forward like a hunter nearing his prey.

Her panting breath roared in her ears. Forcing herself to inhale deep, quiet lungfuls, her mouth drying, Nell watched.

Around he went again, silent as the windless night.

Hearing nothing but the pounding echo of her heartbeat in her ears, she waited. Frustrated at the shake in her hands, she tried to still them. She tried to make herself as small and insignificant as possible behind the cart's wheel, but her cramped limbs were clumsy.

How to escape? To run and not be seen or heard? He had rounded the house again, but what was he looking for?

Inching her way upright, she knelt, bent low to keep her eye on the house. Held tense in fear for so long, her limbs tingled, pins and needles prickled as her blood flowed again.

The roar of a gunshot blasted into the air. Her hands flew up to cover her ears as they split with the noise. The crunch and shatter of wooden shutters, and the tinkle and crash of glass exploded into the night.

She didn't hear the soft glide of footfalls. A gloved hand clamped over her mouth, and a hard arm wrapped around her waist.

Thirty

Flora looked across the flames at Mr Worrell, who sat on a log, holding a pannikin of tea. The night was dense around them, the only noises were Josie's soft snores nearby and the yells and songs of drunken miners further away at a nearby lemonade tent.

'Who'd have thought?' he said, his face creasing in a grin. 'I was about to chase high adventure on the Murray River, but I've found it here, at a Subscriber's Ball in Ballarat Town.'

Flora rolled her tea pannikin in her hands. 'Thank you for walking us back here but there wasn't any need. I'm sure me mam would've fought off a pack of wild troopers tonight.'

He laughed. 'I've no doubt she would have, for you, Miss Doyle. You have to admire a strong woman.'

Flora felt her cheeks warm. 'Well, I should take to my bed.' She looked around at her tents, at the tubs, barely lit by the firelight. 'And you should get going.'

'Are you sure you won't have trouble tonight?'

She shook her head. 'Not sure, but what would either of those men dare do here in the dead of night? Too many others about.' But she remembered the enraged look on Lewis's face as she'd emerged with Josie as they'd flown out of the crowd.

They both sat quietly for a moment.

'Dangerous place for two lone women anyway. Why do you stay?'

'Because I haven't earned enough to leave. Because it's dangerous for a woman anywhere.' She sat up straight, looked around again. 'I told Nell not to come back tonight. I shouldn't have done that. She would've been safe here. Now I worry I frightened her off and I'm wonderin' where she is.' She looked over the lowering flames, the smoke barely visible and wafting away on a gentle breeze. 'Her father was bellowing at her to stop, and he's been here, threatening her. Then there was her nephew, Lewis, right there behind her father tonight, shouting at her.'

Mr Worrell tapped his cup. 'Allow me to stay here this evening, for you and your mother, just for my own peace of mind. Find me some blankets and I'll sleep by the fire. If Mrs Amberton returns in the night, or anyone else comes, I will be here.'

Flora didn't answer. Sipped her tea. 'So what is it her father would want? Is it something to do with why you're here?'

'Well, I—'

'Is it likely to get me and me mam in the way of trouble, Mr Worrell?'

He tilted his head. 'Hard to say. And please, call me Matthew.'

Then Flora heard a gun being loaded and a man stepped up to the firelight.

'Not a word, Flora. Not a sound,' he said and swung around. 'You either, Matthew.'

Thirty-One

Matthew Worrell stood up slowly, warily, his eyes fixed on the figure in front of them.

Flora shot to her feet, glaring across the low flames. 'Ye think I don't know it's you, Lewis, behind that stupid mask.'

Lewis pulled the kerchief from his face. 'I said not a word. Clearly your Gaelic ire makes you deaf though I must say the fire-light makes you look truly fierce.'

She ignored his derision, stood with her hands on her hips. 'What in the name of all things holy do ye think you're doin'?'

Matthew tossed his tea into the fire. 'Is this wise, Lewis?'

Lewis swung to face him, the gun dangling casually from his hand. 'Of course it's not wise. But wisdom won't get me the gold, will it? Force will.'

'There's plenty of gold here. It's a bloody diggings,' Flora snapped. 'You just have to get your hands dirty.'

The revolver came up fast as he cocked it, and waved it at Matthew. 'Such language. I see you are wise enough not to try and tell her to shut up,' Lewis said.

Fear caught in Flora's chest. 'What are you doin'?' she breathed.

His eyes glittered with firelight, and he barked a laugh. 'It seems I'm shortly to be married, dear Flora. So I need to clear some debts, almost all of them incurred by my demented uncle in his debacle of a life. And his gold will ensure that happens.'

Flora's mouth dropped open. 'Married?'

Lewis tossed a glance at Nell's tent. 'Nell? Come out, now,' he called softly.

'She's not here,' Matthew said, his hands by his side, his eyes on Lewis.

'You sure about that?' Holding the gun steady at Matthew, Lewis squatted, picked out a burning stick and tossed it at Nell's tent.

Flora gasped as the canvas lit up. She stared back at Lewis, dumbfounded, horrified. Then frantic, she turned and dashed to her own tent. 'Ma!' she yelled. 'Ma!'

Lewis pulled another burning stick from the fire and straightened up. 'You were telling the truth, Flora,' he called. 'No Nell.' He pointed the gun again at Matthew's empty hands. 'Never a good idea to be on these fields without a weapon.'

Flora was crying, screaming inside the tent. 'Ma!'

'Where is it?' Lewis demanded of Matthew. He waited a beat before he waved the gun impatiently. 'Come on, man, I see you're thinking of a way out of it, but there isn't one. Just tell me where it is, and all this will go away. I know Nell has my uncle's gold. And I want it.'

The stink of burning canvas hung in the air. Fabric smoked then peeled away from itself, dropped from the timber rod and fell over Nell's bedding. Embers landed on her chair and it caught alight. A makeshift little table by her bed began to smoulder.

Matthew wiped his nose with the back of his hand. 'She hasn't told me,' he said quietly, cool-headed. 'I was to come back for lunch tomorrow, here at the laundry.'

Men from further down the camp began to shout they'd bring water, they'd bring blankets, but before they could gain momentum, Nell's tent collapsed, the flames smothering themselves. The little chair and table burned brightly before dying out, the bedding scorched and smoking.

Lewis yelled, 'Stand down, no need for help. It's out.'

The camp site was a known tinderbox. Testy shouts of 'good on yer' and 'watch yerself' faded off as the growling men retreated.

He looked over at Matthew. ''Tis a good thing you haven't moved.' The burning stick twirled in his fingers. Lewis flicked it across to Flora's tent.

It landed short of its target and Matthew bounded over to stomp it out.

'Oh, don't worry,' Lewis said, his voice softly eerie. 'I know our Miss Flora has got her poor old mam out the other side of the tent and they're probably high-tailing it to somewhere they think is safe. A shame they were so worried,' he said and tilted his head. 'I was simply checking that the man they had at their campfire was a good man, not some ragamuffin thief.' He chewed a cheek then said, 'I see all is well here. Pity a spark set off the fire in Nell's tent. Always a problem here in the camp, unguarded flames and all that. Everyone knows it.' He pointed the gun again. 'Be sure to tell Flora that unless I learn of the whereabouts of Nell's gold, and soon, it'll be more than an accidental fire.' Lewis turned to go then turned back. 'And another thing. I wouldn't bother the troopers with this. My standing in the community is so far unblemished, and they'll believe what they're paid to believe.' Then he left, and his shadow melted into the darkness beyond the firelight's reach, and his menace with it.

Matthew let out a breath. Clenched his fists to stop the shakes.

Flora burst out of her tent. 'Are you all right?' She rushed to Matthew, grasped his hands, then dropped them, stepping back.

He nodded. Looked at his hands. 'I'm all right. Not as calm as I'd hoped, but all right.' He stared at her tent. 'Your mother?'

'Could barely rouse her. But I got her up just before I saw the flame under the tent.' She pointed to where the second stick had landed. 'We were ready to run out the other side, like he said, but now he's gone, Ma's back in bed.'

Matthew nodded, listened for the light snores, but couldn't hear anything yet. He felt for the log he'd sat on earlier and slumped to his backside. 'Not something you want to stare down every day.' He rubbed his face hard. 'I'm glad you're safe, Flora.'

She sat beside him. 'And you too, and that you're here.' Her shoulder brushed his. 'And he's getting married. That's a surprise.' She shook her head, stared into the fire. 'He's an odd one. His uncle was mad, insane I would say. But Lewis has a ...' She searched for the word. 'A certain coldness to him. He never hurt me, or anyone else that I know, and he's not a coward like his uncle. But what was he talkin' about, about Nell? I don't understand. Would he have killed one of us just now?'

Matthew wiped his hands rigorously on his trousers. 'Don't know. Glad he didn't.'

'At least that fire's out,' Flora said, pointing to Nell's things, and the glow flickering over two little piles. 'All but done, anyway. Oh, Nellie, Nellie.'

She stood up and Matthew stood with her. They stared across at the ruins of Nell's tent, at the little sparks coming from the remains of the bedding and canvas.

'I wonder where she is,' Flora said, and her hand crept into Matthew's.

Lewis wasn't his best in the dark. But the moon had risen, and he could see well enough. He knew which direction home was in. Behind the row of tents was safe and he took confident steps towards the township, still ever mindful of holes in the ground.

What had he just done? What possessed—

The first missile hit him just above the right eye. He went down on his knees. Before he could bellow, before the pain exploded in his brain, another hit him in the back of his head.

Pitching forward, he saw stars on the ground, somehow. He fell heavily on them, the earth tilted, shuddered, and pain shot into his face.

He wondered if he'd just died.

Thirty-Two

Held tight against a powerful male, unable to make a sound with the hand over her mouth, Nell shook. Terrified by the gunshot and paralysed by the man in whose grip she was, she barely heard the voice.

'Nell, it's your old friend. No noise, now. The night carries the softest whisper.'

The bushranger. Even here. She nodded, and felt the hand loosen and drop away from her mouth.

'I'm going to crawl back in line with the cart so we can't be seen from the house. You need to crawl back with me.'

She turned her face, caught the tickle of the kerchief on her chin, but his cheek was bare. She wanted to look closer—

'Can you do it?'

She nodded, looked away.

'Let's go now while he's occupied inside. But he won't be long.'

A glance back to the house and Nell saw a light flicker to life.

'A candle. That's good.' His voice was close to her ear. 'If we go now, the candlelight will prevent him seeing anything of us. We can run. I'm going to take your hand, and we'll get up and go. All right?'

Nell pushed to her feet behind him, kept low, felt the burn of more pins and needles. He crouched ahead of her, thrust his arm back and her fingers found his hand. They moved off slowly at first, keeping their bodies low. Once on the road, away from the building site, he pushed them into a loping run for a time.

She didn't stumble, didn't hang back, kept up with him until he slowed, and stopped. He pushed open a little gate and as they stepped into a house garden, it swung shut behind them. Up a step, and then inside an unlatched door.

In the hallway, lit by a candle on a narrow table, he locked the door with one hand. He slipped off the kerchief, pressed his mouth against her neck, his hands on her hips, her waist. 'Nell.'

Breathless herself, scared out of her mind for hours, needing the privy, wanting a wash and a drink, she pushed back to see his face, her hands on his chest. As she stared into those green eyes under the auburn brows, they looked back at her with something she couldn't fathom. She took in the empty broadcloth sling hanging from around his neck and under one arm, and dropped her hands, her eyes wide as she recognised him. 'Mr Seymour.'

He rested his head against hers a moment and pulled back. 'I really should introduce myself before accosting a lady. Finneas Seymour, at your service. It would do me a great honour if you were to call me Finn.'

She allowed her gaze to roam over the weathered face. Allowed the beat of her pulse to respond to the decidedly delightful familiarity in his eye.

'Well, Finn,' she said, her throat so dry that her voice wobbled at first. Her chin came up and her mouth was so close to his she could feel a tingle in her lips. 'Please direct me to the outhouse, then to a bowl of water for a wash, and afterwards, to a cup of tea.'

Thirty-Three

Finn leapt from his seat. Nell had knocked on the open parlour door while he was deep in thought. His hand shook as he sat the glass of rum on a table beside him. 'Please, come in,' he said.

Hesitating in the doorway, she clasped her hands in front of her. 'Thank you for the use of your water. I feel much better.' She dropped her hands to brush quickly at her skirt, yet, by the light of the candles in the room, her dark clothes already seemed much less dusty than before.

She passed by his open arm, and the faint tangy scent of his soap on her reached him. 'I'm afraid there are no feminine accessories here for you to be properly refreshed,' he said, and cleared his throat over the catch in his voice.

Her gaze strayed to the mantelpiece and to the two framed pictures on it. 'Though there once might have been,' she said. 'Is that—?'

'My late wife, Louisa.' He crossed the room to the mantel and laid a hand by the frame on the left. 'She's been gone nearly three years ago, now. This house was where we lived.' He took a breath. It was the first time he'd mentioned Louisa as 'late' to another woman. He looked at his wife's face in the picture, and his heart gave two heavy thuds. Then it calmed, and something of the pain in his chest let go. All seemed well, still. All seemed right.

Nell followed his gaze. 'I didn't know her but your home feels as if it would have been a happy one.'

Finn felt his eyes burn. 'Does it? It was.' Taken aback for a moment, he pointed at the next frame. 'And this is my father and mother, John and Celeste Seymour.'

She nodded, studying the likenesses. 'I did know your mother a little. She knew my mother, Cecilia Thomas.'

'I have no recollection of her, unfortunately,' he said. 'Or of you and your family.'

Shaking her head, Nell said, 'Understandable. My mother is dead some years now, my two brothers were born after me, but died a long time ago, as infants. I don't remember them. My father does.' She gave a short laugh, as if she regretted what she'd just said. 'As for meeting you, our paths barely crossed, just once, I think, at your sister's funeral. You wouldn't remember me from that.' She stopped. Looked as if she thought she was talking too much.

'Susan. Susie. Yes.' Finn felt his chest swell with emotion. 'Unfortunately, I have no likeness of her for my mantel.'

'I am so sorry for what happened to her.'

Her words touched a deep chord in him. 'There's no need for you to be sorry for that.'

'I survived what she did not. To be standing here …' Her voice choked off.

He went to her, his hands firm on her arms only for a moment before he dropped them, remembering himself. The bushranger might well put his hands on her, but Finn Seymour was trying to woo her; he had to rein in. Yet in that instant, feeling her warm under his hands, her arms strong and lean, he nearly gave in to grabbing her to his chest, holding her and rocking her in his arms. Instead, he said, 'For you to be standing here is a victory over people like him. Do not be sorry on her account without gratitude for your own.' He stood to one side. 'Please sit with me.'

She took a chair close to where he'd been sitting, and a sigh escaped as she settled back. Her boots were worn, but the dust had been wiped away. Her black skirt fell just shy of the heels as she found some comfort. Her nails were short, and her hands, now folded in her lap, were reddened.

He glanced away, took his seat once again. 'I don't have much food here, a few eggs. I usually eat out. There's not a lot to offer you except tea. And rum.'

She nodded. She'd bundled her hair into place again though wisps had escaped, and a loose tendril dropped along the line of her neck. 'Only some tea, thank you, before I journey home to the camp.'

'I will happily provide the tea, and then the company home,' he said, though he didn't want to let her go too soon. 'But tell me, you were running hard, away from the ball, when I saw you outside the main tent. What had happened?'

Drawing in a breath, she said, 'My father was being his threatening self, and Lewis Wilshire appeared to have cause to fight with him and then with me. I was closed in. I just had to get out of there.' She flattened her hands on her skirt. 'I thought I saw you with Mr Worrell when I left.'

Finn shifted in his seat, murmured a noise. 'I needed some air, myself. You might have noticed I wear a great sling, and why I wear it.' He nodded across to the side table on which the broadcloth was draped.

'I saw you at your sister's funeral. You wore a sling then.'

'Ah. That was a very bad day for many reasons.'

She frowned. 'And then there was some episode at the hold-up but no sling.'

'That episode nearly cost our lives. It's a cursed thing.' He studied his hands. 'I left the ball tonight because of it. Not many have been witness to it when it strikes me. I hope to lessen its impact on others,' he pointed again at the sling, 'although, it's not easily done, if at all. I am sometimes vilified for it.'

Nell waited, her eyes on him. Candidly, patiently, she waited for more from him.

'I was with the British army for a short period of time. Some cousins are in England and I thought to lose myself there with them after Louisa passed away.' He glanced at Nell. Attentive, her blue eyes locked on his. 'We saw a number of engagements prior to what is now the Crimean War. It appears I have some sort of affliction after surviving those skirmishes. The tremors can be debilitating, and frightening, for me as well as for those who see them. It seemed that another episode was about to descend on me at the ball. I left before it did. And when it didn't, and I watched you running by, I followed you.'

He'd told her too much, he knew it. She was too quiet. She'd dropped her gaze, was intent on her hands. She looked away to the mantel. She would think him cowardly, and not fit to—

'It's a wound then,' she said, still looking at the pictures on the mantel.

'Not a physical one.'

She looked back at him. 'And one not yet healed.'

He hadn't thought of it like that. 'Yes. That's possible.'

'I too had wounds.'

Finn took a sudden, deep breath. 'A man who harms a woman ... he's not a man. Had I avenged Susie earlier—'

'I'm glad he's gone,' she blurted, and her chin shook as she gathered herself. 'And so will the memory of him be gone. I have scars, not physical ones either, but scars all the same. Wounds will heal,' she said firmly. 'I'm sure yours will too.'

She'd only glanced at him. His heart swelled as her confidence bolstered him. 'You have strength of mind.'

'I just wanted to survive. I had to,' she said, and fiddled with her skirt. 'So, I was in that surviving part of my mind, not my right mind, at the hold-up.' A bloom of colour crossed her cheeks.

He remembered his own rush of blood the day of the hold-up, the moment she *requested* his help. He felt the blood thicken again and spoke for distraction. 'You had a strategy for survival.'

Her blush remained. She gave a short laugh. 'A polite way of putting it.'

'But it was a strategy. And I fully understood.'

'Surely not.' She shifted in her seat. 'Oh, this is very difficult.'

'Then we need not speak of it again.' He watched her curt nod. 'Except to say that once I recovered from denying your request, I was immensely flattered.' It warmed his heart to see a twitch of a smile from her.

It disappeared when she looked at him, those intense blue eyes on his. 'At the hold-up,' she began, 'you didn't know about the gold, did you?'

Finn shook his head. 'I knew nothing of any gold. I only wanted to kill the man who'd killed my sister and her unborn child and consequently, by way of the grief that inflicted, killed my father.' Emotion spiralled up like a ball of flame in his chest, and a pulse thudded in his neck. He ran a finger along his shirt collar, though it was already loosened.

Nell's eyes squeezed shut a moment. 'I'd never seen the bags before. I didn't know there was gold in the coach until he said so, earlier that morning. I'd no idea it had come from your family.'

'That was new information for me, too. But I will be glad to have it back.'

She looked up sharply. 'You know I wrote to Mr Campbell about returning it?'

'Which is why his cousin, Mr Worrell, is here to act as agent and retrieve it.'

Retreating into silence, she nodded. Her face carried a little frown, and she lifted a shoulder as she thought of something, as she rubbed her fingers.

Hands clasped in front of him, he caught her eye. 'I am only so very glad, now, that I do not have his murder on my hands.'

Nell started to say something and stopped. Started again, but shook her head, looked away.

'Nell.' He held out his hand when she looked back. 'May I take your hand?' She hesitated only a moment before reaching across and slipping hers into his. He held her fingers, unsure until he felt the tension leave her. 'Even though murder was my intention on the day, I'm glad I wasn't able to pull the trigger.' Those blue eyes of hers were clear as she stared at him. A clench in his gut. He wanted to drink her in, or take her under him now, lose himself inside of her, have her writhe on top of him and whisper his name.

'And I'm glad you are not a murderer. But I am glad he's dead.' Nell leaned across and laid her other hand over his. 'Perhaps we should speak no more of him, now. It sours the evening.' Before his pulse could thunder around his body, she inched forward. 'I don't suppose we could make some tea?'

Thirty-Four

Nell's mouth had dried, probably from thirst, or worry, and now nerves, because she'd just begged for a drink after boldly gripping his hand.

'Tea.' Finn barked a laugh. 'Of course. I'm remiss.' He pointed out the back, one hand still holding hers, hard calluses rough on her palm. 'I'll fire up the cooker—'

'I'll come with you.' She followed him outside, letting her fingers fall from his. It left her feeling a little bereft. She wondered if she should slip her hand back into his ... No. That would be like a desperate woman, needing a man. She puffed out a breath.

Finn picked up a candle from the shelf at the back door and led her outside and into a room devoid of furniture except for two chairs and a small, square table by the stove. The candle flickered, strengthened, and light glowed when he placed it on the table. Indicating she take the chair, he turned to stoke the cooking fire. He tested the kettle for water, set it on the stove then took down the teapot from the mantel.

Nell looked around. The room was sturdy, large timbers exposed, and the space big enough for more furniture but there was nothing, not even a cupboard.

He caught her frown. 'I lived in here when I was building the rest of the house. There was a bed there,' he said pointing to one side by the far wall. 'Was plenty for me at the time.'

'You built this house?'

'I did. I wasn't a wealthy man because my father had insisted I make my own money. So I went and found work. Any work. Blacksmithing, shoe-smithing, labouring on other farms. Anything to avoid his merchandise business. Finally got enough to build this place, small as it is. But I was about to be married, so ...' He let his voice trail off as he reached for the tea caddy and pried off the lid with a spoon from the mantel.

The words shouldn't have unsettled her. As she heard them, a sadness crept in. He was a widower who had clearly loved his wife. He had worked hard to put a roof over their heads and done it without help like most others who might have had some privilege.

Watching him swill hot water into the pot, toss it into a bowl on the hearth, measure the tea leaves, she wondered what Louisa's life had been like with him. She stopped herself as the heat rose over her neck. Of course, the heat would be from the stove, and from the kettle now popping its lid as it began to boil.

He looked at her once as he poured steaming water into the teapot. That flutter tripped inside her again. She should make conversation. Should talk about something, anything, but the silence seemed somehow comfortable, and it lengthened. Two people were about to share a pot of tea. That was comfortable. But these two people had already shared some strange experiences. Some dangerous, heart-pumping experiences.

The kettle set aside, he pulled two tin cups from the mantel and poured lightly steeped tea in each. 'I prefer it weak when there's no milk. I hope that's all right for you. Please, sit there.' He indicated the chair at one end of the table.

Aroma from the steaming pannikin reached her. She took the cup and blew into it. No other words would come. She blew again, tried to sip but the tea was still too hot.

He dragged out the other chair to sit near her. 'Here I am talking about tea.'

'Yes?' Her heart thumped. She stared at his mouth, his nose, eyes. The stubble of auburn beard once again on his jaw. She wanted to touch the line of his dark rusty coloured brows. Finn Seymour. The bushranger.

'Tea. As if the extraordinary events of these last months have not occurred.' He lifted a shoulder, as if to say there should be more to it. He leaned an arm on the table, his eyes on hers.

She could sip her tea at last, and though hot, it allayed her thirst. 'A mark of normalcy, I suppose. I'm not usually a risk-taker, but after the events of tonight, I seem to have properly acquired the necessity.' Sipping again, she felt her throat ease. Blew some more and was able to take a swallow. She sighed her enjoyment of it, and her stomach thrilled as she caught his gaze.

'I would like to relieve you of that necessity, madam,' he said, inclining his head, a small smile lighting his features. 'However, it would be just plain Finn Seymour at your service. I advise that the bushranger has retired.'

'Oh. A pity.' There was sharp dismay that the bushranger would no longer appear. Yet, instead she had the real man here, and a man who seemed genuine. Who *was* genuine. She knew she wanted him the way a woman should want a man, to be giving and affectionate. She knew he wanted her, too. To have her and hold her and love her. And he protected her, looked out for her. *Deep breath, Nell.* Her glance was tentative, but she knew that what she was about to say was not. Hoping her hands wouldn't shake, she kept a grip on her cup and said, 'The bushranger was such a gentleman. I would miss him.' At her own daring words, she sipped more tea and watched for his reaction.

He snorted. 'If you'll pardon me, he was a damn fool. He is gone.' His fingers tapped the table as if marking the bushranger's demise final.

She set her cup down. He'd missed it. Completely. 'Well, Finn Seymour, if you'll pardon me, I meant I should like the damn fool back. I had become very fond of him and do not have a care to be without.' She held her breath and stood up. *Bold, bold, bold, Nell. You are running away with yourself again.*

I don't care. I don't care.

He shot to his feet, reached across and pulled her to him, his eyes glinting, the auburn hair rakish in the candlelight. 'He might not be the gentleman bushranger this time.'

Her heart leapt. 'I will take my chances.' She loosened a hand and her fingers brushed his mouth. Whiskers tickled as she found the soft flesh of his lips. 'I have long wondered what that would feel like.' She trailed fingertips over his cheeks to smooth his brows. 'And what that would feel like. And this.' She ran both hands through his hair.

He took her wrists. Eyes bored into hers. 'Nell.'

She felt the hard swell of his penis against her. Warmth curled through her belly and she knew she would take her chances tonight. She knew that whatever happened afterwards, she would be all right.

'Nell,' he breathed. 'You have been hurt by the worst—'

'I choose to leave that behind me,' she cried. Her hands shook in his. 'I will not be afraid to live my life because of it. But if I falter,' she said, staring into those beautiful eyes, 'it will not be because of this.'

His mouth came down on hers, held her there a moment before he kissed her neck, scraped his jaw along her nape. 'Perhaps the kitchen another time,' he ground out, 'but tonight, to my bed. The bushranger still has his manners.' He took up the candle, tugged her back to the house. Setting the light on his dresser inside his room, he let go of her, only for a moment, waiting.

In a heartbeat, she came to him, her mouth to his, breasts pushed hard to his chest. His hands grabbed fistfuls of her skirt. Fingers gathered the fabric until he could slip his hands underneath. He toyed with the cotton of her drawers. Her belly tensed, her hands clung to his shoulders before sliding to the hem of his shirt.

He took it off himself then lifted her, hands under her backside. Turning, his thighs quivered and bunched as he lowered to sit on the bed. Astride his lap, waves of pleasure cascaded through her as he flicked open the buttons on his flies. Every movement sent tingling little pulses between her legs, made her breathless against him.

I never thought this *is how it would feel ...*

He stopped, withdrew his hands and began the task of opening the buttons on her jacket. He kissed her, quick and hard, his fingers working on the small buttons, and then the soft, smooth fabric fell open over her chemise.

His lips pressed on her neck, on the swell of her breasts. Her hands cradled his face and she dipped to meet his mouth. A warm callused hand slid under her chemise along her ribcage and found a nipple. Shivers of delight feathered over her as a finger stroked, and the pulse between her legs became urgent.

He pulled the loose ribbon and brushed open her chemise, cupped a breast and sucked. Her pulse hummed, and her cry stopped him. He looked at her to check then smiled, sucked again, and again she cried out.

He lay her on the bed, shucked his trousers, fell alongside her. Pushing up her skirt, he let a finger glide between her legs where it was sleek and hot. She reached up to take his shoulders as sudden wave after wave of pleasure rolled through. She sank, in wonder, wanting more, needing more. He knelt over her and slipped his penis, warm, hard, and insistent, inside and his body leisurely rocked her. Urgent now, he lifted her hip and thrust deeper, swelled, and drove harder. Then he buried his face in the curve of her neck, tensed, and let himself go.

He sank on her, settled his weight on her, and she waited, happy and awe-filled. When his breathing returned to normal, he rose up unsteadily on one arm. Kissed her nose and her mouth and fell back to the bed. 'Nell, my Nell. The bushranger has surrendered.'

They lay, naked now, under the covers. A candle flickered on either side of his bed. Her head rested on his shoulder, and her fingers splayed over the wiry dark hair on his chest. Strange that it wasn't all the same colour as the hair on his head or of his beard stubble. Her hand travelled down the line of hair, over his belly button, into the tight coils of his pubic hair, and inched back up again.

'And so, Ben and I travel to Melbourne periodically to pick up more supplies. Perhaps only two more times before this winter sets in. Each trip takes about two weeks, all being well, and we go in a few days' time. I miss you already.' He turned to glide a languorous kiss on her.

Nell burrowed deeper alongside him. Her hair, spilled from her pins, fell forward on his chest. The contrast of her blonde locks against his dark and sometimes fiery copper tones fascinated her.

'Then we go onto the fields with a laden cart,' he continued.

'And what about the store? Do you not trade out of there?' Her fingers twirled on his chest, scooted softly to the thatch of hair under one arm.

'Ah. The store. My father's legacy. Not something I ever wanted,' he said flatly, and tucked an arm behind his head.

She said nothing, just continued a lazy whirl over the band of his ribs and flat stomach.

'In any case, I'd already scheduled a visit to the fields for tomorrow. Apparently, all my laundry must come with me, too,' he said, and laughed a little.

She kissed his chest and murmured, 'I intended to sew the nuggets into every garment you and Mr Worrell own. I brought it in my own hems, very piecemeal.'

'That's how you brought it in?' He shook his head. 'Hiding gold in a goldfield. Ingenious.'

'There are four more bars still at Amberton House, where I was going last night. I'm not sure how to get them, now.'

'Where are they?'

'I'd loosened a few rocks in the stand under the water barrel, on the south side. They're in behind.'

He was quiet for a moment. 'Perhaps I can get them. No suspicion would be aroused if I turned up in full daylight to inspect a new purchase.'

Nell raised her head, alarmed. 'You wouldn't buy the place?' she asked. 'It should be razed to the ground.'

'I wouldn't buy it.' He reached over to toy with her hair as it fell over her face. 'But if anyone questioned me, that's what I would tell them.' He stroked her arm. 'Don't worry. I can get them.' He hugged her. 'And after that, when these last two trips to Melbourne are done, I can move on to other things. Perhaps,' he started, 'you'd like to take that journey with me.'

She wriggled, wanting to keep her voice calm. 'I had hoped to make a living for myself.'

'As a merchant's wife you could make a living in the business. You would be invaluable.'

She stared at him. 'Wife, is it?' she asked, stunned.

'Of course. How could I let some other man have you by his side?'

He was offering marriage … She didn't want to think on that now. Didn't want to think what other thing the night of heady love-making might bring to her, either, but she might have to. She snuggled deeper. 'I know plenty of women work their own businesses on the fields,' she said. 'Laundry is not exactly what I would choose, again, I have to say. I should find something else.'

'Women do work their own businesses. But outside the diggings, do they, so much? I'm thinking I—we—might like to live in Bendigo. There seems to be more civilisation there; get out of Ballarat and its race for gold at all costs.'

'By all accounts it is different from here, more town living than goldfields.' Idly, she wondered what she could do there.

'I had wanted to build boats for the Murray at Goolwa in South Australia, but I doubt my current aversion to loud noise would tolerate it.' He held up the arm she rested on and pretended a tremor. 'Land has also been opened up north of here on the river. A place called Echuca. It might be good to invest there.'

'Perhaps I could teach somewhere, after all,' Nell mused, then she sighed and moved against him.

'Why? There are teachers hereabouts already. Besides, I detect your heart is not in it.'

'It's something I could do, I suppose, other than sewing, or baking. Or laundry.'

Finn said, 'I have a suspicion you could turn your hand at whatever you chose.'

Nell remained silent. Perhaps she would widen her scope and find something she'd be happy doing. Perhaps it could be working with Finn. Still, a woman had to be careful what she attempted. Too much had happened to her to believe hard work and expectations alone would make all things right.

Finn was thinking far ahead of her, far ahead of where they were now. He was right to offer marriage, but as she'd said to Lewis—it seemed so long ago now—she had to be allowed to administer her own finances. Would *any* husband agree to it? Did she risk losing someone like Finn Seymour if he wouldn't agree? She would have to study that thought at length.

Another time. For now, he'd turned on his side, his face in her hair, and his strong arms wrapped around her. His velvety smooth erection nudged her bare leg.

Thirty-Five

The sun had risen minutes before, and dawn was streaking golden light over the pitted earth. Ahead, the miners were stirring from their tents after a night's rest.

'People might talk,' he said.

Nell shrugged. She sat alongside Finn on the hastily laden cart as it bounced and swayed over the road. 'I don't care if they do. None of them cared about speaking up before. Besides, it could be that you simply gave me a seat on your cart from a friend's house.'

He cast her a sidelong glance, tugged on the reins and the cart horses turned into the fields. 'I wonder where Mr Worrell got to last night. I'd offered him lodgings.'

'Perhaps he escorted Flora and Mrs Doyle home.' She knew she sounded distant, but it was for the best. She'd woken up feeling she'd moved too fast. Despite the glorious night she'd spent in his bed, she was unsure. Of herself. It had niggled at her through her sleep.

Finn glanced at her again. 'You won't be going back to the Wilshires for anything, will you?'

Nell shook her head. 'I'm finished with them. If there's anything I need, I will buy it.' She looked across at him, and her heart warmed. 'Especially as I wondered if it was Lewis at Amberton House last night.'

'You're not safe, Nell, not with Lewis angry, along with your father. I'd have a word with them, but I suspect it wouldn't help.'

'No. It wouldn't.' His interference on her behalf would only madden things. 'Once this gold is out of my hands, there's no need for me to feel unsafe.' She gave him a small smile then stared ahead as something caught her eye. Leaning forward in the cart, she squinted up the hill.

Shouted greetings reached them as miners, slipping braces onto their shoulders, headed away from their tents and straight for his cart. The horses reined in and Finn leaned across to her. 'This lot won't take long to sell off. Ben's on his way, so I'll be up at the laundry soon.'

She stepped out of the cart, not waiting for him to help, and stared at Flora's laundry site, her eyes blinking in the glaring morning light.

'What is it?' Finn asked, following her gaze. A group of men had arrived and were pulling tools from the cart, weighing them up. 'Nell?'

She grabbed her skirt and started to run. She stumbled, righted herself, heard Finn call out, ran on. The closer she got, the clearer the situation became.

Her tent was gone. The tubs were empty, the fires out. Mrs Doyle was perched on her tree stump, sewing. Flora, arms folded, kicked the dirt at her feet. She could see Mr Worrell on his haunches trying to coax the fire to light.

She couldn't see anything of her tent. 'Flora,' she called. 'What happened?'

Flora spun around. Mr Worrell stood immediately.

Nell flung herself over the last few yards of dirt and stopped, dry-mouthed, as she saw the pile of blackened, burned canvas.

'Was there an accident? Is everyone all right?' She scanned all three faces.

Josie rocked back and forth. 'We're all right, lass. We're all right.' Her fingers darted over her lad's shirt, the needle flashing.

'And good morning to ye, Nell.' Flora dusted off her bloomers, a couple of back-and-forth slaps.

'Flora. I ran and ran from the ball. I got to Amberton House and—'

'Lewis came.' Flora was frowning at her feet, scuffing the dirt again. 'This is his work.'

'Lewis did this?' Nell spun to Mr Worrell. 'Lewis Wilshire?' He nodded.

'Threatened us with a gun,' said Flora. 'Threatened to burn my tent down too, and Ma with it.'

The blood drained from Nell's face.

Flora flung out a hand. 'What have you got here, Nell, that he would threaten us?'

A glance at Mr Worrell and Nell knew he hadn't said anything. Her good friends had been put at risk. She threw her head back and let out a yell of frustration, of rage, and stomped over to the remains of her tent.

'He said he'd be back for it, or else,' Flora said, alarmed, and coming close to raising her voice a little.

Nell kicked over the frame of the chair and it collapsed in a puff of white soot and ash. Her cot and its bedding were nothing but shapes at her feet, recognisable only by the pattern on a remnant of the old patchworked quilt she used. Her booted foot thrashed out at it.

Flora came closer, her voice now low. 'Nell, I need to talk—'

Matthew reached her. 'Mrs Amberton, let me help you.'

Nell toed the chamber pot, gave it a good foot and it sailed up in the air before exploding into bits of charred porcelain. She dug her heel into the hollow of the dirt that had been underneath it, then fell to her knees, scraping at the hole. Grabbing a piece of lightly scorched bed-frame timber, she scooped the dirt out of the hollow.

'*Bloody* gold. Bloody, bloody gold,' she muttered through her teeth as she hacked at areas of the hollow that had hardened. 'All this trouble for the sake of it. As if there's not plenty of gold for everyone. I will unearth this lot,' she scratched harder, 'and fling it back,' as she dug deeper, 'to where it came from,' she ground out. 'Blast you to hell and damnation.'

Flora tried again. 'Nell, what are you doin'?' She bobbed down beside her.

'It's *under* here. What Lewis wanted. It's under *here*. It belongs to the Seymour family, but Lewis wants it.' Nell kept shovelling furiously.

Mr Worrell hunkered down beside her. 'Mrs Amberton, let me dig.' He pulled the scoop from Nell's bleeding fingers and began to scrape.

Flora took Nell's arm firmly, helped her stand then dabbed at her scraped fingers with her pinny. 'You brought gold *in* to the diggings?'

'I'm not mad,' Nell grated and brushed out of Flora's grip. 'Where else could I hide it? Where else would no one think to look?' She squeezed her hands together, tried to stem blood flowing from a finger. 'Someone was even at my old house last night, sneaking around. If it wasn't for—'

Josie chuckled by the fire. 'All them hems. All them hems.'

Flora glanced at her mother then stared at Nell. 'In the *hems?*'

Nell nodded. 'And that's how I was going to get it out again.'

'With my help,' Mr Worrell said, brushing dirt off a tin box, still partially covered in the shallow hole. 'And Mr Seymour's, in our newly washed and mended laundry.' He flicked a look at Flora. 'It was to ensure you and Mrs Doyle were never in danger. We just hadn't counted on Lewis coming here. I'm sorry for that.'

Nell stared as more of the box was uncovered. Then she looked around her, checking for anyone watching. 'And where did Lewis go?' she asked, her mouth a tight line, her foot tapping.

'Left. As cocky as only he can be,' Flora derided. 'If I ever see him on a dark night again—'

'No need for that now, lassie, no need for that now.' Josie rocked over her rag.

Flora went to her, laid a gentle hand on her shoulder. ''Course not, Ma, it's all right.'

'It's all right,' Josie repeated. 'It's all right.'

Mr Worrell opened the tin from the hole in the ground. He whistled low.

Nell peered inside. There, nestled in the quiet space, dull, clean and snug, lay the nuggets, innocent in their neatly packed state. Probably less than half the five thousand pounds' worth, she was sure, and it all belonged to Finn Seymour. The rest he would retrieve from Amberton House himself.

She looked over her shoulder and down the hill. Mr Steele had just arrived on horseback where the men were purchasing tools. After a short conversation, Finn hauled a bag off the cart, tied it onto Ben's horse, mounted and made his way up.

Run run run.

She wanted to pick up the nuggets, one by one, and hurl them down the hill. Instead, she took in a deep breath, tried to calm the anger boiling within, swallow down the panic.

Andrew. Lewis. Gold. Pa. Bushranger.

Nell looked around her, wanting to see a solution. She wanted it over and done with. It was impossible now to get the heavy box out of the ground without attracting attention. The gold would have to stay where it was. Finn had dismounted and was striding towards her, the bulky bag of laundry on his back.

Shouts of concern for the burned tent reached her ears. Flora fended off anyone coming too close, saying that all was well, and that the laundry would fire up soon, that Sunday lunch would be late. She darted a glance at Nell as Finn approached.

Nell's eyes widened, not at Finn, but at the troopers who made their way towards them on horseback, behind him. Miners stepped out of their way, some waving fists at the troopers, others miming shooting them once the mounted police had passed them by. Her blood ran cold.

Thirty-Six

Finn glanced over his shoulder to see the troopers. They must have followed him up from his cart. He looked back at Matthew, who indicated with a tilt of his head that he should go to a spot behind where Nell was standing.

She had stared past him, as had Miss Doyle and Matthew. Mrs Doyle kept her seat by the fire, muttering as she stitched.

So Finn trudged over and passed Nell. She glanced as he dropped his bag of laundry over the hole in the ground, and on top of the tin box. He smiled broadly, jauntily at her. 'My laundry, ma'am. You said it would be returned to me—'

'As you can see, Mr Seymour,' Flora snapped, and stood with her hands on her hips, angling towards the troopers. 'There was a fire here last night. Destroyed one of our tents. The laundry is not yet open. Will have to be another day before it's done.'

Finn turned to Flora, his smile widening. 'Ah, Miss Doyle, if I remember correctly? I haven't availed myself of your laundry for some months. I'm sorry to see there's been some bad luck. I hope all is well?'

Flora cleared her throat. 'Well enough,' she grumbled, deferring politely.

281

'If the trouble has delayed your service, the next day will suit. I will certainly manage until then.' As the two troopers reined in, Finn turned to them, his hands flexing. 'Good morning. Is it another license *hunt*, already, gentlemen?' He pulled a paper from a waistcoat pocket, unfolded it and held it out.

Flora marched into her tent and produced her own license paper, brandished it, even though the troopers made no attempt to check it, or to dismount.

Matthew held up his hands. 'I'm a visitor.'

A trooper, both hands bandaged, sat at an awkward angle in the saddle, hugging the reins. He leaned forward. 'No license *check*. There's been a complaint.'

'I'm sure there's been plenty,' said Finn.

The troopers had their eyes on Flora.

'Complaint? About my laundry?' she asked of them. 'What is it—some weak-kneed down-and-out miner hasn't got his trousers back and he's sent in the police?'

The injured trooper focused on her. 'A gent'man said he was accosted here last night.'

The other looked around. His uniform was smudged, poorly patched, and Finn could smell both the men from where he stood.

'What gentleman?' Flora asked. 'Me ma and me were back here, late, after the Subscription Ball. No gentleman was here except for Mr Worrell. He walked us safe home.'

The troopers looked at Matthew. 'And still here, I see,' the first trooper said. 'At dawn. *Miss*.'

Flora burned red.

Matthew winked at her as he turned to the troopers. 'I certainly made no complaint, sirs,' he said.

The trooper rolled his eyes. 'The *complainin'* gent'man said he was minding his own business after being in these parts when he was throwed stones at.'

The other trooper struggled to keep down a chortle.

Finn watched as Matthew frowned slightly as if trying to remember something. Flora blinked at her mother. Nell stood, hands on hips.

Josie rocked a little back and forth at the fire. Chattered softly. 'I must be cookin' for the bairns, Missus McGinty. I must be darnin' their smocks fer Sund'y best.' Josie's chatter was barely audible, a lyrical noise as she discussed housework with her imaginary friend.

The trooper went on. 'Got hisself a right shiner, all closed up and bloody. Might lose it, he told us. And got hisself a nasty lump on the back of his head. Seems he copped one as he was comin', and another as he was goin'. Bedridden, he is. His mother says he's right not well. Some Chinamen got him to the hospital tent afore he crawled all the way there hisself.'

Nell's brows drew together in a dark frown. 'Does it look like we throw stones at our customers?' she asked, archly. 'Which of us ladies—'

Hand-bandage pointed at Flora. 'Miss 'ere has a good aim with the slingshot, I heard.'

Flora's mouth dropped open. 'I just said we'd come back from the ball. I wasn't aiming any slingshots in the dark.'

Matthew made a coughing noise. 'If I might approach you, sirs.' He stepped up to the horses. He looked around and then beckoned Hand-bandage who leaned down to hear. 'I will attest that Miss Doyle never left my company last night.'

Flora's face bloomed a deeper red, but she held her tongue. Josie's lyric chatter in the background kept up in the otherwise eerie silence.

The trooper shifted in the saddle, and his glare moved around the tent sites. 'How'd the fire happen here?'

'Me ma got confused. Took to cookin' in the tent 'stead of out here.'

Everyone looked at the mad woman chattering quietly, rocking by the fire.

'Should be locked up afore she kills ever'body. Place will explode in a fireball,' the other trooper said. He lifted his chin at Hand-bandage. 'Let's go.' They turned their horses and ambled back the way they'd come.

Miners lined the way along the creek until they were well past, then the jeering began, a few rocks thrown. The troopers kicked their horses into a trot.

'Ma,' Flora started and went to kneel by her mother.

''Tis all right, now.' Josie settled herself more comfortably and continued with the lad's shirt.

Flora let out a breath and stared at her mother. 'Ma, did you get out of the tent after Lewis left last night?'

'Felled him with the first,' Josie said and mimed her manoeuvre. 'Hit him afore he hit the ground with the second.' Flicking her hand in the air, she completed the move. She sniffed and looked at her daughter. 'Lookin' after me lass.'

Finn looked surprised. 'She uses a slingshot?'

Flora bit her lip. 'It's a deadly aim, she has, better than me, still,' she said quietly. 'She wouldn'a missed, especially with the good moon last night.' She turned away, wrung her hands. 'But she might yet have killed him.'

'Won't have killed 'im, weren't goin' t' kill him.' Josie said softly. 'Gentle tap on the brow, is all. Always looks a sight worse at first.'

Finn gave a slight bow to Flora. 'Remind me to be very careful when in your company, Miss Doyle. Would you introduce me to your mother?'

'My mother, Mrs Josie Doyle. Ma, this is Mr Seymour.'

He turned to the older woman. 'A pleasure, Mrs Doyle. I am Finneas Seymour.'

'I saw ye at the dance.' Josie nodded at him.

'You did, indeed.'

'I see yer arm is mended.' She pointed.

He gave a small smile. 'Sometimes it is mended.'

Matthew walked behind Nell and looked at the bag of laundry sat on top of the tin of nuggets. 'Thought you said you didn't have much laundry,' he said to Finn, who shrugged. 'Now, for getting the tin box out of that hole.'

Finn said, 'Help me load up a barrow, and push it back up here. We can exchange goods, so to speak. None will be the wiser.'

'I don't need picks and pans,' Flora said quickly.

'But buckets, and a rake or two. Maybe some stools for sitting by the fire.' Finn looked at Nell. 'I could even bring another tent, and the makings for a cot. I'll be back in a few minutes.'

Flora darted a glance at Matthew, who nodded and followed Finn down to the cart.

Nell wondered, dumbfounded, how easily the men thought the gold could be moved.

Looking anywhere but at Nell, Flora said, 'Not getting anything done standin' around. Would ye tend to the billy and start on the taties for the lunch?'

'I'll get changed first, but why are we still doing lunch?' Nell asked as she headed for Flora's tent.

Once inside, she heard Flora reply, 'To look normal, and be carryin' on the business as usual.'

By the time Nell changed out of her widow weeds, pulled on the bloomers and apron, and gathered enough potatoes from Flora's stores, the men had returned.

In less than fifteen minutes the gold retrieval was done. Flora had flapped sheets and swept ash and moved boxes and the empty wash tubs as cover for the activity, all the while the two men were emptying the barrow and had hauled and loaded the tin of gold into it.

Finn tipped his hat in a mock salute at Nell. She only nodded, and looked away. 'Mr Worrell,' she called. 'You will have a receipt for me?'

'I will,' he said, coming closer to keep his voice down. 'I am to write the specifics regarding the transaction before we leave here with it.' He pulled out an envelope from his pocket. 'If someone has a pen and some ink? I seem to have forgotten to bring them with me.'

'I have. I use nib pen and ink for my ledger,' Flora said.

'Of course you would.' Matthew smiled at her.

Satisfied, Nell began to drag the tubs over the fire pits. She snatched up a bucket nearby, and then another.

Flora called out. 'Nell, no need for that now. We're not—'

Nell marched to the creek for water, a large pail in each hand.

Finn caught her up. 'The laundry looks like it could use the barrow, too,' he said, and tried to take a bucket from her. 'Fill the buckets, load them into a barrow. Easier than carrying them. I'll supply you one.'

'I'll buy one. It's a good suggestion.' She kept walking.

At the creek, he took a bucket and scooped up the water. 'How many of these?'

'Eight to begin. Each tub.'

'Eight?'

'Washing needs a lot of water, and water is scarce.' She dipped the other bucket into the dirty water.

'Nell, stop a moment.'

She looked back at the laundry. No one was taking the slightest notice of them. Matthew was helping Flora, and they laughed at something together.

Last night. What she'd taken for herself was not hers, much as it had been wonderful. Her bushranger had disappeared on a breeze and in his place was a real man, one whose life had been much different to hers. One who had known a good love, one who deserved a great love. Not someone who had been damaged by an ugly marriage, not someone who had thrown herself at him, and not once, but twice.

She shook her addled head. What had she said? That her wounds would heal properly. She wasn't so sure now. Decisions she'd made were bad ones. She'd hidden the gold on the fields and had endangered friends who were dear to her. Then she'd decided to—*dared* to—give herself to Finn. She shouldn't have trusted herself there, either. Shouldn't trust herself now.

'You have your gold. I have fulfilled my promise to Mr Campbell. I think it's best left as it is.' Her heartbeat boomed in her ears and this felt wrong, too, but too much was happening, too much to take in all at once. She'd brought destruction here; that was the only thing she knew for sure.

He frowned at her. 'Nell.' He lifted a hand towards her, but let it drop. 'I'm not about to leave this as it is.'

'You are a rich man now.'

'I wouldn't be a rich man if you weren't honest and true. All would have been lost to this …' He waved a hand around, 'this end-of-the-earth place. But I don't want to lose the chance we have because of it.'

She stared up and felt the tempting tug of his gaze.

'In a few days,' he began, 'after I have the gold from the Amberton House, I'll have the lot assayed. I will go to Melbourne for stores, for more tools. The trip will be long enough if all goes well.' He bent to catch her eyes. 'But time will go more quickly if I know I'll see you again on my return.' He went on, while her only reaction was to glance away. 'With the gold, I need not continue as a merchant here. But I have stock orders that will fill two more trips, and I can't leave Ben to do it alone. Then I can be free of the diggings, free of sudden gunshots and deaths and corruption.

I can go where I choose, try to find a peaceful place, with someone I love. Don't let fear guide you now,' he said earnestly. He
touched her hand, caught her eye. 'Come with me.'

'I will have to think about it. But not now.' She started to
march the two buckets of water back up to the laundry until Finn
caught up and took them from her.

Nell watched as Finn climbed into the driver's seat of the cart
alongside Mr Steele at the bottom of the hill. He picked up the
reins, took one glance back at her, then turned the horses. The
cart pulled away.

Matthew had walked down with him, starting up a conversation with Mr Steele as they'd loaded the spare implements and
had hauled the tin box aboard. Handshakes were exchanged, they
seemed as friends, and he'd waved them away as the cart moved
off the fields.

Flora stood beside her, watching the cart leave. 'He's a good
man, that Mr Seymour. He always was nice. Cut above all those
others what come onto the fields, those that aren't diggers. Don't
speak down to anyone, if you know what I mean. And now
he's got plenty of gold again too. Wished he'd have left all that
laundry.'

Flora's sidelong glance seemed odd. The cooking fires crackled
behind. Nell's heart was a lump, pumping hard, but she kept her
voice steady. 'We'll be busy enough as it is. I'm glad to be working,' she said, her chest feeling tight. 'At least I'll be able to buy a
new tent, and a new cot. Mr Seymour said he'd have one of each
sent up before he leaves for Melbourne. Means I can still get on
with the laundry, Flora. Still work here.'

'Nell,' Flora took a deep breath, 'I don't want you here.'

Stunned, Nell couldn't move her head. 'What?'

'You brought trouble. I know you didn't mean to, but you did. Lewis, on a rampage. Your father before him, and we don't know what he's goin' to do.' She rounded on Nell. 'Me mam could be up for murder if Lewis dies—'

'No one knows who attacked him. What Josie said, her mind—'

'Don't, Nell.' Flora frowned. 'I'm sorry for ye, I am. But I can't risk my mam. I can't.' She waved Matthew away as he started up the hill. He veered to talk to a group of miners by the creek. 'We stayed up talkin' all last night, me and him.'

Nell's heart was beating so hard she felt faint. No place to live, no work, no money. She'd sent Finn away without an answer. In a woolly-headed daze she heard Flora go on.

'Mr Worrell says he can find me and mam lodgings in Bendigo. He said he could pay me for ledger work, that I might find more work there with him and his lawyer cousin, or maybe I could work with a business family, on Mr Campbell's recommendation.'

Nell stared at her.

Flora chewed her lip. 'Might have to move quick because of what's happened, but I don't know when or how, yet. I've a bit put by, and I can sell off some of this.' She lifted her shoulders. 'I've thought about it. I like it.' She looked at Nell. 'I like him. Very much.'

Nodding, Nell turned back to look down the slope, saw the back end of Finn's cart slip around a corner and disappear. 'Then I'm glad for you, Flora,' she heard herself say.

''Course, Mr Fancy-pants Seymour seemed to take a shine to you, couldn't take his eyes off ye,' Flora continued as if she hadn't heard. 'So I thought maybe he should help you out. Mr Worrell says there's more gold in that tin box than Mr Seymour knows. Seems your husband was hiding away lots of nuggets from who knows where.' She dug in her pinny pocket. 'Before they'd come back with the barrow, I took a souvenir for you.'

In her hand sat a drawstring canvas bag and as Flora folded it down, Nell could see six good nuggets through the opening, small, snug in her palm. Flora cupped her other hand underneath to hold them.

'Wouldn't that be stealing?' Nell's voice trailed off. She didn't want that on her conscience too. The morning sun beat down on her head and neck. Another sweltering day was on the march.

'Not if they were Andrew's. And who's to know?' Flora dropped the nuggets into Nell's pinafore pocket. 'Don't be stupid,' she said as Nell tried to stop her. 'You know what this much gold can mean for you. You'll find lodgings with it, for a start. You have to go, Nell, now. Today. And don't come back. Too risky after last night.'

Nell couldn't grab hold of anything to make sense of it. Flora stood quietly beside her a moment before sighing, and trudging back to the laundry. Nell followed and began to look for any possessions she might still have that weren't burned to ashen dust. She bent to kiss Josie's warm forehead and hug her tightly. The old woman's grip on her wrist was a tug at her heart that nearly undid her.

From Flora's tent, she gathered up her widow's blacks, retrieved the promissory notes, then once outside, pitched the clothes onto the fire pit. She watched a moment until they caught alight.

'I hope I did enough potatoes,' she said to Flora, and glanced at the heavy pans as they waited to go onto the coals. The vegetables were coated in glistening lard, warmed by the heat of the fire.

'Nell, you understand. I have to look after me and me mam.'
She nodded. 'I do.'

She walked down the hill, her heart heavy, her pocket heavy. Where to go? What to do?

Survive. She heard her own words from a day that seemed oh-so-long ago—*I will do everything I can to survive.*

Finn set his mouth, itching to click the reins and get going, but Matthew was still talking to him.

'By a quick reckoning, and only on the feel of it in my hand, I'd say there's much more than a few hundred pounds worth in that box. Once you get the bars, Mrs Amberton's got you your inheritance and then some.'

Earlier, Finn had told Matthew where the rough cast was hidden. 'The rest would be hers, then,' he grunted. 'I'll get it back to her.'

'Once it's assayed properly, of course,' Matthew advised. He stood back as Finn made to turn the cart. 'I have copies of the receipts for Joseph. Is there anything else I can do for you?'

Finn shook his head. 'Do you need lodgings tonight?' he asked.

'I'll sleep by the fire again here, then in the early hours I'll move the ladies into town. Miss Doyle wants to stay a while longer, but I feel the urgency to move as soon and as quietly as possible.' He looked across to Ben, who waited in the cart beside Finn. 'I'll take you up on that offer of your spare cart, Mr Steele.'

Ben nodded. 'A fine thing, Mr Worrell. I'll make it as comfortable as possible in the back. You'll have to sleep on the road somewhere, but you'll be in Bendigo in good time. Your word is good, I know you'll pay me.'

'I will mail a banker's note as soon as I am back at my work.'

Finn said, 'Ben and I will load up and go to Melbourne tonight. I'll visit Joseph when I return after the last buying trip.' He held out a hand and Matthew gripped it. 'Thank you.'

Matthew hesitated. 'I know we were successful, but it somehow doesn't feel like it,' he said.

'It's a strange thing, a hollow victory. Till next time, Matthew.'

The cart pulled away and they drove to Ben's stables where they would divest it of its excess implements and conceal the tin box.

Finn would drive to Amberton House and take the gold bars from their hiding place and then prepare for the trip to Melbourne.

Ben sat alongside, silent until now. He looked across at Finn. 'Reckon you've got a reason, but why are we in such a hurry to leave tonight?'

Finn wiped a hand over his mouth. He thought of soft blonde hair, bright blue eyes and a determined frown on a beautiful face. 'To stop me doing something I might regret.'

Ben gave him a long look. 'And that tells me all I need to know.'

Finn wanted to march back to the laundry, put his case to Nell again, make damn sure she knew what he wanted, no mistake. But he'd regret it. She'd said she'd think about it, and she needed to do it without any added pressure from him.

Ben was waiting.

'I'm thinking of marrying again,' Finn said.

'All right, I think I understand the connection—marryin', regrettin'.'

'Not what I meant.'

'So, let me keep guessin'.' Despite Finn's look, Ben carried on. 'Yer only *thinking* about marryin'.'

Finn flicked the reins, kept quiet.

'And I reckon I might know who the lucky lady is. I didn't know you were courtin'.'

A brief glance at Ben, and Finn said, 'Not yet. But I hope to.' Then his mouth set.

'It's Mrs Amberton, isn't it?' Ben said. 'She was up at Miss Doyle's laundry just before.' A curt nod from Finn and Ben tsk-tsked. 'She know you're that dashed bushranger chappie?' He grinned and slapped his thigh as he caught a glare, and another nod from Finn. 'Hah! Yer sweet on her and ye dunno if she'll say yes. That's what's up yer nose, isn't it?'

Finn turned the cart down Ben's street, Steele and Son's shed ahead. 'I'll be thinking on what to do while we're gone.' He looked across. 'Pray we don't have rain either way. Can't afford the money nor the time to be bogged.'

Thirty-Seven

As she walked, Nell put everything from her mind but the next step. And the one after that, until she had reached Mrs Willey's store on Bakery Hill.

Hot, thirsty, and not a little worried for herself, she stepped inside to peruse the goods for sale. A sensible dress was what she needed, or two, and a blouse and skirt—*if* she could find so ordinary a thing, such was the splendour of the merchandise on offer in this shop. New boots and new underclothing would be required. That would see the first promissory note taken care of. She headed for the tables and the racks to choose her garments.

When she took her selections and laid them on the counter, the shop assistant looked at the note Nell handed her. 'What is this?' the woman said, eyebrows arched.

'It is a note for credits, I believe,' Nell said evenly, though her stomach fluttered. 'My late husband must have returned some goods, and this is the receipt.'

'Just a moment.' After a glance up and down at Nell's bloomers and her pinafore, the woman disappeared behind a curtain, the note in her hand.

Voices low and urgent reached Nell's ears and again, flutters waved in her stomach. The urge to run was strong, but she had no reason to do so. She touched the envelope and checked the other note inside. At least if there was something wrong with the first one, the second one should be perfectly fine.

A pleasantly dressed woman, older than Nell, came out from behind the curtain. Her demeanour was anything but pleasant, and Nell was struck by the anger in her voice.

'Where did you get this?' The paper was scrunched in her hand in front of Nell's face.

'It was in my husband's possession, and now he has died, I am in need to redeem the credit.' She flustered a moment. 'But if there is something wrong with that one, I have another here in—'

'These have been stolen from this store, and fraudulent credits have been written on them, Mrs ...?'

Stolen. Nell shook her head in shock. 'I am so sorry. I had no idea. Please, take the other one. If it is indeed stolen, I cannot abide to have it on my person.'

The other was snatched from her, read quickly, and the angry set of the woman's mouth returned. 'I've a mind to have the police come and speak to you.'

Nell backed up, her hands, palms out, in front of her. 'I had no idea,' she repeated, shaken. 'I mean no trouble. He is dead. There'll be no trouble.'

'And just who was he, this dead husband of yours?'

Flinching, Nell just shook her head. 'A most terrible man.' She turned and fled the store, her heart in her mouth as her feet pounded back down the way she'd come.

There were many other stores, but none she had notes for, none from where she could easily exchange gold for goods. That would be too suspicious, especially if the women at Mrs Willey's store alerted others. She'd got past the first merchant by exchanging the tiny nugget for bed linens and the chamber pot, but that must have been just luck.

Damn Andrew. Damn him, damn him, damn him to hell. Her head rang with the thud of her pulse.

Too nervous for tears, too worried for her next hour, day, week, Nell kept her feet flying. The nuggets weighed heavily on her, bouncing in her pinny pocket as her hand kept it closed. Even trying to exchange them would bring the law down on her. No bank would open an account for a woman. No honest merchant would take this amount of gold from her—widowed or otherwise—and exchange it for notes, and no dishonest one would leave her any.

She stopped by a horse trough, leaned on it to catch her breath. It was no temptation for her, even though her mouth was dry. She was craving water. Clean water. There was only one place she knew she could get herself a drink at no cost and no notoriety— a long cool draught of water—and that was from the barrel at Amberton House.

People looked at her in her bloomers, at her flushed and sweaty face, prompting a tut-tut from some of the ladies. Once her breathing was steadier, she brushed herself down and headed in the direction of her previous abode.

It was around midday, and broad daylight—surely it would be perfectly safe there now?

As she rounded the corner, Amberton House came into view, sitting smugly in between the two empty lots. The builder's cart and supplies seemed to be untouched to the right of it, and there wasn't a sign of life on the other side. She looked back over her shoulder in the direction she thought she'd taken with Finn Seymour, back to his house. How many times had she passed his house and not known who lived there? Coming this way, she didn't have to pass it, but going to the township and not the camp, she was so close.

She had to shake off that thought. Staring at the dwelling, her
fate now in her own hands, she straightened up and walked resolutely around to the back door of the house. Sure enough, a window had been smashed. No one had been back to board it up. And
goodness knows what might be in there, having taken up residence
the night before. She peered in, but nothing seemed amiss.

The barrel at the back of the house was a welcome sight. She
opened the lid, dipped her hand for the bucket, dropped it and
hauled back a pail of water. Scooping one-handed, she slurped a
drink, splashed a little over her face and neck. What she wouldn't
give now for another bath. She looked around, assuring herself
she was alone.

A bright patch of yellow caught her eye. *Oh.* The golden wattle
was in bloom again.

Courage.

Midday. Finn leapt from the cart and waved Ben off to the general
store to secure an order to take for wholesale purchases. He strode
into the Bank of Victoria. Though it had been robbed in October
just after he'd returned, it was still the best place to park the many
gold nuggets.

He produced Mrs Amberton's receipt for it, and Joseph Campbell's letter of its provenance, and once the manager was satisfied,
requested the clerk assist him to bring the bags inside from the cart.
The manager said that it should be received behind closed doors,
but Finn couldn't wait for the bank to close. He wanted it locked
down, in the vault and safe, now. He wasn't coming back to do it.

Watching as the manager and the clerk wrangled the bags
inside, the warning sensation in Finn's arm surprised him. He
pressed it to his side, scrawled a signature on the bank's ledger and
uttered an apology to the manager for having to hurry.

The walls of the bank wavered in front of his eyes. He had to get outside. He pushed through the door, and the shots in his head, which he knew weren't real, rang loud enough to shatter his eardrums. Enough time to get around the other side of the cart, he slumped against the wheel of the cart, and wave after wave of tremors hit him. His boots scuffed the dirt as he tried desperately to stay upright against the wheel.

Distant shouts reached him, but he couldn't discern the words. He slipped further down the wheel, and from under the cart saw the nervous stomps of the horses' hooves as his shudders rocked the cart.

Shouts again, and this time Ben slid to his side, grappled him into a sitting position, fists in Finn's shirt front. 'I got you sat straight, Finn. Just take them deep breaths.'

An hour later at Steele and Sons, Ben pushed the pannikin of tea at Finn. 'Bad, this one. What happened?'

Finn shook his head and flexed his hand before he took the cup. 'Seems to be gone now,' he said. Leaning over the rough-hewn bench that served as a table, he blew into the tea.

Ben sat in an old chair and hooked an arm over the back of it. 'Don't reckon you should be goin' anywhere for a while.'

'Have to. We're right down on all the tools and got orders up to here.' Finn tapped his forehead. 'Need to get stock back here fast.'

'Bollocks. You need to get into your pa's store fast. You haven't looked at a damn thing in it since you came back. You dunno what's in there. And you nearly knocked yourself out this time,' Ben said, his voice hardened. Finn remained silent, flexing both hands. 'Look, you got most of that gold back. You told me Wilshire is out of action for a while, so take a break. Hire a couple of lads for me to take to Melbourne and you sit here awhile.'

'It's my business to look after.' Frustrated, groggy in the head from the episode at the bank, Finn couldn't trust his body to look after him, much less look after his business.

Ben pointed at him. 'You have one of them bad turns on the road and you might just leap off the cart and kill yourself. Or the cart might roll over you.'

'You had the brake on today, like always.' Finn studied his hands. Steady. Why was his head woolly?

Ben snorted. 'I say you don't go. Not tonight, anyway. Leave it a day or two.'

Finn lifted his chin. 'Might be right.' He took a swallow of tea, black tar, the way Ben liked it. Grimacing, he reached for the rum and splashed a little into the cup.

Ben held out his pannikin. 'Always better with rum.'

They heard a shout from outside. Matthew Worrell ducked into the shed. 'Afternoon.' He held up a pint pot. 'Got some lemonade.'

'Better step inside then,' Ben said. 'What flavour lemonade?'

Matthew pulled a cut log around to sit at the table. 'The rum flavour. The whisky flavour didn't taste very good.'

'Only a pint pot?' said Ben.

'I have work to do later,' Matthew answered. 'Thought you did too.'

Finn rubbed his face, knuckled his eyes and rolled his shoulders. 'What brings you this way so early in the afternoon?'

'Two things. First, I came looking for company other than the laundress and her mother. Was putting my case forward about leaving tonight, and I met with some staunch resistance. A little bit of distance for an hour or two might work in my favour.'

'And the other laundress? What does she say about you moving her friends away?' Finn believed Nell would take over the laundry. He was glad to know where she would be when he returned.

Matthew dropped his chin. 'That's the second thing. Mrs Amberton was asked to leave the laundry, Finn,' he said. 'For everyone's sake, hers included.'

Finn sat still a moment then palmed his hands flat on the table. 'And did she leave?' At Matthew's nod, he barked, 'Where did she go?'

Ben turned to stare at Finn. 'Mrs Amberton was asked to leave?'

Matthew answered Finn. 'I don't know. She left the camp altogether. I don't believe she said anything to Flora—Miss Doyle—about where she was going.'

'I thought they were friends,' Finn growled into his tea, thinking hard.

'Miss Doyle's protective of her mother. And she seemed to think you care for Mrs Amberton, if you'll pardon me for saying, so I was to tell you what had transpired.' He waited a beat.

Finn nodded, wiped a hand over his mouth. 'No idea where she went?'

Matthew shook his head. 'None.'

Ben scratched a brow. 'Only place I know would be Amberton House. And why not? It's empty still, far as I know. Maybe she'd go there ...' He looked at Finn. 'A man needs to go look, just in case. An' yer would regret this, if yer didn't go.'

Finn agreed. 'Aye.' He got to his feet, glanced between the two younger men at the table and pointed at the grog bottle. 'Don't drink all of that.' He steadied himself against the table as the room swayed in front of him.

'Whoa, Finn. Wait up,' Ben said and shot around, bear-hugged him from behind, under the armpits. 'Sit. Gather yourself.'

Matthew thrust up out of his chair. 'What is it?'

Ben had Finn back in the chair. 'Gets the turns or something. Came back from the war with it.'

Matthew, agape, said to Finn, 'You've had another attack?' When Finn shot him a look, he inclined his head and shrugged. 'Joseph made me aware.'

'Yeah, he had an attack,' Ben answered, terse and low. He slopped more tea and then rum from Matthew's pint into Finn's cup. 'He's all right, now.'

'You need a doctor?' Matthew asked. 'I'll go for someone if you direct me—'

Finn shook his head. 'They'll want me in an asylum,' he wheezed.

'He don't need no doctor, just some sleep.' Ben shoved the pannikin under Finn's nose and waited until he took a drink. 'You need bed, mate, more'n you need to be gallivantin' around after some woman and the rest of your gold.'

'I'll just take a minute.' Finn's hands clasped under his chin. The room had stopped swaying, and some of the sick feeling in his guts disappeared with it. This was the worst he'd felt so far. He couldn't get a grip on it, on what was happening. When he was right in the thick of extreme danger or if he was on the periphery, he could never be sure he wouldn't shake like an earthquake. *What was it?* 'I need to get my sling.'

'Let's do that.' Ben nodded. 'I'll drive you to your place. But we'll leave off the trip to Melbourne for a couple of days.' He stood up and went to the cart, the horses still harnessed from the morning. 'Ready when you are.'

'I'm coming too,' Matthew said.

Finn stood, taking care. 'All right,' he said to Matthew. 'But afterwards, accompany Ben from my place to the laundry. If Miss Doyle is worried about undue attention, you should be there. Ben can help if needs be.'

'Fine with me,' Ben said. 'But if Wilshire is laid up, who's Miss Doyle worried about?'

Matthew looked at Finn, who said, 'Nell's father. Alfred Thomas.'

At Finn's house, once he had the kettle on the kitchen cooker, and water heating for a wash, he said it was time for Ben and Matthew to leave.

After he assured both of them that he was indeed capable of tying his own sling and sitting in his own chair all by himself, they left him. Not without reminding him where they'd be if he needed them.

Fat lot of good they'd be if he did need them. The walk up the hill was at least half an hour for a fit man. But Finn wasn't intending to need anybody.

He rummaged in one of the camphor chests Louisa had used for storage and pulled out a sailcloth bag, a thin rope as its drawstring. Once his sling was strapped, he pushed the bag into the sling, donned his hat and took to the street on foot.

Amberton House was not far. If Nell was there, he would once again try to entice her away. If she wasn't there, he would prise the gold from the wall anyway, and add it to the vault in the bank. Then he would move on and set about to look for her.

Thirty-Eight

Nell was hungry. That was the pain in her belly. Hunger. She sobbed a laugh. A pinny pocket full of gold, atop a rock wall with thousands of pounds worth of hidden gold in it, and no food in her stomach.

Right now, she'd happily part with a little of the gold, risking capture, to get her hands on some eggs, or some ham. When had she last eaten? She couldn't think when.

Giddy with hunger, she took up another scoop of water. Perhaps she would take the smallest nugget to that merchant who'd changed the button of gold for her. She'd argued about the rate of exchange until she got a more satisfactory one. He'd remember her. Where had she put her license? That would have been in her tent, all burned, thanks to Lewis. Would she need to show it? She'd have to do something quickly. Wouldn't survive here without funds, food. Shelter. Safe shelter.

Finn Seymour. Had she just made another stupid decision?

Slumped on the wall, her head hanging, she hadn't heard the horse's approach until the voice from a few feet away grated on her nerves.

'Wondered if I'd find ye here, after all, Nellie Thomas.'

She squeezed her eyes shut as she recognised her father's voice. 'Did you, now?'

'Aye. But you look a little poorly. Bit like I'm feelin'. Don't mind that I don't get off me horse. I'm a little tender after a right boot in me nethers at the ball last night. 'Twas that mad old woman laundress.'

Nell nearly laughed. 'Could have been anyone wanting to kick you.'

He hissed in a pained breath. 'Ye test me patience, girl.' He looked grey in the face, his clothes crumpled and thick with dust as if he'd slept in the dirt.

She looked up. 'You're despised six ways to Sunday.'

'And I've just as many friends, Nell Thomas, a number of them troopers. What does yer smart mouth say to that?'

Nell looked away and shook her head. 'The gold is back with its rightful owner. All nice and legal. Whatever agreement you had with Andrew Amberton, it's moot. You've lost.' The gnawing in her stomach made her feel sick. She wanted to retch. Instead, she scooped another mouthful of water and as she bent sideways, her foot scuffed a rock in the wall. It dropped to the ground.

Her breath hitched as she straightened, not daring to look down. She put her foot on the rock, brushed at her skirt. Glanced. Oh God. A gold bar was exposed. She shuffled over a few inches, her dress covering it.

'Oh, I know there's no more gold in the house. I had a look in here last night to be sure, once I could stand up proper-like and walk again.'

Nell couldn't feel sorry even for him, her own father. The thought of Josie's kick …

'So, unless you have another gold nugget hidey-hole for me, it looks like I need to find yer another husband.' He leaned towards her, eyes wide.

Though his menace and his threat chilled her blood, she gave a short laugh. 'I think you've lost your mind believing you'll ever be able to do that again. Your last choice was detestable, nigh on a murderer—'

'Murderer. Bloody rot, girl. A strong man—'

'—Without making mention of any of the other idlers you tried on me before that.'

'Ah,' he sneered. 'Nigh on thirty thousand people here, most of them menfolk, good strappin' lads and none of them was any good enough for yer, was they?'

Nell stared. 'Is that why I got sold to the man *with the money*? Because I refused all the drunks and the no-hopers around our camp you brought to look me over? Half of them had deserted their wives and families. Sound familiar, does it, Pa?'

Alfred shifted in the saddle, carefully.

'You can't force me now,' she said. 'I'm a grown woman. I'm a widow. I'm independent.'

He scratched his ear. 'That so? Heard your tent at the laundry burned down. Went up to see. Sure enough. Gone. Abandoned. So, I put a stake on it. Both yours and yer friend's.' He pulled a paper from his pocket and waved it at her. A license, perhaps. 'Just in case you might've buried something there.'

You're too late. She aimed a scowl at him, nonetheless.

'Independent now, are ye?' He wiped his nose on the back of his hand, stuffed the paper back into his waistcoat. 'How you gonna keep yourself now Andrew's gold is gone?'

What else had he heard, if he'd already heard so much?

'It was never Andrew's gold, and you know it,' she accused. 'You were both as bad as the other.'

'And like I said afore, Nell, I know you. You got some of it somewhere and it were owed to me.'

Nell felt a wave of dizziness hit her. The afternoon sun, no food, and talking to her father. It was enough to send any poor body dizzy. But she couldn't stand up and go for the shelter of the house without risking the gleam of the rough cast at her feet catching his eye.

'You ailin', girl?'

She glanced at his squinting face. Her stomach rolled again. 'Just go. There's nothing for you here.'

He straightened up. 'What ails ye? Ye're still me daughter. Ye can't be gettin' sick, now.'

'No, a sick money-making bag won't help you, will it? But if you get off that horse,' she said, as he made a move to dismount, 'so help me God, I'll find the strength to get off my deathbed to kick you myself.'

Nell heard the rumble of affront as he righted himself in the saddle. 'Kick yer own father, would yer?'

'Well, I haven't got a gun to shoot you.' She doubled up again. 'Now, get away from here. Bad enough I'm at this hell-hole of a house. Don't need you as well.' She began to retch.

Alfred reeled the horse about, his voice rough. 'What is it, girl?'

'A contagion,' she rasped, hoping he'd ride off, scared witless.

He slid off his mount and came a little closer. 'Nell. Nellie.'

'Get away from me,' she cried, with an eye on him. 'A contagion, you could fall ill, too—'

He backed up. 'I'll get help. I'll bring Dora—'

'Just leave, and don't come back.' Nell slumped, and rested clumsily on an elbow, mindful of her foot covering the gold bar. Under half-closed eyelids she watched him.

Alfred hauled himself up onto his horse, and said to someone else she couldn't see, 'Get away from here. She has a contagion. My God, could be the plague.' And he rode off at a gallop.

Nell opened her eyes and there stood Finn Seymour, his arm in the sling, shock on his face. She pushed upright. 'So. That's my father. He rides off leaving his deathly ill daughter in the hands of a bushranger.' She waved a hand in his direction. 'I am quite fine except for an attack of the giddies. The heat and hunger, I think.' She turned and scooped another handful of water. She lifted her foot and pointed at the rock. 'There is gold bar number one.'

He barked a laugh, relieved. 'Plague I can't do much about. Hunger I can fix if you can hold on for a little longer.' He came closer, extended his hand. 'Gold can wait a moment. There's shade over by that wattle. May I help you there?'

She glanced at the disappearing dust cloud behind her father's horse. Taking Finn's hand as he helped her stand, she walked light-headed alongside him to the yellow flowering wattle where he settled her in its shade. 'All the bars are easy to find,' she said. 'The rocks are loose but hurry in case he really does get help.' The sweat broke out on her brow again.

'You doubt a father's concern?' Finn withdrew the sailcloth bag from his sling.

'I doubt his, completely.'

She watched as Finn knelt by the wall and picked at loose rocks until another four gold bars were found. He studied them as they lay lined up in the dirt, then he lifted them into the bag. Standing, he shrugged the drawstring over his shoulder and came back to the wattle for her.

He held out his hand. 'A one-armed man, an ailing woman, a bag of gold and a stroll in the summer heat. We're not mad,' he said. 'Come on, we'll go to my home.'

A stroll it was, mostly in silence except for the obligatory chat about weather and health. They stopped once or twice as Nell tried to ward off the dizziness and when at Finn's house, he directed her to a chair in the parlour. An open door and window allowed a faint breeze inside. After slipping out of the sling, he divested himself of the bag of gold bars, and knelt on the floor to load them into a camphor trunk.

'You seem to be always rescuing me,' she said. 'I feel at odds with that, though I am grateful.'

'It's not gratitude I want. I care for you, Nell.' He reached over and touched her hand. 'I don't want you to withdraw from what we started. There's no need, if you want the same as I do.' Unable to find words at that moment, she watched as he got to his feet. 'Tea first,' he said. 'And I have boiled eggs ready to eat.' He called over his shoulder as he headed for the kitchen. 'Until I go to the stores, it's the only food in the house to keep me going. Bachelors don't cook overly much.'

Settling back in her chair, she closed her eyes a moment. Survival had propelled her off the fields; yet her own actions confused her. How could she survive on her own, and thrive as a woman? It would be nigh on impossible to have a decent life. Of course, she knew it must have happened for others, but she couldn't think for a moment of anyone she knew who had such a life.

Finn returned some long minutes later, with three shelled eggs on a plate, and a pannikin of tea. 'Eat. Starvation is not uncommon on the fields.' He set the tea on the table beside her.

She nodded her thanks. 'I didn't mean to starve. I just forgot to take something to eat.' Her heart raced, and her head hurt at the temples. 'I should be eating in the kitchen, not in this room.' It seemed to be getting smaller around her.

'You are not a servant, Nell. And there are no society matrons to frown on us.' He held the plate up to her. She took an egg, tore it in half and ate. 'As for where you eat, that's up to you. Treat this house as yours. Stay here.' He paused. 'With me.'

Unsure exactly what that meant, she said, 'You have to go to Melbourne for trade.'

He lifted a shoulder. 'You could stay here if you prefer, or come, as my wife. Whatever you choose.'

Nell flushed. 'We would not be married by the time you needed to leave.'

'Ah, but we would marry as soon as we're able,' he said.

Nell pushed the plate away only to have him push it back again. 'We have not known each other long,' she began, a shake in her throat.

'Marry me. Or do you think I am some sort of ruffian who would not offer marriage after what has passed between us?' He shook his head. 'More importantly, I'm happy for it.'

She snatched a breath. 'I know nothing of you—'

'Nell, you do.' He looked perplexed.

'—and you were intent on killing a man. You might even be such a man as him.' At his stunned look, she cried, 'I don't know, I don't know, my judgement is so impaired. I don't know what to trust. I know I'm afraid and I tried not be.' She heard her voice shrill and shake and run away with words that tumbled over one another. Her heartbeat was a thunder in her ears and she clapped her hands over them. She heard Flora's words about him echo in her ears. *He's a good man* ...

'Afraid? I have never seen fear in you.' His voice was steely, eyes intent on hers.

'I am afraid,' she said, angry and hot. 'The consequence of being married to that ... thing, and I fear I can't think straight, I fear that it's always my fault, that somehow I despoil everything I touch because I must be so terrible a person, and not worthy—' She stopped, hearing her own words, though not her words. *Andrew's words.* She wondered in horror if she had truly finally gone mad after all.

Finn reached for her hands, but she snatched them away. 'Nell, you are not any of those things. You are brave, and you are strong.'

He waited a moment, as if measuring his words. 'I am not such a man as Andrew Amberton, if he could be called a man,' he said, his voice low, soft. 'I never would be or could be. Yes, I'd intended to kill him because he was the murderer of my family.' He looked at his hands and the slight shake there. 'And just so you know, if ever you, or any member of my family to come, were being threatened, I would kill, and kill again to protect those I loved.'

She stared at him, then at the mantel, at Louisa's serene smile at her from the photograph.

'I have an uncertain future thanks to my journey onto the continent. It might prevent me from earning an income later. I have no way of knowing.' He looked up, his green eyes bloodshot. 'I might be a difficult man at times. Stubborn. I might yell when I argue, I might not always confer when I should.' He took a breath. 'But I would never harm you. I would always protect you. I am not anything like the abomination that was Andrew Amberton.'

The quiet, contained, measured words thrummed over her. Panic still hovered, and she struggled. And yet … And yet … She wanted this good man. She wanted the life he offered.

Finn cleared his throat. 'We have not known each other long, I agree. And we find today, now, that there is much about the other that we don't know. But do you not feel the warmth between us, Nell? I do. Do you not feel something deep down inside that is real, and solid, and demands the chance to grow?'

She tried speaking again, her voice was shaky still, and her mind clutched at deflection, at excuses. 'I am penniless, besides.'

'And what has that to do with it? In any case, you have a pocket full of nuggets.' He pointed at them then reached over and tapped the plate. 'Eat more.'

She reached for another egg, took a bite, chewed and swallowed. 'Those nuggets—Flora took them out of the tin box, gave them to me before you shifted it with Mr Worrell.'

Finn seemed to think about that, then unbelievably, he shrugged. 'I see.' His eyes were still on her but there was no judgement, or accusation. Only what appeared to be mild amusement.

Taking a deep breath, she said, 'I have nothing to bring to you. I have come from a terrible marriage and I—' She stopped to choose her words. 'My father is a scoundrel bent on corruption in every situation he finds himself. I grew up with that. My husband … I don't know if I have the strength in my mind to begin again. I would question my every action, I would wonder about my every word.' She clamped a hand over her mouth, then dropped it again. 'I want it, I just don't know if I can do it.'

He said nothing for a few moments. 'I believed you when you said you'd had to survive. You are a survivor. You said you had wounds and that they would heal. They will heal. You and I will not lead the life of your past, we will never revisit it. You need never be afraid of it. Or of me, or the consequences of anything you might do and say.'

She sat listening, her hands clenching, releasing.

Finn leaned forward. 'My wife, Louisa … we were lucky we had a good marriage. A safe marriage. I was a good husband. She was a good wife.' His look at her was candid. 'But I need more. I want to be closer, I want the trust and the love of it. I want those things from you, with you, and I want more. Good things, wonderful things, laughter, love. Life. Passion just at the touch of your hand when I see you at the end of my working day.'

Nell bent her head as her heart squeezed. Her eyes met his again. 'I've not known those things, in life, or in a marriage. Only despair. My mother despaired, I know. Perhaps even my father despaired, maybe that's why he's like he is. And I was afraid in my marriage, and I was afraid my mind was going, too. I fought despair.'

'Ours won't ever be that. I have light in me again because you're in my life. God knows, we should grasp the chance to live it well.' He bent over her hands and kissed them. 'I already feel love. It's at the start of its journey, I know. Nonetheless, it's there for me ...' He hesitated. 'I don't have flowery words, Nell.'

A hard thump of her pulse sent a fierce heat to her face. It was true, what he spoke of. She wanted the same. Her fear was great, but her hunger for it was greater. 'You don't need flowery words. You are right,' she said. 'Love has started its journey.' Heat bloomed in her cheeks and burned, but the roof didn't fall in, nor did the floor disappear underfoot. 'Perhaps if we just let a good thing happen.'

His chest expanded. He stared at her reddened hands, his fingers pressing hers tightly. 'You need do no more work at the laundry tubs,' he said quietly.

Oh no! 'But I'm used to work,' she cried, and tightened her fingers under his. 'I want to work, to earn my own money, never be at the mercy of someone else, and never beholden. I cannot risk being left destitute. It is not negotiable for me.'

'Then choose some other work, Nell. I'm not against it, but if you didn't take a job, ever, you would never be at my mercy,' he said earnestly. 'And I would protect you by law, as a husband, if something happened to me.' He gave a deprecating laugh and let go of her hands. 'I'm assuming you'll marry me. And then if you do, you don't need to do laundry.'

She let a beat pass. 'None?' she asked, a brow raised.

Finn stopped short. 'Oh. Well, I already use a laundry service or two. I should continue to do so, and you should too. You need not do laundry.' He shifted in his seat. 'You said you might teach. Look at that for later perhaps, if you feel you want to. There's bound to be a national school here sometime in the future.' He let out a breath. 'My sister and I learned to read and write from my mother. She would read to other children, scratch their letters in the dirt when there was no paper to be bought, no pen to be found.'

'And my mother taught me.' Nell thought of her mother, whose married life would not have been easy. Suddenly Nell wondered what her mother had been like as a person, an individual. Her thoughts quietened. She gave his hands a small squeeze and let go. 'Teaching is not really for me and I would rather not return to laundry. Though little presents itself outside of service work, I will look for something else.'

Finn's gaze was intent on her. 'You said your mother's name was Cecilia. My mother's name was Celeste. Has a ring to it, doesn't it? Cecilia and Celeste. Names that sisters would have,' he said.

Children.

Nell breathed deeply and felt the thump-thump of her heart-beat again and the rush of heat to her cheeks. This new feeling was unsettling. Her hands refused to stay still while she mulled it over. She reached over, split the next egg, ate half, then sipped from the tea cup he'd put on the table for her.

He still leaned towards her. 'You want to work, I heard you. What else do you want, Nell?'

Those kind, green eyes were intelligent, intense. He offered her things she never thought would come to her, things that would make her heart sing like it had with him the night before, things that would take her breath away.

'I want to take a chance, but I don't want to fail.' Words rushed out of her. 'I don't know what a happy life looks like, or what it's meant to be, but I want it. I want to make a happy life, with you. I'll make mistakes. I might be fearful, or too forthright. I'll argue my point. I might not—' She brushed her hands down her pinafore. He reached over, took her hands again and linked his fingers with hers. 'You might have to have patience,' she said.

His grip was strong. 'We will have to have patience for each other.'

Her thoughts ran on. 'It would be unconventional, it would be going against what most people do, if I work while I am married.'

'What of it? The bushranger and his bride have been nothing but unconventional so far,' he said. 'I am not afraid of it and there are many here already who are unconventional. The diggers' wives who work, for instance. I even know one or two who keep their own purse.' He squeezed her fingers. 'I've been thinking. I should like it very much if you were working, by my side, in Seymour's Implements and Merchandise.'

It would be a good job. Respectable. 'I know nothing of that sort of work.' She would come to him with an open mind and an open heart, but she had to be sure of her future, of herself. 'I will think on it.'

'For wages,' he said, and his eyebrows waggled.

She laughed then. 'You charm me, sir. Perhaps it would suit me well.'

'Your sudden smile charms me, Nell, and there should be more of your laughter.' He bent to her fingers and kissed them. 'We will work on that.'

Finn slipped out in the late afternoon. He brought home a cut of mutton, potatoes, some ham and fresh tomatoes he'd bought from a street vendor.

They supped late on roasted meat and potatoes, and talked, laughed some more, sipped tea. Finn had a rum later; Nell declined. She tried to feel at home, instead felt herself a guest. But there was a more pressing situation than worrying about her status in his house.

'I must purchase some new clothes, soon.' She took a breath. 'So if I could impose on your generosity for a short time.'

'I am happy to exchange notes with Mrs Willey for you if—'

'No, not there, thank you,' she said quickly. Not the shop she'd practically been thrown out of as a thief. 'But somewhere. I will, of course, repay you once the gold is changed.' She nodded at the nuggets on the table that had been unloaded from her pinafore pocket. Suddenly mindful of how she'd acquired them, she tried to say something, but he was already talking.

'Of course, if that's how you prefer it,' he said.

'It is.'

He studied her a moment. 'My gold merchant is an honest man. I'll exchange those for you before we decide on the trip to Melbourne.'

She nodded, let it go for later. As long as the nuggets sat on his table, it would be easy to relinquish them back to him.

The candles had burned low. The conversation faltered in the flickering light and Nell decided it was time to prepare for bed. 'If you have water to spare, I should like to bathe after such a day. Would you direct me to a bowl and a pitcher of water?'

He got to his feet and smiled. 'I'll heat some more water, and I can do better than a bowl and a pitcher. I'll get the tub for you.'

In the spare room, she stripped down. Deciding to rid herself of her underwear—there was no one to chide her for it—she stepped naked into his man-sized bath tub. The water he'd provided was warm, and only deep enough for a good wash, but she sighed at the simple pleasure of being in clean water with a bar of soap. She washed quickly.

He'd handed her a towel earlier, a swathe of soft cotton, and although loathe to step back into her worn clothes, she dried off and dressed. For one quiet moment, she let Finn's proposal sweep over her. Her heart answered; her head remained quiet for once. She would take his offer, and not look back. Her chest swelled with an anticipation, but not a girlish one without care or caution—one with a calm, sensible attitude.

What rubbish, Nell. When have you ever been calm and sensible?

When she returned to the parlour, refreshed, though in her dirty clothes, she asked, 'Where should I sleep?'

He leapt off his seat and came to her, touched her cheek, slid his hand down her arm until it found her fingers. 'I should like you to sleep with me, Nell, in my room, in my bed. Our bed.' He produced a ring from his pocket. 'It is a man's ring, I'm afraid. A young man's ring. It no longer fits me. But I hope it fits your wedding finger.'

She gazed at it in his palm, a simple heavy ring in gold, a square signet engraved with FJS. Picking it up, it felt warm in her fingers, as if he'd been holding it while she bathed. 'Are these your initials?' she asked.

'Finneas John Seymour.' He slipped it on her left hand, the ring finger. 'With this ring, I thee wed,' he said quietly. His voice feathered over her.

The cold slide of fear entered her heart. *It can't be anything like it was before—*

Her mother's voice. *Stop. This is not Andrew.*

There'd be no turning back once they married.

It will work. Go forward, Nell. Don't turn back. Make your promise to him. Make it in your heart. Her mother's voice … The fear fell away as if it had never been. *It will work. You will make it so.*

'With this ring.' Still she faltered as she stared at his hand over hers. 'I thee wed,' she said and felt a shake of her hands. It was a vow. Not married in the eyes of God but married in her heart. She stared at the gold signet. A glint of candlelight caught the engraved initials. 'It looks very handsome, though—'

'Though?'

'It's a little loose. I wouldn't want to lose it now.'

He rested his forehead on hers. 'We can wrap some twine inside it.'

She nodded, her eyes still on the ring on her finger. 'I am a tangle of nerves. It will be an exciting adventure, won't it? We're sure of that, aren't we?'

He kissed her again, long and languidly. Then he took her hand. 'Aye. It will be an adventure, and we're sure. It feels right. More than right.' He pressed his mouth to her shoulder a moment. 'Let me take to you to our bed, Nell.'

It was in the dark silence of deepest night when Finn awoke. Aware of the lithe, sleeping woman beside him, he cursed his stiffening arm, his shuddering leg, and the violence within. It propelled him off the bed in a desperate bid to keep the tremor to himself and not wake her. *So soon after the last one …*

Under the glow of starlight, he saw Nell rise. 'Finn?'

'Stay in bed. This is not good to witness,' he ground out. He pushed himself to the wall, and rolled onto his side. The table rattled as his body shook; a bag of something fell to the floor from the dresser as he bumped it.

Then Nell was by his side. He saw her feet first, then the slim, strong legs. A shirt of his was all he'd had to offer her for night-wear and it fell just short of her knees.

She knelt quickly, wedged between him and the wall, her arms wrapped around his chest. She moulded to him, the tremor buffeting her. She hugged him tight until it subsided, moments later, and the last few shakes petered out.

'This is my nightmare, Nell,' he whispered hoarsely and sat up tiredly, disentangling himself from her. 'I'd no intention to hide it, but didn't think you'd witness it so soon. I'm sorry for it. It feels at times like I am half a man because of it.'

'Not so,' she whispered back. 'It's a small part of the whole man.'

Thirty-Nine

Ballarat, Camp Hospital tent

Lewis could hear quiet chatter. His mind was still fuzzy—thanks to laudanum, they said—and so was the sight he had in his good eye. The bed creaked slightly as he moved, and the chatter stopped.

Canvas walls waved in and out on a breeze. He felt giddy each time he noticed it, and vomit threatened to surge in his throat.

'Oooh, look. His good eye's opened.'

Whose voice was that—a young woman's?

Then a familiar face peered in. 'Son, are you feeling well enough today?'

Lewis tried to focus and blinked at his mother. Then his gaze shifted to the young woman, and an older man hovering at her shoulder. *Ahh. Annabel and her father Rufus Someone-or-other.* 'Well enough for what?' he croaked.

Annabel beamed at him, clapping her hands together. 'I'm so happy you're awake, it's been days and days and days.'

Enid held up an envelope for him to see. 'This came from Mr Campbell's office this morning. I thought we should wait to see if you are well enough to hear the news.'

Lewis squinted his good eye at the letter. It was addressed to him. He looked at his mother. 'It's been opened.'

She reddened but was smiling. 'I thought it best.'

He glanced at Rufus, who nodded his head. 'You are coming out of the worst of it, they say. You're a strong man. A little more rest and you're good as new.' The gap-toothed smile appeared.

Grunting, Lewis struggled to sit up a little, the thin pillow behind not much help to him.

'Read it to me in private, Mama,' he rasped. At the stoic looks on the faces of all three, he added, 'So not to burden these good folk.' His tongue felt thick, and pain was creeping back. He'd rather pain, welcome it over the dulling, damning effect of laudanum. The nurse had told him he'd not be given any more.

'Not a burden to us,' Rufus said expansively. 'We're family, now that you're betrothed and all to my daughter.'

I am? 'Please remind me of my proposal.' He knew he would be excused for being ungallant on his sick bed, but he added, 'Perhaps it would help jog my memory of such a momentous occasion.'

Enid didn't seem to notice. 'You were on the stretcher, my boy, waiting for a hospital bed. You took Annabel's hand. It was lovely for us all to hear. Even the nurse was delighted with it.'

He sank against the pillow. *Wonderful. All those witnesses.*

His mother looked back at Rufus, and Lewis thought he saw something in her gaze. A softening, a light he hadn't seen for perhaps his whole life. The pinched countenance had gone, and it looked as if years had lifted from her face. Dear God. Did he now have to contend with the prospect of a stepfather as well as a father-in-law?

Annabel still beamed, and somehow her happy face cheered Lewis a little. She was indeed a beautiful girl.

'Read on then, Mama.'

"'Dear Mr Wilshire, to reference the matter of your late uncle, Mr Andrew Amberton's estate. It is my great pleasure to advise a most fortunate turn of events for you, most extraordinary and most unusual.

"It has come in the form of a waiver of the repayment of the loan, for which you are the remaining guarantor, as secured by the late Mr Amberton. It has been fully and unconditionally forgiven, as it were, and it is in writing that no further action will be taken against the estate, or you as its guarantor, for the purposes of retrieving payment.

"In short, the loan has been fully repaid to the Seymour family, and receipts are in hand as proof.

"As for the other matters, they can be attended once your mining is fully operational again.'" Enid looked up. 'It goes on in legal jargon, says he has written to the creditors and is very hopeful the mines will pay everyone to redeem our good name, et cetera. But this other is the most wonderful news, Lewis.' She tapped his forearm.

He nodded dumbly.

'And there's more good news,' she continued. 'On Mr McNaught's advice, I paid the license fees again, ensuring that our mines still operate while you recuperate.'

Lewis's good eye met Rufus's stare.

'Yes,' Enid went on happily. 'And he has very kindly offered to oversee until you are back on your feet. Our mines can still produce to keep us.'

Everyone was beaming broadly. Lewis closed his eye to shut out all that happy, smiling, *beaming* optimism.

A rough hand clamped his shoulder lightly. 'It is my pleasure to help, Mr Wilshire. And a pleasure to have the company of your good mother, if you approve it. We have become firm friends while we wait for your health to return.'

The good eye opened again and met with Rufus McNaught's forthright gaze. 'I'm sure if my mother has approved ...'

'I have,' Enid declared. 'I do.'

Lewis held Rufus McNaught's look. 'Then it is a very happy family, indeed.'

McNaught nodded. 'And *all* family business will stay that way, son,' he replied.

Lewis knew right where he stood with that seemingly innocuous comment. He groaned a little, felt ill, trapped but resigned to his fate for the time being. When his gaze settled on Annabel, he saw a light in her eyes, and a strange thought descended.

Flora never looked at me that way.

McNaught was talking. 'Now, if the ladies will excuse us for a few moments, I should discuss some business with you, Mr Wilshire, if you're up to it. No need to unduly burden your good mother or my daughter with it.'

Lewis shuffled against the pillow. The sooner he was done with whatever McNaught had for him, the sooner he could go back to the oblivion of the last of the laudanum dose. 'Of course. If you'll pardon us, Mama? Annabel?' The women wandered arm-in-arm to the end of the tent then ducked outside. *Amazing.* Fixing his one good eye on McNaught, he waited.

The older man leaned closer. 'I'm glad that you're looking as fine as you are, yessiree, no mistaking that. But I reckon looking through a rifle sight might not be something you'll be doing too much more of from now on.'

Despite how suddenly his heartbeat pounded through him, Lewis's stare was steady on McNaught.

'Good thing I was here when you came 'round, yesterday,' McNaught continued, and scratched at the bushy beard. 'A nurse was finishing up the bandages for you, and she asked me to listen to whatever you were mumbling about. She was a bit worried.'

Blood pumped harder under the receding painkilling dose. Lewis's chest expanded, and his hand bunched slowly in the bed covers.

'I leaned closer to hear you say something about making a clean shot, and "no more uncle". Fact, you said it three times.'

His open eye blinked once. 'Strange thing.' Lewis pushed himself up again, tried to wrangle the pillow to give him support. 'A nightmare, perhaps?'

'Yessir, I'd heard your uncle was an unpleasant fellow, got himself shot by a bushranger in a hold-up. Not by you. Of course not. No, that never entered my head.' McNaught reached behind him and plumped the pillow, grabbed another from an empty neighbouring cot and shoved it in behind him. 'So, I said to the nurse that it sounded like a delirious mind, which she agreed it could have been. Or maybe you'd said snot and carbuncles or the like, and that I couldn't make anything of it to worry about. Think that satisfied her.' He shook his head slowly. 'Couldn't have you with two unexplained problems, now, could we? Especially now that you're soon to be married to my daughter and building up a respectable business again.'

Lewis grunted. 'I've heard that laudanum can give some folk the deliriums.'

'Son, my thoughts on the matter exactly. Annabel will get you all cured of that. She'll look after you properly.'

'She will, at that. Lovely girl. Be assured, she'll be well looked after too. Be assured.' Lewis closed his eye. Exhaled quietly. 'Carbuncles,' he repeated, musing. 'Damnable things.'

'They are at that.'

'I would hope that information doesn't get around.'

'No one will hear it from me,' McNaught said. 'Son.'

Forty

The weather had been favourable—warm, clear and no rain—on the way to Geelong. It was the easiest way to Melbourne, and to the wholesale stores from which Finn purchased his goods.

Ben Steele had agreed to drive an extra dray, smaller but sturdy. He thought it a good idea to push hard on the way there, to spend more time loading extra merchandise. He took Finn aside before they left to say, 'At last, a happy light in your eye, Finn. It looks good on yer.' He'd nodded approval at Nell being with them.

Nell's spirits had greatly improved too, once they'd left the hills of Ballarat. The noise of the fields had drifted to a silence that only their voices, or the horses' hooves, had broken.

In Melbourne, the drays had been piled high, and their return took longer, as expected. Lumbering bullock wagons ahead slowed their days even more, and now once in more gentler terrain, Finn and Ben could pass them without undue havoc.

On board the dray Finn drove, a chest for Nell was packed with new clothes, simple and functional, as she had chosen. She refused to fuss over things that would not be practical and prudent. A few new blouses, skirts, aprons, two new bonnets, and her precious cottons for underwear had been carefully selected. Warm jackets were added after encouragement from the shop assistant. Two pairs of new boots too.

Finn piled new blankets and linens for the bed into another timber box and slipped a pair of dancing shoes in for Nell. Not that there'd been more dances since the Subscription Ball but there would be, and then they would dance together as husband and wife.

There'd been good news on the return trip from miners walking to and from the fields: two of the thirteen diggers incarcerated in Melbourne for treason over the Eureka Lead incident had been cleared by a jury of any wrongdoing. Everyone thought the others would be freed as well.

That gave some people an excuse to let off steam. Gunshots and drunken shouts of merriment had dogged their campsites for a couple of nights on the track. Finn's tremors had broken out late into the night. Before the creeping dawn was upon them, Nell had fought them with him, on their mattress under the cart, away from sight.

Then last night, back in Ballarat, they'd all taken to their own much longed-for beds for a quiet night. Finn and Nell, exhausted, wrapped in each other's arms, fell asleep and barely stirred until dawn.

This morning, the merchandise would be driven to Finn's store in the town and unloaded. Finn had agreed, on the drive back from the city, to begin the task of operating from there. Ben had been very vocal that it was the right thing to do.

Before he left for Steele and Sons, Finn kissed Nell hard. 'A promise of things to come tonight, good Nell,' he said, cupping her chin, his other arm around her waist. 'If you've a mind, though, come visit the store. I might be in need of your company.' With a wave, he set off on foot.

Nell, dressed in a new blouse and skirt, looked about the house. She would live here with Finn—marry formally one day soon, they'd agreed. She wandered into the parlour and stared at the pictures on the mantel. The one of Finn and Louisa caught her eye.

He was the same man, but different, of course. The horror of battle was still with him somehow, his family gone. Nell and he would make a new one. Her face grew hot at that. He'd thought his fortune lost, too, but now it was found. He'd told her it was a wiser man with whom she lived.

Nell wondered about Louisa and her life with Finn. The woman seemed to smile at her from the photograph, her gaze serene. Nell smiled back, nodded to the picture of his parents, and headed for the front door.

Today she would walk to where Flora had made her laundry and confirm that she and Josie had really left. She'd walk to where she'd pitched her tent, where she'd been hopeful of a different life among the detritus of the old. She would venture onto the digging fields for one last time, to take a walk over the damaged, sad hills filled with empty holes and dashed dreams, and finally leave all her old life behind. All of it. She needed to do it.

Pulling on her old boots, she was ready. It was a reasonable walk and she wasn't willing to risk blisters forming if she wore her new boots.

It was overcast. The din of the fields increased with each of her steps. Her mood plummeted despite her best efforts. As she stepped over the camp litter of tin cans, broken bottles and torn sailcloth and canvas, she began to regret her decision. She stopped to check her bearings.

A little had changed in four weeks; a few tents had gone and the folk she had waved to at one time were no longer there. Other tents close by, new to her, stood slightly aside from the original sites, as if the owners didn't want to stand in the same footsteps as their predecessors.

Looking up the low incline to where Flora's tubs had been, she saw a couple of tents there, one larger than the other. Perhaps it was her father's. He'd said he'd relocated to this site. Deciding to press on, she trudged a bit further up the hill until she was within a few yards of the tents.

No Flora and Josie here. She gazed at the smaller tent and walked to it, realised it covered a hole which had some sort of small corral over it. As she peered in she saw it was a deep shaft. Men had been digging deeper for gold for over a year now that the surface stuff was harder to find. Shafts were everywhere, their openings hidden from sight by canvas gone grey and splotchy with damp. She glanced about, reckoning that the tent was over the site where she'd pitched hers. The larger tent was just about where Flora and her mother had lived.

Sadness crept in. But Flora would have gone on to something better for herself, just as Nell had. She knew that Josie would be more comfortable, too. How quickly things had happened for all of them. New lives far distant from the ones they'd led only weeks before.

It is done, here. Over for me.

Nell jumped at a voice.

'Ah. I wondered if ye'd made a full recovery and ye needed yer old man after all. Is why ye're here, I take it.' Alfred stepped out of the larger tent, a pipe stuck between his teeth and a tobacco pouch in his hands. His clothes were not so old any longer, and his boots still had both toes in them.

'I don't need you. It's curiosity, that's all. A friend of mine lived here, gave me shelter, kindness. You might remember.'

Alfred grunted. 'She and her mad old-woman mother have gone to Bendigo.' He stared at Nell a moment, then flicked a wrist at the other tent. 'It's why I got in here. I said so, remember?

I came up here and pitched the big tent where hers had been. Thought I'd look around.' He stood as if carefree, a jaunty tilt to his head.

She couldn't help the sarcasm from creeping in. 'Is that so?' Nell asked, 'Did you not bring your wife?'

''Course, I did,' he answered sharply. 'She's gone to Mrs Willey's. Got some female garb to buy.'

Nell was a little surprised. While Dora had always been intent on spending, she was shopping in the best of the shops. Interesting. She wondered who her father had fleeced this time. Well, no reason to stand and make chit-chat with him. She had the answer she sought; Flora was gone, and Nell had made her own goodbyes. She turned to go.

'I put another tent over this spot, here,' her father called.

She turned back at the curious tone in his voice.

'Reckoned it was on your patch that burned,' Alfred mused, thumbing towards the canvas over the wooden framework.

Nell looked across and lifted her shoulders. 'Perhaps,' she said, though she knew it was.

'Got curious, meself, about a real soft little hollow there. Thought maybe there'd been somethin' hid in it. Long gone, o'course.' He took his pipe and knocked it against his palm, a plug of tobacco shooting out. 'It made diggin' a bit easier to begin with. Came up with a nugget, a beauty, I did. Big as me fist. Not more'n a foot down under the soft stuff.'

Nell gave a short laugh, the irony of it not lost on her. 'Well, I'm thinking that now you've found this beauty of a nugget, you won't be pestering to sell me off, then.'

Alfred pointed a finger at her. 'Harsh words, daughter. I'm back to bein' a man o' means again after losing the run all those years ago.' But he couldn't quite hold her gaze.

Nell didn't bother reminding him that he'd been a poor manager of his means. It had been a fine squatter's block near Buninyong until he'd drunk and gambled away his family's livelihood.

He stepped towards her, seemed a little unsure of himself. 'Not needin' to sell you off no more, Nellie.' His features were a curious mixture of apology and pride, and something else. 'Thought maybe you mighta been needin' me,' he said, and lifted a hand towards her, before withdrawing it. 'Needin' your old pa.'

She didn't even shake her head. 'Goodbye, Pa.' She heard the finality in her voice. She turned to go.

'Wait, Nell.' A hesitation. 'Nellie.'

Without looking back, she walked down the hill, the way she'd come, her father's voice still calling. Well, perhaps if he came running after her, she'd stop, but he didn't. Instead, she heard another voice calling.

'Miss. *Miss!*' A male voice, rough and wheezy, and from behind her. 'It's me, it's Tillo.'

She turned. 'Mr Tillo.'

'Tilsbury, miss. But they call me Tillo.' He caught up with her, his chest heaving under his shirt. 'I was lucky to see you there, just leavin' old man Thomas, the cranky old git.' He held out a folded bundle of fabric to her. 'It were Miss Flora and Miz Josie asked me to give you this if I ever saw ye back this a-ways. Miss Flora said you might be back here the once.'

Nell took the bundle. It was the lad's shirt. Tears sprang suddenly, and her throat ached.

'There's a paper wrapped in it too,' Tillo said, pointing at the colourful rag so finely, lovingly stitched. 'There's something writ on it, dunno what it says, but I'm thinking it's a letter.'

She pressed it to her chest and looked at Tillo. 'You don't read?'

'Nah. Tried it once. Not for me.'

'Thank you for this.' When she realised he still stood there, she asked, 'Do I need to pay you for this, Tillo?'

'No, no.' His hands came up in protest. 'Thing is,' he said, his voice gruff once again, 'we could do with laundry tubs around here again, miss. Now that our Miss Flora's gone, and all.'

Nell wrinkled her nose, sniffed to stop the drip. 'Perhaps you could help another person set up a laundry shop. There's plenty could use the money. I have another job now.'

'Aye, that might be all right, but yer sorely missed on the fields. Well, if you ever do come back, remember us poor diggers needin' clean clothes once a week.'

She smiled. 'I will. Good day. And thank you again.' As she walked away, she felt in the bundle for the letter. Sure enough, she found one page, folded in half, her name neatly written on the outside. She gazed at Flora's stilted hand, *To Miss N Thomas from Miss F Doyle.* Opening it, she stood still as she read:

Dear Nell,

We have left with Mr Worrell for Bendigo, I think the date is February sixth. Ma is fine. She has a new shirt to sew now. If you come to Bendigo to visit, you will be able to find us care of Mr Worrell at Mr Campbell's offices.

I hope you are well.

Your friend, Flora Doyle.

There was a mark underneath, an 'X', and beside it in Flora's hand was written *Josie.* Nell folded the letter back inside the lad's shirt and hugged it close all the way home to Finn's house. The tears on her face gathered a little dust as she walked.

Forty-One

Nell stood on the step to Finn's store alongside him. He fumbled a little with the key, but the clunk of the lock signalled he'd opened the door.

'It's not quite how I want anyone to see it,' he said. 'I should have it cleared out, cleaned up first to make some space. I started when I got here this morning but found a few reasons to go to the stables instead.' He smiled ruefully. 'I'm glad you thought to go there.'

Nell had visited the store but at no sign of life, she'd ventured to Steele and Sons and found Finn there, unloading stock. Together, she and Finn had walked back to the store.

The doors swung wide and the masculine smells of leather, steel, iron and oil met her. On the threshold, locked-up heat and dust hit her first. The hot mustiness of it sailed by her as if it had been waiting to escape once the doors were opened.

A great timber bench ran along the right-hand side, spanning the length of the place, and piled high on every inch of it sat timber boxes full of axes, shovels, picks, mallets, pans and sieves. Behind it were shelves stuffed with trousers and shirts, hats and underclothing.

There was no clear avenue to navigate anywhere.

Finn wove his way to the back of the shop and thrust open the doors there. Light flooded in, illuminating all the way through the place back to where Nell stood in the doorway.

She swung her gaze to the left. She imagined the bales of canvas would be tents from the wholesaler, stacked one on top of the other. Puddling cradles, barrows, buckets, winches, all thrust haphazardly into piles on the floor. Rope, bags, tarpaulins, sails …

It all stretched before her. She took a breath. 'There is so much merchandise in here. The place is stuffed full to bursting,' she said, calling over stacks of camp stools as Finn made his way back.

At her side again, slapping off the dust and cobwebs, he said, 'Truth be known, I haven't wanted to face it. I've gone to Melbourne with Ben buying so I don't have to stand in here and hear the echo of my father's voice. Or to realise how ill he might have been. There's a lot of stock hoarded here.' He fiddled with the large key then set it on the counter. 'Ben's right to be frustrated. It should be sold off.' He gazed around. 'I'd forgotten just how much there was.'

The oppressive heat of the closed environment seeped out, the open doorway not enough. 'Finn, the air in here is so close.'

'Wait.' He climbed onto flat stacks of canvas on the long timber counter, reached over and pulled a dangling rope. High overhead, a window creaked open. 'I'll get all of these, that'll help.'

One by one the windows opened as Finn picked his way along the bench, tugging on the ropes on the wall. Nell felt the stagnant air move upwards.

Silent, the heavy, dumb stock sat waiting for her response, as if anticipating something from her. She took a few steps further into the shop then wandered where she could. She gazed upon some things that gave no clue as to their purpose.

'You'll learn what's what,' Finn said, dropping off the bench and coming to stand behind her.

'Will I?' She turned to him. 'And you will be gone most of the month, each month, while I stand here and sell this on?'

He looked around as if seeing it for the first time. 'I might not need to go so often. There's plenty of useful stock in here, now that I take it in.'

'You sound as if your heart's not in it, Finn.'

'It has to be. It's a livelihood. We've got the gold back, I know, but I intend for us to save some for the future. All this good fortune could change overnight.' He opened his hands as if it was in the lap of the gods. 'And it's not as bad now I'm in the store again. I've pushed aside being here for long enough.'

Nell noticed a narrow flight of stairs. 'What's up there?'

Finn followed her gaze. 'My parents' quarters. They lived here for a while. Not long, as it turned out.'

'Is there anything left up there?'

'Mostly what my father had with him after Ma passed on. We don't need to go there.'

Nell thought there was a lot more unsaid on that subject, but let it go. 'If you want to shift some of this, we have to throw open the doors to the public.' She swivelled, hands on hips. 'Let's put your shingle out and we'll see what walks in the door. Or rather, what walks out the door.' She swished her skirt about her ankles. 'I should have worn the bloomers.'

Finn ducked his head. 'You're the woman I love, a lady merchant you'll be for a time, and a wife who works. Are bloomers really what you want to wear here?'

The woman I love. Out loud, just like that. Her chest tingled all the way through, and she recognised the *happy* in it. She took a moment, amazed, then snapped back to the present. Bloomers, yes. She eyed the bench he'd stood on, and the mountain of stuff surrounding her.

'Bloomers are practical,' she said, pointing at a heavy timber ladder leaning against the far wall.

'So is a lad up the ladder, under your orders,' Finn reasoned. 'Or Ben. He's only too happy to start on this and earn from the extra work. He's bringing the empty cart around for another load to go to the diggings.'

'Bloomers are practical,' she repeated. 'Any woman who wears them knows it. I will have to wear comfortable work clothes.' Was he trying to dissuade her? Surely not. He certainly wasn't ordering her but … She stared at him, a little startled.

'We know wagging tongues can be cruel, Nell. Bloomers are new to the fields, to Ballarat.'

She relaxed. 'New, and sensible. Nobody will mind on my account, Finn. And I don't care if they do. Sensible folk will see I am hardworking in my husband's business and have been saved from the dreaded laundry tubs. And Ben is welcome to go up the ladders, I have no care for that.' She stepped close and wrapped her arms around his waist, touching his nose with hers. 'We have to move with the times, start this new life properly.' She looked up at him.

He gave a mock frown. 'You mean *I* have to move with the times?'

'Yes, my handsome bushranger. You do.'

Ben was happy as a lark as he drove four cartloads from the store to the fields that week. After days of sorting, cleaning, and oiling, it was once again a busy, well-utilised shop. Stock was now at a manageable level and Finn had taken to counter sales himself. That meant only one more drive to Melbourne before the winter respite. They would next revisit the wholesalers once the rains had subsided to allow a safe return journey.

The upstairs area of the store had been left alone. Nell had made no comment as Finn had strung a thick rope over the stairway. 'A task for another time' he'd said. She went about her busy day. Clientele was growing, and Finn had promised he would build a footpath along the width of the shop if the winter was kind.

She'd made good sales that amazed and delighted her. Old acquaintances from the fields were surprised to see her there, and a few told her how her father was faring. Very well, by all accounts. She shrugged at that. Her father would soon hear of her whereabouts, if he hadn't already. And what was there to worry about if he did visit? Not a thing.

But the couple who appeared in the store one morning after Finn had gone to the diggings nearly took her breath away.

Lewis had a young, dark-haired woman by his side, her arm in his, her smile wide. 'Good day, Nell,' he said. 'I'm very happy to see you.' He gazed around. 'This looks a very fine store now.'

Stunned into silence, Nell noticed first the pink scar that cut into his right eyebrow. Other than that, he seemed just as usual— the confident charm and the pleasant demeanour. Did he not see the mockery of his visit? The effrontery? This, the man who had burned her tent to the ground and threatened Flora and Josie.

Before she could speak, he held his arm out a little, indicating the woman at his side. He said, 'May I introduce my fiancée, Miss Annabel McNaught. Annabel, my aunt, Mrs Nell Amberton.'

Nell covered her chagrin and extended her hand. 'Miss McNaught, a pleasure.'

'And to meet you, Mrs Amberton.' Annabel bobbed a little as she briefly took Nell's hand. Her American accent was a soft burr, and she sounded as pleasant as she looked.

'I go by the name of Mrs Seymour, now,' Nell said, and straightened up. She returned Lewis's own surprised stare. 'Mrs Finneas Seymour.'

'Oh. My mother has mentioned nothing of any banns in the newspaper—'

'No banns.' She was short with him. None of his business. She and Finn had agreed to be married in Melbourne as soon as somewhere suitable could be arranged. Without all the to-do. Until then, she would carry Finn's name as she saw fit.

Annabel's glance darted about, but she kept her smile wide. Nell's heart tugged. Perhaps the girl was uncomfortable in the company of a woman so recently widowed, one who'd attached herself to another well inside the mourning period.

But the younger woman wanted to chat, and her girlish delight was disconcerting. 'And, well, you would have seen our banns, wouldn't you, Mrs Seymour? And my father's and Mrs Wilshire's?' Annabel asked excitedly. 'We will all be married only weeks apart, sometime next month.'

Nell hadn't read a newspaper in ages. She turned to Lewis. 'Is Enid to be married as well?'

He shrugged a little and made a face. 'As it turns out, to Annabel's father.' Lewis patted his fiancée's arm. 'Annabel, I was mistaken. There are no items in here that would remotely interest you. Perhaps if you visit your choice of store along the way and I'll catch you up there.'

It seemed Annabel was happy to make an escape from the boxes of digging implements and the shelves of male clothing and working tools. She said to Nell, 'I should like to make your acquaintance again, Mrs Seymour. Perhaps later when you are not visiting your husband's store. If you'll excuse me, I do have errands I must attend.'

Nell kept the smile. When she was not *visiting* her husband's store. 'Of course, Miss McNaught. Another time.' What hope did women have to be independent when most of their kind were not only governed by men under the law, but also by their own complicity?

Annabel retreated with a smile and a wave, swishing outside, a light scent of rose following her. As the younger woman disappeared, Nell turned her glare on Lewis, her voice muted with outrage. 'You come in here behind the skirt of your fiancée?'

His hands shot in the air, and he lowered his head. 'An opportunity to get in the door. I came to apologise, Nell. To beg forgiveness.'

As she crushed the fabric of her pinafore in her hands, her voice scraped low and hoarse. 'You burned my tent with the intention of forcing me to hand over something that was not mine to give.'

He shook his head. 'A moment of madness,' he offered quietly. 'I'm sorry for it.'

'A moment?' Nell queried derisively. 'You threatened Flora and Mrs Doyle.'

His head came up. 'Where are they? How is Flora?'

'I will not tell you anything of Flora, Lewis.'

He rubbed his scarred eye, shifted his weight, and clasped his hands in front of him. 'I was ashamed at my own behaviour, even as soon as I walked away from your campsite that night. I fully deserved that slingshot.' He nodded at her surprise. 'Oh, yes, I knew it was a slingshot, and whose. They told me two hard-flung stones had brought me down. Could be no one else but Mrs Doyle.' He kept his head bowed. 'I had breached all my own boundaries, which are wide, I admit, but I had descended into a despair, if you will.'

Nell had nothing to say to that. She had known despair too well to lend her voice.

He went on. 'Something came over me at the ball. My life seemed to be slipping away, not only Andrew's total debacle, and the huge debt he left, but the sudden prospect of marriage and an insistent future father-in-law.' He waved a hand and went on. 'The thought of supporting a wife without means, my mother's life destitute … I snapped. I became—' He stopped. 'I am *not* my uncle.' He looked at her. 'You of all people should know I would never become my uncle.' At her infuriated silence, he continued. 'All my life I'd watched that madness. What I portrayed the night of the ball was different, borne of another desperation.'

'It is the same thing,' she cried, vehemently. 'It is still violence.'

'For what it might be worth, I have vowed never to raise my hand in anger again.' He looked out the door where Annabel had gone.

'You must ensure it, Lewis. Your uncle's demons defiled all he knew.'

'I know it.' He looked at her, a frown gathering his brows, a strange light in his eyes. 'He was dealt with, properly, finally.'

Nell saw something else there in his gaze, a coldness, and not for the first time, she wondered who, deep down inside, Lewis really was.

Finn came through the front door, a burlap bag over his shoulder. 'Good afternoon,' he said to Lewis's back. 'I hope my wife has seen to—' He stopped at the look on Nell's face and turned to face his customer. 'Nell?'

'This is Mr Lewis Wilshire, Finn,' she said, keeping her voice low. 'Lewis, this is my husband, Mr Finneas Seymour.'

Finn stared.

Lewis straightened and, recognising Finn, looked stupefied. He glanced at Nell, and back again. 'Mr Seymour, I must beg your pardon. I hadn't realised that you were now Nell's—my aunt's husband. I had not recalled, when Nell spoke of you earlier, that

Finneas is your Christian name and that you are—were my Aunt
Susan's brother.'

Nell's glance flicked to Finn. Her stomach rolled, and a queasy
bile rose in her throat.

'Mr Wilshire. Your business, sir?' Finn looked calm. Nell knew
he was not. She could feel the burn of his rage humming between
them. He dropped the bag to the floor.

Lewis regained some of his composure. 'To see my aunt.
To inform her of my impending marriage.' He sounded formal
and stony.

Finn cast a glance at Nell then addressed Lewis. 'I don't know
if social mores any longer require that you still call my wife your
aunt,' he said flatly. 'I should say not, after all that's occurred.' His
shoulder hitched, small tremors threatened. 'And as far as I am
concerned, you, sir, are no longer any relation of mine.'

Lewis stiffened. His face had blanched. 'As you wish.'

Nell held her breath as Finn stepped closer. 'Your uncle was
the unlawful cause of my sister's death, and, I'm sure, that of her
unborn child.' A muscle worked in his jaw as he seemed to clamp
down on more words. Between his teeth, he said, 'I wanted to
kill him.'

Lewis's eyes were red-rimmed. 'He deserved it. For your sister,
for Susie's loss, I am truly sorry.' Breath shot out of him. 'I could
not stop him then.'

Still staring hard at Lewis, Finn shook his arm out of Nell's
light touch. 'And he was the perpetrator of grave harm to Nell,
who is now my wife. You, sir, did nothing.'

Alarmed, Nell murmured, 'Finn.'

Lewis began, 'I must—'

Finn launched at him. Hands bunched in Lewis's coat, he
shoved him hard against the long timber bench. Grappling, they
bounced to the floor, knocking a box of axe heads that spilled

along the polished boards. 'And then you went to the laundry and burned my wife's possessions,' Finn blasted, as he snatched Lewis off the floor, jerking him upright on his backside.

'Stop!' Nell shouted. Paralysed, she could only stare at what was unfolding in front of her.

Trying to steady, Lewis grabbed Finn's wrists. 'It was but a moment's madness at the laundry, and I regret—'

'You would have planned to go there and do harm.' Close to Lewis's fearless gaze, Finn snarled, 'You have the same affliction as your madman uncle.'

Lewis's breathing was rapid, but his voice was low and controlled. 'No, I don't. He was a coward, insane, but I am not a—'

Finn knocked Lewis hard against the bench. 'And you did nothing,' he repeated. '*Nothing*. You dare bring that evil to my family once again.'

Lewis's glare snapped up. 'I'm delivering your freedom of it.'

Finn ignored him, shoved Lewis down again. 'I should kill you here and now,' he raged, nothing louder than a hoarse whisper.

Nell heard it. 'No, Finn,' she burst out. 'No more violence for us.' Her voice snagged in her throat. But she knew Finn. *Her* Finn.

He dropped Lewis to the floor as if burned. He clutched his now shaking arm by the elbow and glared at the man at his feet.

Lewis glanced up at Finn's arm. He looked to have had a sudden recollection. 'But you … are not a murderer, Mr Seymour.' Words, shaky but clear. After a glance at Nell, he pushed off the bench, got to his feet and waved an arm to have Finn step back. 'It's true. For Nell I was very nearly too late.' His voice broke. 'But I did not do *nothing*.' Pointing at Finn's arm, he said, 'You recall at the hold-up that he was stopped, and not by *your* bushranger.' He stood his ground, his face pinched. 'It could be said that it was done in your defence.'

Finn still gripped his elbow, but the shakes had diminished. '*You* shot him?'

Aghast, Nell stared at Lewis. There'd been no clues, nothing to give away what he'd done. Killing Andrew had saved her life. Lewis could have killed her for his inheritance at the same time. Why hadn't he? Her legs wobbled. What he'd done at the camp-site, after the ball ... had he finally snapped?

Her knees threatened to give way. 'Lewis,' she said on a breath, shocked. Reaching for the counter top, she steadied herself, sud-denly light-headed. Lewis was still trying to settle his rumpled clothes and catch his breath. He glanced at Nell and shook his head, as if neither of them should say more.

Finn saw it, looked from Lewis to Nell. 'Nell, did you know—?'

'No. Sweet Christ, I didn't know,' she swore, barely a whisper, meeting Finn's worried eyes. It gnawed at her. 'I wished I'd been capable of saving myself. Saving myself from what I allowed to happen—'

'You didn't *allow* anything. You *didn't* allow it,' Finn seethed. 'The blame for it lies with Amberton, with all of *them*. Not you.' He held out his hand for her.

She took it, squeezed it, and looked at Lewis. 'And Enid? Does she know?'

Bright spots of colour appeared on his pale cheeks. 'Much as my mother is not a saint—God knows she could have tried something to stop her brother—I would not cause more harm by telling her. Let it be, for all of us, that Andrew Amberton was killed by a bushranger.' His mouth grim, he gave a rigid but slight bow to Finn. 'Nell had no knowledge of my intention, I can assure you.' Coldly polite into their dazed silence, he said, 'And now, I trust we need never speak of this again. Good day.' He turned on his heels and his boots marked a steady beat out of the shop.

A moment passed before Finn roused himself to follow and slam shut the door to the store. 'And I trust we need never set eyes on him again.' He flipped the sign to closed. He turned back to Nell, his eyes bleak. 'I wondered, before, if you were protecting Lewis.'

'I would *never* have come to you if I'd known there was murder on my hands,' she cried fiercely. She swiped hair from her eyes and rubbed her forehead. Angry tears filled her eyes. 'Andrew's poison still infects everyone he ever barged into. It takes a person's reason. Their trust in themselves. Others mistrust *you* for what's happening to you, believing you're deserving of it.' She stared at him. 'It belittles everything I am.'

'You are not belittled, you are fine and strong. It was all Amberton, only him, and he is gone.' His voice softened. 'And I trust you. I only thought for a moment that perhaps you didn't trust me.'

'No, no, no, Finn.' Nell let her breath go, depleted, and reached behind to lean on the bench. 'What Andrew did to Susan, to me … is it always going to be with me, still working in my mind long after he's dead? Leaching me?' She felt sick, nausea threatened to choke her.

'No.' Finn strode to her, took her by the shoulders. 'He is gone, and you—*we* will drive out what is left behind. We have begun already.' He bent to catch her eye. Both hands went to her face and his thumbs brushed aside the tears on her cheeks. 'We have hope, Nell. We don't need tears.'

She rested her forehead on his. 'And Lewis? No one should have to pay for taking Andrew from this world.'

Finn gathered her close, arms around her in a strong embrace. 'Even if I wanted to go to the police, it cannot be proven that he killed his uncle. My love, Lewis knew his information was for our ears, and our benefit, only.'

Forty-Two

Ballarat, March 1855

Nell's nausea had not stopped. Since Lewis's visit to the store that day, she had been sick every morning, and sometimes into the afternoon.

'Finn,' she said and rested her damp forehead against the door-jamb, weary of the queasiness. 'I have some news.'

He smiled as he looked up from the desk in the store. 'Let's hear it.' Then he frowned a little and stood. 'Still feeling ill?' He went to her and rubbed her arm.

'I am sure that will pass. Or I hope so, as the baby grows in me.' She wiped her mouth, pulled up her apron to dab the sweat from her neck.

'A—' Then his face broke into a grin. 'Nell. Really?' He took her in his arms and rocked her. 'Oh, that's wonderful, Nell. For us.' He rocked her again.

'Don't. I'll be sick.'

He held her at arm's length. 'Here, come and sit down. Can I get you anything?' He angled her into the chair on the other side of his desk.

She swallowed uneasily. 'Strangely, I want a piece of Mr Chadlow's licorice and a pickled onion.'

Finn blurted a laugh. 'How about a sip of water, and then I'll see what I can do about the other.'

She nodded, dabbing some more at her neck.

'How long before—?'

'Perhaps seven months.'

He kissed her forehead. 'Then we will make haste and make us a proper family.'

Late March, Nell and Finn travelled to Melbourne. It was their last buying trip for the store before winter. There they married, and mid April, amid bouts of morning sickness and the consumption of many pieces of licorice and many pickled onions, they made their way back to Ballarat.

Ben lent a hand to unload the morning after their return. Boxes of tools and other merchandise were all situated in place in the store. He greeted her as she came in from the back door. 'Morning, missus,' he said, a grin on his face as he bent to lift a box of mallets off the floor.

'Morning, Ben.' Nell wiped a damp rag around her neck and over her face. She'd just heaved up beyond the doorstep.

'Heard the news? All thirteen miners, those what got arrested after the battle, got off, the case got laughed out of court.' The box of mallets landed on the bench with a thud.

'Yes, it's a grand thing that they were not charged. A good day for them. For us. I didn't know you were so concerned about all of that.'

'Me either, till I heard the news. Gave me shivers up and down me arms. But the poor newspaper man, Mr Seekamp is still in prison. Got six months for seditious libel—means incitin' against the government.'

'Yes, Ben.'

'But folk reckon they'll get him out sooner. So, Peter Lalor won his day when he spoke up for poor man's rights. He's still hidin' out somewhere but they're talkin' amnesty for him. Mind you, lost 'is arm in the process. Better'n his life, though.' He bowed his head a moment. 'And some bloody trooper still has the flag somewhere—pardon my language, missus—but it'll come back, take its rightful place.' Ben was beaming at her now.

'Then I expect we'll see some changes hereabouts,' she said. 'And call me Nell. Missus is so old-fashioned.'

'Aw, 'twould have to be missus, in company, though.'

'All right,' she conceded and headed back towards the tea room for a sip of water. 'Where is Finn?' she asked, over her shoulder.

'Up the first floor,' Ben answered, and slid a crate of ropes across her path just as she exited.

Stepping around it, she headed for the stairs. The first floor? Indeed, the rope barring entrance to the stairs was lying at the foot of the steps. Gripping the rail, Nell headed up, aware that long disused floorboards creaked underfoot.

The heat rose as she climbed. 'I hope you've opened windows up here,' she called.

At the top of the stairs she bobbed into open space. It was just an open floor, no internal walls, jutting out over the shop. There were windows on the far wall that overlooked the back of the building.

Finn sat on an old bed, his hands clasped on his knees. 'Some of Ma's clothes are still here,' he said and pointed to a small dresser, a drawer opened, and a lady's nightgown still neatly folded in it. 'Her hairbrush, too.'

Nell saw the brush. It sat in a porcelain dish with an assortment of combs and pins. Three little bottles, all different colours, lined up against the grainy mirror. A small round box, covered in fabric, sat with them. Her throat constricted. Her own mother's things, like hers, had long gone. She could see the lines of dust on the dresser from where Finn had moved the items.

He didn't look at her. Instead, he gazed up at the open windows. 'I didn't tell you that this was left exactly as it was the day I left for Melbourne to go to England. As if Pa just came up here afterwards and waited until he died. When I first returned I couldn't face it.'

'I can understand that.' She glanced around. 'But if your parents lived here, where was Susan?'

Finn pointed behind to a place in the shadows, over what would have been the back of the shop, their tea room. In the dim light, Nell could see a heavy curtain. 'Just a bed, and a dresser for her after Louisa had passed away,' he said. 'Before that, when I was on the diggings, Louisa stayed at the house because she couldn't abide the noise and the dirt of the camp. Susan stayed there with her, good company for each other. Then Louisa became ill. I came back into the township to look after her and Susan moved in here. When Louisa died, I left. And Susan got married.' He took a deep breath. 'I didn't see that Pa was failing after Ma died. I didn't. I just couldn't stay one more day after Louisa had gone. Couldn't be in the town, in the colony, couldn't be in the country one more day. I left. I just left him with his grief, left my sister with hers.' He flicked a glance towards the ceiling. 'Too wrapped up in my own grief to see anything clearly. No wonder Susie flung herself into that marriage. Perhaps she thought she'd escape the grief of the whole family. She couldn't have known what a terrible decision that would be.'

Nell stood at the end of the bed. 'They would not have blamed you for leaving,' she said softly. 'They would have understood.'

'They needed me, and I didn't see it. And I tried my damnedest to shift the guilt of being away. Susan had passed away only days before I got back. I didn't care if I lived or died by that time, so I tried to take vengeance on Amberton. Thought maybe we'd kill each other. That didn't happen, thanks to his nephew.'

'Isn't self-pity, is it, Finn Seymour?'

'Sounds like self-pity.' He studied his steady hands. 'It was frustration, for the loss of lives I couldn't save, for all the grief. Had I not run, I might have stopped Susan.'

'And you might not have.'

He nodded. 'Perhaps that's true, too. But I wouldn't have gone away, wouldn't have returned with the relics of war haunting me.' He held up his left hand. It was steady. 'I could have done so much more,' he said. 'I could still do so much more.'

'Then we should revisit your idea of the Murray River paddle-steamers,' she said. 'We could visit that port in South Australia. You said that Mr Worrell would have liked to—'

'No.' Finn shook his head. 'That's past. You and I have another dream now, and nothing will jeopardise this,' he said, reaching over to smooth a hand over her belly. She put a hand on his. 'Matthew said something that made sense to me when I visited him in Bendigo months ago. He said that the man who supplies the diggers easily wins the gold. I like that idea. Perhaps we'll invest in Steele and Sons and help Ben supply a road service from here to Bendigo. And when that's done, maybe we could move there.' He slapped his thighs. 'That's what my father would have done. He'd have made the adventure where he was, not gone off half-cocked looking for it. I think it's a good idea.'

'It's a good, *safe* idea, Finn. Is that what you want?'

'Yes, a safe one. For our family.' He looked at his hand again, and rubbed his elbow. 'This thing can't be trusted around machinery or engines, anything given to sudden loud noises. I'll make a good living here. *We'll* make a good living here,' he corrected. When he looked at her his smile was wide, and there was light in his eyes.

Satisfied he wasn't mired in some dark oppression of the mind, Nell smiled in return then held her breath, fearing another upsurge of bile. 'I must go downstairs again and try to find a cool spot. I don't think I could live up here in this lingering heat, right now.'

'We have our house. And I wouldn't live up here, Nell,' he said and stood up to take her hand. 'I'll clear it out, and it can be used for storage, or for a man's quarters, if we hire.'

'Are you sure you want to do that?'

'As sure as I am of anything. It's time to make this new life work.'

'I have an honourable woman in my hands, Mrs Seymour,' Finn said in their bed that night. His hand traced her hip, his finger warm and gliding.

Nell was admiring the signet ring on her finger. 'A queasy Mrs Seymour. I hope that part is soon gone,' she said, trying to jiggle the ring. 'There's no need to tighten this with twine anymore, it seems.'

'An honourable, plump woman in my hands. My life is happy.' He cupped a full breast and kissed her cheek.

'It won't be so happy if this daily sickness continues.'

He rose up on an elbow. 'I've heard it said that if a wife is sick early when she's in the family way, it means a baby girl is coming.'

Nell quirked a brow. 'And where would you hear that said, Finn Seymour, in the pub tent and all the men talking about it?' She wriggled to get comfortable and thought a moment, back to a darker time in her life. 'Let it be a girl first,' she said. 'I feel it is a girl, an October girl.'

'I would welcome either girl or boy as long as you're both in good health. Dangerous things, babies.' With his free hand, he brushed aside the blonde tresses at her neck and leaned over to kiss her there. 'If it's a girl, she will be brave like you, and a stout defender of her rights.'

'We will see that she is. From her very first steps.'

He rested on his forearm. 'I will write to Joseph tomorrow, have a paper drawn up to protect you and our children should I not be around to provide.'

Nell reached up, her fingers touching his day's scratchy, stubbly beard. 'Nothing will happen to you.'

'Who knows what this blasted shaking business will bring me? It may yet get worse.'

'Then we'll take necessary steps, as you say, and have a care for the future.' She smoothed her hand over his cheek. 'We have the store and the mining license, and if needs be, we can stake a claim again, dig for gold. We will teach our children to look after themselves.'

'We will,' he mused. 'And there's talk of a new license system that will benefit us all. It never touched me much before, but I see the worth of Lalor's politics now, the meaning of the whole business at Eureka. Rights have been hard fought, and he will get up the vote for the working man.'

Nell's eyes widened. 'A vote for the working man, is it? I wonder if Mr Lalor's fiancée would like a vote for the working woman, like I would. It's all around us here, women working alongside menfolk, earning their own purse, yet we have no vote, no say of our own.'

'A force to be reckoned with.'

'Hah! We must stand up for ourselves, band together as much as we can. At least here, on the diggings, we can do that.'

'The diggings are different. Things are not done in the conventional way. It's not like that everywhere. I think it will be a long-fought battle.'

Her energy ran out. She sighed and turned on her side, facing him. 'What about living in Bendigo? You once said you'd like to go there. I would too,' she said, and blinked away the sleepiness descending.

'As much as we'd like to go, we need to stay here awhile. For one thing,' he said, a merry glint in his eye, 'if we were to move there, or elsewhere for that matter, there wouldn't be work for a married woman outside of the home.'

A futile spot of fury bubbled inside, then it broke. She shifted onto her other side to get comfortable. 'We need our say heard, to have our lives made safe, in law. And the law upheld.' Only a flicker of dark memory invaded their privacy and she pushed it away.

'You, my love, will always be safe here, will always have a say in this house. However, we will still have to vote for government policy as one, not two.'

'One day it will change.' Nell rubbed her hands back and forth across her belly. 'Our daughter will have a better say in her life, I'm sure of it. She'll be a strong one.' She closed her eyes and sighed again. Suddenly, fatigue waved through her.

He lay back, an arm behind his head. 'Our daughter, Cecilia Celeste Seymour. It's a long name,' he went on, considering. 'It has a ring to it, all the same. Her grandmamas would be proud.'

'We'll call her CeeCee,' Nell murmured. 'Nice and short.'

'I like it.' He gathered her closer. 'We need a ready name for a boy, as well, just in case.'

Nell huffed a little. 'We do, but no child of mine will be named after my father,' she said, and snuggled closer. 'We will think harder.'

Finn said, 'If it's a boy, he will have his own name, start his own dynasty.'

'Of course, he will. He'll be very fine, my dearest Finn, just like his papa. CeeCee will be very fine, too,' she said sleepily.

'CeeCee Seymour.' Finn gazed at the flickering shadows on the ceiling thrown by candlelight. 'For all I have now, I am grateful. I am a lucky man,' he said, his voice drifting. He reached across and snuffed out the candle then settled back, gathering her alongside.

'Aye, you are, my love.' Nell turned again, tucked against him and kissed a spot on his chest. 'And I am the lucky woman who loves you.'

Author's Note

There were many women such as Nell and Flora who worked for a living on the goldfields in their capacity as miners, publicans, newspaper journalists, shopkeepers, and a myriad of other roles. Violence within families was rife on the fields and was rarely punished other than orders for the perpetrator to desist. It often culminated in abandonment of the wife, and children if there were any. At least on the fields if a woman held a license she could mine for gold, own a shop and sell wares to support herself. If not, she could starve if she couldn't find paid work. Otherwise, it was making and selling sly grog, and engaging in prostitution. Many did starve: men, women and children. In 1856, the Miner's Right replaced the hated license system (the poll tax) and was a 'necessary qualification for voting...' There was nothing in the legislation to bar women from purchasing a miner's right and therefore voting—the miner's right was not gender specific when it first replaced the mining license. However, the Act was quickly amended in 1865 and the word 'male' before the word 'persons' was inserted in the Electoral Law Consolidation Act 1865. It would be almost another forty years before some women achieved suffrage—in South Australia in 1895 for both Indigenous and non-Indigenous women, and in Victoria, where better rights for men were fought for under the Southern Cross flag in 1854, non-Indigenous women gained the vote in 1908. Not until the 1960s were Indigenous people allowed to vote.

Acknowledgments

With grateful thanks to the following. Readers who are, of course, most important in a writer's world. Thank you for your kind words in feedback, for your delight in my stories and my characters. Susan Parslow, your love of a good story makes mine what they are. My heartfelt thanks to you and your red pen. Fiona Gilbert, my research travelling buddy. And thanks also to her husband Tony who holds the fort while we take off and time-travel to the 19th century. Clare Wright and her wonderful book *The Forgotten Rebels of Eureka*. An inspiration for the story of women on the goldfields at the time of the Eureka Stockade and beyond. Dorothy Wickham's *Women of the Diggings Ballarat 1854*, a marvellous insight into the women who lived and loved and lost. Jon and Sarah Lark and the team at Kangaroo Island Spirits (fabulous gin), for taking on a time-traveller at the cellar door who transports herself to and from the 19th century. Amy Andrews, in early draft days, you set me straight once again. Sovereign Hill, Ballarat and the knowledgeable, keen staff whose love for the facility shines in the presentation of this wonderful tourist attraction. The excellent Gold Museum, a wealth of historic information, beautifully and sympathetically presented. Museum of Australian Democracy at

Eureka, Ballarat where the breath-taking story of Eureka unfolds on the site itself. Honouring the history, and their love of the site was evident in the passionate members of staff. Matthew Worrell, my accountant, who lent his name to the ledgers man in this story. They both do a fine job of the books. The Kangaroo Island community, the bookselling teams at the Kingscote Gift Shop and the Kingscote Newsagency, and the Kangaroo Island Library, as always for their staunch support. To Jo MacKay, Laurie Ormond, Dianne Blacklock, Kate James, Sarana Behan and Johanna Baker at MIRA (Harlequin Books, a division of Harper Collins) and their teams for all the assistance and professional guidance throughout. To the fabulous Michelle Zaiter and the evocative cover of The Widow of Ballarat, another unforgettable touch of magic. And lastly to family, including Hamish the much loved Wonder-dog.

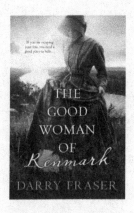

Turn over for a sneak peek.

THE
GOOD
WOMAN
OF
Renmark

by

DARRY FRASER

Available December 2019

One

Renmark 1895

Maggie O'Rourke's heart pounded. Standing over the body, the iron rod still clutched in her shaking hands, she was ready to swing it again if she had to.

The rutting had ceased abruptly when the *thwack* copped the side of his head. A last grunt had escaped him, and a soundless Robert Boyd collapsed over Nara, the woman he'd snatched. His breeches were taut over thick thighs but in his frenzy, the back seam had given way and his buttocks gleamed white.

Nara kicked and wrested her way out from under him, shoving his head off her. Her dress had hoicked up to her waist, and her heels skidded as she rolled to get away. The cheeks of her backside scraped on the gravelly dirt.

'Get up and run. Did he—did he get you?' Maggie waved the iron rod, her gaze never leaving the big body.

Nara scrambled to her feet, pushing at her dress as she tried to dust off. She pressed her hand between her legs. 'He nearly stuck it in, but you got 'im before—'

'Oh God, oh God. I'm so sorry. Are you hurt?'

Rubbing herself, Nara squeezed her eyes shut a moment. 'Maybe.'

'Oh God. Bad, Nara? Are you hurt bad?' Maggie felt sick for her friend, sick for herself. But she wasn't the one that monster had defiled.

Nara rubbed again, considering. 'He didn't get me. Just fell down on me.'

Maggie, blinking hard, peered at the body. 'Is he dead?'

'I reckon.' Nara straightened her dark dress under the dirtied pinafore. 'You got 'im good.'

Pointing the rod at Boyd, ready in case he leapt to his feet, Maggie seethed. 'He is an evil man.'

'Just a dead one now.'

She stared at Nara. 'Why did you do it? Why did you get in his way?'

Nara and her husband, known only as Wadgie, had been friends with Maggie almost from the day she'd had arrived to work at Olivewood a few years ago. The Wadges had been in trouble before, defending themselves. They were rabbit trappers, poor people making a meagre living from what they could scrounge off the land. They were often vulnerable to unscrupulous rogues, some said even more so than the blacks.

'He bashed Wadgie. Accused him of stealin', and that was a lie. This time he were after you. But the troopers will kill me if I kill him, so better he chases *me*, and *you* bash him.'

Maggie squeezed her eyes shut a moment. 'I know, I know. But he got you. I'm sorry he got you.'

Nara waited a beat. 'Me. You. He don't care.'

Maggie could hang for this, especially if no one believed they'd both been in danger. Robert Boyd had begun pestering Maggie a month ago and, despite her rejection, had kept it up. Earlier today when he'd arrived unannounced at Olivewood, he'd become more than a nuisance. He'd tried to touch her, had made a grab for her arm.

Maggie had snatched herself away. Hands on hips, she'd faced him at the foot of the verandah steps. 'Mr Boyd, I have said before today, and very politely, that I am not interested in your attention or your company.' She squared her shoulders. 'Even if you were not married. Yet still, you have persisted, unwelcome, uninvited, and now you dare lay your hand on my person. Go away.'

He had mimicked her hand on hips. 'Ain't you the feisty one? Nice and built well, too, takin' a man's eye.' His gaze settled on her chest a moment before he grinned at her. 'All that mussy black hair tied up tight, and them big blue, invitin' eyes. Can always tell the ones what've already lifted their skirt. Got a certain look about 'em.'

Maggie's mouth had dropped open. *How could he possibly know any such a thing, and how dare he say so, anyway?* No one knew what had happened between her and Sam, her old beau from back home, no one.

Sam. Lately, he'd popped into her head at the most inopportune moments, and she'd just wanted to reach over and ruffle his thatch of blond hair and see the mischievous grin once more.

Boyd hadn't known about *anything* to do with Sam, of course not—he was just being his vile self.

'See? I was right. That look on yer face gives you away.' He gave a derisive snort. 'A tart, all right. I'll get what I've come for. All your fancy blatherin' about rights an' such mean nothin' to me.' He looked around with an exaggerated swivel of his head. 'And looks there's like no one here to stop me.'

'I'll stop you,' she cried, the blaze of anger streaking her cheeks. Maggie was strong, but she knew she'd be no match for him. Her heart thumped hard. *It's broad daylight for God's sake, how could he even think he'd get—*

'I don't think you'll be able to stop me.' He'd taken a step towards her. 'Now, I've been nice, and you shouldn't keep knocking me back, playing me. So, I'm just gonna take what I want.'

'Get away from me,' she ordered at the top of her voice, and backed up the steps scuttling to the front door.

'You're a neat little piece, ain't ye? Little thing like you won't be too much trouble.' He was on the verandah in two strides.

'I'm no little thing,' she shouted. 'I'll defend myself.' Behind her back, her hand had found the door latch. She well knew there was no one around to help. The Chaffeys had gone to visit another family across the river.

Boyd barked out a laugh. 'Defend yourself, will ya? Now that is funny. Might be nice inside this big house. What do you say?'

Nara, one of the housemaids, had appeared in a rush from the side of the house, her feet thudding loudly. She'd stopped, her eyes wide, a forge tool—an iron pick-up rod—in her hand.

Boyd flicked his hand at her. 'And there's another little thing. Get, before I bash you like I did your bloody kin,' he snarled.

Ignoring that, Nara crept forwards, her glare fixed on him.

'Nara, get away,' Maggie rasped. 'Run!'

But Nara strayed closer still, risking capture, daring capture. She got within his easy reach then sent the rod slithering across the boards to Maggie, before she turned to run off the verandah. Boyd grabbed Nara, threw her over his shoulder, and loped across the dusty concourse towards the rows of older trees near the stable. Nara yelled and kicked and writhed, and then he'd thrown her to the dirt.

Maggie had snatched up the heavy rod and darted from the verandah.

Boyd had already dropped his weight on Nara and she pounded him with her fists, then gouged at his eyes. He brushed her off with one hand, fumbled with his flies and shoved his pants open.

As he pushed her dress up and thrusted, Maggie let out an enraged cry and, still running, had taken a wide swing.

Thwack! And he'd dropped like a stone.

Now, she shook the rod at the body. Her heart thudded, her pulse pounded. 'But he hurt you, Nara. I'm so sorry.'

'He's sorry,' Nara said and lifted her chin at the inert body. 'Good for you and that iron.' She pointed at the pick-up then. Taking a deep breath, she winced but stood tall.

'But he—'

'We're not gonna stand here and talk like ladies,' Nara flashed. 'We're gonna run away. No one will believe that he attacked me.'

Maggie still wielded the rod. A dog barked somewhere off in the distance. It would be Bucky. *Bucky, Bucky, Bucky, don't come, my friend, don't come.* 'Yes, get going, Nara. Get far away from here.'

Nara flicked her hand between the two of them. 'Let's go.'

'I can't. I need my money. I need my job.'

Nara rolled her eyes. 'You made a funny, Maggie. The job with Missus Ella is finished for us.'

Maggie knew it as soon as she'd said it. *Of course it was ridiculous.* There'd be no job with Mrs Chaffey after this—she'd just killed a man. She'd go to prison and then be hanged. Dear God, having no job was the least of her worries. She stepped from the body, felt her mouth dry. *Is he really dead?*

'We 'ave to go, now,' Nara insisted. She backed away, brushing at her clothes.

Maggie tossed the rod aside as if it was aflame. She'd just killed this self-proclaimed pillar of society—this *family* man. He lay dead at her feet. Not liked by many, if at all, but she'd killed him. A blow to the back of the head. Who would believe that it was in defence of another? She would run. She'd have to.

A chill cooled the sweat on her back. She spun about and eyed the young olive trees at the front of the house. Too open, no hiding places. She swung around to stare into the scrub at the back of the house, past the olive crushing plant and beyond the packing sheds.

That way was down to the creek. She'd have nowhere to go once she got there, no way to escape. The river. She'd go the other way and get to the river. It was a bit of a run, but if she got a move on … If she could just pull herself together.

Nara had run some paces when they both heard a bellow, 'Oi, you two!'

Maggie sucked in hard breaths, rooted to the spot. Robert Boyd's brother Angus, that strange postal clerk, was pedalling fast on his bicycle towards them, waving an arm in fury.

Nara turned. 'Hurry, this way.' She beckoned urgently.

Maggie shook her head, stuck fast.

Angus Boyd bore down on her. 'No, no, *no*,' he yelled.

'Maggie.' Nara began to go back for her when a tall sun-browned man appeared from the scrub, his hair a black frothy mess and a smoke clamped between his lips. Wadgie, Nara's husband. She squawked as one of his sinewy arms hooked around her chest. He lifted her off the ground and charged behind the shed, out of sight.

Snapping out of her stupor, Maggie hitched her skirt and bolted in the other direction. She charged through the young olive orchard, her booted feet thudding the earth.

Angus howled behind her. 'What have you done?'

She heard the pushbike slide on the gravel and, with a quick look over her shoulder, she saw Angus fall to his knees at his brother's body, his hat flying off and his stringy blond hair falling over his face. Now, her eyes glued on the track ahead, she ran fast, not even daring to look sideways.

Is he dead? Is he really dead?

Where to go … Where to go? Police? *No, the constable is twenty miles away.* Mrs Chaffey? *No.*

Pounding feet. Breath hitching. A stitch in her side. Dirt on her face, in her eyes …

Dog barking, far away.

Ma. Pa. I need help. I need help.

Sam. Sam, I'm not so brave. I need help.

Two

Angus grabbed his brother's arm and tugged. 'Get up, Robert.'

On the floor of the shed, Robert Boyd tried to focus on his brother hovering over him. 'Where am I?'

'Packing shed. We grabbed you up from out there thinking you were dead.' Angus dropped his voice and goaded, 'Bein' dead would be no good, would it?'

'You followin' me?'

'I told you. I'll always follow you, see what you get up to. I know there's no cure for your type of madness, I just try and keep you out of trouble. Not very well, by all accounts.'

'You wouldn't know madness if it poked you in the bloody eye.'

Gruff though he sounded, Robert felt fear in his guts, and not because of his brother. He could easily have been killed after that swing she took at him, the iron rod could have crushed his skull. It must only have glanced off him but laid him out just the same.

'Who else helped grab me up?' He struggled to sit.

'Watson from the farm over the way. He came to get some olive oil for his missus. He didn't see nothin', just them two running away.'

Robert grunted. 'Jesus. What did she hit me with?'

'This smithy's rod.' Angus pointed to a single-bit, long-handled pick-up at his feet. He leaned back on a bench and folded his arms, a smirk on his face. 'Good thing you weren't finished off.'

Sarcasm wasn't lost on Robert, but he ignored it. Grunting, he rolled over to his other side, sat up and began to button his trousers.

Angus pointed at his brother's flies. 'Your missus won't want to know you been at it again. You know what she's like about all that.' He shook his head. 'What in God's name were you thinking, trying that on, trying to roll her out there?'

'Didn't do no such bloody thing.'

'Well, that's what I mean about your madness, Robert. It bloody looked like you were trying to roll one of 'em to me until that high-and-mighty Miss O'Rourke drubbed you,' Angus said, his face thrust close to his older brother.

'So you saw it?'

'You were out in the open, bare arse in the air.'

'Not that. *Her* beltin' me.' Robert grabbed Angus's shirt. 'It don't look like anything to you, not now, not ever, except that uppity piece bashing me.'

'You never learn, do you? There's summat wrong with you, summat deep in your mind.' Angus pried off his brother's hands.

Robert felt his blood boil up. 'Don't start that shite again. And what do you care, anyway?'

'I don't care except I can't have that Miss O'Rourke beat me to it and take your guts for garters.'

Robert stood up. 'Jesus Christ.' He braced his head between two large hands, stumbling as his balance skewed. 'She won't have my guts for garters any more than you. Where'd the other woman end up, anyways?'

Angus swiped a forearm under his nose and let his glare slide away. 'Her husband came out of the scrub yonder, carried her off.'

Robert grunted. He shoulda bashed her old man harder when he'd had the chance. And that bitch, Maggie O'Rourke, she was the one whacked him with that iron rod. He'd heard her yell a moment before the clang landed. The pain had exploded between his ears and down he went. It's all he remembered. He glanced over at the discarded tool. Christ, his head hurt. His teeth hurt in his gums. He ran his tongue over them, sucking. No blood. No loose bits. *Bitch*. He sniffed, hawked and spat. She'd done it now. She was dead meat. She was going to pay for this, and a hefty price.

Fire flamed in his belly and prickles of heat stung the backs of his hands. He clenched his jaw. No one showed him up. No one. And if he ever caught that other woman, she was going to pay, just like he'd made her husband pay. He stopped himself then. He'd got away with it, only because he knew they hadn't gone to the troopers. Well, they didn't frighten him with their long stares. 'Cept they did. A bit. He should go to the troopers himself, have them moved along, especially if he made sure it was known the woman had helped try to kill him. Dirt-poor nuisances.

He snorted, and a clot of blood shot out of his nose. He wiped the remaining dribble on the back of his hand.

But Maggie O'Rourke, you upstart Irisher baggage, I'm going to hunt you down.

'What you going to do now?' Angus asked. He pulled his bicycle from where it leaned on the shed wall and straddled it.

Robert roughly swept dirt and debris off his clothes and straightened up. 'I'm going to go about my business. There's wool and timber waiting to get loaded at the wharf, and maybe my stock to off-load.' His ears rang. His head pounded. Suddenly he bent double, vomited, and sagged to his knees.

Angus didn't move to help. 'Hurry up, then. I can see old Harold's just got to the crusher and is staring over this way. Must be wonderin' what we're doin' here. And the bloke with that new camera thing was skulking about the place, too. I passed him when I was coming in.'

'What bloke? Who're you talkin' about?' Robert got to his feet, leaning an arm on the wall to steady himself. He took a couple of deep breaths, and his head stopped spinning.

'He takes photographs.'

'So?'

Angus shook his head, slowly. 'What if he took one of you at it?' He looked over his shoulder, across to the olive trees, and then over to the house and the shed beyond. 'Could be anyone saw you this time.'

'Ballocks,' Robert growled. 'Nothin' happened, no one saw, and no one took a photograph. I've heard you can't take 'em quick, anyway. And even if they did, no one would want to say anything, just like before,' he said, the sneer visible. He straightened up. 'What's his name, this photographer?'

Angus shrugged. 'Dunno. Heard he wants to set up business in the town. Takes pictures of anything.'

'Bah. No money for that in a town like this one.' Robert stalked off, mindful of feeling a little shaky.

'Comin' from you, waitin' to be the big rich merchant here. Where are you going?' Angus called.

Robert didn't bother turning. 'I'm going to see if the boat's brought in my stock,' he yelled over his shoulder. *Going to see if I can find her quick …*

'Well, you might want to wear your coat then, hot as it is,' Angus called out. 'Your fat arse will get sunburned otherwise. And keep your hat on low. I have a feelin' you'll have two beautiful shiners tomorrow that you might not be able to see out of.'

At the gate, Robert wrenched his own bicycle upright and climbed on, shoving his coat under him. He set off over the dusty road, his legs pumping the pedals. This mode of transport was no longer fit for purpose.

If I'm going hunting, I need a horse.

Three

Dragging in great gulps of air, Maggie slumped against a tree, its bark rough under her hand as she steadied herself. She wiped sweat from her forehead and squinted into the tangle of scrub behind her. No one was coming.

She recognised her surroundings. She usually came this way to visit the banks of the much-loved river. She was a long way from the road, she knew that, so going north, the river was ahead of her. It wouldn't be far that way.

She pressed a hand over her heart and firmly tried talking it down from its rapid hammering. Her jaw ached where the pulse banged under her ears, and her throat was dry. Squeezing her eyes shut, she listened with all her might to the sounds of the bush around her. Except for a few birds and buzzing flies, she couldn't hear a thing—but the voice in her head that kept shouting she'd killed a man.

Why doesn't it feel like I've killed a man? Stupid. How would she know what that would feel like?

It wasn't as if it had been done by someone else. But it felt as if she'd been standing outside her own shoes and some angry, terrified, righteous *other* woman had slammed that rod down on

Boyd's head. No. She'd done it, all right, and there was no time to stop for any ladylike trembles. Not that she'd ever been ladylike, but she had improved since being at Mrs Chaffey's. To get ahead in the world, Maggie knew she had to be a little more refined than the tomboy she'd been in the past. All the same, it was not her intention to have weak-kneed wobbles or to stop and grizzle, as her mother would admonish in her quiet, lilting voice.

Deep breaths, Maggie-girl. Be brave. When were you ever not brave?

Her mother. *Ma.* Maggie crept a hand under her pinafore and felt for the tiny drawstring purse she always wore. It had her savings in it. On her mother's advice, she'd always kept it on her person, ensuring that she would never be without money in any situation. Rubbish to the thinking that a woman shouldn't mind her own money. How was a person to get by if she didn't have any money? Couldn't trust the banks, that much was clear to anyone these days, and had been clear for a while. And, because she was a woman, she wasn't allowed a bank account of her own; her father or, if she had one, her husband would take care of it for her. *Bah to that.* So it made perfect sense to carry her own money, and to hide it.

Maggie closed her fingers over the sturdy, soft leather purse. Its contents would be her salvation now. There might only be four pounds, six shillings and sixpence in it, but she knew it was her fortune, every penny hard won.

Yes, yes, you have money. But where are you going to go? You just killed a man.

Her side pinched where the stitch still hurt. One thing she'd yet to learn was how to run without killing herself. Breathing deep into her abdomen, the stitch eased. Still she waited, alert, her eyes darting towards every flit of a bird and every rustle of leaf litter. Then she heard the faint whistle of a paddle-steamer.

Ears straining, she heard it again. The river wasn't too far away now. If she kept going …

And then do what? Stroll out to the riverbank and wave? Would the news of her having murdered a man reached the townsfolk already? Would it be racing along the river as fast as a bushfire?

She leaned back on the rough tree trunk. Dear God. What to do? What to *do*?

Home. Go home to your parents, to Echuca. No, no. They'd catch her there. They'd take her away to gaol and hang her not long after … What a terrible thing that would do to her parents.

But would she be a criminal in the colony of Victoria? She didn't know. And no one to ask. *Oh, excuse me, protecting myself and my friend, I've killed a man in Renmark, South Australia. Does that make me a criminal in Victoria too?*

She had defended herself and always would. She was a strong woman and no man was going to inflict a denigration on her, or on anyone near her, and get away with it. Maggie was the one who didn't allow stray hands and fingers of others to linger when they'd tried touching her as she'd stood in a packed crowd somewhere. If they believed it was their right to handle her and other women like they were possessions, why do it so furtively? No, she'd concluded, they knew they were wrong, and she would say so every time.

Apart from her father and her brother, there was only one man she'd ever wanted near her, and it was Sam. Down to earth, happy, laughing Sam, with his broad chest and his kind brown eyes. *Oh, stop bringing Sam into this.* For goodness sake, she'd given him marching orders too.

But now what? *Think, Maggie.* A sob escaped, tearless and scratchy, and she swallowed down the next one. *Think, Maggie O'Rourke. Dammit, dammit, dammit.*

That was a very good mimic of Sam's mildest cursing, his voice now in her head. Oh, and now tears might come—*Sam, I only wish ... all right, I know I've opinions that are just as strong as yours but no less valid because they're mine.*

She'd sent Sam packing after their last little tryst, and he was not a happy man. But sending Sam away had been the best thing to do. For Sam. Well, for her, really.

She'd always tried to do the right thing in her life ... like helping sick people, or defending those weaker than herself, especially in the play yard at the Camp Hill school in Bendigo, where the family had lived before relocating to Echuca. Or like picking up that iron rod and cracking it over the head of that monster attacking poor Nara. Surely the law would see why Maggie had done it. Surely any policeman would understand the need to—

Her stomach plummeted. The police would ask what the woman had done to attract the ire of the man who attacked her. The law would ask why a so-called decent man like Robert Boyd would lower himself to such a thing. With no witnesses in their favour, it would be the servant women's word against that of a *so-called* pillar of society—so-called by himself, that is. Maggie had seen and heard enough about how working class women fared under the law, let alone the poorest of women like Nara. She and her husband eked out an existence however they could. This terrible economic depression had displaced so many for years.

Oh yes, there were some decent magistrates, but they were moved along in the country circuit too quickly for Maggie's liking. She had often been asked to assist with transcribing at the makeshift courts when the male clerk could not attend. That drew raised eyebrows, and on occasion, objections. How ridiculous that was, and she'd said so—she was merely using the skills her mother had taught her. Besides, the loutish, lazy clerk hadn't shown up, so who would have recorded proceedings? There wasn't even a reporter for the newspapers for miles around.

This was how the law worked. Women had some rights under the law, but they were not upheld as much as the rights of men. Maggie had been vocal in her views about it, a firm believer in her rights, *human* rights—that was how some of the suffrage ladies described it in their articles and letters.

Mrs Chaffey had quietly warned her that perhaps the local people weren't so keen on the things she believed in. After that, Maggie had tried to temper voicing her own opinions, but she couldn't help it. She'd let anyone know that she was all for the vote for women, and she'd scoured the newspapers for any word of it.

What would her rights be in gaol? She'd have none.

Bah! The law would ask why she had taken it upon herself to inflict grievous harm upon a person. Was it because she was in some nefarious scheme with her accomplice to steal from the man, or worse? Maggie squeezed her eyes shut. Didn't matter a boot that the man was a ruffian, a low scoundrel masquerading as someone with morals. His poor family … although she doubted anyone would have alerted his wife that he was a dangerous brute.

Maggie wasn't the violent person, *he* was. She wasn't someone who hurt people. She was a woman who stood up for herself and her friends, for people who had befriended her, like Nara and Wadgie.

She opened her eyes but all she saw was how quickly he'd sunk into death. How quickly the light went out of his eyes. Maggie had never seen a dead man, only dying or dead animals, but the light snuffing out when life departed had looked the same. *He was dead.*

She drew in short shallow breaths. Staring at the dusty ground at her feet, at ants scurrying by, at crackling-dry fallen leaves, Maggie suddenly knew with alarming clarity that life as she knew it was gone. In its place was a strange unknown, with no safety, no shelter. No haven into which she could crawl.

Hearing another faint blast of a paddle-steamer whistle, she pushed off the tree and grabbed at the strings on her apron to tug it open. She needed to get rid of it—it was white, and therefore a flag, waving that she was likely a servant, a maid. She pulled it off over her head and was about to fling it into the bush when she stopped—it could be useful. She lifted her skirt, and retied the pinafore underneath, hiding it from view. Besides, she shouldn't leave anything behind for someone to find, to track.

She looked down. Her dress was presentable, a classic check in a dull brown with a bodice of box pleats nipped at the waist. It wouldn't attract too much attention, if any at all. She brushed quickly at the full skirt, smoothing its creases and ensuring the pinafore wasn't showing. Feeling it tied there, it seemed as if it had a role in a greater plan that she hadn't fully thought out yet. It felt faintly ridiculous to be thinking such an odd thing. Is this how a murderer thinks and acts, as if outside of oneself looking in? As if the crime committed had been carried out by someone else?

A waft of breeze found the loose tendrils of her hair. She must look a mess—she'd been running like a mad woman and would have hair to match. She deftly picked out the hairpins and poked them on to her bodice, dropped her long hair and finger combed it. Knots and snarls nearly defeated her, but it was becoming manageable. She plaited it swiftly, wound the finished braid to the back of her head and stabbed in the pins once more. It felt tight, but it would have to do.

Now, move quickly. The quicker, the better. She could beat any news of her terrible felony reaching the local people near the river if she acted fast. But oh, for a plan. She had to have a plan. She had money. She looked respectable. No, she didn't, not yet—she needed her hat, and a bag of some sort. A lady always carried a bag when she was travelling.

Her own hold-all—something she had fashioned from an old dress of her mother's—was still back at the house. She had to have it. Apart from anything else, it held her latest letter to Sam, yet to be mailed.

'What is wrong with me?' she whispered, aghast. She'd hit a man over the head, she'd run from the crime, was hiding in the scrub and now worried about needing her bag and her hat. *Dear God, my mind is skewed.*

Finally, impatient with herself, she took a couple of steps away from the tree. Nothing happened. No smote from high above. No voice suddenly calling her out from behind. No thundering of policemen's boots crashing through the bush. There was nothing except a whisper of leaves on the breeze, perhaps a wallaby skittering away. Again, she put one foot in front of the other until she was heading towards the river, her pace swift, her steps light.

Out of breath after what seemed like ages, Maggie stopped, puffing, and rested by a fallen log, hidden by a copse of straggly mallee near where the bank dropped away to the river. To her left and a little distance away, paddle-steamers and their barges were tied up with ropes thrown to the low water mark and secured to posts sunk deep.

It wasn't a robust-looking river in these parts these days. Drought had decimated the flow, but the water level was still high enough. The single wharf of sturdy beams and cross-trusses rose above the water further along. Men were unloading what looked to be household furniture from one barge, and others were stacking bales of merchandise—wool perhaps—ready to be loaded.

Further along, there was a group of people milling about, out of the way of the workmen but keen on their industry. Perhaps someone would recognise her. Maggie took a deep breath. Hopefully no one would take too much notice unless she got in the way of the workmen. She would go down quietly and identify for herself which boats were which, and which way they were headed, and when. If boats were going upriver to Mildura and onto Swan Hill, and even to Echuca, she wouldn't go that way. The police might think she'd run to the closest border and might even be waiting for her there.

And she couldn't take passage on the coach—it didn't depart for days and she couldn't wait. She was sure to be known as a criminal by then. She'd have to go by boat the long way, down-river, perhaps all the way to Tailem Bend and somehow, by some stroke of luck and good fortune, find a way into the colony of Victoria. Then go to Melbourne, and write to her parents from there. Have her father come for her. Maybe Sam would come.

Was it the best idea—going downriver? Well, it would have to be for today.

It was a *foolhardy* idea, that's what it was. Her mind was still skewed but working fast. She pinched her nose and shook her head. *Just do something, anything!* Trying to calm the terror mounting in her belly, she stood tall then froze as a low voice spoke almost in her ear.

LET'S TALK ABOUT BOOKS!

JOIN THE CONVERSATION

HARLEQUIN
AUSTRALIA

@HARLEQUINAUS

@HARLEQUINAUS